## FROM DIFFERENT WORLDS . . .

**ELIZABETH DOWLAND.** Daughter of a prosperous landholder in the Massachussetts Bay Colony, she fled betrothal to a man she detested to become Kayaskua, beloved second wife of a man they called savage.

**WAKWA MANUNNAPPU.** Hunter of the Massachuseuck, favored to succeed as sachim of the tribe, he was a peacemaker betrayed by injustice, a gentle man driven to kill for Elizabeth's love.

**QUNNEKE.** First wife of Wakwa, she found it in her heart to make a welcome place for the frightened white girl.

**ANNANIAS HUDSON.** Enraged by Elizabeth's refusal to marry him, he plotted revenge against Wakwa and viciously humiliated Elizabeth when she was defenseless.

**GILBERT WORTH.** Determined to see the right thing done by his niece Elizabeth, her son, and her husband's people, he held his honor before his life.

*Other Avon Books by*
**Lois Swann**

THE MISTS OF MANITTOO

# TORN COVENANTS

## LOIS SWANN

**AVON**
PUBLISHERS OF BARD, CAMELOT, DISCUS AND FLARE BOOKS

AVON BOOKS
A division of
The Hearst Corporation
959 Eighth Avenue
New York, New York 10019

The Charles Scribner's Sons edition contains the following
Library of Congress Cataloging in Publication Data:
Swann, Lois.

    Torn covenants.
    Bibliography: p. 420
    1. Massachuset Indians—Fiction.  I. Title.
PZ4.S9715To  [PS3569.W258]      813'.54

First Avon Printing, December, 1981

*For Burroughs Mitchell*
*Remember Dogwood*

# ——— Acknowledgments

I EXPRESS special gratitude to Timothy Seldes, my literary agent, who made my ideal of this work his trust.

My children, Peter and Polly, I salute for their bravery and loyal participation in the circumstances and the process leading to completion.

I am proudly indebted to Arthur M. Grossman, M.D., F.A.A.P., Emeritus Attending Physician of Cedar Sinai Medical Center, Los Angeles, Emeritus Member of the Academy of Pediatrics, for his verification of eighteenth-century medical arts appearing throughout this book, and for his specific guidance and that of James McB. Garvey, M.D., with respect to physiological and pathological matters in several chapters.

Lucille Blocksom, weaver and teacher, has helped with her gracious perfectionism, confirming by tests certain inventions of the author regarding spinning, dyeing, and weaving, and with her patient, long-term loan of her exquisite reference works.

I thank Lukas Foss for information relating to the harp and to early American musical composition, and Robert F. Sheil, J.D., for the lively check he kept on the legal practice and facts used here in relation to real property and entail in the context of eighteenth-century law. The same sort of generous concern on the part of Reverend William Walsh, S.J., Librarian, St. Ignatius Parish Library, New York, assisted me greatly in painting the Jesuit missionary face with a sure brush.

Many fascinating hours listening to Steve Shipp, trapper, Milford, Ohio, discoursing on the hunt, and his kind loan of materials concerning long guns, must not go unmentioned.

Why do they thus renounce sleep,
the delights of honey and love. . . .
Why all this toil and distress,
and whence comes this mighty assurance?

Maurice Maeterlinck

_____ **Chapter 1**

THE FOREST, the place of wild growth, was touohkomuk to the Massachusetts Indians, an uncultivated space, the haunt of many different kinds of wood. The close village of Sweetwood had been named by English settlers for the birch and wild apple, blueberry bushes and sugar maples that were rampant at the sides of the pines that caught the air of the sea in their green tops. It was a living woods, one where regeneration still took place and the evergreen did not hide the forest floor from the sky. The firmament passed above, shedding sun or mist through the branches, keeping the ground beneath a breast that nurtured. Anyone who walked it sipped new life from its silence magnified by the footfalls of the deer.

The place was southeast in Massachusetts, not far inland of Buzzards Bay where the waters are warmed by the Gulf Stream and the weather is not unkind even through most of the winter. In January, 1747–48, the rolling land submitted to snowfall as it did to fog that in warmer weather flew like God-sized feathers.

Scents of sweet wood smoke ascended into the dark. Snow streamed and sank the unpeopled wild under white as strong as light. One with this backdrop, ermine darted, daring the wolf. The powder layer on the bent back of a wild rose arbor slid and dissolved at the alien sound of human voices.

"Why are you going away?" a woman asked a man.

He did not speak. His hands drew the red stroud up over their heads, creating a warm cave out of the wool blanket.

Her hands combed away the snow that had collected on

1

his long hair. "Tell me how this journey is not a fool's errand."

He touched her face, seeing the blue of her cold stiffened lips with his fingertips. He felt the desperation creasing her forehead, and his thumbs passed gently across her eyelids, judging her pain in the low dropped curves of skin which in all her moods shaded her spirit in dignity. His face bent into the hollow of her neck. "Elizabeth Dowland!"

The man, a Massachusetts man, a red man, exhorted her with the sound of her English name. A century earlier English faces had appeared on the blue hills that hugged the sea, her great grandfather's face among them. Through payments and written parchments over time the Massachusetts coast was cultivated in the English manner; fences, cattle, spires marked the land that the whitemen cleared of trees. And the humming of the bees they brought to make their foreign vegetation reproduce, transformed the sound of the woods. The bond that had grown between this Indian trapper and Elizabeth Dowland, a landholder's daughter, was founded in the air of the year when they met, 1746, long after fascination, domination, and blood had harrowed a gulf between their races. Their marriage was a climate distilled from crossing winds. Their attraction pervaded them, soft and full of fright as a mist. Yet, their daring to unite had floated them above their differences and they existed in sun.

"Elizabeth Dowland! Is it so foolish? More foolish than my taking a girl like you to wife?" He held her head behind, his fingers warm in her hair. "Charles Dowland's daughter, and promised to another . . . a whiteman . . . the most snake tongued minister who ever drew pay from a church!" And he laughed.

"Do you poke Annanias Hudson at me, when I talk about danger to you? To our life?"

"I do." He lowered his head away from her shoulder, tender about leaving her alone and within an afternoon's walk of the preacher whose grief at losing her was an unquiet thing, a marsh bubbling in its infected heart.

"Then," she swallowed the shame of the truth of his concern, "shall you go, Wakwa?"

"Elizabeth, I shall go to the north and east, into Maine.

2

I am after a simple thing . . . to meet with our Indian neighbors, though they be squabbling with you English in the sea towns. I shall talk to the Abnaki and I shall come home."

Like a fish struggling away from the bait although the hook is already embedded in its flesh, she pulled his purpose this way and that, arguing, vexing the taut line of his idea, after its weak points, to break it. "The Abnaki are part with the French! Needing them! Helping them like family! Your loyalty is with the British Crown!"

"Forced loyalty."

"But it makes a bar between you of the south and the Indians to the north. A legal bar. There is a treaty! And on it are your father's name and your uncle's mark. If you cross over to talk to the neighboring people it makes you and yours traitors."

"It makes us children," he did not chide, "children wary of the children of their parents' enemies."

"Nevertheless! The treaty is of honor."

"The treaty is of 'Submission.' "

She moaned and she panted.

"Elizabeth," his voice let the words slip down to her, not pelt her, not tear her, or crush the regathering of her strength, "I am not happy that foreign kings rake my forest of fur and in the bargain tell me with whom I may safely speak without being hanged on Boston Common for treason. Soon the king will treat us no better than we hunters treat beaver. In dreams I see the forest cleared of Indians as the seaside has been stripped of trees . . . I need friends of my own kind!"

Her hands that held his face to hers were frozen in their insides the way a heart is cold when there is no hope in struggle. "I know," she said, "I know," leaping into his net, "I know, but did you think I could wave you off to hell without a whimper? This is a risky, risky thing, leaving everything behind because of a nightmare. . . ."

He shook his head at her in the dark, recalling her walk into the wilderness toward the new and away from her own.

She could not see. "Are you clear about what you are doing?"

He had always lived in the woods, but he was the man

of his band with the greatest talent for words, not only in his dialect, but also in others and in English. Now, he picked his language carefully, and phrased an answer to his wife with movement. He arched above her, and he tended her no differently than he tended his fields of sweet tobacco, or the corn. He sowed her with the germ of himself, his body the tool. And all the while his long-sighted purpose was crystal in his mind.

"Wakwa, do not go away!"

"It is done."

"Then if you must go, cannot you wait a bit?"

"I am gone." He cried without shame and his arms furrowed the snow as they released her.

Surprised, Elizabeth reached down, touching emptiness between her thighs. He had withdrawn from her as adroitly as the winter sun from the earth at a day's end. She contracted like tree bark, curled into herself, her knee at her forehead, her soft-shod feet guarding the opening that exuded his honey.

One time, the January before when her father had died, Wakwa had forced her to cry. He had goaded her to mourn out loud, had helped her to let go of her father with the sounds. This night, he taught her too, sat up out of the silver mound they had become, took a handful of snow and washed his English wife between her legs. He did the same to himself, bathed his penis with the frigid stuff.

"Aieee!" He cursed and quaked from the cold. "When better to leave women alone than in winter!" he said, lightly, ending her own shocked screams.

The other wife, Qunneke, Tame Deer in English, heard them coming home. They sounded merry as they made the descent into the winter valley. She wrapped herself in a feather cape to meet them at the door. She knew they would come in by her way. It was respect to her since they had been private together.

The tall, tan woman stood staring, gazing at the commonplace objects in the room, the way one stands spellbound by fire. Her unmoving eyes took in the drying feathers, bunched and hung, the bowls carved of burls, the sleeping mats tightly rolled, unused tonight. Like a general's, her jet eyes reviewed the rows of skin bags she had

4

filled with pemmican, the portable food for Wakwa's delegation of forty men. Qunneke flexed her fingers. They had worked almost to the moment of the men's departure. Their separate souls had accomplished the preparation of the incorruptible meal. They had ground and shaven and pounded flesh and fat and fruit into cakes of exquisite qualities. There was no recipe. There was the feel of the meat, the spread of the berries. The women in the Massachuseuck town gave Qunneke credit for the best pemmican. It nourished, gave instant energy, piqued the taste with sweetness. But it never cloyed or caused thirst. Qunneke's pemmican was prized because it meant safety.

Left of the center fire a suit of clothes lay folded. Qunneke had sewn it out of skins she had cured herself. It was for Gilbert Worth, Elizabeth Dowland's uncle, a golden, a generous man. He had let Tame Deer stay in Wakwa's house though his niece loved Wakwa and lived with him, too. Gilbert understood what other Englishmen might not, that behind the wall of trees it was better that one woman not be discarded for another, even if that first wife could not bring herself to accept a husband's touch. For the time, and perhaps for all time, Qunneke would keep her place and self-respect and preside in her house. Gilbert Worth had held out his hand to them all and expected nothing to fill it. Qunneke decided to put health there. Without being told, without inquiring, she knew that Worth would have an expensive suit made for the journey he was taking with Wakwa. It would be very pretty, but bovine, and heavy skins could not be rightly tanned for soft, quick drying near a hasty fire on the march. Deerskins, pulled and pulled and rubbed with the right stuff, brought a man home sound and safe.

Her nose, straight from its bridge, planed without flaring nostrils, as if by the hands of an ascetic potter, caught the scent of snow in the house. She turned her slow, full-breasted body toward the door. Those children were standing there, Wakwa and his Kayaskwa, Charles Dowland's daughter. Qunneke's look flew and settled on them like a dusky bird. She reached them, kissed them, and drew them in.

\* \* \*

LOIS SWANN

They had a meal around her fire. None of them could squander their last night together in sleep. Steadily, wordlessly, the married trio swallowed the warm pottage, nasaump, the unparched corn softened and seethed in water from the running stream. It was the life bread of the area. The English who knew anything of the Indians and traded with them in Wareham, the port town, had raised families on the good native samp. Elizabeth's father's fields still produced the greatest yield of corn in the neighborhood, though Charles Dowland was dead and the planting was left to another hand.

Wakwa heard his daughter Sequan cough from another room, a little annex ordinarily used for storage. Illness was not mixed with health, but Sequan had ceaseless care from two mothers, a grandmother, Wakwa's father, and the helping girls. The Taupowaw had been paid and came from time to time to apply wild onions against the child's skin, and to oversee her sweatings and rinsings, but the infection did not pass.

The father looked guiltily at the women. He took gold from his purse and put it into Elizabeth's palm. "I cannot stay and stay until Sequan is better. We will miss the advantage of winter travel. Believe me, though there be bloody trouble in Maine, the English and the Indians and French are busy hunting for profit and have left off killing men until summertime. I will leave my cousin his horse. Weeping Heart will run any errand that you may want of him. His brother will bring your meat, but Wuttah Mauo knows the byways. He can get anything else you need."

"Dear, I will not need gold to fix her."

"Elizabeth, use the gold if you need it. There is black money, too. Qunneke knows where our trunk of suckauhock is buried. There is enough shell money there to cure an hundred. If there would be a cure."

"Oh, now. Sequan will get better. I lost Henry my brother and my mother to pneumonia. I can see your little girl is not as bad as they were. And we came very close to saving Henry. My uncle's wife makes a conserve out of white roses. . . ."

The man held her chin on the plane of his long fingers. He was powerful and tall, but not rudely built. His body was a legacy in flesh of pure blood and single spirit from

6

hundreds of centuries of his people's holding to that district. His muscles were long, under a fine, hairless skin, struck with amber. His eyes were clear as tea. He was thirty-three, and the features of his face, like the rest of him, were long, even, and definite. Serenity muted his beauty. But his smile was jest. Pretty teeth feigned unwillingness to be seen. He smiled then.

"Elizabeth, I am going this journey to make it a smoother thing to live with you, what good will it do if you are worn out when I return?"

Elizabeth tossed her head as if to rid her mind of both notions. She turned aside, looked into space, and Wakwa quivered as he did when he had seen lions move.

"Elizabeth," he took up her weightless hand, respecting it as an instrument of force, and spoke in a different tone, "take care of yourself. If it is to happen, time will heal Sequan. It is your sister-wife who needs you. Help her to want happiness, any happiness. If she stays with us or no she is part of me and so . . . my heart sways down with hers at her pain."

"Take care of Uncle Gil. He is finely made and forty-seven."

"I will take care."

Wakwa cast a look around the room, lost his glance high in the curve of the roof, and then looked down to the half-Massachuseuck, half-European baby, the son Elizabeth had borne him. He stood and took his greatcoat down from the pole where Qunneke had it drying. He turned up its hood and his expression became remote from them. The women rose and stood still as he held them both at the same time, one of his hands sliding down Qunneke's body's length of hair, the black strands wefting between his fingers as he pulled himself away.

He turned out the door onto brilliant sun. He dreaded to make the first step and mark the flawless snow.

_____ **Chapter 2**

THE FORTY, Massachuseucks, Scatacooks, Nipmuks, Narragansetts, Wampanoags, Nausets, and men of the New Hampshire hills, went to collect Gilbert Worth. The toil of crossing the river, of going through the hunting ground and assembling on the frozen meadows of his farm, was a mark of respect to the English uncle of Wakwa Manunnappu. Worth had volunteered to be their voice, to speak in French for them in Maine where French was the tongue even of God.

Worth's courage in taking on the dangers of their five hundred mile walk did not fetch them. They would miss their snug homes as much as he. It was his defiance of the hangman's rope, his spitting in the eye of the Treaty of Submission his English king had required the Indian Peoples of Massachusetts to sign after their defeat in Philip's War, the Great War of 1675, that sent them to Sweetwood en masse, in fealty. Gilbert Worth had not just closed his eyes and let his niece live with them, he stepped into their circle himself. They could see the foreign gentleman's middle finger thrust in the face of the Submission of twenty-five winters' duration. Their torn families were treated as a snarling rabble and Gilbert Worth liked it less than they. So they honored him for risking his name, his gold, his wife, his land, and his life for their grief, which was also his.

Most of them went on snowshoes. Horses were hard to get and not convenient in the woods, but some of the leaders had a few for chattel. The Massachuseuck had horses, though, grand beasts bred for hunting, gifts from Gilbert Worth on the solemnization of his niece's marriage to their spokesman, Silent Fox. The men on snowshoes packed the path and the mounted ones followed behind, Wakwa last. They walked uneasy that their shadows left traces for some spy. But Wakwa appraised the merciless eye of that morning's sun noting how it chased down anything dark, burning up any shade. He regarded it as their wise ally, secreting them by a blind of light. He was thoroughly happy to be squinting across Worth's blanched field to pick out the sprawling white house.

The house was not old like Elizabeth's father's, built a hundred years before. It was Worth's personal creation on coming to the New World. He had bought the land for house and farm in '27 from Charles Dowland. It was the northern part of a vast triangle subdivided out of Plymouth Plantation by the original Dowland emigrant. With resigned good humor every spring, Gilbert Worth watched the rich top layer of his land erode into the low places southeast. Worth joked that Charles had sold him the stony highground in retaliation for his enticing Dowland's lovely sister Hanna to be his wife. The inability to raise corn was uncommon in the region, an adversity which brought doubt on a farmer's election to the ranks of the redeemed. Though quite pleased with the state of his soul, Gilbert Worth turned to science to right this depleted soil. Worth's pleasure became the invention of ways to retain the nutrients of his land from where on clear days the sea was visible. The barren ground, once good only for grazing Dowland's goats, became the turf of fruit trees, peach, and cherry and apple. In May the acreage blushed pastel with its success. Blueberries, strawberries, and cranberries matured in summer in quantity to fill a fair-sized ship. His flax paid his taxes to the king many times over. Gilbert Worth used to purchase grain from his brother-in-law's surplus or from Annanias Hudson, the Presbyterian minister whose manse was down the dell. That arrangement had been dropped. Gilbert Worth got his corn elsewhere after Elizabeth Dowland ran from home to avoid a marriage with the preacher. Hudson, the respected Harvard scholar, turned sour when Beth rejected him. He behaved in erratic ways for his station. And with Beth's marriage to the Indian, Gilbert thought it best to leave his neighbor out of his business.

In the atmosphere of his house, Gil's masterpiece, new patterns of existence cut themselves as heat does glass. Worth had planned a home that would treat its surroundings kindly. Low, obstructing no conformation of the terrain, it had been cast onto the hillside with the grace of a stroke of chalk. It was white shingle and roofed with cedar like many Cape Cod dwellings but here was a sumptuous use of windows to retain every prevalent light. It was an American villa, pure to purpose, the purpose being excellency.

Gilbert Worth sat midway up the half-flight that connected the main hallway of his house to the sleeping rooms. His new Jaeger, a German-made fowling gun, lay in the vestibule across the psaltery he was carrying along for music. A rustle of gown as his housekeeper came to wish him well roused him from thought.

"Sir, there's currant pudding I have had Matthew put into your saddle pack. Don't forget it's there. But heaven knows, even if you did, it would keep in this cold. See you keep, sir."

Gil slipped an arm through the rail to reach down to her, behaving more like a departing nephew than a master. "Cooke, I cannot imagine a reason for it, but if Mistress Beth should come to the house while Mrs. Worth and I are away, keep her visit mum among the help. Not a word in the village."

"Why can't she stay, sir? It was I were with her all the time she was growing up. There is her baby now to do for."

"It is the lawyers who have to say when she may come, if ever. . . ."

"Sir!"

"Mrs. Worth is gone from us down South to help bring about such a day."

Cooke shook her head.

"Now, Mrs. Cooke, Beth is fine where she is. But some emergency . . . not even Winke must know."

"Especially not Winke, sir. Pardon, but she is a bit upset about your letting her go as housekeeper here and bringing me up from Dowland Farm. She says you have turned her over to ghosts. She has grown very partial to Mr. Hudson. You should watch her, master."

"Thank you, Cooke. The time has come for me to leave the watching to you." Like a little boy, his forehead against the stairrail, his hands gripping the turned posts, he watched the matron retreat. He did not know how he and Hanna could vacate their farm without Cooke and Matthew, the black houseman, to run things in their absence.

"Master!" Matthew pushed open the door of his tiny office partitioned out of the northeast corner of the sitting room. "Can you hear?"

Gil lifted his green eyes to the eyes of the man he had bought out of slavery. He stood and tilted his gold-haired head. The skin twitched over the delicate bones of his face as he paid minute attention. He shrugged a buff-coated shoulder.

"There!"

Sweat broke over Gil's blond brows. He blew out breath. Ringing, delicate ringing of ropes of copper bells played upon the hush. Wakwa's black tossed his rein. "Well, that's it, then." Gil's hand shot out to shake his servant's.

Matthew held open the sitting room doors and Worth came down to see. Beyond the window, the great cherry embraced the Indians under its massive skeleton. All the men, in regalia as various as their origins and experience, stood rigid as silver under a hail of snow crystals from the tree. Wakwa had dismounted and stood in easy expectancy, larger even than his ordinary self in his buckskin and fur coat.

"My niece can certainly sew," Worth's deep voice piped.

Wakwa's flamboyant colt strutted and screamed his whinny.

"I was working, sir, and I looked up and they were all right there, like that."

"Knocks the wind out of you, doesn't it? And Matthew, I am going to need all mine. That bastard Plant walked out on me just at the choice moment. I really could have used his French. He's Canadian, you know."

"The mistress says your French is very good, master."

"Around the Paris Opera, but will it stand up in the woods? Plant's a prick, that's all. Mrs. Worth says I am better off without him. But that's because she argued with him over the miniature of her beautiful niece and that man out there. I didn't see it. But your mistress said the ass of

11

a painter turned Elizabeth Dowland into a miller's daughter. Fattened her up. Shortened the nose. Got rid of her brows. Said eyebrows are hateful."

"Is he a hairdresser, sir?"

"Haw!" Gil clamped a hand onto Matthew's shoulder. "A handy thing it would have been to have him along! And of course, it's always good to have an artist by, etching the campfire scenes into history."

They stayed quiet.

Then Matthew growled, "These Massachusetts men, if they do not take care of you. . . ."

"Matthew, it is about time I took care of myself."

Matthew went into the hall for his cloak, and Gil lifted his chin to get the collar buttoned tight.

_____ **Chapter 3**

THE MOUNTED forged ahead of those on snowshoes. Like post riders, they put miles behind them and then rested, waiting for the walking men to catch them at the stopping point. The riders readied fires and food. Then, their horses were turned over to the ones who had walked, and the process repeated itself. Yet, no man sat Sucki or Brun or Grandee but their masters. The horses of the sachim, his cousin Awepu, and Gilbert Worth were led unencumbered for part of each day. Their freshness meant the safety of the pivotal three. Safety for them was the life of the venture.

From the first morning, Wakwa, Worth, and Awepu made inseparable links in the chain of men winding their way north. A stop by one man to readjust a shoe, to wring his stockings dry, or to empty his bladder changed the shape of the general progress. The men's effort made the only voice with the birds, the wind, the running water. Awepu, cautious of fowlers, tuned his ears to the click of a rifle hammer; Wakwa registered the breaths of his forty men, judging their energy and their tempers. Gilbert Worth heard novel music in the bristling air.

However, nine nights at the campfire with the Ninnuock men left Gil aching to hear the sound of English. The lush Indian voices slipped around the dialects of their mother tongue, still strange to him, and Gil's humor darkened. He was smaller than all of them to start with, but he felt diminished in age, too. In the broad blackness of the night forest, the legato flow of unintelligible words recaptured him into his babyhood. He existed in a nebulous zone, shivering from primitive memory of nights long ago when language poured on his infant ears and he was at first pleased to have it touch him, then proud to lie in his cradle amidst company. He felt again his straining to interpret meanings so that he could laugh with those people that he loved. And there was the wringing of his insides when his child-strength had failed to understand them, though he could see, and delight, and talk himself, but his elders called it babble. Gil heard that baby wail in his heart.

The nurse had always taken him from the hall. Now, not to scream his frustration, Gilbert Worth absented himself from one of the small fires, and started a conversation with himself.

"A bottle of this, and a dab. Oh, for a nip!" He had his back against the straight trunk of a white pine, and he delved into his traveling kit for balm to rectify the damage the cold had done his hands. "And the dagger." He ran his nailfile across his throat first, before his fingertips, because he coveted the silver flask looped by velvet onto the bottom of the box of necessaries. He forbore to drink. "Sweet thing, you! Come away, I'll lay my hand over your breast and warm you up." Gil got his psaltery down from his bay. Back under his tree he tried to warm the strings before plucking some music out of the instrument.

"Gilbert?" A soft voice embarrassed his loneliness. Awepu had come next to him. "Why do you go away from the fire? The men wonder. Your nephew, Wakwa, is concerned to lose you."

"Friend Awepu, they do not miss me. I may as well be a

duck flying over the same route as they, for all they include me in their conversation."

Awepu rubbed his chin to cover a grin.

Gil complained, "They are a hard bunch to get to know."

Awepu dug the butt end of his smoothbore into the packed snow and crouched near the whiteman. "They do not know themselves. You think because they are all one color they are wetompauog? Those men are not the dearest of friends. Some of them are from the sea towns, and some were born by a river, like Wakwa and me. There are a few from the mountains whose eyes are always on the stars. And there are swamp men whose minds are thick as mud. Most of them are sachimmauog, important fellows. They are not so familiar with seeing so many great people in one place. They are watching one another. They are watching what they say, and that is hard to do when hardly five of them together know what five others are saying." Awepu wore a sweet smile in his torchlight. "There are more tongues in these woods than there are Indians to talk them. But there is one word we have all in common, and that is Wakwa. Wakwa, the old, old name for fox, the black fox who is seen at dawn and is rarely taken because wakwa is protected by the light. And that is why they laugh, Gilbert. Not at you."

Gil admired the lean fellow in moosehide. "Thanks, Awepu. Your English has gotten pretty fine since the day I met you."

Awepu latched a hand over one of Gil's wrists. "It is because I spent so much time with your brother Charles and with Hanna and you. Come back over to the fire."

"Oh, I will. I will. I've got to pay attention to her, first." Gil showed the psaltery, flat and square-edged. "I've got to heat her up before we go to bed, or next time she won't play."

"Gilbert!" Awepu was amazed. "You sleep with your music box?"

"The strings, man! They'll snap if she lies on the ground in the wet and cold." He turned to the instrument. "Bony bitch! I have felt the bruises you have given me in bed." His head rested against the tree and he beheld the pitch dark. "Oh, Awepu, I have settled for a thin and miserly

14

mistress, who only shrivels more if I do not tickle her skinny ribs."

"You are not sorry for coming with us?"

"Not a bit." Gil's new gold beard sparkled in the faint light, and his mouth turned up in a jest. "I wouldn't be snug in a four-poster with Hanna all lace and perfume at this moment for anything."

Both men laughed low.

"But you are here."

"Wakwa."

Awepu caressed Gil's grizzled jawline with his thumb, then he preened the fur of his own hat. "How big a voice does the wooden woman have?"

Gil held his forefinger and thumb a quarter inch apart. "Her cries of delight are small."

"Then play upon her, friend, but do not lean against the tree. Ninnuock do never do so in wartime." Awepu left him.

Gil took the minstrel's tool on his knees and made it serve his rich bass voice as best it could. He sang a French lullaby, to himself, he thought, and his fingers, starved for practice on his harp, were pleasured by their working.

"Some of the men have fallen asleep to your song, like children." Wakwa appeared next to the psalterer.

Gil looked up from his labor at the rustle. "That is good. I have never had any of my own to lull to rest." His fingers kept moving.

"Nissese, you always carry that sadness with you."

"I did. But now there is your son. Moses is my heir, someone to step lightly on my land when I am buried under its dirt. The void is less."

"I hope he is more than that to you."

"Christ, yes! But the other must be assured. Not for my satisfaction but for his good. For his mother's good. For all your good. He's not even related to me by blood. He's in the Dowland line. I tell you, Hanna is more intent than I that Charles' will be rightfully settled. Single-minded women in that clan. I couldn't keep her back till spring. She was so worried that any wasted moment would lose us that new lawyer. New to us. He's really a solicitor of some merit, very strong in complicated property cases. Has a son just a few months older than your Moses."

"It seems far for her to go."

"We're going far too. Oh, listen it's got to be done, Wakwa, and it was a stroke of luck to find someone of his distinction willing to study this case rather than passing it over for something easier but as lucrative."

"Then it is well."

"I'm not convinced." Gil's teeth worried the lining of his mouth. "She's traveling on roads no more than logs side by side, when there is a road. I've exposed her to cold, ice, and filthy, far-between inns. And strangers. Why, we're better off here in the woods. At least Elizabeth is home."

"Oh, nissese! Who there knows that it is her home? And with that snake Annanias Hudson nearby?"

The men were close, Wakwa squatting on the snow, one hand hidden in the left breast of his jacket, the other dangling between his thighs. Worth let his eyes dwell on the long, strong fingers of the Indian which blocked sight of his crotch. "You and I will be all right," he ventured, "we have only to go rub up against a tree."

Wakwa's hands became a cup to hide his smiling face. "In wartime, uncle, we must deny ourselves even that."

Gil sang again, free of the strings. Unconsciously, he accustomed the men, regents among their own, to the language they were all bound to go to hear in Maine.

Their fresh meat was eagle. Their beds were pits gouged out of the snow. Every night, in each new location, they dug again. They turned hot embers from the fires into these holes in the ground, and scattered cold soil thinly over that. They lay two by two in the hollows like companions in a communal grave.

To be as cold as they were, without respite, and to move breath by breath into a region colder as they advanced, worked changes in the journeyers. Above the techniques of keeping the extremities warm, of fueling their organs and muscles by frequent feeding, of performing the routine of sheltering the horses from wind and common hazards, a detachment of mind began to function. These headmen and advisers, who were husbands, sons, as well as fathers, existing in constant physical crisis, had the spiritual need to forget. They forgot comfort. They supplanted pleasure with progress. They did not remember activity that did not have pragmatic purpose. Private loves and gratification burned as hotly but remotely as starlight. Individual differences of family or family circumstances faded away. They drifted with the cold, like a wolf pack, instinctually refined in their relations with one another, adopting one will. They scented survival northeast; not flesh for subsistence, but hope and dignity, the life blood of their race. Like the pattern of the distant cosmos, which gave them direction, such emotions guided them away from their ancestral homes.

Distancing their minds from what lay behind increased their separation from those places by actual miles. At the last week of January as they experienced the moon slip from its third quarter into the darkness of newness, three hundred fifty miles had been crossed.

_____ **Chapter 4**

ELIZABETH DOWLAND walked into the wood the morning after Wakwa had. To gain the other side of the wide, ice-edged river, she walked a bridge that Wakwa's father had built long before Wakwa was born. It spanned a narrows under the palisade where a hunting lodge perched. In constructing the lodge, Pequawus taught Wakwa the builder's art. Arm and eye and hand measurements made a slope-roofed, square-cornered, high-walled structure that would outlive the sagamore, his son, and many generations to follow. The natural steps up the incline to it were effaced by snow and a gliss of ice, but Elizabeth took this short way to answer her sudden wish to see the forest house she once lived in and reluctantly left the September before.

She talked to her young son as she climbed, encouraging

17

him not to mind the cold. She had him nestled at her breast held by bands of crossed cloth. Her snowshoes and her punk fire and a little food were all that she packed on her back. The boy was heavy, close to twenty pounds at four months of age. He drank freely of two mothers, but the sharpness of his eyes, and the evidence of wit in his infant smiles, replenished the wills of the sister-wives who had the job of contenting him. His English name was Moses Bluehill, but because of his mother's and father's histories and the nature of their bond, the boy was known in the Indian town as Wolf-of-the-mist He-hopes, Muckquashim-ouwan Noh-annoosu.

"Dear Moses," she confided out loud, "this woods is where you were born. I'm glad to say not in the otan nor in Sweetwood. I wonder why that pleases me so? Mayhap because there was room and peace, and you and I were together, alone for the last time. Here is the house! See? Where you came to be and where I brought you home that white day I bore you. Here we are again, you and I. Without your father. What a father you have! Will you remember him when he comes walking back? Of course, you'll know his voice. What waste I am without his voice!"

Elizabeth pushed open the single panel Wakwa had put in for a door to make her feel safe when she had first come to live there. They had passed a year of life in the two high rooms while they gradually let their folk know of their union. Within the split wood walls they had reasoned how to win approval of their self-made match. Moses' safe birth marked the end of their stay.

Elizabeth sniffed the air. It was lively, the lofty rooms bristling with active use though she was gone from them. The house had been retransformed into an efficient place to repair nets, to store poles and flint, to hang finished skins, and to harbor weary hunting men. Bone hoes, birch brooms, and rakes of antler made utilitarian decoration on the walls. The drape Elizabeth had sewn and appliquéd to give privacy in the back of the dwelling was down and packed away to preserve it. Now the rear chamber, hers, flaunted its wealth to the casual visitor—Elizabeth's low wheel, the distaffs, the iron and copper kettles, bunches of dried flowers misting the rafters with color. The storehouse which she had touched in various ways to form into a home was, again, a workroom on a grand scale, cheerful, ringing with the laugh of the hunter who most recently had employed it to his purpose.

"It has gone to the tribe," she said, "as have I." Elizabeth turned her back on it, unsettled by the sight of her belongings fitting so well among the rest. Outside on the stone step, she put on the webbed, elliptical shoes that would make possible her snowy path east. She reassured the dozing baby. "One act leads to another, dear. The first act was good, so it is all as it should be."

Elizabeth meandered down paths that stretched away from the house. The urgency of her errand could not seem to push her fast. She was not passive. She risked her own child to the cold, going after remedies for Wakwa's daughter. She was taking direct measures to avoid calamity. But walking the ways cloistered by snow prevented hurry, and she bent into the slow rhythm of it. Her eyes watched the frozen bouquet that the woods was, silvered sumac, the differing skins of the trees, the succulent and thorny thickets, while her steps took her down the veins of memory. She traversed sixteen months of experience in the wild.

Elizabeth stopped moving. She stood with the baby's weight on her chest, feeling no pull toward the farmland that she was visiting. She was content where she was, in the tangle of denuded trees, unfettered, responsible, and alone.

Out of duty she took a step. Instantly she was confronted by an anonymous landscape. She grinned briefly, supposing that she had lost herself because the wilderness was where she liked to be. "Silly mama that you have, daydreaming. Come, drink, dear. I need to sit down, anyway."

She opened her inner jacket to her son, nestling like a treasure under her coat. Night rangers, owls, foxes passed in front of her, brazen in the drifts, empty-bellied, the snow protecting their prey. Moses sucked loudly inside the cocoon of her clothes.

Elizabeth did not know how long the pair of yellow eyes had been staring at her. A musky, not unpleasant odor introduced itself to her senses. She sat motionless. Moses squealed satisfaction with her milk. A long, gray-furred muzzle moved toward that sound. Elizabeth caught sight of the dust-colored timber wolf near her shoulder. Centers of heat burst inside her as she identified the features of a kind of animal she had never seen closely. She returned the fixed regard of the eyes, which seemed to belong to the face of an unfamiliar man. Half hidden behind a bramble, the wolf extended six feet from his nose to the tip of his tail.

There are some woodland animals who are attracted over small distances by the helpless sound of the young of other species. A small rabbit in peril makes a noise irresistible to a carnivore. Elizabeth's baby, Wolf-of-the-mist He-hopes, made his meal of her milk with the frantic racket of a being in danger of extinction if his belly is not immediately filled. Like the rabbit, Moses had drawn the wolf. The great animal stood fascinated by the audible pangs of the human.

Elizabeth crushed the baby boy to her. She expected a lunge of fang and fur and then, destruction.

The wolf uttered a deep-pitched bark, his hot breath leaving visible trace on the cold air. He swished past the mother and child, spraying snow about them with a sweep of his tail.

Elizabeth tied her clothes with a shaking hand. "Hush, Noh-annoosu!" she begged. She went out of the glen toward open space, her self-assurance shattered by her fear of the beast. Strangely, the baby was pacific, and cooed against her breast. "Oh, hush!" Looking into the wind, she saw the wolf.

He had distanced himself, but he paced close enough within view that Elizabeth could differentiate his gray from the dull sky and snow.

Elizabeth broke toward her left hand. The wolf bounded, streaking the air with his speed. He ran an arc disappearing at the vanishing point of Elizabeth's route.

Making a cry, she turned a half circle and walked the extreme opposite line.

At times, the wolf showed himself. Sometimes he moved quickly, cutting off her progress in a particular direction. At other moments he stood in her way, challenging her, barking like a dog defending his master's house. Each time he met her, Elizabeth altered her steps to accommodate his presence. She thought, "Does he wait for me to fall? Am I driven in smaller and smaller circles?"

When her knees seemed unable to straighten, or her thighs to lift, or her ankles to bear her and the baby, she gave in and rested against a tree. She had no peace. A flurry of soot-colored swifts shocked her, covered her in their fierce dive out of a hollow tree, batting her as they flew skyward, by their hue lost against the overcast. Looking after them, Elizabeth saw chimney smoke against the sky's lighter gray.

She took in breath perfumed by the farm, seeing that she had come to Sweetwood. She looked for the wolf. He did not show himself.

All she had of him was his howl, bass sound, a heaving outward of some terrible diary, a mourning. It trailed away and looped wildly back to her, victorious in farewell.

She was sad without him, and unsettled. She wondered at the wild thing's pushing her home.

Matthew Freeman left his cabin window and leaned around his door to stare. A slim, dark-brown tree trunk was moving toward him, sliced somehow from its roots, and walking across the snow crust. "Hegh! Hegh!" He tore his coat off its hook and flailed his way through the hardened snow to defend the farm. He neared and the bark softened into a flow of fur, the knot became a well-cut female face, its skin abraded by the constant wind. The branches were arms that ended in pale hands. He felt them hard from the freeze, as they held his own.

"Matthew. Don't you know me?"

"Anywhere, Mistress Beth, anywhere!" He looked more at the joining of their hands than at her face which shone from some secret.

Swaying from the wideness of her webbed shoes, she guided him back toward the forest.

"Mistress, please won't you come to the house? Is there trouble? Are you alone?"

"Not quite." Smiling at her burden, Elizabeth showed Matthew the round, sleeping face at her bosom.

The freedman clucked with pleasure at the infant, then thought of the mother. "Mistress Beth, please do come in. You must be tired. This is a large little man that you have."

"The dangers this side of the woods are much more tiresome to me, dear Matthew. Never mind. Enter our long room!" Elizabeth went back to the corridor of bare trees where she had set her fire of smoldering seaweed she had stored in clamshells. "Time for tea."

"I will make you tea in the sitting room."

"Mine is made from snow." She took things from her pack, a birch vessel for boiling, the leaves to infuse, and a small but heavy gourd. "I have a stew here, Matthew. I'm glad to share it with you. But in any case I must eat for I've got to go back and be there before dark and there are things that I must carry."

"Mistress. Why cannot you come to the house?"

"I cannot go to the house until I go on my husband's arm without fear of getting shot in the back by the neighbors as I stand at the door."

"Who will see? Who will see?"

"It is not who will see, dear Matthew Freeman, it is that no one should even look." The amply-lit windows across the field invited her. "No. I shall stay here. Going would cause stories that will only undo my aunt's careful plans. What discomfort I have caused her over paperwork."

"But imagine the discomfort Cooke would cause me if she learns I left you out in the snow and cold. She'll come after me with a cleaver!"

"Matthew, no one would come after *you* with a cleaver. Not even Winke."

"I hope you are right, Mistress Beth," he said in accents identical to his teacher's, Gilbert Worth.

"Matthew? You are not afraid of Mrs. Winke?" Elizabeth laughed to the burly black man, but he cast his glance down.

"Not that, Miss."

"You are glum."

"It all seems strange, miss, very strange."

She dropped her cooking things and her eyes rimmed quickly with red. "It does to me, too. That I cannot come back home. That home is no longer home."

"What would you have me bring to you, Elizabeth Dowland?"

His insubordinate address of her flattered her, for it made them related by virtue of the pain of their exiles, not seedlings of the rare, acrid herb, 'long suffering,' and of his losing the struggle to make it grow.

". . . So the skins are brought to the church in the fort. I bring them to here, after that. I pack them myself, I have become, after thirty-six years, a good craftsman. You see the crates are marked with the English word 'cod.' This furry cod is then transported to an island where the Penobscot still live, and from there it goes to France on a French ship."

"And all this Locke does for you because Kirke is a Catholic?"

"No! I give him seven and one half percent!"

Gil's white teeth showed under his untrimmed moustache. "Do you work on Dire's soul, Father?"

"His? Hopeless." The old man searched for something under his cot.

"Has he devils, too?"

"Sweet boy, he *is* the devil!" The trader-priest pulled off his shoes, added thick woolen stockings over the ones he already wore, and changed to boots of moosehide and fur.

"Won't they clean for you, Claude?" Gill looked around, distressed.

"I cannot have anyone in here."

"On account of the furs?"

"On account of other things, too."

"But how do you sleep?"

"Rarely. When you don't have a woman there is nothing in it, and I am too busy. Pull that curtain, please. I am sorry, Zheelber, I have to do something."

Expecting anything, Gil moved to where he saw a curtain partitioning one corner of the room from the rest, like a booth at a bazaar. "C'est-ci?"

"C'est-ça."

Gil walked the heavy drape open, pushing toward the window wall, but he stopped before he reached it. The alcove he had exposed was a sacristy. The accouterments of sacrificial ritual rested on their altar with the order and the beauty of the cosmos. Rescued from the remoteness of the cathedral, the tools of the Roman Catholic Mass appealed to Gilbert Worth for what they were—the components of a table setting in the home of an aesthete. There was no extravagance in form to inhibit function. Bleached linen, lace, gold. A leather-bound book codifying conversation for the special banquet. The juices of olive and grape, pressed and fermented. And, housing the food of the communicants to this high-minded repast, the hive of the tabernacle.

Claude de St. Aubin swept past the Englishman with a relish and a reverence for his duty that lent grace to his bulk. The latch keys jingled, a diminutive brace of warning bells. And the tabernacle door swung wide.

Ruby and lapis inset around the bowl of the chalice absorbed the light of the whale oil. The lesson in this opulence weighed on the freethinker. Gil fell slowly to his knees. His glance dropped from the holy place like a youth's from his first sight of a woman. With his eyes closed, Gilbert Worth inhaled the perfume of the mystery, which in its prime had subjugated and enlightened the civilized world. Even crouched low, away from splendor, Gil was not free from the persuasion of human arts. The elegant legs of the altar table were figured in marquetry intricate enough to spellbind. Gil looked up, exhausted by the evidence of faith which was taut with civil power.

"Monsieur le Déiste," Claude whispered kindly, "I have just consecrated the hosts before going out. Do you desire absolution?"

"Your Excellency, I . . . I am not deserving of it."

"No one is. Do you want it?"

"I resist the wanting of it."

The pastoral fingers formed into the hierarchy of blessing, and Latin vowels played the tension between them. "I give it to you, Zheelber, against the time you need it."

Out in the hall, Dire stood in his doorway winding a clean neckstock around his throat. Jeanette could be seen behind him, her hair uncapped, remaking his bed.

Looking like a mountain swathed in fur, the bishop, preoccupied with some errand, rebolted his room and marched away from Gil. He wielded a heavy leather case, containing an altar stone and other equipage of religious service, as another man would carry his gloves. "Do not hold dinner, Dire, I cannot tell when I am back!" He barreled down the hall.

"Dinner is a little later than usual tonight, Claude. Take your time."

The priest muttered as he made his short-winded way to the steps.

"Have you got what you want out of him?" Dire spoke to Gil.

"There has not been a chance to say a word."

Locke nodded gleefully, recognizing some pattern of behavior, and made for the steps while doing up his cuffs. "Honestly, Claude, you know this gentleman has walked half a thousand miles to see you. Let him say his piece."

"Not now! Do you see it is night? You do not have to go out, why should you worry!"

"Disagreeable Frank!"

"Escroc Juif!" The priest blew a kiss.

"I do not think that this is helping, Mr. Locke," Gil fretted. "Besides, this is not a subject to broach in a hallway."

"That is up to you, Mr. Worth. I got him to stand still. I'd grab him while I could."

Gilbert Worth looked from the factor to the cleric.

"Zheelber! Will you keep me here forever? Say what you have to say!"

Gil sucked his stomach in. "My message is far too important to hurry. The man who sent me to you is far too important to fail."

"Nothing is so important as what I have to do. While we argue in the hallway, a man is dying. I am on my way with Extreme Unction."

"Good heavens! Go!"

"Speak!"

"Like this?" Gil appealed to Locke, but the agent was on his way back to his room for his peruke. "The sachim of the Massachuseuck is in this region to talk to your Indians about peace. The Abnaki won't move without you. Will you come in with me?"

"When?"

"As soon as feasible."

"Can it wait until morning?"

"Morning?" Gil tried to keep up with the priest.

"Do you feel better now? Do you see how little time that took to say?"

"But . . . what of the dying man? What of the unpacked furs? Without the least thought you consent to go into the woods with a stranger, an Englishman?"

"As to that, my boy, that decision was made at my ordination. Those are my babies. My sheep. But of course I go with you, to protect you from them, and them from you. As to the furs, Dire will pack them. Do you hear?" de St. Aubin shouted up the steps to Locke.

"Excellency, I am going, too. This sachim is an old friend of mine whom I am very anxious to see." Dire was resplendent in black.

"Diable!" Claude hurried the rest of the way down and crossed the vestibule to the door. "God will pack them!" The French priest turned back from the door. "Zheelber, this man I am to visit tonight gives me a pain. He always dies a little every February!"

The sun rose at their backs. Dire's lanky blue roan was heavily packed with salted cod and strouds, neutral gifts of good will to his surprise hosts. Claude's horse, sturdy and short, seemed to know the route himself. The priest and Gil argued over the origin of the madrigal, while Locke paced ahead and dropped behind, a nervous scout.

"Be easy, Dire." Claude interrupted a rebuttal from Worth. "We are being watched. My lambs are following us as we go, though we cannot see them."

"Why is it, Claude, I have the feeling they ought to be watching something else?"

Sudden clouds grayed all perspectives, and the smell of coming snow pushed the trio fast toward their objective.

The farther west Dire Locke went of the town boundary, the less ease he showed. He had a business to run, and he was riding the path in pursuit of it. But his packing craftsmen had been due at Kirke's house before first light to crate the Frenchman's furs. They were being dished an extra half per cent commission to get the job done before the tavern crowd got wind of it. They had not come before it was time for Claude to go into the woods. Jeanette held the keys to the priest's room, as she did those of the rest of the house while he was gone. Yet, Dire did not like passing his responsibilities to staff.

_____ **Chapter 14**

GIDDY CHILDREN, released onto the plain to play in the February thaw, disturbed the noontime naps of the wives in the otan. Elizabeth resisted the impulse to amble, to pick premature flowers. She was shy of golden air, unwilling to have it touch her. She would not offer herself to mock spring. She cleaned, combed, and carded the wool in her house, and then asked the women to come and spin.

Seventeen girls and young wives, and old women, arrived, curious. Elizabeth made each of them a spindle out of a notched, clean stick of ash. Their whorls were lumps of clay driven through by the sticks. Her apprentices held these simple machines earnestly, trying to see their value.

Barren of words, Elizabeth sprinkled oil on some locks of clean wool and began to work. She tied a piece of her own yarn to her stick spindle. She teased a bit of the oiled fleece around the string. She twisted the spindle toward her heart, and the fibers grew down, chasing the fingers that drew them out. Then she released the new-made twist, left it on its own, and it ran upward on the string, strengthening itself, forming into yarn.

Some stood to have a better view, some were forced close, enthralled by the magic string, some took to the walls and whispered. Soft, guttural praise went round, "Ooooo."

Elizabeth never counted how many times she started the rough practice wool on each of the spindles. She took the seven-inch locks, and teased, wrapped, bent the spindle to her heart and drew down, and when her practiced nature cried a silent alarum, she released the infant yarn to its upward run, to its own life. The undyed wool that she held snaked into her imagination, colored itself with her hopes for it. Instead of waste, it was transformed into finished stuff, ready for the loom, loomed. The plum-color wool made cloth various as damask, as she alternated the twist of the warp fibers, letting light into it, and freeing light out of it. The single color turned into fabric striped many tones, because of the way she moved it with her hands.

Then, the task as it really existed stepped naughtily in front of her. Elizabeth saw the raw stuff she held and she began to laugh. Her pupils laughed, too. Some put their hands on her arm to assure her they understood where she had been. But they pulled away. Her body was lit, warm, alive like fire.

Wuttah Mauo strolled the camp like an amiable dog, in the luminous sunsets. He had delayed at his father's house, keeping his secret, avoiding travel to Boston in the cold. And now that it was warm, it seemed a waste to go to join Prudence Hanson. He wanted so to run the meadow. An idea stuck in his head that if he could run, if he would run, he could break through the cloud of the rum. And then he would look his smart fox of a cousin in the face, again. For that pleasure, he might endure something, go without something, not pick up a bottle, hurt willingly. The scented woods above him stayed brighter than the valley. Wuttah Mauo walked toward them. He had a craving to be in them, no time elapsing between this breath and there. He moved over the sodden ground, away from the darkness welling in the protected basin. He ran. He fell over his own feet and sank one knee and moccasin into the muddy path that had been ice a week before. "Cheepie!" He swore at the devil that had made him fall. "Always in my way." He tried to turn his mind away from the pain in his lungs, and stayed mired there, looking wistfully toward the trees riding above the dark. "What fishing there would have been!" He was embarrassed to go home covered with mud, like a five-year-old. He thought of Elizabeth in her quiet room. She would clean the slipper for him. But he was much closer to Panther Eye's hut and he hobbled over and called her out.

She poked her gorgeous face out of the pit of her house.

"Bad woman," Weeping Heart's teeth caught the last of the light, "help me with my shoe."

The next evening, as the moonlessness brought cover, Wuttah Mauo scraped at her door, again. She came outside, quiet, careful, knowing she was not to be visited by any man. These were the last months of her trial and she wanted to carry a clean heart to Wakwa, for judgment in the spring.

Panther Eye was already pacing the inky meadow when Wuttah Mauo climbed the hill on the third night. He took her hand and brought her to the riverbank where he had left his brother's small canoe in wait under the branches. He jostled it into the water, and it leapt upstream like a striking snake. The woman thought it was madness to travel dark water. But the slender bark thing fled toward still bright places, and she let go of its sides and rode its dangerous courses with delight. Freed of the ground, their wounded spirits masked by the dark blue air, each of them laughed. They were dread comrades and did not mind the tumbling out of the boat's bottom when it tore its skin on the rocks.

Their tattered clothes hung on the willow branches, dripping dry. Wuttah Mauo blessed the black moon. He parted her thighs, denser than the dark, and brought her joy at her breach of faith with Silent Fox.

"Wakwa's wives are quarreling," Wuttah Mauo said as Panther Eye worked to strike fire with flints.

"I do not believe it. Qunneke wouldn't talk, even to argue."

"Lo! Wisdom! That is the truth, pretty cat, they are not speaking at all."

"Weeping Heart, you sound surprised. You can never have been married. Two women in a house? Sharing a man? I think it very queer those two are fighting each other when he is gone, not when he is here."

"They are very close. They gather together, they suckle each other's children. I do not think they know anymore whose baby is whose."

"It makes my stomach sick." Panther Eye put her head against the cool ground.

"Waban wants the squabbling ended before the great man comes back. That is why he has kept the feud a secret. He had Pequawus bring Sequan to him for a good lesson."

"Did she kill someone? Or is she starting early? Did she go after Moses?"

"Evil thing, you are. The daughter was mothering Moses. Elizabeth is distracted by this spinning work my father has set her. So Sequan was playing nurse, not that there weren't serving women enough to take care of him. She built a little wetu for her half-brother, in the sun, just out Elizabeth's door, and she dragged him to it like a doll, and set up a nice little cooking fire," Wuttah Mauo rubbed Panther Eye's shoulder flatteringly with a finger, complimenting the successful blaze she had started, "and was stirring up a meal of a few grains of corn and some berries from her mother's stores when, whoof! The wind god blew in the walls of the wetu, made of the English saunks' precious cloth. Flames! Screams! Rushing! The women pulling the baby out. And slap! The daughter of Dowland Farm takes the tiny hand of the daughter of our glorious sachim, and cracks it good!"

"She struck a child? Her husband's child? Another woman's child?"

"Sequan did not understand. She looked from her mother, to Elizabeth, and back again. And what else could Qunneke do? She is the first wife. She is a quiet woman. She turned on her heel and went to her own part of the house. It was then Sequan saw that she had been insulted by the second wife whom she uses as a plaything. And Sequan struts right out after Qunneke. And Elizabeth, she is left with silence."

"She is a nasty thing."

"Do you think so, Panther Eye? She can do no better than she was taught. Those people hit their children with reeds, with leather belts, whatever comes to hand, if the poor things take a crumb extra of bread, or they do not say their miserable prayers. Any such thing. I tell you, I have seen it happen."

"So. Then those two do know whose child is whose."

Elizabeth showed the fledgling spinsters how to use the wheel. Each had her turn at holding the distaff under her arm, treadling with her foot, moving the wooden wheel, overseeing the tautness of the twist. The tops, the long fleece, combed as devotedly as a woman's hair, were roved and ready for nervous fingers to guide them into new being, the made yarn. The women began to love Elizabeth's room. There was something beneficial there. As the days went by, they noticed that the new yarn each one stored in her own basket overnight improved with rest in Elizabeth's house. The corrective power of happy sleep seemed to work on the uneven, knotty yarn, as it did on their own babies. In the morning, their spinning had rid itself of trouble. It was soft and formed as perfectly as the silk of the maize.

Admiring their handiwork with the heat of beginner's pride, the women missed noticing that Elizabeth took on the defects that their skeins threw off. Her skin lost its texture. It was transparent to the pattern of veins carrying blood away from her temples and her throat. Her bones were stiff as strained fibers. Color leached from her eyes.

Tame Deer never involved herself in the weaving experiment. A complex of principles kept her away from the work that was calculated to give new muscle to the tribe. The skill was Elizabeth's, it was her honor, like a mother's, to show unschooled hands an alien art. For Tame Deer to sit next to Elizabeth would be stealing, to sit at Elizabeth's feet would humble Tame Deer before their husband and the otan. Qunneke excelled in the old things, and kept to them. The life of the wives was balanced and there was no division between the saunksquuaog. But there had been a small violence, the chastisement of Sequan, and apologies did not close the wound. Each of Wakwa's wives was glad she had a door facing opposite to the other's.

The dark hours that seemed to cure the yarn were not quiet. Moses cried at the midnights. His wails got their strength from some courageous hunger. He pleaded for more than the kind of milk that sprang from women's breasts. His outcry echoed through the great, round house. Qunneke felt the pain of it in her breasts, and she woke her father-in-law.

"Pequawus, help me speak to her!"

"Sleep. Sleep."

"Pequawus! Something grows in there. Something new squats in there with her. Some strange lonely thing is the closest friend she has for her English soul. Take me in."

"It will be there in the morning!"

"To hear you is like hearing Wakwa talk! Do it now!"

Grudgingly, Pequawus bundled into his blanket and brought Qunneke to the passage. The baby had grown quiet, so they made no noise. They parted Elizabeth's curtain without the polite word of warning. Moses was in his rush basket, turned away from the glare of a fire overloaded enough with wood to make daylight out of the heart of the room.

Their eyes began to follow a shadow on the far wall, the west wall. Two shadows. They were black and thin, stretching apart, then moving toward a center point like the branches of a tree. Unceasing motion flowed, and flowed again, with the consuming intent of the ceremonial dancer.

"Ssss!" Elizabeth, dressed for day, was at her wheel, dandling a soft, slender cord of wool, testing its caliber. The airy stuff was invisible to the intruders, but as her motions drew their circle, and began again, yarn was gathering, perceptibly, seemingly spun of the spirit of the woman who drew it into existence.

"Ssss." The sound, in unison with the creak of the wheel swaying slightly in its sockets. That hiss was her pain at her untwisting and respinning of the inconsistent yarn of the day. Stray noils caught in her parched skin but the hands would not stop or ruin the evenness of the worsted.

Pequawus held Qunneke back. "The spider works!"

"She is in flight! Not stuck to any web. She is the gull as Wakwa has named her!"

The pair went into their own room and replenished their fire.

Pequawus shook his head. "I say she is the Spider. She is working to make a web. And the pattern of that web shall trap life into it. But there must be a hole, a flaw to give the weaver's spirit room to breathe. Then her soul can fly! Our Elizabeth admits no flaws. She must make one or she will die."

Qunneke spent the next day outside, working over an iron kettle to render the fat of a bear. She was determined to cure Elizabeth's hands. She shook the cold, gelatinous substance into the pot and fended off questions from the gossips who passed by.

"Tch, tch, you are always working so hard, Qunneke."

"With two wives the work may double, but so does pleasure." She sent them away gasping.

As soon as Moses cried that night, Qunneke got up and went to Elizabeth's room by herself. The white wife was nodding in the rocking chair trying to hold Moses to her breast. Her arms dropped to her lap. Qunneke hurried there just in time to catch the boy.

Elizabeth came awake, and her face shot with red at this new inadequacy. Qunneke restored Moses to her and turned herself away. She had seen nothing.

"Thank you." Elizabeth cradled Moses, tucked his blanket around him, and dropped back into the chair. "Let me make you something warm to drink."

Tame Deer heard kindness behind the English words. She took Elizabeth's hands into hers and examined them. They were the hands of a wizard; parched, crooked from cold, scales of skin marred by cracks that showed red where joints bent. They looked like devils, though they did work like gods. Qunneke began to stroke Elizabeth's hands with the heavy oils of the mink and the bear.

Elizabeth's voice filled the room, uttering the sounds of grateful flesh. The unfettered noises she made did more than tell of benefit to herself. They themselves became the balm of touch.

Qunneke kissed each hand and gave it back. Elizabeth's eyes wandered to the wheel. Qunneke took work of her own from her carrying pouch and began the decoration of a belt, with tinted quills. She stitched in the firelight, breathing lightly as a wanderer eager to hear the sound of leaves in the wind. "Hhhhaa!" At last the sound came. Her husband's bride spun. The voice was not pain anymore, but exaltation.

# Chapter 15

WINTER POURED BACK into the Massachuseuck valley in the shape of rain. Elizabeth and a brigade of women lined the open meadows with buckets to catch the water that fell out of the sky like weavers' manna. Gallon after gallon of rainwater was needed for the rinsing and the dyeing of the finished yarn.

Elizabeth moved the yarn through the glowering pigment with two wands of sanded wood, causing the subtle flight of the dyestuff into the wool. She weighed light, judging the exhaustion of the dyebath and the effect of the spun stuff on the sight, until it touched the color ideal fast in her mind. The weaving went forward.

Outside, the maple sap began to run, skunks left their dens, and the night sky went dark, as the moon reset itself for another revelation of its shining body.

"Wait, Panther Eye, and you will eat with me in my father's house. There will be meat and fat and fur to keep you warm. You will be the mother of the sachim." Wuttah Mauo put a heaping basket of acorns down in front of her.

Panther Eye considered his gift, and his proposal.

"Boil these a little at a time, and they will last you till I come back from Boston at the end of spring."

"You have a face like wisdom, but you talk like a boy. You know I have never borne a man a child. You will have to get a son out of someone else."

"That is taken care of."

Panther Eye settled her stare on him.

The gambler showed his suit and told the story of Prudence Hanson.

"What do the Massachuseuck want with more half-breed

babies! Manunnappu cannot be blamed for his with such a stone for a wife as that Qunneke. But he chose her and the second one too! If I sat with the women's council I would not bring his name up for election as a sachim."

"You have as little use for him as I do?"

Smiles played her mouth. "I would not go so far. He does have the longest, straightest legs of any man I have ever seen."

"Another sign how stupid he is, that he did not let your husband kill you in Rhode Island!" Weeping Heart showed her his back and took to the fields.

Panther Eye followed without hurry, but she came.

He felt her next to him. "I thought you were the one woman who could keep her hands off my pretty cousin."

She dared him by silence.

"You see," he succumbed, "we quarrel like husband and wife already. It is settled, now. But we will not say anything. I want my newborn boy in my hands, first."

March wind sent chills over Panther Eye's frame. "I think I am afraid. Weeping Heart, do not go. Stay here."

"Fear lasts." He left her, sure she would be there in that spot when he returned.

Panther Eye cursed him aloud as he galloped out of camp on the white gelding. Sleepy people complained about the clamor of the running hooves. Elizabeth did not hear for the clack of the shuttle.

# Chapter 16

WAKWA LAY on the wood floor of the long house, on a litter of blankets. His eyes were open wide, happy. He smiled his secret ecstasy to Awepu.

"What is the matter?" Awepu fretted. "You look as if all the bones have been taken out of your body. What did they feed you in there, those Abnaki? What did they do to you in that small room, all alone?" Awepu sat close to his cousin. "The last time you went somewhere without me you found Elizabeth. Now what have you found?" Awepu polished the trigger of his gun with his thumb.

Wakwa committed himself only as far as a sigh.

"You are tired."

"I . . . am . . . untirable . . . untirable . . . untirable. . . ."

"Is that all you can say? Say something that will get us out of here. Get us home. Did they give you rum? Jimson?"

"Awepu!" Wakwa's eyes spilled their liquid coating. "They gave me man root! Man root will overpower the deer!"

The kind of thing that Awepu understood was that to shoot well, a man had to practice daily. To place a killing shot he had to know how to use time, to let seconds pass in order to hit the heart of any target. His sparing time had made space in his experience for his friendship with Charles Dowland. It had made this journey away from his wife and four children necessary. In his style, Awepu was acutely aware of his duty to Dowland's grandson, and that was to hunt whatever beast stole too close to his future. Smelling strangeness in the woods, Awepu went to shoot.

The five-leafed corolla peculiar to the pines of Massachusetts arrested his eyes. A feathery tuft of green needles, bullied by a wind which was carrying snow, danced like a kihtuckquaw for him. Its responses to the gusts tempted him to test his eyes and his aim on it, making delicate judgments as to the direction it would blow. The resilience of its branch, the fringe of his own coat, his long, free hair, flying back, the nerve in his neck, gave him prewarning of the corolla's movements and communion with them. He smiled broadly when he had had enough of this looking exercise, and pulled his hand over the succulent, smooth needles as he would have done to a female's dug.

To bring in food, and to keep in form, Awepu made a solitary hunt in a retreat of blue-green teals. He was not out to plunder them. His skills were too refined for that. Breaking cover, he shocked the birds out of guarded sleep in their ice marsh with his man-presence. They rose in stages, their squawking falling back down to alarm their brothers and sisters. Only when their bright wings went black against the pale sky did Awepu make his nine-second load, choose a bird, and, as it began its final pumping, high and away, shoot.

He left a brace of them to be plucked by Wakwa's guards, taking only jerky for himself for a supper. Awepu moved at night in an easterly direction, his bayonet ready and his aim honed for trouble.

Awepu threw his weight on one foot and used the muzzle of his gun to prop his hands and chin. He mulled over the trio that paraded by on the deer path. Locke did not belong in it. But he was there. He looked worried that he thought he might be stopped.

Awepu thought of Dire Locke as an honest man. He had not cultivated the bad habits of so many other traders when the English king had laid an import duty on cured American peltry. Raw skins entered England free. The duty sped the process of the trade. The fur-hungry European public now was fed raw skins out of the crates. The quantities were far greater than possible if the pelts had been American cured. Native curing took time. The duty was a false and selfish holding down of prices. The levy put the squeeze on the merchants, who could not command prices high enough in England with raw skins to meet the modest demands of their Indian suppliers, let alone make a living themselves. To save themselves, most licensed and unlicensed traders made up the difference from the pockets of the hunters. To shrink the prices of the skins the traders laced their barter with rum. Drinks of rum. Unregulated numbers of kegs of rum. Rum kept the mood of the woodland hunters high for days. Awepu saw the only use for that stuff was to make the ignorant, the worn-out, stupid enough to accept any pittance that was offered for their skillful labors. Locke was a different sort. He was Kirke's man, besides. Both of them responded to the pleas of sachimmauog from Virginia to Massachusetts, and controlled the trafficking in rum though their Parliament wouldn't attempt it. Somehow, rum swindlers who worked Locke's boundaries got shot. Barter with Kirke Company was sober. Furs were traded for blankets and guns and powder and dried flesh. And so, each season Locke's reputation spread farther and farther west, and there was no space he could not cross. He was received anywhere because the word had it that Dire Locke "filled gut."

Awepu let the whitemen pass, without a word, but trained his eyes in the direction of Pemaquid, where Locke kept turning as he rode.

The old pine wood was dark even in the day. Waste undergrowth did not grow. Centuries of layered brown needles deadened sound. The columns of the evergreens looked all the same, and the squirrels that ran were mirror images of one another. Snow had established itself, flew sideways on the sea wind, erased the deer path in its cold flow.

Awepu ranged away from that easy entrance to the forest. He left intruders who would come that way to the discretion of the Abnakis nearer to the encampment. He searched for some wild thing, something unconscious of the rules of that dreary turf. He began to think of putting up a lean-to so that he could make a fire and chew his pemmican in peace. He looked for a likely grove in the dun twilight and was rewarded, doubly, for his effort. A complaining voice reeled from trunk to trunk in a clump of pines, and a man shivered against a tree. "I hate the woods!"

"As for myself, I love them." Awepu's voice came, disembodied, but the steel of his bayonet against Hal's neck was convincingly real.

Hal's gasp lifted into a trill of terror, as he snapped his head around to see who spoke. Flakes of snow delineated Awepu's features, made contrast to darkling eyes, marked the never-ending cascade of his hair, like black water running far back into the night ocean. Hal screamed hotly. His gun was lifted away by expert hands.

Awepu blinked at the noise. He detained the fisher against the tree. "Who is with you?"

That the wildman, the savage of a settler's nightmare, spoke better English than he himself turned Hal's mind to confusion. "Oh, my God!"

Never having inspired fright in a rabbit, Awepu was amused. "What are you doing here?"

"Nothing!"

"Be quick!" Awepu's knee found Hal's groin.

Hal whimpered, "Hunting."

"Hunting what?" Awepu saw no lines, no contrivance for traps, only the gun and the man's powder horn, full and dry.

"Beaver."

"Near no water?" Awepu scorned his lie. "Hunter! You came after Locke!"

Hal piped, "Who is that?"

"You are English and came after beaver and know not Locke to whom you would trade it?" Awepu threw Hal down and tied him like a deer to be roasted.

"Please! I am lost. I only want to go home. I will not bother this place again. I was trying to find my way out."

"If you were a wise man, hunter, you would tell me that you traveled with twenty. That they were vicious as she-bears and nigh, so you could frighten me away. I am sorry for your discomfort that you are worse than a fool. You have no regard for me." Awepu left Hal with his face in the snow.

The veteran of Louisburg had the gumption to call out, "Heigh! Heigh! I'll talk to you!"

"Be fast. Your brother is running away."

"My name is Hal Dunn. You're right. I'm not a hunter. I . . . I'm a timberman. I come lookin' for timber trees is all."

Awepu's eyes narrowed, doubting the names and the work.

"Injun, you're not from these parts, are ye? I can tell. Ya talk the language real good, real well. You're from other parts. Who are ya?"

"Hal Dunn, I am the man who will kill you if I find that you lie and are not alone. Tell me, timberman, how do you hunt trees? Do you shoot them?" Awepu took random aim and fired Hal's gun to test if it were loaded. The shot lit the clearing red.

Wakwa's lanky cousin took the trouble to search where he could for an associate to Dunn. But the task was impossible because of snow and night. He made a shelter for himself and the lying fisher while drifts built, burying Deil.

# Chapter 17

WHISPERS WERE PASSED and passed along that riders were coming from Pemaquid, and Wakwa walked to put himself at ease. He deemed it very efficient of Elizabeth's uncle to have accomplished his goal overnight. Wakwa Manunnappu could not have been more pleased with the start of his political career.

He turned up his hood, disliking the feel of cold air on the back of his newly bared neck. He minded his haircut more than he would admit to Gilbert Worth. As he crossed the frozen ground, Wakwa reckoned time, allowing for the gathering of the tribesmen, talk, the growing of ideas, disagreements, smoking, decision, leave-taking, and the journey south. His calculations had him in Elizabeth's arms before the roses would be in full flower.

Wakwa stepped off the footpath. Horses snorted around the curved nave of the forest created by the pines. He faded in among the tree trunks, not wanting to surprise, or to be surprised. But his heart gorged on blood, seeming to expand and palsy in the same beat, causing him lingering pain when he saw Dire Locke. The dark-coated agent rode third in line, as unwanted a presence as doom. And Awepu was nowhere. Wakwa had counted on finding him in Worth's escort.

"Gilbert loves me." Wakwa steadied himself and let his uncle-by-marriage pass by with the cleanshaven, corpulent priest. But he came to the path edge to stop Dire Locke. "Was not the peltry I sent with Gilbert Worth enough for thee?"

The roan reared but Dire dug his knees in. "No! I have come to get your hide, too!"

Wakwa pulled Dire off the horse as if he were a child.

Habituated to the feel of fine stuff, Dire's hands coursed Wakwa's hooded coat during their embrace. "It'd fetch a pretty price. Sell?"

Wakwa spread the interior to Locke's view. "Who do you know rich enough to buy this?"

"The question rather is, who do you know rich enough to embroider in this fashion?"

The farmer and the priest were oblivious to anything but their singing. They looked back for Locke's applause.

"That is he!" Gil introduced Claude to the picture of Silent Fox, from far away.

"Gesu!" The priest let go his rein and smoothed his jowl with gloved hands. "Musician, what are you doing here? With your niece married to such a man you would do better to go home and write an opera."

French Indians began to surround their confessor. The headmen in the camp were called into the twilight snow, to add pomp to the premature meeting of Wakwa and St. Aubin.

Gilbert Worth walked to Wakwa, making a link between the Indian and the French adviser to the Abnaki. "He likes to be thought a prince of the Church. When you meet him, the protocol is to bend your knee and to kiss his ring."

"What do you suppose I have, Gilbert, that he can kiss?" Wakwa went bravely and with a smile.

Claude's sweet, gray voice grew to the breadth of the timber walls of the Abnaki house where all the men mingled, hearing the solemn sacrifice of the Mass.

"What is it they speak, Dire," Wakwa whispered, "the language of the priest's craft?"

"It is the language of all craft. It is Latin, very like Narragansett. You could pick it up in a few weeks."

"Then I must, for even with it I am one language behind my Abnaki brothers. They have French, as well."

"Old friend, you are ahead of them. They have forgotten their native tongue."

Wakwa and his men from the south were embraced by Claude's song as if it were a cousin. It was the way they sang, melody driven from tone to tone by the power of feelings, a plainsong, unmeasured, unmathematical, its changing pitch drawing pictures. Wakwa's confidence surged. There was much appeal in treating with the French.

When Claude was relaxing, down from the altar, Wakwa said to him, "Father, we consider our gods differently, but we sing to them the same."

"Well-observed, exquisite pagan, and well-sung, my dear deist." Claude harbored Gil's hand against his chunky waist. "Next time you will play, too, on the strings, yes?" The priest only looked at Dire bleakly.

"Don't you have any names to call me, Claude?" Locke left for his quarters with the southern delegates. He sat up late with Wakwa and Gil.

Wakwa put it to him. "Why did you come, Dire, just to see my face?"

"What better reason could I have?" His diplomacy unfurled. "And while here, allow me to give you my belated wedding gift for your second wife."

"That is kind, Dire," Wakwa said mildly, "may every sort of fish leap into your nets."

They grinned at each other with their eyes while Wakwa unwrapped the corner of several breadths of cinnamon-colored silk. "It is like her. I thank you. But such an uncomfortable journey you have made to carry this thin and fragile stuff."

"You know my affection for you and your family." Locke pulled a gunnysack from in back of him and untied the knot for Wakwa. "I cannot overlook Tame Deer." He drew out a hemp-colored object that resembled a doll of husks. Its legs and arms tapered into stiff strings. Dire sat it on his palm.

"Man root?" A crease cut downward on Wakwa's forehead.

"That's right, Garent-Oquen, as you Indians say."

"Man-with-his legs-and-thighs-separated."

"Right. Ginseng to the Chinese."

"They gave this to me to smoke a day ago."

"Tame Deer will know something better to do with it than to send it up in puffs of smoke." Dire twirled the root by its own hairs. "The Chinese trade for it. Every root brings its weight in gold."

"Figuratively," Gil interpolated.

"Not figuratively. In Peking, high-quality North American ginseng is sold on the open market for its weight in gold. Fetch me a pound of this five-leafed root and I will give you five dollars. What do I give you, Fox, for a pound of beaver?"

Wakwa looked silently at the agent.

"What do you give him?" Gil wanted to know.

"A shilling." Locke looked back at his Indian friend.

Gil was pink in the face. "Who needs beaver?"

"Exactly." Dire stuffed the mature, well-dried root into the woven bag, and tossed the heavy sack to Wakwa.

"This were a costly gift." Wakwa weighed it.

"A good investment. Of anybody I know, Tame Deer will have the patience to give me back man root the quality of that."

"You want us to trade in this?"

"Haven't you heard? The bottom has dropped out of the French Company. France forfeits her monopoly on this trade because Canada has fucked herself. The people up there have stripped the place of the root. They were greedy, they picked Garent-Oquen before he was old enough. The seeds could not mature. End of wild ginseng."

"I shall become a hunter of roots for Kirke?"

"A man with two wives has got to scrape where he can. And man root cannot run, he does not require to be shot, or strangled or skinned. Only leave him three years in the dirt, dry him respectfully and slowly, and he'll send you back five dollars a pound from the Orient." Dire drove hard.

"But what do the men from China want with my ginseng?"

"What do you care if they shove it up their asses, as long as they pay what they say!"

"Dire!" Gil was shocked on Wakwa's account.

"Pardon me, Chevalier!" Locke reminded Gil of his testy sword. He warmed to his work. "Fox, listen to me. These people see that the root is formed like a man. They love him as much as you do. You will not bend your back gathering their man root so it will be wasted. They use ginseng like medicine, like herbs. They sweat it, they drink it in tonics, they cut it up with wooden knives and brew it in earthenware vessels, and with that they restore their women after childbirth, they assist the blood, they strengthen their lungs, they try to forestall age. And last, but never least in my book, they mix a potion of ginger and orange and the magic root, that . . . you won't be offended, will you, Worth?"

"For Christ's sake!"

". . . That they aid their . . . what they call Yang essence . . . their wuskannem, in Narragansett, their semen, that it endure."

Laughter burst out of them. Wakwa managed to say, "Having two wives, how shall I hinder any man from that!" Hands clasped over a bargain completed.

"No wonder they pay in gold!" Gil lit with invention. "Why not bottle it? Wakwa, you gather the roots, Locke, you transport the ginger, and I will supply the orange peel from my hothouse. We'll advertise in the *Gazette*. There is a fortune in it!"

"My dear Worth," Locke returned, "you are not being improved, at all, by this journey. You came a gentleman and go away a merchant."

"A bearable fate. I still think about that furniture of Kirke's."

"Ah, yes, the bricks."

"Bricks?" Wakwa missed the imagery.

"What Kirke calls each cabinet and chair given to him by the Chinese in the building of this trade. Thomas has been there for some time dealing with a very dangerous group of fellows. Bodies float in the harbor there when the yellow man feels duped. Kirke has now got his guarantees and is ready to supply."

"Kirke is in China?" Gil could not digest the fact.

Wakwa was drawing a map on the soft nap of his moccasin. "China is very far away, Dire?"

"Very far, my friend." Dire watched him.

"Thomas Kirke must have many more ships than I have thought. For if some are always filled with planks and lime and fur, bound for England, there must needs be others to fill with man root."

"He is always at the top of his form." Locke used Worth for a buffer against Wakwa's clearsightedness. "Kirke and I have been conversing via letter about just this topic. His paucity of ships. In a way, it is his good fortune to be English, for he is not restricted to English ports in trading.

Being English saves Thomas Kirke from turning into a smuggler. But what good is this without enough ships for cargo? And! The high costs of shipbuilding in a London yard! Well, Silent Fox, there is a limit to what he can outlay in capital." Locke could not look at his native friend, and studied his stockinged shins instead. "The *ideal* place for building ships is this trove of hardwood where we now sit together."

"And of course, Kirke is an Idealist." Gil seethed.

Locke turned cool toward him. "Of sorts, Worth. You see, Silent Fox, there are little islands just out into the Great Water not doing the slightest good to anyone for they won't grow anything but sheep. Kirke proposes to buy a little cluster of these uninhabited islands, even one, and do his shipbuiding out to sea, as it were, using nearby wood, and possibly," Locke looked up, "native labor. Steady work. But from whom do you buy an island off the coast of Maine these days? The French and the English cannot decide which of them owns what. Thomas, that great friend of mine and yours who would like to get our necks out of the trapper's noose, suggested himself that I approach the local Indians about such a purchase. You can appreciate the delicacy of all this for me. I could immediately be killed by the French or the American farmers if it should get out that I negotiated with the French Indians directly. This place is worse than China, I assure you. Of course, Claude de St. Aubin can't touch it with a pole. I was sitting in the tavern, playing cards as I am wont to do when sorely troubled, and came your excellent uncle-by-marriage telling me you were a stroll away. Put a word in for me? Great Spokesman?"

Gil was indignant, but he watched his manners, and stayed quiet.

Locke appealed to the sachim who had come to ask nothing of the northern tribes. "You do understand I would ask no favor unless I were in extremis."

"That is more Latin."

"You understand everything."

"Yes." Wakwa clucked his tongue at Kirke's man.

"You may forget I ever said this, Silent Fox. All will continue as usual. Your position here may be more fragile than mine." Then Locke smiled. "There are plenty of other factors anxious to get my place. The Trade will continue whether or not I am shot."

"Dire, the Trade will continue over the face of the moon if the earth is someday swallowed up. I have a cousin, Dire, Tamoccon is his name. He wants to be a captain on a tall ship."

"A captain? A redman a captain? Could he be satisfied with somewhat less? You know the times. A captain is no captain unless his men are willing to obey him."

"Mayhap, Dire Locke, by the time the child Tamoccon is a man and ready for command, the times will have changed for the better."

"Kirke shall have his name," Locke promised.

Wakwa rose and walked away, treading softly among his sleeping men. He leaned against a wall with his eyes closed.

Locke joined him. "Wetomp, leave it go if it is trouble to you."

"Dear friend," Wakwa said, "only one thing troubles me. Where is the father of Tamoccon? Where is Awepu?"

"Hal Dunn, I am going to do you a favor," Awepu decided in the morning. "Pardon me, but I am now hitting you on your head to send you back to sleep, lest you come to greater harm being awake."

Awepu moved like a bear on his snowshoes, rolling his gait because he was too tall for this kind of portage. Yet he carried Dunn for hours, stopping once, only, to adjust a webbed shoe and knock the fisher unconscious again. At last, the Abnaki guards appeared and stripped him of his burden.

Awepu stopped to hear Wakwa's voice behind the curtain in the place the miawene had begun. He smiled. His dialect curled around polite forms, brought out a little laughter from the headmen, after Gil turned the words to French. Wakwa invited them to his own lands, singling out the brill, and the salmon, the shad and the clams as their especial food, when they should come. With clever comedy he admonished each type of fish and sea life to consider itself honored to be dedicated to such good people as the northerners evidently were. He named river and ocean creatures by the hundreds and thousands in a silly and staggering line, exciting the men's laughter. He shared a few happy tales that were common in southern Massachusetts, to let them know him, to get their hearts open to his message.

Awepu heard quiet. A few throats cleared, a cough or two erupted. Wakwa did not go on. Or could not. He seemed to have no way to get to his message from his greeting. The Spokesman would not speak. Before the pause was too noticeable, someone said that food and drink was in order after such a pleasant talk as the beautiful southerner had gifted them with. As the attention wavered from Wakwa, and the buzzing of the hosts began over whatever would appease their bellies, Awepu went into the meeting room and laid the limp fisher at Wakwa's feet.

The whole company was sucked to the spot like water into a vortex. Wakwa held his cousin to himself over the prostrate man.

"He will have a pain in his head when he wakes up, Wakwa. For your sake I hope I have not overhurt him."

Dire Locke probed Dunn's shoulder with the toe of his shoe. "You will not have addled any very special brains, Awepu. Where is Deil?"

"I found only him, Dire. Your face is dark. This is no friend of yours?"

"Hardly!"

"This is something I have done, isn't it?" Gil held his temples.

The priest was on his knees, searching Dunn's clothes. He found frozen remains of Eucharist and his chapel paten.

Locke breathed, "Jeanette!"

Claude ate the desecrated hosts from Hal's pockets, and gave orders while he chewed. "Take him to my loft in my longhouse. Take care of him, keep him warm, feed him. On no account let him see anything, or hear anything. And mind! This mule here has nothing to do with Monsieur Locke." Claude did not trouble them with whole truths. "It is Zheelber that he and his friend are after. They stole his gun, and the Sweetwood farmer cut one of them but good."

A cheer went up in Gil's favor.

"Don't be dunces!" the priest scolded. "The whole idea is to make out of these shits of fishermen, saints!" Claude forced Dire against his cushiony shoulder. "You stop worrying about your Bonbon. If I know anything about Jeanette, it is that that little one got the advantage of these two troublemakers."

"The stuff in his pockets! The paten, the. . . ."

"Get your boots on, Dire," Claude snapped. "We are all getting off our asses and out into the snow for a nice walk around. We had better bring that other one in alive if you value your friend, the Fox."

"Claude," Dire said tiredly, "I am no woodsman, I'll be no good hunting down Deil. I have got to go back to the house and . . . clean up whatever mess they have left me."

"Dire!" Gil gripped the slighter man from behind. "I couldn't be sorrier."

"No apologies, Mr. Worth. It was now or later. The Trade was doing my Jeanette no favor at all." Dire went on, ahead.

Claude stood over Awepu. "Take these, dear, and put them on." He forced a pair of woolen stockings on the Indian. "Go on! You are wanting to go back out into the cold air, and I am terribly sorry about it, but you will not come on our jaunt if you are not sensibly dressed. Poor lamb, I am getting you something hot to drink."

Awepu drew the thick, warm stocking over his hairless calf. "Wakwa? Tell me why is it that Locke came, at all. I was afraid for you when I saw him in the woods."

"My cousin, he came to say that man root will overpower the deer."

Awepu's exasperation equaled Wakwa's enjoyment.

# Chapter 18

THE ONE HUNDRED moved in silence listening for trouble. It tolled back to them across the moist air in signals like women's voices shrewing. The men spent themselves toiling over the difficult surface toward disaster they could not see. A stench began to serve them for sight. And then vermilion blinded them. Blood washed their vision in quantity more gagging to the fighting men than a battlefield. Blood made red plush of white ground and rained down through the knuckles of the tree branches. Monstrous grunts of Locke's roan brought their hands to their ears. The grown men ringed the thicket, nonplussed as children by the sight of death in progress. The roan was down, murdered, and his blood flowed.

"Godgodgod!" Before any other man moved, Gil got free of his horse, waded into the muck of bloodied snow, holding his fowling gun high over his head.

The legs of the blue-flecked horse kicked, then stiffened. A bayonet bobbled in his spleen and with each horrible gyration started by agony the steel tore him more.

Some hunters searched the crimson thicket for the roan's owner. Gil set his trigger and took aim. Men ran out of range, but Awepu stayed watching Gil's wait before the shot. It was as Awepu's muscles tensed that Gilbert Worth exploded the charge and ended the horse's torment with a single ball.

The Ninnuock men ran west, after Wakwa and Awepu, tracing red ruts in the snow, marks of a man being dragged. Gil stood near the carcass. Père Claude approached, and wiped Gil's blood-splattered face.

"As you speak English, Father, and are an honest man,

103

there is really little purpose in my being here in Maine. Herr Jaeger, however, has done himself proud."

The priest took Gil's elbow and led him from the carnage. "Zheelber, it is the gun, I am afraid, that is the root of this trouble. Come, Dire needs us."

Locke lay abandoned for dead twenty yards away. Wakwa stayed long enough to feel life in his flesh, then hurried after the malignant spirit which had turned its breath on his mission.

Locke's abashed guards were all around him. Claude set them to building a palette and bringing deadwood for a fire. He spread his cloak to insulate Dire from the snow. In moving him, the priest discovered Locke's injury, and moaned. Gil turned from extracting his traveling kit from his saddle pouch. The agent's left leg was bent askew like a child's rag toy. The bone of the calf had given way, snapped from the kick of the wounded horse.

"The snow saved his back." Gil unscrewed the top of the silver flask, and poured the spirits into a silver, round-bottomed cup. "Why wasn't he stabbed instead of the roan?"

"He looked already dead." Claude became lost in the words of sacrament.

Gil sprinkled the brandy on Dire's lips as carefully as if it were holy oil. He forced some of the liquor behind Locke's teeth, and cradled his head and shoulders. In time, the factor wheezed to consciousness.

Dire opened one eye, then let it slide closed. "Why in the hell if you carried brandy such as that did you make such a fucking nuisance of yourself to get some at the tavern?"

"This is good stuff. I was saving it for a connoisseur."

Dire sighed his approval of Gil's gracious dialogue. He spotted Claude. "Not Extreme Unction!"

"Never mind. I am all through."

"Well, I am not!" Dire took the brandy in gulps, burning the lining of his throat with a rich fire. "Save your blessings for Deil. I am up to get the bastard!" Dire moved to stand but swiveled and bent against the ground like cork broken. "My pivot leg for a reel. Damn him!" Locke's eyes were bright with pain. "He's mad as a sailor drunk on salt water. Oh, somebody shoot my poor horse."

Gil closed his eyes. "I've done that, Dire."

"Shoot me too!" Locke turned his face into his shoulder and wept. "If I cannot walk, I cannot work!"

The priest bent over him. "Extreme Unction is not just for the dying. It is for giving strength to the living. Even living Devils."

Dire's thin hand closed on the plump paw of the priest. "Whilst he stabbed that poor beast, rabid Deil made me understand that Jeanette had thrown them out of there before they could touch your furs. I am so glad." He craned up a little to see Worth. "If you know some stout matron with an unpleasant breath looking for a post, send her my way, Gilbert. Jeanette goes home to Canada as soon as is safe."

"Dire," Gil offered, "let me make it up. I will go back in and get her. We can take her to Wareham for you."

"Do not trouble yourself, kind sir. One of these American towns is as bad as the next."

Gil worked Dire's breeches up over his knee.

"Blow it off, but don't do that!" Dire squirmed on Claude's fur coat.

Gil paid no attention, but continued slicing at the boot leather with his steel knife. One of the Abnaki undid the center ornament from his necklace and took Gil's place. The thing he cut with was a beaver's tooth, the curved incisor, which carved away the stiff boot and clinging clothes as if they were pudding.

"What good is it?" Dire pushed himself up to see. "Now the leg will only freeze."

Gil left the agent's side for his horse and unstrapped the psaltery. "Do not run away, Dire. I am going to set it."

"To music?"

Gilbert stood the box-like instrument on its side and began to pry the thin wood of the lid away from the frame.

"Zheelber!" Claude squealed.

Gil disassembled the psaltery matter-of-factly. "I need splints. Flat, smooth wood."

Dire's eyes grew round. "You mean *set* it?"

"I set the leg of a ewe once. I did not want to lose her lamb."

"Farmers."

"The odd thing is that I have had a physician as my

house guest for weeks at a time. If he weren't so far along in his age, he would have been here on this sojourn."

"Barbers overpaid."

"Ah, not this one." Gil kept Locke in conversation. "He is a scientist with an enquiring mind. At least, he admits what he does not know, like the good student. He is a disciple of Tame Deer, tries to learn the mysteries of her herbs. He is also one hell of a good flautist."

Dire smiled until he cried. "I am not cut out for heroics. I know I will scream and make a fool of myself, and I must not make a noise for Wakwa is out there hunting down Deil."

St. Aubin forced a stick of hardwood between Dire Locke's teeth. "My dear, I do not think that you will."

The men who traded with the French priest helped him pin the agent of the English-allied Indians to the ground.

Gil's green eyes moved to the priest's face, and in the next moment he straightened the leg.

Wakwa spotted the wool-coated figure of the fisher on the beach of a pond, a quarter of a mile round. He wanted to take Deil alive. But Deil's voice circling through the woods on the wind like foul smoke was crazed curses. The hunters saw him drag his frozen feet in direct line for the pond. Deil saw it as a calm sea but he wondered where the buildings of Pemaquid had gone.

Wakwa moved onto the strip of snow and sand, dropping his weapons. "Stand still!"

Scores of smoothbores being cocked behind him triggered manly memories in Deil. "Is this the greetin' I get? I'm marchin' home a wounded man an' you're all hidin' from me!" He toiled for the water.

"Stop!" Wakwa sprang over the uneven snow.

"Arrêt!" The signal went among the Abnaki, and guns slid from shoulders. The marksmen stood at ease.

Deil leaned around, bent like a bookkeeper, to trace the concerned voice. Forty feet distant Wakwa was so tall to the splitter, so straight, so brown, so unaggressive, so graceful in his bound, that Deil reassured himself, "Just a large hare." He trundled on.

"Stop him!" Wakwa screamed to his fellows.

Deil held up. Through his trance he heard the voice of a

living man. He turned around. An Indian man. Deil made straight for the pond.

The French Indians guessed the English words that Wakwa shouted, but they knew that the pond would be stoppage enough. Awepu let a bullet skid across the ice-bound water. It did not deter the fisher. Deil crashed through the frosted skin of the pond water. Wakwa dived for a hold on Deil's gore-encrusted leg and followed him under.

Some men ran for wood. Others raced to the shallows to pull Wakwa out. Gasping, already purpled, he tugged Deil by the hair, the waist, the scruff. They threw Deil aside, stiff as salt cod, and tore Wakwa's clothes off his body and beat him soundly to keep blood moving in him. They wrapped him in stroud and whipped him with sticks, lashing him into a run toward the blaze beginning at the edge of the wood. They watched him for the sign of his shivering.

Wakwa stared into the fire, reliving the instant of his failure with every muscular reach of the flame.

"A stiff-necked chap at his best." Locke mocked Deil's frozen corpse. "It is a failing somewhere in my soul, I know, mon Père, but I do not feel the least sympathy for him." Dire peeped at the body, as he was carried near to Wakwa. "You certainly know how to pick your uncles, Fox. As soon as Gilbert Worth matched up the Chinese puzzle pieces that the late Fisher Deil made of my leg, he wired me up and played a minuet on me." Dire threw his blanket to one side and revealed the leg. It was blue and shiny and swollen, but as straight as his right one. The calf was encased rigidly on each side and underneath with the flat, hard segments of the mutilated psaltery. The parts of this brace were fitted with tiny holes laced through by the instrument's wire strings. Dire leaned up on his stretcher and plucked the taut lacing. He collapsed back onto the pallet at the twang he produced. "Jesus, Fox, I am sorry, I am sorry!" he groaned.

Wakwa covered his friend and stroked his blood-soaked hair. He looked at Gil for encouragement.

"Pay him no mind, Wakwa, he's just awfully drunk."

Claude was busy easing the departure of Deil's troubled

soul. He repeated the words and the gestures he had performed over Locke, before.

"Father Claude," Wakwa questioned, "why do you bless the enemy of your friend?"

"Learn, young man, Jesus said even as the Romans nailed him to his cross, 'Father, forgive them, for they know not what they do.' There is Christianity! And when this wilderness walks with those words, comes peace."

Wakwa raised his voice to the Jesuit. "Learn, French taupowaw, that peace does not lie abed with ignorance. This man Deil knew what he did. It was whereof he acted that cut his hand and built his rage, and wasted animal life and his own, and left Dire as you see. This wilderness is condemned to unending war because there is hardly a man in her acknowledges his wrongdoing. I condemn the spirit of this body to wander this frozen ground until his fellows can stop to listen to an Indian without shooting him down, or running away like a frightened animal into a pit. These American men will not be forgiven for their ignorance, or for their fear! Deil may wander the wind for an hundred winters, or a thousand, but wander he will with an unhappy sound, until he pays me his calm attention! Your Christ is not a fit god in these woods. In Massachusetts, my land, it is no good that a man kiss his injury. It is only good, no matter the clay he is made of, that a man crave my secrets, know me, befriend me. Then he will have claim to suck the bounty of this blue earth. And she will give to him like a good mother to a motherless child. And with such a brother I will run." Something had turned in him, opened him, that had not moved him to speak at the long house. Deil lay in the snow, still and heavy as iron, the key.

Gilbert Worth repeated these sentences in the purest French that he could muster. He had tasted the effect of Wakwa's spokesmanship with each mile he had walked toward Maine. But imagined plaudits never rewarded him like the sight of the faces near the bonfire, gone redder with pride.

_____ **Chapter 19**

VAUGHAN THOMAS KIRKE got his island. But on the advice of Silent Fox there was nothing exchanged to indicate a sale. It was not a sale but a letting of use. Kirke Company Ltd. was granted the use of the sea-surrounded land for certain guarantees: work, the seasonal seeking of permission to use wood, and payment for raw supplies in any form requested by the northern tribes.

"I warn you against any written covenant on the treaty. I vow for Kirke that he will keep his part, and Dire Locke will vow to him on your account. Ink runs in the least drizzle."

Of Wakwa's main idea, alliance with English-American towns against a larger, more distant enemy—why not? Castin's peace had lasted twenty good years. But cooperation would be a long time under consideration. At the end of an octave of days of talk they gave Wakwa permanent welcome, and free run of their wild woods if the Cape Cod tribes got too pinched in the belly, or became fodder for the masterly Iroquois.

And then, the Abnaki and the northerners left for a new site, northwest in a region of lakes, until the affair of Deil had blown over in the town.

Gil inquired as he and Wakwa packed for their own departure, "What is the enmity between the Massachusetts Indians and the Six Nations to the west? Is it their strong alliance with England? I thought you Massachuseuck were neutral."

"Gilbert, rather, we are neuter since Philip's War. And that is to be neither strong nor weak, but a people between,

109

siding nowhere, but like sexless creatures resisting all advances." Wakwa worked and talked.

"Then you are stronger than all coalitions."

"Except our backs are broken, for we are walked over by all sides. And why? It is a story you must ask Awepu to tell. He keeps them all. Have him tell you of sixty winters ago, when Philip walked himself to the Six Nations, alone, in the middle of his war, knowing that with Iroquois aid the English towns would be leveled and the plantations at an end. Ask him about the nameless Iroquois sent to kill Philip, and of Philip's killing the assassin, instead. Ask Awepu to explain to you why the Six Nations then called Philip a murderer and refused to meet with him, or to help exterminate the towns. Gilbert, my uncle, you have your farm by courtesy of the Iroquois keeping faith with the English, and breaking it with men of their own race. Who am I to guess their reasons? We are a divided people. I am neuter, now, but I offer my soul to the service of those who trust me, so we may someday walk like men."

"Elizabeth Dowland thinks you quite a man, already."

"Oo. Less her, that leaves only one million, nine hundred ninety-nine thousand, nine hundred ninety-nine white people to convince to think the same."

"You caught that census in the *Gazette?* Do you get it delivered to the sachimmaacommock?"

"The trade blankets that Dire sends are wrapped in it. The ink is good for keeping the moths away."

"You hate them?"

"Moths?"

"The Iroquois, sachim!"

"Gilbert, I hate no one. I only will serve no one."

"That's strange, I thought I just heard you say that you are hell-bent to serve everyone."

Their gear was tidied and ready.

Claude, the captive, the corpse, and Dire Locke went on the road to Pemaquid.

"You are sure, Dire, you won't need me to give some testimony?" Gil asked from the side of Locke's litter.

"Thank you all the same. But I want this solved the best possible way, that means with money. The delicate point is just how much I should offer for the blood-wite. Too much and the shire-reeve will smell you about. Too little, he'll smell me."

Claude seconded, "Don't you fellows come, or there will be a riot."

Wakwa tried to talk the priest into accepting escort for his caravan of wounded and dead.

"The more pitiful we look, the better," Claude refused. "We 'av it all figured out. Like a good boy you will stay here with your chicks, and we will get your horses shod at Thomas' house and back out to you. If all is well, they will be led back here, and I, personally, will ring the mission bell. I will ring it and ring it as if Louis himself were sailing into port. And then, you babes go right away, south."

"This is farewell?"

"Renard! Between you and me there is no farewell. I will see you again, before the face of God. What sweet discussions we will have about many things. There is much for you to learn."

Wakwa shook his head merrily over this single-mindedness.

"Silent Fox, send me away with some hope that you will not live a proud prince like the rest of them."

Wakwa's eyes were overcome with a softness. "Claude. The words are in your book, how are they? How are they . . . ? 'Our heritage has been turned over to aliens, our homes to foreigners. We have become orphans without a father; Our mothers are like widows. . . . With a yoke on our necks we are persecuted.' You know the words, how are they, Claude? 'The crown has fallen from our head . . . but thou, O Lord, art enthroned forever. . . .'" Wakwa could not go on.

The old Jesuit finished for him. "'. . . Renew our days as of old; For if Thou wert to reject us completely, Thou wouldst be going too far in thine anger against us.'"

Dire's nasal voice needled, "So, Claude, you got what you came for, a golden soul."

"You got what you came for too, you Lucifer!"

"No I didn't."

Wakwa was at his side. "What is it, Dire, that I owe you?"

Locke tallied on his fingers. "The agreed-on price for your political coming out. . . . I get back one shirt, one handkerchief, one yard flannel cloth, and a baker's dozen buttons."

For two days, the southerners camped outside the town waiting for the bells. At the dawn of the third, they sharpened their knives and oiled their guns. They planned a night raid and occupation of Kirke's house.

The February twenty-first sun reached its high point. It hung like a disc of brass in the white sky. A sound struck the shimmering air and the waiting men looking up seemed to see the sun vibrate like a gong. Again. Again. The bell intoned past the forbidden border—Free to go home. Free to go. Go!

_____ **Chapter 20**

LIKE WARNING SMOKE of softer seasons to come, fog shied into Buzzards Bay on the mid-afternoon wind. It was kind cover while the woman-shaped land dressed for spring. When the fog parted in shreds by sunset, some secret jewel had been added that would show pastel, next day, under warm dawn air off the sea.

But the evenings were not devoid of color. The cold river took gold and purple from the sky, and the reflective bellies of shad going to spawn riffled the waterway silver in its deeps. The greening marsh reeds, bowed under moisture, possessed skins of yellow and piths of russet.

The color of this renewal, in each spring she had known since her birth, attached Elizabeth Dowland to the region with umbilical strength. Her transmutation of its hues and textures into dyes and cloth and garments was the dedication that did not constrict her. Her only dictator was the weather. He told her when and how and what she would gather, render, and sew. She was like the Indians who were her family.

She crept into the wetuomemese, the little hut where she would spend the time of her menses, and thought of her aunt's solitary journey south, to help to place Dowland Farm under her control. Hanna's effort to win a woman proprietorship of the estate seemed an ironic turning of Elizabeth's purpose.

In this March Elizabeth was of the mood of giving back, of replenishing the lit land out of the womb of her hands, with her creations. She could not foresee herself coping a segment of it to own individually, chaining the enormous, stolid body of ground to herself and her issue, forever. As she sat and sewed the dress for Panther Eye, Elizabeth saw the difficulties in peaceful parceling and inheriting of land as the resentment of the earth at this puny imprisonment. To her ears, the vexations of going to law over land sounded like rattling of shackles by the soil, which was endowed with muscles greater in grandeur than any man's.

Elizabeth's conviction grew strong as she plied the breadths of cloth with her gold needle. "I am a case in point. Look at how I tremble at being locked away like this for five days every month, month after month, because I am such a large mystery—ah, yes," she sent a smile to her sleeping son, "I, the creature who bleeds without dying."

The dress formed into a festive thing, satisfying to the sight as vibrant fruit. Elizabeth made it into a soft sacque with a high neckline that spread, monk-like, into a cowl. This collar could be drawn over the wearer's head like a hood. The body within it would make its shape. But the dress was equipped with woven ties to wrap at will from bust to waist, or crossing the abdomen, binding the hips. It was many dresses in one, planned to be merciful to its owner's imperfections.

Elizabeth made her douche in the water that swirled under a river falls, and rushed home to show the family her work. Pequawus was in the sachimmaacommock alone. Shyly, she displayed the finished gown for his opinion.

"Wame!" Pequawus called it whole, a total and unified piece of work.

Elizabeth held it like an animate thing, or like a large doll in which a child searches for a spirit. She looked and

113

looked again into its darkness to see it clearly, to see through it. Tenderly, she laid it out flat, its long arms outstretched. It was shroud, yearning. She sighed a weaver's sigh over it. Then with the determined self-sacrifice of the most proficient artisan she took her knife and began to cut holes into the fabric so flawlessly woven.

She left a pattern over the heart of the dress—a fertile pod in filigree, with runners extending out, like one she had seen on Qunneke's bark vessels. The beautiful bosom of the woman who was to wear it would be glimpsed there while hideous memories would be covered over in all other places. The Ninnuock design would have to be bound now, using twist from the same color wool.

Elizabeth put down her knife and rubbed her hands to warm them for the rest of the work. And Pequawus rested his hand on her hair, content for her soul.

No one would come with her to deliver the dress. Excuses were whispered across doorways. Wetu by wetu. As the sun sank, Elizabeth walked home, annoyed by this snobbery. Qunneke was preoccupied combing the snarls out of her long hair preparatory to washing it.

Elizabeth said to Sequan, "I could wait until your father comes home, but who knows when that will be? I will do it by myself."

"I come?"

"Thee?"

"Me!" Sequan began the search for her moccasins.

"Good for you!"

"Good for you!" Sequan echoed.

They went out into the violet shimmer, disconnecting their hold of one another only to let the evening light play in the palms of their hands.

A seepage of smoke from the thin shell of the house showed them that Panther Eye was at home. Elizabeth called in English. Sequan used the native tongue.

Elizabeth and Wakwa's daughter turned to watch the western horizon flush magenta while they waited.

Elizabeth sighed, "Let us go home, Little, no one wants to bring this dress and no one wants to receive it."

Sequan scuttled backward to look up at the smokehole. She made a dash around the circumference of the hut.

When she arrived back at the front mat, she simply parted it and disappeared, inside.

"Sequan!" Elizabeth followed her. They collided just inside the door.

"Zabeth?" Sequan tugged at Elizabeth's red cloak. "Why does she not sweep?"

Elizabeth went dumb at the menace in Panther Eye's look.

"Zabeth!" Sequan insisted.

Elizabeth backed the little girl toward the curtain. "Sequan, you should go."

"I am come with you!" Sequan stamped her foot.

"Sequan! Go."

"Zabeth. . . ."

"Go to your mother, baby."

Panther Eye spat.

"Zabeth?"

"Go!"

The child ran out.

"So quickly? Did she not give you to eat or drink from thanks?" Qunneke asked her daughter in her dialect.

Sequan crawled into her grandfather's lap, pouting.

The combs began to draw through the hair. "And you came back alone?"

"What is the matter?" Pequawus stroked the small head pressed against his belly.

"If you act this way, Sequan, next time I shall not let you go."

"I will not want to go!"

"Sequan! You know I must wash my hair, and we must eat, and you waste the night stirring up storms!" Qunneke twisted and her five-foot-long fall of hair streamed down her back as she stood to go to the little girl.

Sequan showed her face for a moment.

"Little," the mother crooned, "tell me why you are low." She held out her arms to her. "Where is Zabeth?"

Sequan fled to the comfort of her mother.

"Trouble between this one and that one, again?" Pequawus said to Tame Deer. "I thought we were past that."

"What troubles you?" Qunneke rocked the child.

"My mother, why does Panther Eye not sweep?"

"Oh!" Tame Deer's hands slid smoothly over the round body. "That is a long tale. She has many worries. Some night Awepu will tell it thee, around the fire."

"Why could Zabeth not say that?"

"What did she say, Sequan?"

Sequan began to cry. "I'll tell the women's council on her, I'll tell my father!" The girl wailed, angry at her longing for Wakwa's second wife. " 'Go!' she said. 'Go!' "

Quenneke put the little girl aside. She leaned at the door, looking up the slope, vexing her finger with her teeth. "Pequawus, I think you and I must go there." Her eyes became drawn to a growing sparkle on top of the dark rise. The entire camp heard the screams. "Qunneke!"

Qunneke took the hill like a hind. She forced her way up toward a figure trailing flames from its long clothes. She was naked to the waist but she did not hold back from the tails of fire wiggling round the hair of Wakwa's second wife, like vipers. It seared her own skin but she threw Elizabeth down and tore the smoldering dress out of her singed hands and pounded fire with it. Qunneke caught Elizabeth's smoking body close.

The other wife cowered under this new beating, then grasped for the cool softness of the embrace, pressing ash-filled eyes against the roundness of Qunneke's breasts. She did not know who she was. She shouted from behind the blind of unpartable heart.

Fathers of families ran from their houses. Youths clustered on the hill staring at the smoking tatter of the white woman, the saunks whom they called New-leaf-through-whom-the-sun-shines among themselves.

Qunneke mobilized them. "Get Waban. Go for the taupowaw. Find me Mosq. Send a runner for the whiteman who makes her medicine." She peeled the stinking remnants of Elizabeth's woolen clothes away.

Men who had never walked to Elizabeth came forward to help at this moment, lifting the fuming, rigid, bright white woman onto a blanket, which they held up at the corners, saving her the agony of touch. They yelled as the willow-thin body lashed out of their invention.

Pequawus saw her fall and watched her claw at the ground as if she would dig out a hole to bury herself. What was not burned on her was going black from beating. He waved the flaring torches back, and uttered tears. He said, "Nippisse!" He ripped his own wrapping off, drew it wide, and let it descend slowly on air and settle on her. He dropped to his knees and slid his arms underneath Dowland's daughter. By the power of his will he denied his age and rose with her and walked as smoothly as shade crossing the moon.

"I have seen that look before!" Waban accused him as he gained the hill with the help of his stick. "What has happened now? Why is it always you with some horror in your arms? You had that look the night my sister died! Who now? Our-Elizabeth! Elizabeth!" The old sachim touched her dangling hair and hanks of it came away in his hands.

Pequawus passed down toward Wakwa's house and Waban pushed himself to the top.

He chased down the story for himself. He found the charred club near the ruin of the dress. "Our great, new hope!" He forced the rag on his second son, Nuppohwunau. Waban took his stout staff and broke it in half with only his hands. "The jagged end of this I will ram up the ass of the mattanit who has spoiled Elizabeth!" He scurried along the traceable route through a litter of char and stones toward Panther Eye's hut. The men with the pitch and bark torches struggled to keep up. "Mattanit! Mattanit! Devil! Get her. Get Panther Eye and bring her to me!"

They tore Pequawus away from Elizabeth's hold and ushered him to mishe-miawene, a council on a grand scale. It was Qunneke's and Sequan's part to witness Elizabeth trying to avoid constant and piteous screaming.

# Chapter 21

WHEN THEIR PHYSICAL ALLURE WANED, Ninnuock women were not thrown aside like chaff. They were an integral part of the well-being of the tribe. To be past childbearing was no disgrace. Proud histories trailed each elder female like her grandchildren. Since she had filled the communal barns with corn and beans and potatoes, had satisfied the stomachs of her husband and children with bread and fruit, had built the bark domes that kept them warm and dry, her eyes shone with practical wisdom. Her dances and her songs and her personage had lent grace to family life, and inspired the pleasure that augmented the poetry of her race, and the race itself. Now that she danced no more, she illumined her people's future out of her store of confidence built in the past. It was in the natural evolution of their life's seasons that the autumn of the women was even more vibrantly colored than the balmy neophyte days.

The women's council adjudicated intra-tribal difficulties. It reciprocated the counsel of the men. The women delegated which men should come before the general population to seek acclaim as sachim. And, at times, usually in densest sorrow, when sickness or war had left them leaderless, one of their number served as woman-sachim herself.

The mothers created the hierarchy of power, out of men whose virtues they knew down to the strength with which they had once sucked a teat.

This was the group which was to consider the actions of Panther Eye.

Panther Eye waited for her trial under the watch of some of the young wives. She was too experienced with the jealousy of other women to waste vital time listening to

118

their sneering and their gossip. She gave attention to a disagreement breaking out between Waban and Pequawus.

"Do not try to bring her here!" the sagamore insisted to the old sachim. "No one must move her! I have carried her. She is most tender . . . it is as if the flesh and bones would pull apart like over-boiled meat. You cannot."

Waban squeezed Pequawus' arm in sympathy; he nodded. Then he ordered Mosq, "Bring her."

As Elizabeth was brought through the passageways to Waban's room horrified sound from the hangers-on stirred, and awed the waiting judges. Panther Eye began to devise her defense.

Waban brought the two of them together in the orange of an arena lit by a good fire. The shrewd old ones sat on the fur-covered floor close enough to see even the movement in the muscles of a witness's face. Waban had Panther Eye by her wrist. He lifted the cloth that covered Elizabeth, showing her naked, stiff body to everybody.

Blood had dried where it had run. Skin was black and green over her bones. Lymph pooled in fissures on her flesh. Her blistered eyelids made a grotesque mask of her face. Her hair was char.

Waban touched her injuries and said to Panther Eye, "Did you make this, and this, and this?"

Pequawus wished for the freedom to hide his face. It was not Elizabeth's disfigurement or the sight of her suffering alone that he did not want to see. He wished he could avoid Waban's brutal, swift management of the affair, his bringing the court down on Panther Eye as surely as if there were no trial. Every moan he brought out of Elizabeth with his uncouth touches was a blow with a club to Panther Eye. But it served.

"I ask you, and I ask you, and you do not answer me! Woman, did you this? Did you make ugly what was beautiful? Did you hurt fingers that once could work? Did you?"

"I cannot answer that question, father." Panther Eye looked him full in the face. "To answer an act and to answer for guilt are not the same."

Waban looked at the roof of his lodge, then at his brother-in-law. "Pequawus, I should leave her to you. She wants a feast of words!"

"You should leave her to my son. Panther Eye is his

ward. He must answer for her or throw her to your mercies."

"Your son is not here."

"He will come."

"We do not know when."

"When he is finished his business for this tribe, he will be able to take care of family business."

"His journey was not my doing, Pequawus! And this crime is not family business! The mother of a sachim lies ruined, at least she is at the edge of ruin! To attack the mother of a sachim-to-be is to attack the future of us all!" Waban waved Mosq away with the pitiful armload. "Will you speak in your son's place, Gray Wolf?"

Pequawus said coolly, "I cannot."

Waban whirled away from him onto Panther Eye. "And you, the woman made of wood, will you save us a night's sleep? Tell us how you paid Elizabeth for the kindness she showed you?" Waban threw the burnt gift at her feet.

"I paid her what I owed her."

Waban gripped his knife handle. He wanted to rip it from its sling and slide the ground steel up her, to cut her at the matrix.

Panther Eye turned the soft underside of her naked arms to him and then to the judges. "I ask for no garment other than my skin."

"It is time you covered those marks up. Time to get married, to be happy, to be decent. You want that. I know you do. You asked Wakwa before he left us to think on a husband for you. That is all Our-Elizabeth was doing, getting you ready for your joy, covering up your past with a garment, beautiful to wear."

"And I say, father, she is covering her tracks. She and I have each broken laws. I do not deny my guilty pleasures. And I have paid!" Panther Eye let her long, black hair sway away from the scar. "I beg my corn, I chase down my own meat, I carry wood on my back. I have been alone. But this white woman, this English witch, denied her god, her father, her mother, her promised man, and her grounds for . . . your nephew . . . her pleasure. She never pays and shame grows on her like moss. Covering me, she thought she would strip herself of her crimes. I have done well, I think, to give her just what she needed."

Waban stood befuddled about how to proceed. His neck was stuck in his own trap. He looked to Pequawus.

Pequawus sucked his pipe. "I say, bring Elizabeth back, brother. She should be here if it is she who is being tried."

Waban's head cleared. "Panther Eye, unhappy soul, who seeks love and never finds it, I say, Elizabeth offered you love, not a dress, and your stone heart could not feel it. I say you are always gloomy because your heart is good only for a weight. Give me a good reason why I should not toss you and it into the river." The old headman sat down comfortably and with a chuckle.

"Father, how great a man you are to look into love as the dark cave where all our trouble begins. So many strange things happen there. You call my heart a stone that cannot warm to love, and I say, Elizabeth herself is a stone dragging her husband and his family down. She whips his daughter, and rules his wife."

Buzzing. The women's council demanded to see Qunneke.

While he waited for the next display, Waban put it to Panther Eye, "Who told you Sequan was beaten?"

She covered her misstep poorly. "One hears these things in the wind."

Qunneke trembled, standing in front of so many inquisitive eyes. She looked for her mother among the sisterhood of judges. Qunneke's mother turned her eyes down and away.

Pequawus complained, "Why do we have Tame Deer in the center of the room? What has she done?"

Qunneke moved small indefinite steps in her embarrassment. "I went to her as soon as I heard her on the hill. I ran as fast as I could. I have neglected her, I know, but now she lies calling for me and I should go." Qunneke's hand lifted her untended, sweated hair from her face. "I would do anything for my husband's wife."

Panther Eye spoke up. "We believe you."

Qunneke turned to Waban. "Why does she speak to me? Why am I here?"

Her mother said, "To answer, Did Elizabeth strike my granddaughter?"

Qunneke was open-mouthed.

"Yes or no."

"Yes."

"Poor daughter."

"Not poor!" Qunneke's back went straight. "Except if you have brought me here to beat me down like Elizabeth. I will say this one time. . . ." She looked at Waban and Pequawus, weary and hurt.

Pequawus did not offer her help. Now he was eager for her to shed the winding cloth of her private self.

"One time . . . Sequan is a good child. By a game she came close to burning Moses. To burn someone shows bad spirit or bad training. A blow upon the hand is mild punishment for such a thing as my baby did. I wish the lesson could have been taught in some other way, but just anger does not always wait. Look at you all shaking your heads over me! Would you have Sequan not punished at all? Perhaps not, as the camp smells of braised woman, tonight, and Panther Eye stands here, free!"

Panther Eye spoke softly through the silence that met Qunneke's rare outburst. "Saunks, you oppose me. I do not oppose you. Ever since I was a girl it is you my friends and I held before us. Your beauty was the sun and moon for us. I remember your hair."

Qunneke quaked, feeling how dirty her hair was just then, and remembering combing it to wash it, leaving Elizabeth to go out alone.

"And now, it is said that you are seen coming across the bridge with a double load of wood on your back so the fragile English girl will not have to carry. How do you manage the shame they put you through? Do you hear them through the curtain in the passageway, your husband and his bride? Lonely Qunneke, you have not brought forth for four years . . . not a child in four years."

Tame Deer looked for help from the sachim, or her father-in-law, but they were adrift of her pains. They watched the faces of the council. She stood very still, wiped her cheeks with her sooty fingertips in unconscious feminine gesture. The black smeared her more. "It is not my name you gnaw at. You are stalking Wakwa and I do not know why. But I will stand between you and him because he is the savior of your life, and I am joined in that. I am his wife."

"You are loyal as the best of slaves."

"I say service to one another makes for happiness in a house."

"Is serving happiness? You have been alone so long you do not remember any other way."

"I am not lonely. I can never recall feeling alone. I am the wife of a loving man and his second wife is subject to me in all fitting things."

Panther Eye cocked her head.

"All proper things."

"And the proof? Why do you not conceive?"

"When have you conceived?"

"We have not lain with the same man! I may be barren. Or it may be my men have all been sterile as that yellow-haired farmer who follows you about."

Pequawus threw down the pipe and demanded, "Stop this, Waban!"

But the sachim only tickled his calloused thumb with the cutting edge of his knife.

Qunneke spread her feet on the matting for the fight. "I do not know how a child is formed or is not formed. All I can say to you is, Elizabeth is all that a second wife should be."

"No doubt she is all a first wife should be."

Qunneke put her hands against her eyes and emitted a soft sob.

Waban tried gently. "Daughter, do you understand? She is saying that since Sequan, Wakwa has not lain with you."

Qunneke had learned something since her first ingenuous "Yes" to her mother. She began a very careful verbal walk. "When I wish connection with my husband, I grant myself to him. Should he pass the boundary between us without consent?"

"Tame Deer, I know a man does not violate the one he loves, but if he does not lie with you, if you are his sister, not his wife, then he is false to keep you, and have you wait upon this other one. And if he is false, he is not fit to lead."

Qunneke saw what she had to do. "Shall I recount the times? The very night of his wedding to Elizabeth, Wakwa remained with me." In the narrow corridor between truth and falsehood, Qunneke's statement flew to the heart of what might have been. "Rain began to fall. Elizabeth went

123

to sleep. We talked of Gilbert passing by. Wakwa asked for me."

A look passed between her and Pequawus. Her mother rose and left the room. Panther Eye held a hand over her breast as if Qunneke's answer had struck her there.

Qunneke went to Panther Eye for the first time. "Miserable woman, do you not know that he loves you, too?"

Panther Eye ran against the wall, lost in another crime and another trial. She dropped to her knees, covering the seam in her scalp with her arms. "I have never had to do with him!"

Qunneke took control of her, held her firmly against her scorched skirt, cradling her fearful face in the palm of one hand. "Panther Eye, your experience is far wider than mine in one certain way, but wisdom in love can grow in quiet spaces as it has for me in the time I have chosen to spend alone. Love does not mean only one special kind of concourse. Wakwa can love you without bending over you, or wanting to. He can extend to anyone, to me, his wife, to Gilbert, to you and be traitor to no one. And not to himself, either. It is that way for women, too. For me and Elizabeth. Why should I not love her? She is young, she is pretty. She delights me. When Wakwa is gone I have her face, her scent, her touch. She is like a knot, another twist in the cord that binds Wakwa and me. I see him reflected in her eyes. It delights me when she delights him."

Panther Eye slithered out of Qunneke's grasp. "It is Wakwa who must endure the romance of his wives!"

"Listen to me." Quietly Qunneke held her point. "I must go to her. Because I love her. But if you ever learn to keep yourself to yourself you will come to know that there is no torn ground between one love and another. Loving man or woman or child or place is all one thing. Love is an unbroken plain, like our winter valley under snow. The reach of a heart is endless."

Qunneke left quickly.

Waban took Wakwa's wild ward aside. "Panther Eye, say something, anything that can save you." What she whispered in his ear about herself and Weeping Heart made his leonine head shake, no, no. She laced up her doom with her plea to be mother to Waban's half-breed grandson to come. Sweeping these surprises into his brain with the speed of the wind that he was named for, Waban held her face between his hands and kissed her lips goodbye. "It is too late and too soon you come to happiness. You have been untrue to the great man who saved your life, and how shall I forget, was raised without a mother. Beauty, change your climate. Be bothered by men no more."

Panther Eye fell against him and he wrapped her with a stout arm.

"How will you have it?" he asked.

"Quickly!" Her lashes wet his neck.

While the curious stood outside under the night silver Waban returned her pained embrace in front of them, slipped his knife from its sling, and with hunter's finesse, found and broke Panther Eye's heart with the flint.

A darkness drenched the soil at the door.

_____ Chapter 22

QUNNEKE DISASSEMBLED the walls of the passageway between the two rooms of their house that night. She pulled off the outside bark and rolled the inner mats. She uprooted the poles. She did this duty of closing sickness out with a low heart. She covered the doorways of the now distinct east and west domes, which had once opened hospitably onto the hall, a free conduit for household traffic. She lay next to Elizabeth in the isolated room, and lapsed into sleep on the younger woman's whimpers.

Reclusion in pain became Elizabeth's reality. The entire agonized mass of her became her. Her exterior was like a viscera exposed to air; soft, slick, shocked, aching from life. She stayed stiff and still in a labor toward relief. Hot, dirty ashes swam through the fluid of her eyes and parched it away. As the tear ducts produced more, the filthy particles were delicately dislodged and they knifed through the slick coating of the eyeballs. Blood and lymph ran her scalded scalp. Black and purple bruises rode her contused bones. Attempts at speech from her battered mouth sent screams to the roof. Burned hands curled over breasts hard from not being milked.

In the morning, Pequawus opened the curtain onto the sight of Elizabeth trying to suckle her son. The man turned and left. Out in the chill sun, the sounds of Elizabeth's suffering returned his mind to decades past. The spur of anguished sound moved the widower to lucid memories. The days of his prime became more pertinent to him than the garbled present.

He was thrown back into competition with a young Waban. Again, he was the father of a nursling boy, Manunnappu, who at four moons of age was already his image. Pequawus was next to his wife, Nippisse, Little Water, who met the promise of her name and was his source of refreshment, the place where he stopped to immerse himself, coming away replenished. Friendly as her brother, she had a tender heart, and like the pond she spawned life and liveliness from her deep center to her bubbling periphery. Pequawus heard once more the uproar of a certain Taquonk feast, the prelude to the public election in which he and Nippisse's big-faced, big-hearted brother were the contenders. He watched her lissome back, again, as she mounted the meadow alone, wandering from the gaiety to gather alder and wintergreen for the pesuponk, the sweat cave where the fragrant steam would clear the minds of the delegates who would bring the decisive vote. Pequawus had not seen her face as she walked away that day. He had shouted out "Nippisse!" so she would turn toward him for a momentary parting. His mind always eased him away from recollection of how he had next seen her.

"He is frightened of her," Qunneke was saying. "Moses does not know her. If he sucks she pulls away. If he does not suck she cries for him and the tears run and the eyes . . . oh, Pequawus, the eyes!" Qunneke passed into her own room with Moses.

The gray-haired man went to the woman from whom he had held aloof until recently. Her abused face was swollen, the skin of unmarred places stretching to compensate for bulbous conformations elsewhere. Her heavy wool cloak had prevented her ravaging by fire, and the horrific effect of her blackened, reduced hair, and the fissures of her scalp where flame had winged from the ends of locks to the roots, destroying the skin, caused more permanent harm to the viewer than to the victim. The blisters on her wrists and fingertips did not frighten him, but they made her dependent for the most fundamental needs. Her fine eyelids were humped over the pus and blood of her ulcerated eyes—frog's eyes. Not a part of her seemed free to move or touch without causing harm to another part, or to healing. Pequawus saw the loose tooth, and made a prayer that it would reseat itself. "If the jaw is broken, so is her hold on life. Manit! She is like a rotting fruit, broken and smelling of her ooze."

"Elizabeth Dowland!" The Massachusetts man called to the soul he saw throbbing in this new embodiment.

She was not a creature who talked. Her tongue was hard against the roof of her dehydrated mouth. But the father-in-law knew that she had heard, for her windpipe moved as she swallowed in a useless attempt at speech. Drop by drop, he moistened her withered lips with the water Qunneke had ready. He held her through the pain of assimilation.

He murmured to her spirit with words out of her tradition. " 'Know then that God has overturned me, And has enclosed me in his net. Lo, I cry "Murder," but I am not answered; I call for help, but there is no justice. My way he has walled up that I may not pass on; And upon my paths he sets darkness. My glory he has stripped from upon me, And he has taken the crown off my head. He has broken me down on every side, and I am gone. . . .' "

Her arms reached up at the cadence of the verse that had, by her upbringing, formed the second language of her soul. Pequawus caught her from behind, where he sat with bowed back. They stayed like this, he remembering couplets, fragments, whole passages of the sacred poetry that had been his introduction to her English tongue. And by his choice of the drear, he conveyed some notion of his sympathy to her wounded mind, which was locked in black by her blindness.

Like the scratch of broom, she answered, "Father!" and

though the man did not know whether she appealed to the deceased Dowland or to him, unfamiliarity with her melted, and she became opportunity resurrected, the means for him to salvage a being as he had not been able to salvage his wife, Nippisse.

"She will lose her milk if she does not nurse," Qunneke told Pequawus softly, in Narragansett.

Sequan heard, too, and crawled against Elizabeth's side. A veteran of suckling both her mothers, she primed the distended nipple with a kindly tongue, then began to pump Elizabeth's hard, overfilled breast. Sequan performed the service with care, sensing soreness as her small hand guided the breast against her mouth. Even Sequan's artful management of this life-link caused Elizabeth's burnt hands to rise and her bruised heels to push against the matting, moving her body away. The grandfather received Elizabeth into his lap, as she inched upward. In her tongue, he implored her to bear the pain, but she was out of herself, lost in grotesque moorings, incapable of will. Her body strove for its own life.

Sequan wept against her mother. She left the room as Qunneke dipped a rag in boiled water to clear the yellow strings of dried fluid from Elizabeth's eyes. The little girl returned, half-carrying, half-dragging her brother's solid twenty-one pounds into the sickroom. She prompted the infant, getting him to nurse. Qunneke watched and worried. Moses' yearning hurt this white woman when she was healthy. Elizabeth's response to his grasping resigned the family to the fact that Panther Eye had stolen nurture from Elizabeth's motherhood.

"Mother," Sequan piped, "I am too old for milk. I am four. I shall drink from my hands at the stream. Moses is your baby now."

Qunneke cried in front of the girl, at her own loss.

The child comforted. "Zabeth will be your girl baby. Why should we not give her to drink, too?"

Sequan's fingers pressed mother's milk from Qunneke into a basin. Together they watched the nourishment from the bowl go down.

*　　*　　*

"Nippisse is a small circle of water. A pond. It is Little Water, opposite to the Great Water, the sea." Pequawus threw Elizabeth his history as a lifeline. "Nippisse was my wife."

He was at his accustomed place, behind her at her head, lightly pressing Elizabeth's temples with his long fingers.

"She left the plain to gather sweet wood. The election of the sachim was nigh. She left our son, your husband, with Qunneke's mother, because, already, he was large and heavy and she . . . she was slight. I do recall Tame Deer making games for him—she was as old then as Sequan is now, and my little one was amiable with her. The noise was great in the field, because it was fall-of-the-leaf. How we feasted in those days! We had carved the loins of thirty black bears besides other meat. Not one bear, as was brought in for your wedding in the fall. We had thirty. Thirty-one had been wounded. Thirty were taken.

" 'Nippisse, do not go alone!' I called out. She straightened her back when she had climbed the hill. I knew it would be bent on the way down after she had chosen her wood. I wanted her to save her strength for better things . . . she had skin soft as silk from the corn. The men slapped my haunch when I trotted after her while Waban blew hot air around about what a grand sachim he would be.

" 'She teases me to the woods, running ahead,' thought I, and then, 'the woman only wishes to be free.' But I walked over the round belly of the hill just to admire her back as she ran. I saw her. Her back. Small. She had run so far. The hands of a he-bear were on her shoulders. His, not mine, was the last embrace she knew. They say I shrieked, I howled like a summer storm. I know that I ran. My speed and my noise frightened the bear and he dropped her into my arms and went away.

"I see her always. She has no face. I try to see. There is only a pit of red. Even the bones of her cheeks are eaten away. Eyes, there is one . . . I kneel with her in my arms for her strong spirit is not gone. It hovers as her brother and the young men thunder by. They go after the bear. I tender her. I would not, I did not lay her down till dark, long after her heart died, and I felt that I was waste."

Many breaths passed to the height of the high room before Pequawus spoke, again.

"That marked the beginning of Waban's sway. His powers were born out of Nippisse's face. Some called me woman. Some stood by me and said that I was true and wise. The sagamores argued before the people which was the better course—to preserve and honor that which is loved, or first, to kill the threat. By a few, they sided with Waban. Yet, Waban has leaned most heavily on me of anyone, all these years. And I try to give him aid, but on my worst nights I wonder if it were not he were right and I wrong."

Elizabeth bestowed kisses on his hand with her shapeless lips.

"I have no regret when I go before Nippisse's grave."

Elizabeth's voice made a scrooping exit from her damaged mouth. "What doth Wakwa say?"

"Ah! The sachim!" Pequawus' hand warmed with pride. "His speech is the comfort of my age. Elizabeth, daughter, Manunnappu saith that if I had not been that which I am, that I never would have followed my wife up the hill. Had I been blustering with Waban, the wounded bear would have finished with Nippisse and entered among us and slain numbers of the feasters. And where would we be, then? Wakwa holds with me against rushing at obstacles."

A spring snow melted, leaving the earth washed and open, smelling of honey.

Waban looked in. "When Wakwa is finally here, you will have walked beyond all this, Elizabeth, beautiful as ever, and as fat as I am."

"Uncle," she said sourly, "blind people hear tremendously well. The deer mice no longer play in my basket of threads. The earth is warm, and they are gone to the meadow. Above my own smell, I catch the scent of spring. He promised to be here when the snow was gone."

"Wakwa will keep his promise."

"Better he does not. What use am I to him, now?"

"Why, Elizabeth! He must at least come home to talk of his business, with me."

_____ **Chapter 23**

SKUNKS FRIGHTED in the night sprayed perfume, which put the homing men in mind of summer. They stopped to camp under stars, on ground gathering to crag into the palisades which made the riverbank of home.

The delegation had shrunk in size, New Hampshire men and Namskekets splitting off west and east, days before. They had left two souls in their wake, one frostbitten man and another who died of a fever. Wakwa buried them, saying that they had reached home before the rest. Now the Massachuseuck waited out the last sleep between them and reunion.

Wakwa sat up late with Gil. "Give yourself five, six quiet days, then on the seventh come to my house and we will make merry!"

"Where shall I come? Will you be requartered for spring or still in winter valley?"

Wakwa looked at Gil, surprised. "I do not know!" He hugged his belly and rocked in expectation. "I will send for you, an honor guard, to show my love for the great service you have lent to me."

"Make it a feminine one!"

They sat close while others fell asleep.

"Well . . . ," Wakwa offered, "I will find soon, whether I have one wife or two."

"Being quite desperate, I will settle for one." Without moving his eyes from the sky, Gil said, "In dry times like these, Fox, you would be well advised to let go my knee."

Awepu appeared out of the woods, his pipe between his teeth. He reached into Wakwa's tobacco pouch.

131

"Awepu!" Wakwa pulled away. "Ask if you need tobacco."

"Who needs tobacco? I have not taken anything out of your sack. Look in."

Wakwa and Gil pulled the string wide and stared at a downy, partly feathered little falcon, newly fallen out of its nest and abandoned.

"Oh!" Wakwa crooned, "I am reminded of someone!"

"It is your wife, and for her. I am taking home a baby kit fox with a chewed ear for Tamoccon. You watch, by summer they will be friends."

"Where are you going?" Gil called to Wakwa's back as the sachim stood up away from them and began to run.

Awepu sat in Wakwa's place. "I would guess, Gilbert, that he is going home."

"I will stand there in the sun with my arms open to my men as they make this last hill, tomorrow. I will say, 'Brothers, I came first to do you honor and be here to welcome you home.' They will not believe me!" Wakwa smiled slyly and changed his stride to descend to the double swell he recognized as his own house.

He was toppled by guards who lunged at him just below the ridge. After brief scrimmage they knew him and sank backward, embarrassed. "Sachim!"

Wakwa went on his way, his happy mood only slightly askew. He fought to go quietly, not to disturb the sleepy midnight of the camp. The region's fragrant wood, its clinging smoke, the breath of nocturnal wildflowers blowing into the valley, the damp earth of the riverbank and the marsh, even household waste entranced him.

He went to Qunneke's door, knowing he should show himself there first. Mosq unfolded himself from the entryway. Wakwa shivered. All these guards were marring his homecoming.

"Go home to your rest, friend." Wakwa turned the anxious bodyguard one full turn around him. "News later. I must go in!" Wakwa's hand parted the mat. He hesitated at the door. "Nen nont appu! I am home!"

Pequawus and Qunneke turned from somber conversation.

"Were you afraid for me? That I would never come? Do

you sit up late watching for me?" Wakwa spoke the soft syllables of their dialect. "I am so sorry to have made you tired!" The son embraced his father. He went to his wife. "I could not wait or sleep camping so close to you." He held her chin in his palm.

She grasped his wrist.

"Ahhh!" He let his breath come aloud and strode the round floor of his home with his arms wide to the air of it. He came upon his sleeping son. "He is grown! He is changed! Is he the tiny thing I left? Where is Sequan?" He turned where he crouched at the cradle.

The disheveled, haggard woman and the gaunt old man looked like strangers to him. "Trouble!" he said, rising, open to calamity. "Tell me. Sequan did not live the winter. The sickness she had when I left swept her from us."

Qunneke soothed, "Poor Wakwa, do not worry. She is cured of that. Elizabeth went for remedies. Elizabeth cured her."

"Manit!" Wakwa basked near the fire, limp from a crisis that had pressed him and passed over. "May I have to drink? I am thirsty from running! So, they are together? My daughter and my wife?" His eyes went wet. "How fine a thing to be home!"

No one moved to bring him water.

"I shall take a little look and be back with you." He walked from their dumbness to the mat that marked the mouth of the old passage. He pushed against it.

"Wakwa!" Pequawus barked.

The son was back, stunned. "What is this? Separate houses?" He kept one foot outside and one foot in.

"I want you to sit by the fire, dear," Pequawus said. "I have much to tell you."

"I am fed to the filling on miawene. Tell me now and fast. What is this gloom?"

"You are come without warning. There are things shall fall hard on you if they are not introduced to you gently. Come to the fire."

"Is my wife in there!"

"If you do as I say, if I might talk to you . . . she may be there again."

Wakwa wandered a few steps toward his father, open-

133

mouthed. "She hath left me. For what? For whom? She is stolen from me?" He gripped his father's lean arm. "The holy man? Askug? The snake? Annanias Hudson has taken her? Is that why the guard?"

"When will you do as I say?" Pequawus pointed to the fire.

Wakwa split from him, making for the auxiliary house.

"Wakwa!" Pequawus was loud.

Wakwa spun wildly around. "I am a grown man. I have found my way, alone, over a thousand frozen miles and I am going to find my wife!"

"I am so weary of tumultuous spirits!" Pequawus berated. "Your uncle shows in you, Sachim!"

Wakwa was back with him.

But Sequan appeared at the door of the main room. "Nosh!" she said testily to her father, her hands on her hips, "you have awakened up Zabeth!" She ranted in English as she passed by Wakwa. "How many sleeps she has skipped and now this one, too!" Behaving as if her father had gone to the brook to wash his hands instead of making an odyssey of moment, the round little girl punched at her bed pillows despairing of sleep herself.

"Why hath she not slept?" The young father encircled the baby in his arms.

But Sequan gave him an answer only of sobs, and pulled the pillows over her head, dreading to have him know of her part in Elizabeth's mauling.

Qunneke went secretly away to Elizabeth.

"Father, allow me to see Elizabeth?" Fright drained the blood from the skin around Wakwa's eyes.

"For that, you do not have to ask. I must ask you . . . require of you . . . that you let me walk first, that I take you in, that you lean upon me and make no sound, no noise. . . ."

"Father!" Muscles trembled under Wakwa's skin.

"Not a word! And when I say, you are to come away, and hear me through. When my speech is done, do what you will. Only do not undo what I have tried to do for my daughter."

Wakwa let himself be led, astounded at the ominous preamble, at the behavior of his steady-tempered wife and his child, and mostly, at the tie fashioned between Pequawus and the white woman in his absence.

"I left her pregnant," he decided to himself, "and she has lost the child, and does not want to face me. Natural."

Pequawus kept Wakwa moving close to the outer wall, bringing him within sight of Elizabeth by a circuitous path, avoiding sudden motion and telltale sound and shock. Wakwa craned to see past his father, who remained in his line of sight. He wondered why the covered thing he took to be Elizabeth was not lying on the bed he had made for her to ease her back during the pregnancy before, and why she was positioned out of reach of the center fire's light and heat.

Qunneke had tried to improve Elizabeth's looks, bathing her eyes and covering them with a fresh linen bandage. But it slipped to the mat as Elizabeth extended her arms in the direction of Qunneke's leaving.

They stopped at her feet. Wakwa's weight fell on Pequawus. His horror, which took his strength, was based on her bettered condition. Blood and blisters were gone, and broken skin had begun to close. But she was discolored and swollen.

Wakwa knelt forward to see. Her face was crowned by two useless heaps that had been her eyes. She was wasted after four days of fast.

"How are you, daughter?" Pequawus taught his son.

"Better!"

Wakwa pressed a shaking hand over his mouth.

"Would you drink?"

"Ahhh!"

"Shall you have milk?"

"Father, I turned."

The old man left his son for her side.

"I did. And I turned back." A laugh came like a metal bell pealing.

The sight of her mouth smiling around the black and swollen jaw revolted the husband.

Pequawus blessed her with a light touch. "Tame Deer will come with water." The sagamore pulled his son up, and moved him away, leaving the room exactly as they had entered.

Elizabeth lay in her darkness trying to enlist with form

her first determination since she had been struck. "I will get it. I."

"Why do you not wash her?" Wakwa stood over Qunneke.

Bright, black eyes, dimmed by exhaustion, looked up at him and then into the fire.

"Take your place!" Pequawus made the reprimand. He spoke on, until Wakwa had in his mind the flow of Panther Eye's trial. "Thank this woman, your wife, Qunneke. Before anyone, she realized who was standing before the judges. This shy doe, in front of all those eyes, saw the arrow aiming at your heart. She said that you and she shared your bed. It is the only lie Tame Deer has ever told."

Wakwa's head lowered into Qunneke's lap and his arms wrapped her waist. Qunneke did not touch him.

"What it must have cost you to answer such a thing and in such a way!"

"Wakwa, I could not have you pay for what I refused to do for you. Panther Eye held them in a spell. But she did not hold me. For I know, husband, you would have loved Elizabeth whether I was wife to you or not."

He cried out. Her sobs caught on points of doubt.

Wakwa started and stood. "Get me to Panther Eye!"

Pequawus gave him the last piece of news, and Wakwa strode around the room with vicious movements, beset by the triple injustice, to his wives, his ward, and his place as a man. "When was this?"

"Four days ago."

"Four days! Why did Waban rush to this? Why was his hand on my knife? Could he not wait for me to find some better way? Where were his runners in the woods to tell the camp how close I was to home?"

"Better to wonder what secret passed between your ward and your sachim. You cannot undo this other. Never did Waban once lift a finger to defend Elizabeth, but gave Panther Eye her say out before all the council and privately in his ear. Wakwa, I have known Waban a long time, and I say to you that he did not kill Panther Eye for what she did to your wife, but for her secret which now beats in him. Watch your way. I think he is failing. He finds it hard to leave his post and give it to you."

Qunneke left the father and son whispering, and went back to Elizabeth.

Wakwa closed his eyes. "So little good has come from this journey it seemed wise for me to undertake."

"Good has come for me, my son. What a fine thing it is to touch Elizabeth. I have, at last, after all these years, a daughter. I wonder how Charles Dowland had the strength to let her go."

"Why, father," Wakwa coolly answered the rhetoric, "he gave her up when she had become stronger than he."

A scream from Qunneke brought the two men to the alleyway and into Elizabeth's room. Her mat was bare. The three frantic people searched the semidark. Pequawus and Wakwa competed for place when they saw her at the north end of the structure, exploring on her belly with blind reaches. Her scant clothes showed her thinned limbs stretching rhizoid, to find water.

They reached her and Pequawus talked to her while Wakwa held her, turned her face to his.

"Daughter! You might have crawled across the fire! You must wait for Qunneke. She will always come."

Confusing the arms and the voice as one man's, Elizabeth listened and affectionately passed her hands up, along toward the shoulders. The musculature was different, more resilient than the elderly man's she was used to. Her hands mounted to the face and her fingers slipped into short, straight hair, turning softly against the neck. "It is not fair!"

Wakwa buried his face against her shoulder, unable to speak.

She tried to escape his embrace. He recaptured her. Pequawus took Qunneke and departed from the room.

Wakwa passed one of her scorched hands through his hair and said, "I am difficult to recognize, I know, as the hair was cut so I might meet the priest of the people up there." He cried against her breast. "It was a small thing to do to make his acquaintance. I grew to love him, like the rest," Wakwa struggled on, "this Jesuit, this Claude."

Elizabeth crossed her arms over her hideous face and offered bitterly, "Did the Catholic convert you?"

"Never!" He forced her against him, hard enough for pain.

"I told him I had two wives who were like sisters to one another, one Ninnuock, and one English, and he said that I should not bother to be a Christian as I was in Paradise already!"

They both broke, and Elizabeth licked his salt tears. Wakwa lifted her almost happily and carried her to the fire and the water.

Elizabeth turned away from the faint light.

"Your eyes are alive!"

"Eyes?"

Wakwa let the matter slide, and helped her drink. "There is so much to say. Dire Locke was there and sent a present for each of you. He gave something to Qunneke that I see you do need more, and I know she will spare some to you. Stay still. Let me get it. You will not lie long like this, for I am home."

He hurried to Qunneke's room to get his basket and his pouch and discovered her pacing near her own door. "Go to sleep." He held her face with one hand. "I will stay with Elizabeth. Sleep through the night. Poor wife, you are so tired."

"Wakwa?" She twined her hands about his arm. "Stay with me tonight?"

"Ah, wife," he said, not hearing special meaning through his haste, "Elizabeth cannot be alone and you need to sleep. Let me work over her. Together we will bring her back. Yes?"

"Please stay?"

"Qunneke?" He wondered at her eyes, burnished like an animal's that is terrified.

She stepped back from him, a little bit. "I . . . I . . ."

He pulled her against his chest, grasping for her desire of him, so long ago faded, but so firm in his memory. As usual, she strained away. He kept his face from souring. "All is uproar. But your brother is back. Soon, again, you and I will do things between only us two, you and I, sister and brother—we will walk and talk in the night, and take Sequan to the Great Pond, all those things. But not tonight. You must rest. I must take your place in there." He looked over his shoulder at the big, dark house of sickness. "I would say come in and rest by her fire but you would not sleep, you would work. I know you."

Tame Deer loosed herself from him.

He nearly choked when he talked, fighting having to swallow her perennial timidity along with everything else. "Have you enough water, fresh, in here, to make a bath for her?"

"I did not wash her, husband, because, until this day, Elizabeth could not be touched. In any degree. Let it go, and stay with me."

"Get me the water!" he ordered, shocked, smelling what her real fear was. "What do you take me for? A stag at rutting time? Some devil of a thing that would prey on the dying for his pleasure, like a buzzard on carrion? Do you despise men so much you believe I could go in there and force myself on a woman who is nearly a corpse? Except for Elizabeth, I see that nothing here has changed!"

A sense of service to Elizabeth made Qunneke brave the cutting edge of his words. "Everything has changed, Wakwa, but, I am afraid, Elizabeth the least of any of us."

At that, he turned on his heel and left her standing alone.

# Chapter 24

COMBS OF WILD HONEY rested in a small pot. Qunneke had them there to drizzle on Elizabeth's burns. Wakwa drained one into the tonic he was brewing. Ginseng pulverized in the mortar, spring water, and the honey stirred over the fire. There was another packet, an herb Locke said had set Kirke dancing and singing, though those were not his habits. Wakwa did not know if he should mix it in with the ginseng. He was no taupowaw. He looked at his wounded wife. He tore the paper and sprinkled the powder on. He stirred until his concoction was slow-moving gold.

While it cooled, Wakwa unfolded Elizabeth's hands and spread her arms wide. She was half-sleeping on her stomach, shielding her head from blows that would come no more. Wakwa scoured her slowly with talc-fine clay and tepid water. He got to know her miseries, touching her abrasions. He began at the back of her neck and worked down her spine, and over her ribs and buttocks, and in between. He washed the backs of her legs and the damaged ankles and the soles of her feet. She woke. He sniffed at her, and washed her all over again, until all staleness was gone. He rinsed her down, letting the water lick her sore body in cool, clean tongues. He polished her dry with cloths until her lineaments shone like alabaster.

"You are so beautiful!"

Her hands fenced her ears from such words.

He pinned her arms against the mat like wings. "Elizabeth Dowland, I have seen men beaten until they resemble bad dreams, and they heal, their faces as sound, as serene as before."

She moaned as she struggled to free her wrists from him.

He let her arms go, but he gathered her body to himself from behind, and put his beardless face against her clean, white skin. "No one can change your inside by means of a stick or any weapon."

"Think you not?" She cried from the effort of speech. " 'Terrors are turned upon me . . . My honor flees like the wind . . . And like a cloud my welfare has passed away!' "

"What words are those? They are not yours. Where did you hear them?"

"Mine."

"That they are not."

"Oh!" She wished him away. " 'I am made like dust and ashes . . . I go about in black without the sun. . . .' How can you know what it is! Your father understands."

"He said these things to you?"

"We prayed. Job, do you not know?"

"What kind of thing is that to pray? Where are the bold stories, David, Solomon, the victors over difficulty?" He began to wash her underside, his hands making their own room for their passage down her.

She grieved and ached as he rubbed her belly. "He knows. I know. Job knew. What other thing to pray when I fear I merit all that was done to me!"

"Fear! I have spent my winter staring into the eyes of fear."

"And what did you see?"

"Fear blinds. So I closed my eyes against it and remained strong! I ate it. I supped upon it. The good of it became the stuff of me and the rest I cast out of my body with its waste." His hands cupped her breasts in his task and he stopped there, her feel unique to his touch. He had never experienced a woman not firm from virginity, youth, or motherhood. He knew the meaning of this exhaustion by its strangeness to him. Wakwa fell onto her back and mourned the loss of her milk with a dolorous closemouthed cry.

Little hot tears skidded across Elizabeth's eyes eliciting a worming howl from her.

Qunneke sat straight up from sleep.

Wakwa reached a wooden cup and gave her sips. "Take it all, Elizabeth. It is dry-tasting like dust, but Dire promises this drink will slake all the wants of your body and your mind."

Elizabeth took hold of the cup herself after time, between her palms, and nuzzled the liquid into her mouth like a rabbit.

Wakwa smiled. " 'Ah, you are beautiful my love, ah, you are beautiful!' "

"Not that!" She dropped the drink and pleaded against Solomon's song.

"Can you not pray with me? Every word that my father knows of your great book he taught to me."

"Do not speak that now! My God! I am the witch upon her broom!" She covered the char and stubble on her head.

He took her hands away. " 'Your hair. . . .' "

"Do not say it!"

" 'Your teeth. . . .' "

"Rattle in my mouth like an old woman's."

"Your lips. . . .' "

"You mean the lips that were."

" 'Your breasts. . . .' "

141

"Are useless!" She denied him.

And the man covered her back with his body. " 'Until the day blows, and the shadows flee, I will betake myself to the mountain of myrrh, and to the hill of frankincense. You are altogether beautiful, my love, and there is no blemish in you.' "

His weight gave pleasure to her aching back and limbs. She accepted him there.

"Elizabeth, whether I see you again as you were, or I do not, I know only this." His right arm passed underneath her, against her chest. " 'You have heartened me, my sister, my bride, you have heartened me. . . .' " And then he became silent and still.

"You are here!" Her hand explored between her legs. She had not felt his soft entry into her. "You are here!"

"I have not forgot when we parted you had no knowledge I had left. I have come back within you the same way. I will not strain you. Only let me stay awhile."

She felt him relax upon her, demanding nothing but a place to rest, to lie after the long journey he had survived.

He lifted his buttocks to depart her, to come down by her side to sleep, but her right arm stretched back and held his hip.

"O wife?"

She encouraged him with an eloquent hand.

He met this invitation with a patient seeding, producing her first painless pleasure in many months.

And after this intercourse, they laughed like wicked children.

"What was in that drink?" Elizabeth asked.

They collapsed together in sleep. The fact of their reunion did not settle. They remet before dawn, face to face in the lightless room, too much in haste for prelude. They made simple hot exchange, the ecstatic mating of mayflies.

Elizabeth lay white and arrow straight, but not stiffly. Her back conformed to the covered earthen floor, as a bird's on the path of the sky. Her arms and hands were abandoned to the space beyond her head. All the light that the smokehole allowed seemed to pool in her palms. They were bowled, containing her secret, offering it.

Qunneke came close to dip her fingers into the luminous air the palms contained. Wakwa slept against Elizabeth's side, his thigh thrown across her pelvis like a barrier. He woke at Qunneke's silent touch of the brightness Elizabeth held, as if she had disturbed a living part of himself.

He opened his eyes. "I did not mean it to happen!" He passed his arm between his legs to hide himself from her as he unwound from Elizabeth.

Qunneke crossed over to him and held his face, each of her hands on each of his cheeks. "I believe you." The words were petal thin.

"Do you?"

"I do." She let him go. "I did not mean to come in here. I am not prying."

"I know."

"It is true. There was no smoke from your roof. The sun has been up a long while. I went out for water and I saw no smoke, and I thought you two were dead."

"Dead?"

They each stayed stiff at the notion. Then Wakwa yawned and stretched and grinned and laughed. Qunneke joined in.

Qunneke not only brought the wood for their fire, but also burnt a potpourri of sweet-smelling stuff there, incensing the room like a bower. She made a breakfast fit for a bridal pair. The samp was sweet with strawberries that she had laid by in the fall. Clover covered their tray, but the purple flowers were not meant for decoration. Qunneke made them eat them and the greens for an end of winter tonic. They made a communal bath, unsnarling, combing, washing, rubbing, rinsing, drying until the morning passed.

"Qunneke." Wakwa freely touched her long, black hair. "We must do something about Elizabeth's."

Wakwa treated the skin of her wounded scalp with angelica tea, while Qunneke looked through the house for some accurate measure to help the even trimming of the unsanitary mass that once had been hair. Qunneke put her hand into Wakwa's traveling pouch. She clasped the nesting falcon. Before Wakwa could introduce the cheeping thing to Elizabeth, Qunneke pulled out its first real feather.

Elizabeth's balding took place gauged by the markings on the straight feather shaft. Wakwa watched, miserable, remembering his delightful task on the day he found this white woman in the woods, helping her, taking burrs from her tresses one by one. Not a hair had been cut.

Qunneke went to dress. Wakwa chose Elizabeth's clothes. English ones. He helped her to draw on the simple things she had sewn in her first months in his woods. The drawers, the sacque, the thin shirt of linen and the soft black skirt of gathered wool. He tied her high moccasins at her calves, recreating for her blind self the feeling of what she had once been.

Qunneke came in. There was some awful difference in her. Lighter, taller, quicker, she seemed a happy sister of the woman he was used to. "Matta!" the man shouted. She had taken a knife to her hair. It was gone. She pleased him. Wakwa ran his hands through the scant remains of the great token of her beauty.

"Are you angry?"

He brought her against him, fondling the short locks that fell even with her jaw. "I was right, last night, Tame Deer. Nothing has changed. You are still the worthiest woman I know."

She barred his compliment with her forefinger. "One of them. We three! We will start a fashion! Hold me!" She huddled against him, missing the silky growth she had known since childhood. "I did not do it all for Elizabeth. I thought that I could live without it since Panther Eye told me she loved it so."

"Saunks! What will you do? Come to the lodge with me and my wife? Let me show you where Elizabeth leads me, even blind."

"No. You go to the woods with her. I shall set the site of the spring camp. I shall place the houses fairly, none of the wives will complain. What is your desire for ours?"

"That you be there."

She made no reply.

"I want it to see the river."

"And Elizabeth will want space around it. She likes quiet in the morning."

"And you, dear wife? What do you require?"

"I know not. But I shall leave here to help me know."

"Leave? To where? For how long?"

"Am I not freeborn?"

"You will go guarded."

"Until I will be guarded no more."

He kissed her hands in agreement.

Wakwa walked toward his own destination, holding Elizabeth high in his arms, shielding her covered face from the white, March sun. He walked through the center of the camp toward the bridge, not stopping at Waban's dwelling, keep Elizabeth straight and steady.

Some of the otan people watched from behind their doors. Others braved walking with him for several paces, to touch his arm or his back in sympathy for the shock of his homecoming.

The bundle of cloth and fur clasped him about his neck, looking to the gathering neighbors like a curse being carried.

——————————— **Chapter 25**

"SON OF A BITCH BASTARD had a good idea," Gil warbled while Matthew poured hot water into the white wood tub. "Imagine that old pork belly, Hudson, getting up a private bathing chamber for Beth, running water, running out at least, a stationary lead-lined tub, a dressing room attached. Hanna never said a thing. What a Dowland she is! My wife bathing in her kitchen, while that fat ass of a preacher dredges out in a special bath room."

Through the steam, Gil gazed at his kitchen's slate floor,

its worktable with stout turned legs, the gleam of copper and silver cookware, and the gray solidity of iron utensils, marveling at the commonness of his bathing arrangements.

He ranted, disregarding the Swiss oil of apricot that Matthew poured into the scalding water, and the rubbing down he received. "Romans had hot running water. Why not we? I'll not mention it to her. Whom do I know who is an engineer? Or will I have to become one of those, too?"

He stood to be wrapped in a robe of Turkish and walked barefoot up his carpeted stairs. He caught a view of himself in Hanna's bureau glass and was astounded by his mirror image.

His clean blond hair and beard glimmered in the afternoon sun which clung in the southeast room. It was a three-month growth, wiry, undisciplined, dry from wind, a bush of gold. All his features except his fine, straight nose and verdant eyes were submerged by the glittering hair.

"Wildman! You could pass either for a nettle or a philosopher. Same thing." He taunted his reflection.

He dressed the part, appearing in his sitting room in a banyan and soft cap of brown and gold striped silk. He lit his pipe, his first gift from Wakwa, and sat in his wing chair across from the great south window, his travel-hardened legs supported by an ottoman. A book was on the table at his left. He did not read but sent smoke rings to the white ceiling. He became fascinated by the substance of plaster.

"Hello, harp." He grinned at the instrument, not having the least incentive to exert himself to play. "And what is that accursed thing?"

Matthew looked in on him with some brandied coffee. "That is the settee, Master Worth. Redone."

"More ruined, Mr. Freeman. Who chose such a cloth?"

"The mistress. She thought a yellow would bring the sun in in February. I am not sure what she will say about it."

"Does it glow in the dark like a comet?"

"I have not seen, Mr. Worth. We kept it covered until we heard Grandee coming toward the barn."

"Cover it up again." Gil sniffed at the aromatic coffee like an appreciative Turk.

"Master?"

"Yes, Matthew?" Gil drank, not bothering to open his eyes.

"The Reverend Hudson has not finished his bath chamber. He is said to be letting it go. He does not want to build it and have to give it up to the use of the new minister coming in."

"Like him." Gil opened his eyes and looked at the black man. "Matthew, do not let this hour pass."

Utter peace descended on Gilbert Worth, enveloped in brightness, surrounded by beauty. The spiced aroma of the coffee filled the closed room, and the small man dozed. Like the flora of the plantation coming into life lazily in a glow of golden sunshine, Gil reclined in comfort, spread to the new season with complete innocence.

"Ah! Truly seventeen hundred forty-eight." It was March 25, the day of the Annunciation, the time of conceptions, the birth of lambs. By the Julian calendar it was New Year's Day. Britain and her colonies turned their backs on announcing the advent of a new year in a frigid season as Pope Gregory had the rest of the world doing. It made no sense to farmers whose eyes and ledgers recorded the real beginning. And the new calendar was the brilliant labor of the wrong faction—the Vatican. And so chaos reigned in Europe, from the collection of rents, to the dating of records and the simple heading of a letter. All winter, every winter, from January till March English people everywhere compromised, hanging time on a hyphen, noting the date both ways. Gil reached for his diary and quill. "Civilized creature." He dipped ink and scratched '47–'48 out of existence, writing a full 1748. "Simpler."

He had left the book home when he had traveled. Awepu provided the medium for recording their adventures. It was peculiar, Gil thought, that months in his journal were blank of events likely to reshape his life. He made an inscription now, a brief hymn, a bar of music, a repeated note—high —representing the single and elevated tone of the moment. He studied the one chord he had jotted, the enrichment of the note, not quite harmonious, but it represented the unsentimental sweetness that he felt. "It might be the beginning of something. And a good day for it."

" 'Read Simpson!' " he put, signed March 25 with a flourish, then closed it and sat with his hand on it, giving himself over to the bouquet of the tobacco blend cultivated and prepared by Silent Fox, the sachim of the Massachuseuck.

Two letters of Hanna's waited unopened on a little tray on the writing table. But Gil watched the sparse green fuzz of grass out the window and the curve of the horizon, which would dot with berries by summer.

Sealed from care, Gil was sure that no moving creature would be coming his way, though he heard the slow quash of an approaching horse. He shut his eyes again, keeping the picture of his untrammeled, unplanted acres alive in his inner eye. The hoofbeats ceased.

Gil let out a thankful sigh. He was so confident that the rider had passed that he opened his eyes. He sat in his torpor witnessing a person, tall, tan, shapely at the outline as a swell of flowing water, prepare to dismount. A slit skirt showed a length of female leg as the figure bent, turned, and slipped from the saddleless back of an enormous dun.

"What woman?" Dreading human contact at that moment as too complicated to be pleasant, Gil shaded his eyes to see through the glare on the glass.

The visitor adjusted the band to a baby board over her forehead. She started toward the house in soft-shod feet, carefully as if the flag path were of whipped cream.

"Qunneke?" The reluctant host was on his feet. He pulled the linen sheet off the settee and stuffed it into his music cabinet. He could not abide the thought of the quiet woman having to touch her knuckles to the panels of his closed door and hurried to get there first. "Matthew, you are a magician."

The Englishman opened first the door's top portion to watch Wakwa's wife come. He opened the whole of it, as she recognized him, and he offered both his hands to assist her across the threshold.

The housekeeper ducked back into the kitchen after she discovered Worth greeting the stranger in the hallway. "Who is that, Matthew?"

"That is the wife . . . of Mistress Beth's husband."

"I was raised very quiet at Needham."

"Cooke, you'd best forget that if you are to serve the Worths." Matthew had seen, recognized, and allowed the dun to pass the tree line to the front of the house. He went out to care for the horse, forbearing to tell this white widow of his own youth before his capture.

After Gil's kiss, Qunneke freed her hands from his to let them roam his faceful of hair.

"Let us get that baby off you. What is this!" Gil demanded as she lifted the child-weighted carrier. "My hair full and yours is gone? My God! Qunneke! What did you do?" Gil saw her neck and its meeting with her back and shoulders for the first time. "I thought your hair was only tied, behind." With the wall of language between them, he had no hope of an explanation. "You are alone? You cannot be the escort Wakwa promised to me. I only arrived home today. Is all well? I have rarely seen you without Sequan."

This was the first word Tame Deer understood. "Sequan weechauau Micuckaskeete-nokannawi."

"Sequan is with Meadow-in-the-Night? Awepu's wife?" Gil shook his turbaned head. "She has a busy day. Five children in the house and Awepu returned." The Englishman considered, privately, why Tame Deer was not in the otan to welcome her own husband.

They stood in the hallway, Qunneke fascinated by Gil's garb, he by her closeness and the absence of her hair.

Cooke came. "I am sorry, master, I did not hear the door. Do you need me, sir?"

"Not a bit." Gil did not take his eyes from Qunneke. "Take my nephew. And get Matthew to help you with a supper, something light, French, for dusk, and make up a room, Cooke. Small things do as if Hanna were here."

Qunneke's face lost its tranquillity. "Hanna!"

"Hanna is not here, my dear." Gil touched her shoulder to guide her down the hall, and his hand hurt with the same pain he had known the day he met her, the day of Moses' birth.

Tame Deer would not move forward. "Matta Hanna?"

"You want Hanna?" Worth snorted at himself for imagining that their prolonged moment in the hallway had nothing to do with the reality of their lives.

Qunneke locked one of her long-fingered hands into the other and declared, again, "Hanna."

"Dear, how will we talk? Where is Wakwa?"

"Wakwa kah Elizabeth. . . ." Qunneke finished her sentence by a space-consuming wave.

"I should have guessed. Oh, do come in, dear lady." Gil walked to the entrance of the sitting room and indicated a direction to her.

Qunneke had never been in an English house. The hunting lodge had the same rectangular perspectives but its roof was pitched twenty feet above its wooden floor making a sky-high arch above. Before stepping Gilbert's way, Qunneke surveyed her surroundings, then entered his unfamiliar dell. But she made a sound of recognition when she was inside the bright room where Gil enjoyed most of his activities. She had wished for such a place.

She stood in the room's center experiencing first visions of an alien domestic life, a sudden revelation that equaled Elizabeth's of the year before. Qunneke wore a skin bag over one shoulder. The bag touched the curve of her buttocks, which were skirted with smooth-faced beaver skin.

Gilbert closed the doors. He thought of asking her to sit, sending for tea, engaging her in small talk, passing a friendly and typical afternoon. The thought disappeared. He leaned against the newly painted doors with an ache in the blood vessel that ran through his left temple.

Qunneke moved a step toward the hearth. The blaze bemused her, burning as it did in a square hole in the wall. She spread her fingers to feel the air, testing the warmth-giving properties of the proscenium fire. Light from its flames wedded with sharp reflections from the objects in the room, viols, clocks, silver, crystal, waxed wood.

The sun and the fire converged on the settee in front of her, turning the citrus-colored silk brilliant. The seat was not in its usual position, but stood where Sam Spinney had placed it when he had carted it back over from Achushnet. It commanded the center of the soft-hued rug, facing Gil's high-backed chair, open to a chat with it.

"Manittoo!" Qunneke exclaimed over the silk.

"Rather it is yellow. So yellow." Gil's voice came quite dry. "Now you and I will have to get something straight." The slippered man reached her and came between her and the chair.

"Yellow." She smiled at his whiskers.

"Do you have any idea of what you are doing to me?"

They stood close, within range to see tiny lines and flaws of skin, and the working of their irides.

"I refuse to be ridiculous and so I will hold you." His hand directed her sheared head down onto his shoulder.

Qunneke wrapped both her arms about one of his and seemed to rest there while he spoke.

"Now I know you did not come here for this." His free hand hovered near the base of her neck, then moved lightly over her back, claiming her soft waist. "And I did not close the sitting room doors for any secret purpose, but you know I need to touch you, don't you?" He pressed his light-lashed eyes against the well of her neck and shoulder. "And you allow me. And I am glad.

"Oh, Qunneke! Why is my share of things always the best? I have not seen a woman, a real woman for over seventy days. And I am left this exquisite contact with this magnanimous you. Why you are here I may eventually guess, but why, why so receptive, why this mood, why did you take off that unearthly, gorgeous shroud of hair?" He looked at her.

She moved her face against the stiff and golden hairs of his beard and let it scratch her fine-grained skin.

He made an inspiration of breath. "You ask for nothing and would let me do anything. A lamb you are. I shall consider eating you."

The backs of Gil's legs hurt pleasantly, as if his body bade him to lay her down right there, relieving voluntary muscles in favor of ones over which he had no control. "May I touch your face? Which I can finally see?" Hands sensitized to bringing sound out of strings felt the sweet curve of her countenance and the structure of the bones which defined it. "Do you not know what silly beings men are? What flesh and lack of flesh turns them to? Look around you, see my particularity so extreme as to be perfectionist, and look at how I look at you!" He pressed her to himself and his upper body wavered dizzily in the sun. "How came you to be in the state you are in with Silent Fox? What waste!" Gil kissed the thin bow of her lips. "He says I may seek you out, you know. He understands affinity of opposites. He wants your happiness. Why, my God, do I?"

Qunneke brought his hands to her bosom and pressed them to her fullness so hard that the blond man saw it gave her pain.

He lowered his head to nestle at the breasts, permanently enlarged by milking. "What a softness! I'd forgot. For the sake of Holy Mother Trade!" Gil sealed his eyes shut.

"Gilbert!" Qunneke's sound and look were desperate.

"Tell me! Tell me! Where have you journeyed these past years that you can utterly ignore the beauty of flesh?" He locked her close under the heat magnified by the leaded window. "Come then, remember!"

They were equal in height, her cheek against his cheek, their thin clothing not masking his physical arousal.

Since their introduction six months before, Gil had worked at resignation to his place as Qunneke's uncle-by-marriage. But this day, too honest, too alone, too caring of her trouble, he did not hide voyeurish behind their familial relationship. He sorted out their attraction through touch. "Wakwa does not do this with you anymore. Odd that I know it so clearly to be true." His words were felt more than heard, and understood through the pattern of caresses his lips left on her skin. "Why do I wait? Because of my wife? Or for your husband? No. For this moment." His leaning against her told her his message. "If I have you, won't it end? I am old enough to believe that sex must sustain and endure. Shall I oblige us in this moment of our need, shall we swim in heaven for a while, then break apart and wonder when we will dip again? What assurance have I that for you to bed with me would widen what we already have? Must I obligate you to lie with me because we are close in our natures, and you are female? I see that all the time. Such intercourse is common as shitting." He blew puffs of cool air over her heated skin. "Joy with you is everyday. To grasp at you now and again is less than I would want with you. What gigantic disrespect to collect you like an edition of porcelain!" He moved slightly back, supporting her arms on his. Air lighted by the sun passed between them. "I know without any further touch what satisfaction awaits at the most inward part of you. How terribly similar to any other such investigations I have ever made in other times, yet I know it would be unique as yourself. Simply because there is gold have I rights to tap it? No."

He kissed her mouth and felt her excellent teeth with a quick, hot tongue, passing into stages of closeness that he had just forbidden to himself. And in the same way, he used words to explain his soul, though he knew they held no meaning for her.

"I could give you instant pleasure. Justified pride!" He smiled through his passion. "I make myself a match for your magnificent husband. How I am flattered at your not drawing back from me as you do from him." His breath stopped. "Why am I acceptable?"

He ran his hands down her body, from her throat. "Ah! Qunneke! It is simply true that I can love a wife and make her glad, and there is no way that you and I can live as constant partners. The full gaining of you at this juncture of our lives is inconceivable and unbeautiful. I am an adamant beast, and I not only insist on loving you, but I want you to love me, too. What would the Paris Opera say to its dandy harper for not floating away on the wave of the romance which you present me?"

He kissed her throughly, as if for goodbye. "Ah, but it is good to have a friend."

She seemed sad enough to weep, struggling to understand not only him, but herself. Concern for his well-being freed her embraces of him and sighs escaped from Gil as she offered affection without requiring a response.

"You are not shy! More, Aphrodite imprisoned. I believe I am right! And you did not come to my house to find Hanna, nor to escape the second honeymoon of Wakwa and her niece, nor to rouse me from my middle age. You came because the sun is here," he stroked the skin of her face and back, "and, my, you need that! Yellow sun, and my harp . . . you want light and music. Artemis!" He laughed lightly to her. "Goddess of the hunt, ever manless, my sister, come to visit Apollo, her brother." Lost in the aptness of symbol, Gil kissed her repeatedly, coming to know the full shape of her face through the unstopping pressures of his lips. "Thy shafts are indeed soft as moonlight. Without pain, you wound my heart."

He held her to himself. "You came to me because you grow closer to Silent Fox! Or are on the path to that. You are not yet sure you want it to be. I am right." He would not confuse her by prompting her anymore to accept him or to demand him. But he did not release her until the sun's position changed and the sweat on their bodies cooled and gave them chill.

He retained her hands even when they sat across from one another, he in the wing chair, she on the settee. "Has Apollo still his silly hat on?" He tried to peer at it.

Tame Deer removed the pouf of silk for him, and looked sympathetically at his lap.

Gil followed her glance, and folded his wrists against the erection hidden by his flowing gown. "Nux, he is still there, but I am pleased to say I am his master not his slave. I imagine, all our lives that he will cock whenever you're about. You must not let him bother you. He is kind to let me know that I am still alive and almost fifty."

A knock came then, and Gil's whiskers were pushed apart by laughing. Matthew had the tea timed perfectly.

"Come ahead, Cooke. Here, put the tea on me. I won't spill." He laughed again.

The housekeeper waited discreetly for the Indian woman to let go of the master's hands. "Are the scones enough, sir? It seemed with the supper early. . . ."

"How delightful to have you, Cooke. Winke would have insisted on the table, been insulted if we did not down a dozen cakes, and been spreading cloths on the floor, huffing about the danger to the rug." Gil took Qunneke's hands back and their arms rested among the creamer and sugar bowl, the Scottish bread and silver knives and spoons.

"Yes, Master." Cooke eyed their involvement. "Pardon me, sir, but I've put your grandnephew in diaper cloth." The door closed.

The cups cooled.

Tame Deer pulled away and reached into the skin pouch. She offered Gil the braid and took away the tray while he sat with the clean, twisted hair in his hands, its length dangling across his legs onto the floor.

"What a keepsake! A lovelock extraordinaire. Is it a gift or a message? Nightshade. It is so entirely black! I have always wished to touch your hair but it is mournful detached. We mourn what is passed and what cannot come again. What are we mourning? Are you not well?"

Quickly, Gil switched places, joining the woman on the couch. "Your eyes are rimmed with maroon. You are tired. Terribly tired."

All the remorse that Qunneke felt for the benign neglect that had brought Elizabeth down, moved her first to hide her face, and then to slip to the floor to sit at his feet, her forehead against his knees.

"Now, now." He petted her. "I sense that there is something bad." He stroked her short hair. "Something you do not like has happened and you share it with me. Shall we go right into the woods, shall I take you home? Will that help?"

Relaxed by the fondling, Qunneke turned to lean her back against his legs and she looked up to the flat, seamless ceiling, losing herself in the horizon it made where it met the wall.

"No, Wakwa gave me six days," Gil said, "and I will treasure each one of them. Were I needed he would have sent a clear message to me. You and I, keen kah neen, we will go back at the appointed time to find what is disturbing you. Whatever it is I must insist that it never divide us."

They remained still enough to sleep, while the sun made its dramatic drop, lighting the lower objects in the room, gilding the grays and blue-greens with which the lemon-colored couch put up such a fight.

Screaming, louder and louder, rent their mood. Qunneke stood. The door opened and Cooke carried an unhappy Moses into the sitting room.

"I tried to keep him quiet. I am sorry to disturb you, sir." Cooke struggled to hold the frantic child.

Gil relieved her of him and kissed the baby's tear-stained face. "Qunneke, will you feed him now? Meninnunk? Mother's milk?"

Qunneke backed away. "Hanna."

"What possible good could Hanna do this baby? She doesn't know the first thing about them."

Wolf-of-the-mist He-hopes fought off the hairy stranger, his angry wail renewed, and he reached for the woman who had suckled him as often as his natural mother.

Qunneke demurred.

"Little Wolf!" The great-uncle cautioned him. "Quietly, quietly." Gil caught up with Tame Deer, who had retreated across the room. "You won't take care of him? You have brought the child to me? Why do you and Beth not feed this baby?"

"Master?" Cooke curtsied. "If I might say . . . to feed the child, she must have milk."

"Oh." Gil tamed the hair of his moustache. "Might she lose it?"

"She might."

"Dear woman. Matta meninnunk? Have you no milk?"

"Meninnunk!" Qunneke drew aside one half of her bodice and caught into her hand the sweet white substance that dripped from her nipple without pressure.

Gil did not feel the child squirming in his arms as he stared.

Cooke commented, "She's got milk."

Qunneke coaxed some of the pearlescent liquid from her nipple, took Elizabeth's child, and tried to feed him from her hand as he lunged for her uncovered breast. The baby sounded wounded and his face shot with red as he battled for his natural right.

Qunneke put him from her, down onto the soft rug. He raised on his plump arms, gasping from crying, his saliva wetting his short, lined neck. His cries made Tame Deer hold her front as she fastened her clothes.

"Damn, I am stupid!" Gil paced, unenlightened.

"Henry!" Qunneke's word was hardly heard over the crying. Qunneke said, again, "Henry." Noh-annoosu began to suck his own round arm from frustration.

"Beth's brother?" Gil questioned.

"You know, sir, I believe she wants the dead boy's pitcher. To feed Mistress Beth's baby that way." The housekeeper studied Tame Deer.

"It is Elizabeth who has lost her milk?" Gil appealed to Cooke.

"It might be, master."

Without time to hitch a horse to a cart, Matthew Cooke took the mile to Dowland Farm on horseback for the silver feeder.

Qunneke sat alone in a windowless corner of the room, inscrutable as a carved figure.

Gil spelled the wait, trying to distract the small boy, carrying him about the room, letting him touch anything he reached out for. "Little poppet looks frightened. Pull my whiskers! That's right! We'll hurt together."

Snatches of English nursery songs and bawdy tunes in French distracted the child for a time. Crying dissolving into regular breathing shook the whole of his stout little body.

The sun was suddenly gone, its light saved for places west. In the dusk, Gil retasted the uncertainty of his days in Maine, and the comfort of Père Claude's Latin Mass. He fed his grandnephew on the plainsong so similar to Indian chants. The baby curled against Gil's hard, masculine chest, lulled at last by something familiar.

Gil's tranquillity transformed to temper as he listened to his servants report. Wink's refusal to let the pitcher go. Without changing his lounging attire, Gilbert Worth mounted Grandee with the baby still clutched in his left arm, and made for his in-law's house at a gait calculated to beat the dark.

He entered and passed the astounded housekeeper without a word. He made for the storage cabinets built into the hall walls between the sunken kitchen and the dining rooms. He exposed shelves of pewter and china but could not see the small decanter in the failing light.

"Hold a candle here!" Gil ordered the matron.

"I didn't know you really needed the baby pitcher, master. I don't even know where it is. I didn't know you was even home from wherever. See how careful I try to be with the family's goods? Just like when I was at your own house."

Gil ignored her simpering.

"I heard you went away. Did you bring this adorable babe back with you? It is dark. Not like one of yours would be. A foundling? You're always doin' some kind thing."

"That must seem remarkable to someone like you." Gil took the several steps up to the main floor. "Give me the light." He stood with candle high, illuminating the room where Wakwa had asked for Dowland's approval of his marriage to Elizabeth. Clean and polished as on that day, the floorboards and wainscot listened for signs of life.

"This is yours, little Wolf. Welcome to your house," the uncle whispered.

He thought of Mary, Beth's mother, buried far from the home she had tended with respect. Gil would be ordering no more teapots from Locke for her discerning pleasure. Those objects, beautiful and brittle, which held the hot refreshment that made New England winters bearable, had been the only self-indulgence of the modest wife of Charles Dowland.

Gil approached her summer dining room in his slippers, as quietly as if Mary were being waked there. She had kept her teapots displayed in a glass-fronted, painted cabinet. Gil looked into it. On the middle shelf, next to her violet pot, her favorite, was Henry's small feeder.

"But of course." Gil thanked Mary for leaving within obvious reach the thing that her unknown grandson needed.

Its long spout was delicately shaped for controlled pouring into the grasping, mobile mouth of an infant. Worth took it out and slid it into the pocket of his gown.

"Will you feed it with the family pitcher?" Winke's fingers worked acquisitively. "It's quite the best silver, I have heard."

"This 'it' is a human being, Winke. HE is hungry. I suppose you never get that way being so full up with horseshit. Next week, when I have time to bother, I will settle up your final wages. You are released from contract."

"I cannot be released!" Winke did not cry as she had done in September when Worth let her go from his happy house to the empty one.

The master snapped the candle stand down on the kitchen table at this insubordination.

"I have a commitment, Master Worth, a business just started, brand-new, a partnership with . . . an old friend, who is just now away. I have used half her money to begin, and if I disappear to some new place . . . well, I know so little of these things but it might not be legal."

"What business?" Worth bit out.

"Bees."

"Bees?"

"Honeybees."

"Honeybees on this land? And I was not told?"

"You were away!"

"My man Matthew was not. Did you consult him?"

"I did not know his like would replace your authority. And some gorgeous queens became available, and knowing your dissatisfaction with me, which I can't figure, I thought to get a good summer season before I might have to quit your employ."

"Good thinking. Where are they?"

"Past the alfalfa, near the smokehouse, sir."

"Fine. Now I can get my ass stung every time I go for a slice of bacon."

"I know you are unhappy when you use such expressions. You never spoke like that when I was takin' care of you, Master Worth."

"I beg your pardon!" Gil met her presumption.

But she turned his words against him. "Don't apologize to old Winke. I remember a lot o' good years with you. Only don't go an' break up my hives?"

"You are in a pitiful condition, Winke." He despised a mind which could contemplate such pettiness.

"Brought low, I know, sir." She served herself with his criticism.

"You impose on your freedom here, starting this honey-making without my permission. I should charge you rent for the space. This farm is not mine. I am its executor. You have squatted your commercial enterprise on Charles Dowland's ground." Worth's mouth worked underneath the blond moustache, as he turned the unattractive dilemma over in his mind. His lips came to be at rest before he spoke again. "In lieu of splitting your proceeds with his estate, I will expect your speedy withdrawal after the summer crop. I will write this out and enter it in the record. It is true that the air your bees fly is free, and the flowers from which they sip nectar, the possessions of everyone."

"You are still the master whom I loved."

Winke's past tense affected the landholder. "And you are a capable woman, Mrs. Winke."

"Then must I go? Let me back into your house? I will be ever so careful what I say." The matron regarded the light red skin of the baby.

"Winke, you must find a new place." Gil held her shoulder kindly for a moment. "You are not a bad woman. You are, simply, too different from me."

Winke watched from the kitchen window while Gilbert Worth mounted his bay, the banyan riding up to his stockingless thighs when he sat astride.

"He'll get rash on his legs for sure. And who'll bring him salve?" Eating her pottage of dried beans and beef, Winke debated whether or not to tell Mr. Hudson about Gilbert Worth's half-breed baby.

When Gil produced the pitcher for Qunneke she took Moses at once, to let the small body warm against hers. She sat on the settee to let him suckle, but Wolf-of-the-mist would not give Gil up. His small fist remained tightly closed on his uncle's silk dressing gown. Gil in no way minded this cozy method of filling his nephew's stomach. He remained as close to Qunneke through the feeding as Moses did, until the tiny hand unclosed and dropped helplessly down, with sleep.

Gil and Tame Deer dined aone, in quiet, each enjoying the presence of a compatible human being. Leaving larger cares, Qunneke studied the engraved patterns in the sterling, and watched the butter floating in the cream sauce which moistened her meat. She listened to the discreet hum of the household, the wind jostling the acres of bud-ready fruit trees outside the glass windows, and the unexplainable voice of the wooden and stone structure which resisted the thrust of warming wind, and moaned in secret places. As if she were a male youth finding her name, reaching for adulthood, Qunneke remained mentally poised for the significance of the sounds.

She finished her supper without wish for home, and assumed a position on the settee allowing her to watch Elizabeth's uncle and the fire.

Gil turned his back on the writing table where they had dined, and made his first advance toward his harp. He uncovered it, touched its main column, sat, and pulled it down into his lap. He stroked the soundbox, and leaned his shoulder into the frame, embracing its slender body like a lover's. He moved away from it without playing.

Gil relit his afternoon pipe. He offered it to Qunneke. She smoked easily, abstractedly.

"We are a pair of house cats, you and I." Gil nudged her moccasin with a slipper.

Qunneke removed her soleless shoes and let her toes explore the patterns in the rug.

Gil brought her upstairs.

Her room shared a chimney with Hanna's dressing room, which opened out into the master bedroom.

Of the nightgowns placed at the foot of the bed for his guest's selection, Gil, himself, chose the least fussy, a simple sweep of white sarcenet, the silk he liked best to touch. He waited outside the room, while Cooke helped Qunneke to dress, making his seat the top stair of the short flight. He looked at the dimmed corridor below and saw his isolation from Hanna in its empty reach.

When the Dowlands' well-trained maid carried away chamber pots and basins, Gil reentered in time to see Tame Deer shield her eyes from the candle and fire brightness, to search the dark outside for the tree line which separated her from home.

As if she were Sequan, Gil tied her gown at the throat after she settled the curtain and came away.

"Now, if you need me in the night, if you are afraid, or uncomfortable, or in need of company, I will be right in the next door." Gil brought her into the hall and she glimpsed his bedroom. "Cooke is at the back of the house if you need my service."

The tired housekeeper nodded as she reached her own door.

Gil could not leave Qunneke to put herself to bed in a lonely way. He brought her back and stood on the medallion of the rug, centered in the square room, over a floor of unstained, polished native pine. He held both her hands as he had done at his front door, and Qunneke moved backward toward the bed. The backs of her legs touched the white spread at the bed's edge.

"Mattapsh, my dear." Gil retained her hands while inviting her to sit.

She obliged him. She sat, expectant of support, but the masses of feathers unbalanced her. She slipped through Gil's hands and rolled backward. Her legs went high in the air. Clumsiness that caused no pain brought a sound that Gil had never heard from the woman. Rollickingly as water, Qunneke laughed.

Gilbert sat by the bed and roared. Qunneke did not control the rich, rippling noises that came with her merriment. The two were silly for a long minute.

Then, Gil collected her in his arms and moved her, encumbered by the plumpness of the goose down, toward the pillow. She straightened her borrowed nightdress while Gil pulled coverlet and sheet down to admit her cheerfully, if not gracefully, to her first night in a European bed.

Settled on her side, the dark-eyed woman watched Gil show her a little crystal bell to be rung for service, and she accepted the lace cap he hesitantly offered to complete her night ensemble.

The quiet of the inactive house was loud to them both.

Gil bent to kiss the shorn, capped head. Qunneke covered the hand which touched her shoulder with one of her own. She blew on it and raised the gold hairs curling a little way down from his wrist.

"Yellow!" she said.

"Not at all. But damned civil. You won't find one of me in a thousand Saxons, so you stay away from the lot of them."

Qunneke kissed the hairy back of his hand and caressed it with the child-soft skin of her cheek, sensing humor.

"So, we shall both ache somewhat tonight. Good for us." Worth left her, the silk of his robe whirling on wind made from his swiftness. He closed the door firmly.

Qunneke made a cry.

Gil was back in a moment. "What, what?" He knelt and ran his hand reassuringly over her back and shoulders, which were clammy through the gown. He held her head and kissed her mouth strongly.

"Pauquanamiinea?" She begged to have the door left open.

"Of course, sweet thing!" He left a second time, leaving her door wide, according to her wish, realizing as he undressed that Qunneke had never slept enclosed by right angles or totally alone.

Gil lay naked, rebelling against the idea of a night-rail after a winter of sleeping in his trousers. He shut his eyes in the afterglow of the dressing room fire, and without wanting sleep, he dozed. Dreams came, of his wife's unopened letters neatly positioned on the writing table, and of

Tame Deer, lying in the next room as filled with wonderment as a belle.

Hanna's pillow was all that filled his arms as he rested under the rising pressure of his long unsatisfied sexual need. Less uncomfortably than during freezing nights in the open, when his unassisted release of semen had rendered his skin wet and shivering, Gil endured his ejaculation.

"Public school kid!" He woke fully and kicked himself free of quilts and covers, bundled the mess into a corner and hurried into the buckskin trousers and moccasins that Qunneke had sewn him. He wore only a thin, blue shirt on his upper body.

Worth looked at Qunneke from her doorway. In the hour that had passed she had not changed position. Her steady breathing told him that she was truly asleep. "Happy New Year!" he said without sound.

He took the stairs softly as a dancer.

Out of doors, Gil careened into an ocean of wind which chased remaining winter back to polar regions. He made little whoops to it, and slapped it with outspread arms and let it turn him around and push him along the thawed earth of his property toward Matthew's pine house at the top of the north meadow.

The houseman was seated in front of his one window, silhouetted against his small fire.

"May I butt in?" Gil leaned hopefully against the door, which was held open to the breeze by a brass hook. He saw Matthew's whiskey bottle open. A small pile of wood curls littered a board shelf, hung under the low window for table and work space.

Matthew half rose and waved the master in with the hand that held a curved knife he had had of Waban at Elizabeth's wedding feast. "The Sachim's wife is still at the house, sir? You have not let her go?"

"She does not choose to go." Gil sat on the step of the open doorway.

"Good."

"Why good, Matthew?"

"I am making a rattle for the boy, is why." Matthew passed a light, hollow object to Worth.

"You are quite expert at this. It is round as a top. Sycamore? Birch?"

"I ought to be expert. I made enough of them for my own babies in bygone days. Out of different wood. This hath taken me since the Mistress Beth came by for remedies for the Sachim's little girl. Have not finished with it, yet. Too busy here. Tired at night."

"Well, you won't have to bear all this alone anymore. I am home and it is spring."

"I count the springs, Mr. Worth. My sons, if they live, are fifteen this season. In no need of rattles."

Gil was too sympathetic and too exhausted to delve into discussion of Matthew's irreparable loss. He planted his moccasin against the doorjamb and waited for the moment to pass.

Matthew exchanged the bottle of liquor for the toy in the whiteman's hand.

"Nice of you." Gil spoke of Matthew's handiwork for Beth's baby.

"It is you who supply me, old master."

Gil allowed the misinterpretation to stand. "Old, hell." He thought of himself. "Master, hell!" He stood and drank from the bottle, enjoying the hot, smooth taste in his mouth, and the damp, kind-edged wind in his hair. He returned the bottle exactly to its ring of sawdust and said, proudly, "You will never guess what your old master has done."

"What?" Matthew raised a bushy eyebrow, his mind on the guest.

"I set a man's leg, is what!"

Like two colleagues without class or color difference they talked of Gil's trip north. While the rattle took shape they also discussed the future of the freedom. It was Matthew's decade spring in Massachusetts. Within the narrow limits of the laws surrounding emancipated blacks they devised a new course to improve his prospects. The signing of a new contract with Worth, equitable with his responsibilities, allowing him a share in harvest profits was agreed on.

"Master Worth, this means, mayhap, I may ask to buy a few acres around my house, from you, so that when I am an old one I can have a garden and a cow. . . ."

"Buy, nonsense."

". . . And I might have a better chance finding my wife and the boys."

"But does it mean, Matthew, that from now on I will have to hang my own coat on its hook?" Gil mumbled pleasantly as the giant fatigue of his long day shadowed him and closed his eyes. He lay down on a wall cot.

"Even should you shine your own shoes, master, you will not stop me from cooking up your fancy French food on short notice as I did tonight." Matthew laughed, soft-voiced. "See what it has brought us both?"

Next day, mid-morning, Gil was alone in the sitting room reading Hanna's letters. He felt like a wallflower at a ball, observing her winter from that sort of distance. He turned the post paper to the light as if some substance might be hidden in the stock. He read the tidy script again.

Gillie,

Nary a thing has worked as it was supposed to, dear. The total upheaval of my visit I will explain when I come home. But excitement! I am staying with a man who holds slaves. I get on fine with the one assigned to be my maid, although I don't need one since I have Priscilla here. The Negress does not mind talking to me, and knows the history of quite a few plantations as she has been sold several times. She let out that one local "massa" buys exclusively in the New York markets. She worked in his house for years and knows another woman slave who has two sons. Something? Nothing? Who knows what information this may lead us to. At last! Tell Matthew? Raise false hopes? You decide.

Michael Beckett's baby is a boy, called "Ho" by the slaves. I adore him. What mild winters Virginia has. Michael raises no crop but horses. How aristocratic. I judge them dull in breed. Nothing approaching V. T. Kirke's, but they are handsome as the English like them. Israel S. and Priscilla M. walk a great deal, together. More later. Oh, the legal business is coming along. But my return?

Tatta,<br>
Your Ana

Gil came away annoyed. The purpose for their separation, the preparation of a case to win Dowland Farm for Beth, was summed up with balmy unconcern as "coming along." Her use of the naughty diminutive of her Christian name at the closing gave force to his pulls at his clogs, as he got ready to walk over the field to tell Matthew his good news.

That afternoon, Gil indulged himself in a game he had devised to float himself and Qunneke over their linguistic struggle. They rode the land, seeing the farm in detail. At each section of acreage which was devoted to a particular crop, Gil dismounted, and by sleight of hand, transferred a dried sample of produce from his coat pocket to the soil. He made a fantastic mime, dressed in his waistcoat and body coat, and country gentleman's hat, slightly upturned, bringing forth beets and berries, beans and potatoes, from under his cloak to the ground, and into the spring air. Qunneke's laugh was less a rarity by the time Gil had exhausted his reservoir of fruits and vegetables.

They raced down aisles of apple trees, meeting where the rows left off. They looked for signs of peach blossoms. Qunneke's favorite crop, the flax, grew near the sheep pens. They picked out a goat to be the donor of Moses' pitcher-fed milk.

Qunneke's mood changed when they neared the barn to close their ride. She was agitated and her horse responded to her, circling and skirting and galloping away. She turned to Gil, her short hair bobbing with the motion of her mount. "Gilbert? Matta weatchimin? Matta maize?"

"Maize? Corn? I raise corn? No, Qunneke. Matta. I cannot do it. I've given it my damnedest but my ground won't grow it. Whatever it needs runs off these hills down to there." He pointed toward Hudson's farm. "Annanias Hudson raises corn high as trees, but all I get are scrubs. No corn here."

Qunneke spread her arms to the whole of the fourteen hundred acres. "Matta maize!"

"No corn. I am a superfluous farmer. Staples I must leave to other men. But I never pick a mealy peach, and I have refined my apples till now they are recognized at city tables like beautiful people. I popularize blueberries, and cranberries and strawberries abroad. Come to see what else!" He seized the woven strap she used for a rein and led her horse to the greenhouse.

He unwrapped his citrus trees for her. He showed her his notes, the compiled data of their progress, samples of exotic seeds, and drawings of the orchards he hoped someday to house under glass. "Can you imagine fresh lemons in January? What price would they bring at Fanuil Market, eh?"

The woman held him, frightened by his fierce enthusiasm that shattered the composure of his face. He quieted. "Long ago, I let slide my interest in corn." She thought to herself as he clung to her, "No corn. No children." He could not raise the basic stuff of American existence. He was unable to alter the forces that produced or would not produce. Yet, he devoted his life to growing things, plants, people, families, beautiful music. He used his farm as ground where he did a dance of celebration, perfecting each movement as it emerged.

A weight dropped from her. She was released from longtime despair over life, native life. She awakened from isolation in Gilbert's arms. She saw possibilities in tilling her own best capabilities—to keep the hearth, to extend comfort to others, to cultivate knowledge tending Wakwa's field, and to retain its beloved proportions by seating sons and daughters on it. She saw Wakwa's face in her mind's eye.

And Gil gleaned their perpetual amity in her touch.

The third day, Gil left off work on a new-style plow, to run home through a soaking rain to have supper with Qunneke. They christened the summer dining room's twenty-first season.

Gil neglected his currant pie to gaze at her. "You are looking better, beautiful as you ought. There are other ecstasies than Cooke's pie crust, and a fifty per cent chance I can create you no blond little babes to explain. Nasty thought when everything's so nice."

Qunneke judged the green steeping in his eyes, and closed her own with dignity.

Every wall sconce and lamp in the sitting room was lit to brighten it for Qunneke's inquiries. She stood in front of leather-bound volumes, knowing from Wakwa the power that the English realized through pages of type. It was still a mystery to her how symbols so colorless and similar could tell many different histories well. She craved paint and bark and hide. But she sat back on the yellow couch to smoke and wonder about what nature of patience it took to paint the mind truly, using continuously recombining letters as a brush.

"This fellow Simpson!" Gil was busy at his harp. He had a thin black book in his hand. "He belongs in the fire!" Gil pitched the text back over his head toward the flames.

Qunneke rescued the Simpson from the hearthstone and found its place on the shelves.

"Right where it belongs! Took me half of last night to dissect his jargon and I discover all he was telling me is discord is not allowed in good music! How came he to that conclusion? How dare he forbid any sound to me! By whose authority is sound or thought forbade a man? Simpson! The arch-catechist of orthodox sound." Gil returned to tuning, loosening the strings, to try anew for an effect. He muttered all the while. "Like the town codes that tell a man he must attend the church on the Sabbath, like the blighting king snatching a tenth of my flax in taxes for his caprices in which I am not included."

Qunneke blew solicitous smoke Gil's way.

Gil's long first fingernail moved against one of the loose strings. It produced a groan. "Yes." Quietly, he loosened every single string and began to pluck. His harp sounded pained in its belly, horrified in its heart.

"Can you bear the noise, Qunneke? It may be only child's play, but may I try, my sister?"

"Yes. Apollo, my brother." She smiled, came and sat at his feet, startling her companion with her first clear and willing use of English.

Gilbert Worth explored a weird range of tones, remembering cold and blood and unknown land spaces. Qunneke used the pained vibrations of the harp strings to help her own winter memories rise and pass out of her.

"Only a possibility," Gilbert reassured the harp and the woman, and quickly tensed the strings and played pieces recognizable, fully formed, rich in counterpoint.

These works broke Qunneke's meditation and she contentedly admired the hands of the man who played forgetting her presence, enjoying the privilege of his own skill and passion.

Paperwork filled the two following days of rain, along with research into the successful plumbing of classical Rome. But the nights were reserved for musical experiment, and theories budded for the notation of the sounds needed to express the realities of Wakwa's revolutionary march northeast.

On the sixth day, though no escort arrived, Gil kept his promise to Silent Fox. He covered the settee and closed the sitting room doors to traffic. "Adieu, Delos." It did not matter to Gil if the room were filled with company when he returned. The long idyll with Qunneke had established the room as permanently theirs.

After their departure, Matthew cleaned the pipe and hid the braid away.

## Chapter 26

THEY WERE CLOSED INTO the hunting lodge by the rain. Elizabeth sat against the wooden wall, knotting the rips in the fishing nets. Wakwa was horrified at her accomplishing accurate crochet, blind.

"We are going out into the rainwater." He took the work out of her hands.

She walked behind him, one of her hands on one of his shoulders, scenting out things along their way. His heart twisted further.

"There are violets. No. Not quite. Not at all."

"Those are dandelions and I am going to gather them. Stand here, against this tree. If you want to sit, slide down, against it."

"Couldn't we find violets? They won't turn my nose yellow when I smell them, and we could use them in a sallet."

"I am not after sallet, Elizabeth. I want the juice from their stems."

"For wine?"

"For something . . . their liquor makes a mighty cure for warts."

"Warts!" She hugged the tree to her. "Warts?" She felt her skin with frantic fingertips. "I have warts? On top of everything, I have warts? I have never had a wart in my life!"

"Shhh." He stroked her wet hair and face but could not resist a chuckle.

"How do you make fun of me! Oh, do get some sal ammoniac from Doctor Stirling. No hair, no face, and, now, warts! Pick me a poison and let me be rid of the whole of me!"

Wakwa molded his hands around her swollen face. "Never, never say that, Kayaskwa, even in jest."

"It is difficult!"

"Ah! Then you will get well!"

He did not permit her eyes their bandage after their bath. He sat with her in the rain, and turned their faces up to it. When the wind came, drying the sky, he changed her clothes and built a fire, determined that she would spend the night outside, believing in the power of the air of his woods to heal her. They did not talk. He did not share her mat or her blanket. He thought he kept a vigil over her. But exhaustion swept him long before she was asleep. He fell from his prop onto the deer moss that made their bedding ground.

Elizabeth opened her eyes onto the night blackness. She closed them. It was not the first time she had raised her eyelids without pain in the last day. She opened them again. There was no image to retain. No helping light reached down through the trees. "Wakwa!"

She crawled out of her wrappings. "Wakwa?" She felt her way over the thicket floor to find him. The kindly moss, erect little strings of green stars, protected her way to the edge of the resting place. She opened her eyes. The blackness grew in bulk. Black loomed darker. Her voice sent out a little yell. She touched his body. She left her hand there, against his chest, which calmed her as it rose and receded. Her palm warmed against his skin. But the forest was too black for her to tell if she had sight or were still blind. She did not know if it were day. She stayed near the man, shivering as each expulsion of his breath flew the back of her hand.

She sat in tears not brought on by sorrow. She sat until globes of silver turned out of the black. The foilage swayed in her view, pearlescent bubbles, bustles, gray gowns mingling in a court. Elizabeth trembled to hear the laughter of these women strutting their silken veils. She cried into her hands, then wiped her face on her sleeve. These were trees.

She remembered only Wakwa's shoulder as she rose and turned away from him, east, toward the brightening. She left her stick behind, and touched the laurel on each side of her path, a prisoner escaping, encouraged by many small, damp hands. Her doubtful, fantastic way led to a high spot over a meadow. She collapsed there, sick from unsupported motion.

She knew he was there, the sun. He kissed her neck. She pried one eye open and saw pale pink. It was her other hand. A new flood of tears wet her skirt. She saw it stain the shadows of blue in the folds. She shut her eyes against the lifting light that bleached the black void behind her lids to brown.

But the long, gold rays beckoned. As Wakwa had said to do, she slid to standing against the trunk of a tree. She made it her spine and formed her hands into a tunnel. At it's end—an open space—first white, then prism-cut into its colors. A stripe of pain across her eyes ended that vision. She looked toward her feet. The ground was blowing purple.

She blinked and closed her eyes. Blinked and closed. She was engaged in a stand of lupine. It etched the meadow's edge, billowed toward the river. She turned into rows of purple tails, walking with the wind, her tears elongating each separate blossom on the stems. From its roundest crest she saw the lupine pour over the rocks to the edge of the running water.

"Wakwa!" She knelt at his side, enthralled by the sight of his face. She brushed it with a kiss, wanting to erase a tiny line where his forehead sometimes bore a lengthwise cleft when he worried. The mark did not fade away. The shadowed spaces beneath his cheekbones were hollower than she remembered. "Wakwa! Where art thou? Toh kutapin?"

He woke and turned onto his stomach, used to her blindness. His arm wrapped her haunch. "Who taught you to speak?" He kissed the cloth-covered knee close to his face.

"I teach myself. I know your name. All your language comes to me through that."

He groaned flattered disbelief.

"Manunnappu. Appu. This is you. One who is still, unmoving, self-possessed. So, if I say, 'Where art thou?' I am asking, Where are you in your stillness? I must say 'toh,' 'where,' toh kutapin, where are you!"

Wakwa pushed himself up on his arms to study the woman who was explaining his language to him. Her eyes were open, orbs the color of blood. "Woi!" he said wistfully, and lay back down wishing that it were, that she could see.

"It is. I see. I see you."

"Kenaeh? Thou seest me?"

"I see you where you lie. I still have not seen where your dreams had taken you."

"You see?"

"I do." She smiled to convince him. "Nunnaum."

He caught her, searched her red eyes for the working of each iris. Then he hid his face.

"It were the rainwater did it."

"Wompan-anit!" He laid his thanks at the feet of the god of daylight. "It were not the rain!" Wakwa touched her furze of hair, her reshaping face. He closed the red eyes. "Is it a good spirit or bad who has let you see?"

She twisted away. "I awake you seeing, and you think a devil has got me? Are you well? Come with me! There is so much to show you. A little way from here are the bravest blue flowers in the world, darker than the sky, spilling down into the river." She pulled him up, her face glossy with running tears. "They're the same name as our baby. Lupine. Uncle Gil told me Lupus is the Latin name for Wolf. I walked in the forest with a great, gray wolf this winter. You think that I am mad!" She covered her eyes and he took her around her waist.

They stumbled toward the bluff of flowers, each lending

support to the other, like people in a storm. They sank down in wild grass at the edge of the stalwart, lupine sea. Pinks withstood the explorations of bees within their cupped petals and squirrels played near the man and woman who lay stiff and tangled, like deadwood.

"Wakwa, I am resolved to change," Elizabeth finally said. "I will find control. I will not make such a mistake again. The dress for Panther Eye was the finest thing that I have ever made. It was one of the finest things that I ever saw, because it matched something, some dream from inside. It was the thing that saved my face from flame, but it kindled the fire. I am renewed by this experience. I am changed for the better."

Wakwa leaned over her. "Kayaskwa! Acts may change, but the nature of anything is what it is."

"You mean there is no hope for me?"

"Listen to me." He drew closer to her and arranged and rearranged her hands on the hillside as he talked. "When I hunt a deer, what kills it? My arrow sticks in its flesh. It is the deer itself who falls to rub its hurt against the earth and drives the arrow in. The deer makes itself food for man. That is its proper end."

"Doth the same order hold, my dear, when a buck or doe is shot down with a gun?"

He did not spare her. "Guns are out of the order of things. Their use is not natural to these woods. You see the result for Ninnuock all around you. Learn from this that Panther Eye did an unnatural act. She disobeyed the nature of things. She tried to escape her life wounds by covering you with the bruises she felt inside. Waban hath set her course straight. This is the only way I can explain why she is dead. By his knife."

Elizabeth's eyes closed. "You are a wonderful speaker, husband." She began to toss from side to side, as sore as if she had been beaten again. "Truly is she dead?"

"She is gone."

"I do not understand your laws which I always took to be kinder than my own. Why does Waban rob her the chance even to be forgiven! Why does Waban bring this cloud over me?"

"It is his first foolish act."

"I cannot believe him to be stupid!"

"Then why?" In grief, Wakwa appealed to her.

"There is something hidden, that you and I do not know. Hidden things want to be found. Make it stay buried!"

He knelt near her and covered her cheek with his hand. "What will we do? Can you go on? Can we live together with her unsettled spirit present?"

Elizabeth sat up and looked straight at him. "When we return to the otan we will sing over her body as your people are wont to do. I will paint my face black and mourn her, and require everybody in the town to do the same. But I will not lose you to her witchery! She has come between us enough. As you said when you left for far away, I have a son to care for."

Wakwa moved back in respect.

Elizabeth walked away from the sight of the lupine, back toward the lodge. "We won't bother the flowers today. You have seen them there before, I expect."

"Are you angry? Angry with me?" Wakwa kept pace with her.

"Only ashamed."

"Elizabeth! Why?"

She took his hand. "Because I am hungry."

Movement on the path below him disturbed Wakwa's work over his tobacco plot the soft morning of their eighteenth day alone. Wakwa buried his bone tools in the midst of the seedling mounds and followed his wife.

Sun or rain bled fragrance from the trees into the New England air, which was lit by the ocean and cleaned by its wind. April mildness, suffused with moisture, and full of daylight, clung to the skin. Wakwa watched the young woman from his distance, through a perfumed mist.

As she dipped for water, shin deep in the brook, her flank was firm. The hands dispassionately scrubbing her healing scalp with sand were soldier's hands. When she turned fully toward him, not knowing he was there, Wakwa felt surprised to see women's parts. Breasts lowered from past nursing held their tear shape, longer tears. The soft inside of her thighs, whiter than the air, made an inviting halo in the partially shaded arena of her bath.

Wakwa looked at her for the first time not as the mother of his son, or his wife, or a woman. To call her by any sex shortened his appreciation of her. He watched her work. What he saw as strong in her body, in her habits, was a personality which fate had delivered up into female flesh. He formed his first true notion of how close she was to himself. The mysterious accident which had made him fit a male form, and her, one of a woman, was the means that transformed their alikeness into a son.

He shed his breech clout and blanket, and joined her in the quick water, dreading inside that it would float her away.

"You are like the stamen of a tulip. The flowers my uncle imports for spring." Elizabeth lounged with Wakwa at the stream's edge. His wrists were on his bent knees, his long hands dangling. She found his phallus through the barrier of his arms and legs. "This part of you matches the filament in shape. . . ." She considered the radical difference in color between her hand and the organ it touched.

He remained still. Elizabth let him go.

She turned her attention to the succulent, reaching projections of plants regenerating on the bank.

His hand spread across her pelvis. "I see that I left you with no little one this past winter. Perhaps that is for the best." His thumb traced the circle of her navel.

"Because I might have lost it from this thing that happened?"

"I mean, just that it were best. I do not wish to overburden you with mother's cares. I saw this morning that you are other things than a woman."

"Am I?"

Wakwa took his hand away and looked toward the flow of the water.

She deposited herself in front of him and drew up one leg for a chin rest. One continuous line from her knee to her hip showed. Tiny green leaves stuck to her buttocks. "If you want to know how well I understand your feelings when Qunneke refuses your affection, I can tell you now."

Wakwa flicked the leaves off her with his elliptical fingernails. "You do not understand. I do not refuse thee."

She laid her palm across his penis, relaxed again, and dark as before its engorgement.

"Elizabeth, how do you suppose that marriageable women of the Ninnuock do not lead a trail of children behind them before they are ever wed, being free with men before that day?"

"Let me think. The powaw concocts a bitter brew from wizened plants, which all the maids drink before their nights of bliss. The potion makes them impervious to the seed of their lovers until the day they swear faith to one mighty and everlasting mate." She rose and muddied her feet in the shallows, kicking droplets of water into a shaft of light.

"Two mistakes only. The mate is not always mighty nor everlasting, and it is the women themselves who know which plants make the dose and are careful to drink it through their unmarried days. The family must start on firm ground with a father to feed it."

Elizabeth returned to sit within the compass of the man's legs. "Indians know a way to bar pregnancy?" Her eyes enlarged with the enormity of the secret.

Wakwa treasured the sight of the transparent skin forming, restoring shape to the lids. "No children are born to those who drink this drink."

"My dear, you control the world. Find your agent, Dire Locke, and have him sell the stuff. Do you know the sorrow, the agonies, the arguments, the poverty you could prevent by letting out this remedy? Women, their husbands, their paramours will grovel at your feet for such a draught as that. Adultery is no more! Its telltale result is wiped out by a toddy of herbs."

"We must have something, some power left to ourselves, Elizabeth." He met her acrid statement. Then he instructed mildly. "Kayaskwa, when bearing children would cause burden among honest folk, not joy, then the drink is taken. It has had other purpose, to. It would be well for you to know. One thousand married people, long before the English ever came to Massachusetts, agreed to end the life of their unborn babes by drinking this drink. Why? For love. Love of themselves, of Columbus. Nux, that son of the people who make the music your uncle plays on his strings, that man with the great faith in the roundness of things. He died far away from the Indians he loved and who willingly worked for him. The men left over them were slave-making Spanish, so cruel that an whole island of people drank this drink to rid themselves of a posterity. After the misbirths the husbands and wives hung themselves rather than create a race of slaves. In one summer they were gone in glory."

Elizabeth leaned against his supple thigh, overcome by this history.

Wakwa measured the straightness of her nose and its angle to her cheeks. "Your eyes are opened."

"I see you changed from the time before your mission. What happened to you there that has ruined your faith in your future? You are as tortured as Qunneke is by the drift of things. I am not Ninnuock, but a part of the drift which confounds your race. Love me or let me go away!" When these last words came out she grasped him strongly, falling hard against his chest, loath to offer him such an alternative.

Wakwa clung to her as well, rolling her onto her back, lying with his full weight on top of her, anchoring her underneath himself. He held her head tightly, disregarding the wounded scalp. "I told you at Taquonk that you would solve my miseries. Simple as the sunrise, you do it!" He tore into the channel that measured distance between them —a legless, armless, breastless, faceless tunnel, darkness to be freely explored. Complete as a single cell bursting its contents into two, Elizabeth trailed a call into the morning which she never heard. It brought sweat out on the body of the man above her.

Wakwa knew her again that night, approaching with delicacy, and Elizabeth suffered him only out of love because she was still ascendant from their morning.

# Chapter 27

QUNNEKE CAME SLOWLY, with the weight of Wolf-of-the-mist on her back. Pequawus and Sequan worked at coaxing the goat up the wooded incline, above the river.

Not knowing how to embrace them all at once, Elizabeth stayed on the heights and hugged herself, sending hellos toward the awkward procession. The old man reached her first. He placed his son's hand over his white daughter-in-law's. "I see she hath made you new, good son." Qunneke kissed Elizabeth on her lips. Henry's silver cup hung from her belt. Elevated by her affection and the sacrifice of the glory of her hair, Elizabeth sent Tame Deer off with Wakwa, and took Pequawus, the two children, and the goat to the lodge.

"You went, Tame Deer?" Wakwa managed, nervous as a boy.

"Very far."

"All alone, for so long?"

"Never alone. I have held miawene with gods."

Wakwa made a sound, and smiled, and rocked her against his breast. "You are full of secrets. What did you do? Find the root that Locke wrapped up for you? Have you been smoking in the sun?"

"I need no smoke to carry me away. But carried I was and I will not come down."

"You sound foolish." Wakwa let her go, uncomfortable at her look. "You must come down. There are things to decide. And nothing floats forever."

Qunneke left him on the path and worked her way onto a shelf of rock out over the river, open to the sun.

Wakwa regretted the habit of their discourse which had

178

robbed a light from her eyes. He came up behind her on the ledge. "When I make no decision, you despise my slowness. When I say, 'Let us decide,' you turn away. I stopped you. You were floating?"

"Why is the sun so very hot behind glass?"

Aided by her slit skirt, Wakwa's hand experimented, touched her thigh, followed her leg to its juncture with hip and groin.

She did not stop him.

His fingers drew tight on her flesh.

"It is four springs since Sequan was born. When the hill goes blue, I know her time."

"I am sorry." Wakwa's hand lapsed its attention. "I forgot. With all this. . . . A daughter, four! I have not seen her in so long. She is grown tall and well. She passes me by and does not seem to know me."

"It is also four springs for us, husband." Qunneke faced the man, younger than she. "It is hard to bear it any longer."

"So . . . ?"

She watched the breeze billow the shirt made for him by another woman. "Tell me about the glass."

"Do not avoid," Wakwa said gently, prepared for their tragic moment, "do not hide."

"There is no need to hide!" She mistook him. "If you must know, I have passed my time with Gilbert."

Wakwa's head tilted to the side. "I know that when a bottle is left on the floor of the woods and sun hits it, a fire starts."

Sun glinted from Qunneke's teeth. Her laugh caught the attention of the others already at the hunting house.

"I am glad you go freely where you will, Tame Deer. But you have done a dangerous thing, isn't that so?"

"Yes."

"Panther Eye is hardly cold!" The husband saw a different problem than his wife.

Qunneke let her eyes roam Wakwa's physique from his toes, up his straight, long legs, his back and shoulders, his neck. She touched it. "You think the town has something new to whisper about?"

"You tell me what is right to think." The man looked into groundless space over the river.

"Gilbert is my uncle."

"Oh, woman!" Wakwa agonized. "He is also very much a man. He has eyes. And a ready will. For you. He loves you. Loves you!"

"Greatly."

"So!" Angry, relieved, Wakwa turned her face back to his. "He has finally loved you?"

"In the same way that I have loved you these four difficult years."

Wakwa threw his hands up.

Qunneke caught them, bent to him, and gave him her first wifely kiss in years. She left him with his lips still parted. "Gilbert Worth knows all there is to know about love!"

Wakwa walked by her on the path, taking his traditional place protectively in front, his imagination sizzling with what may have occurred in the Englishman's house. He did not seek enlightenment about details.

Their baskets heavy with long grasses for making summer hats, Elizabeth and Sequan came back in time for the birthday feast. There were corncakes, and new blueberries and maple sugar candy. The bass had been caught by the men courtesy of the nets Elizabeth had mended. Pequawus set them across the cove at the falls. Wakwa shot the frantic fish with arrows.

"Paewe." Wakwa called Sequan to him. "Little." He engulfed her and rocked her in his lap. "For a gift I will carve you the handle for your own paddle for the big canoe. I will finish with it soon. But today you will ride on my shoulders, across the bridge and all the way home. We must go back, my uncles want to see me."

"Why must I be home and you be at Uncle Waban's? Talking. Talking. I cannot come with you, there, Nosh. I will stay here."

"You cannot live here on the hillside alone."

"Zabeth does, sometimes."

"You tell her." Wakwa appealed to Elizabeth.

"I will not. Go into the town and do your business, dear, and come to get us after? I have no wish to stay shut up in this weather. A few days more? I will keep the children.

After all, I have the goat for Moses' milk. Qunneke should go in with you. Have some rest."

"I cannot leave you." Wakwa refused.

"It will get me more time to grow some hair."

"Elizabeth, what will a few days do for that? And if you mean to stay away until it is long, I will not see you for years of moons. Come home, Elizabeth. There is a new house in a new spot. Bad memories fade quickly. What will the people think if I go back without you? Many people there love you. They will wonder."

"And well they should! You tell them, please, that I am not coming until I finish my hat!"

Pequawus started the pair on their way toward the water, remaining solidly in the path near Elizabeth when Wakwa looked worriedly back.

He made the next days ones of wonder for the daughter of Charles Dowland. Pequawus took Elizabeth on little pilgrimages through the woods, conducting her to places important in the story of the family and the tribe. He showed her where Wakwa and Awepu had learned to shoot, where Wakwa had been born, the place of summer prayer, so much quieter than the fall and winter fetes. They passed by dug-out hills walled with stones and thatch, where the bones of this or that one had been laid.

"Nippisse is up there, that far ledge. We put the little young ones close to the sky to shorten the distance they walk to Kautantowwit. I am too old to climb up anymore. You see, I thought I would die without her, and made up a grotto for us away from everyone."

The gray-haired father took Elizabeth's wrist in one of his hands, and Sequan's in the other. Affectionately, he led them into one grave not yet mortared over.

"Oh!" Elizabeth pulled back. "Sequan should not be so close!"

Pequawus chuckled at his English relative. "This old man was a friend of Sequan's. He is pleased that she comes to see that all is as it should be. Hold Moses so that he can watch what I do."

Pequawus dug his torch into the dirt floor. It lit the cave's fittings, showing the round place to be hung and kept like a house. The sagamore tenderly unwrapped the corpse's face to make sure of the condition of the body. Weathered

181

skin whitened by death showed. From a jar within reach, Pequawus added to the oxide protecting the body from rot. He made a better wrap of the outer covering and dusted its seams with the powdery red grains. He snuffed the torch when they had backed out of the grave.

"Father, when was your friend laid to his rest?"

"At a sad time for you, little Spider, two winters ago, day after your father was buried near the church."

"But there is no decay! The man looks to be asleep! I have dreams of my father's coffin. I never see my father's face in my nightmares. Green mold, only. You see, under the stone at Annanias' church, my father's flesh is gone."

Pequawus walked close to her on their way to milk the goat for Moses' meal. "Dowland's flesh hath only changed its shape. He is part with my grandson, now. It does not matter how he was buried. Yet, it were good for thee to have seen Charles Dowland's face at the end. I did. Elizabeth, your father died a happy man."

_____ Chapter 28

SHAME. SHAME. Grandee carried Worth away from the Indians' winter valley after he had undergone the news about his niece.

"It would make shame for Wakwa to have you see her as she left the camp." Waban refused to let Gil go to his niece.

The Englishman knew shame. For how many months had he played the magician, Merlin, concocting balm out of money, faith, and affection, to protect Elizabeth's enchantment from being scarred by the world? He had styled the Massachuseuck demigods, cast them roles in a myth of his making. Now he felt responsible for Elizabeth's downfall and his insides burned with a pernicious salt.

He rode home fast, condemning Panther Eye for destroying an eden of the mind. He hated Plant too, for walking off with the miniature of Beth. He wanted even that inadequate painting as a memento of exquisite form he did not hope to see in the flesh again.

Gil made for the mounting block at the front of the house, depending on Matthew to care for his horse. He was reserving his own energy to essay the task of composing two letters, one to Doctor Stirling and one to his wife. He looked up from scraping his boots. Orange behind the sitting room window caught his eye.

"No one has hair like that but Israel Stirling!" Gil ran for his front door. He moved the brass latch without breaking stride. Laughter wreathed the vestibule. He swung the sitting room doors back to get at its source.

Hanna screamed, a wigged man in black came to her aid, Israel knocked something over as he stood, and his father, Doctor Mac, struggled out of the wing chair and wordlessly waved a cane. An unfamiliar baby crawled into view.

"Gilbert?" Hanna held back in mild horror of his woodsman's appearance, her image of him marred.

The thought crossed Gil's mind that Qunneke had no trouble recognizing him for himself. But he brought his demeanor under control, and reclaimed Hanna's confidence with a pretty and lingering kiss on her hand.

Her arm came about his neck and she bent over the wild, gold head lowered to her.

"When?" was Gil's first word. He watched her eyes and face, searching out her ready resemblance to Elizabeth.

"Yesterday, in the morning, Gillie." She had to contend with the assorted company and broke their embrace. "The Doctor we brought with us on our way. He has had a sadness, dear. His Ann is gone."

Gil and Mac turned around and around one another in bear-like commiseration.

"She passed back in January. Right after all o' ye left. Bu' it's a New Year. An old man's allowed a laugh now an' again. It's all he has." Tears glittered in his crisp blue eyes. The Scot pounded Gil's back with his fist. His smile was genuine.

"Damn!" was Gil's consolation to his friend.

"Gil." Hanna brought the stranger together with her husband. "This is Michael Beckett. Come all the way north simply to help us."

"Simple as that? Couldn't solve the riddle in Virginia, eh?" Gil pumped his hand cordially, and found his arms full with Horace, Beckett's child. "Light little thing, did you bring your mama?"

"Oh, Gil!" Hanna hushed him.

"Good sir, you could not know. I am a recent widower like the doctor."

Gil gave the child back to Hanna. "You did not mention that in your letters." He did not forgive her easily for causing this embarrassment. "Mr. Beckett, you have all my sympathy. It has been a trying winter. A tragic one. Shall we have cognac all round?"

Gil brought out his best and served each glass, used now to doing things for himself. He watched his wife with the baby, and passed his afternoon doing nothing more strenuous than listening to stories of the hazards of coach travel on the White Plains Post Road.

After a late supper, Hanna and Gil were left in peace. They remained in the cleared dining room, at opposite ends of the table, each of them reflected in the polished wood.

Hanna recounted her stay in the southern colony. "I went to church while I was there. Everybody does. If I were younger I think I would become Anglican. Such beautiful ceremony! Not the coldness and straightness of our Sweetwood church."

"I met you in this church." Gil leaned back on the rear legs of his chair like a ten-year-old.

Hanna paused, then talked about Beckett. "His wife died of pox a month after Ho was born. He sold the sugar plantation right away to a corporation, and you'll never guess who sits on its board. . . ."

"Sir Francis Drake?"

". . . Stephen Poore, Sr., and that is how Gwynn Poore knew to recommend Michael to us. The rumor is that the Poores will move to Jamaica from the Cape and leave Massachusetts, for good and all."

"And little Stephen? Poore Junior?"

"Oh, there is an estrangement, I hear. Young Stephen is in Europe somewhere."

"It fits. Poore is of steel. But, my, there was a time he could play a violin! How is Gwynn taking the uprooting?"

"Michael says she will like it about as well as his wife did."

"You mean it will kill her?"

"I mean that Gwynn's heart is broken leaving the place where she was born."

"It seems to happen repeatedly and to everyone we know. How is your heart, Hanna?"

"It is . . . home."

As she went on with praise for Beckett's research for the construction of the Dowland brief, Gil relived privately his afternoon of holding Qunneke's sumptuous body against his brown-gold robe.

"Where have you got him?" Gil suddenly cut into her story. "What room is he in?"

"Michael? Oh, the one next to ours. It is warm and near the stairs, and does not adjoin. I have Henry's old crib in our dressing room for Ho, so that I can hear him if he needs anything during the night."

"I wish you'd asked. I didn't want anyone in that room."

"I am sorry, Gil. But it is a guest room. There is some reason?"

"Indeed! But never mind. Just so Cooke watches he doesn't make it smell like a wine press in there."

"Gilbert!"

"I have never seen anyone drink like that. Every case I have will be empty if he stays another week. That wasn't some cheap rotgut from the out towns of his illustrious Virginia. It was fine wine and he consumed it like lemonade."

"He is free, dear, but we are particularly abstemious, being from Massachusetts."

"Bull. There is hardly a soul in the Bay who's not a heavy drinker. They're just a little smart about how they do it. I have no time for it, myself."

"Gilbert, I have never heard you begrudge a guest."

"Well, we'll see what he's got to say for himself in the morning. Mayhap he is worth it. I have waited long to find an end to the tunnel of your brother's will. I need it off my back. I have other things I want to do. And since when are you nursemaid for visiting children? Why didn't he bring one of his slaves?"

"You are quite biting. I said to him I would not allow a slave on the farm. He knows about Matthew. He obliged my principles."

Gil came along the side of the oval table, playing on its finish with his graceful fingertips. "There's my lovely girl. You make me proud. But see you do not substitute yourself for one of his bought servants."

"Gilbert, what do you mean by that?"

"Ana, I do not need two lawyers in the house. You know very well."

"When you met Michael," Hanna was subdued, "you said the winter had been tragic. I have talked and talked. Now I want to know what has happened to you in all this time."

"Not one *little* thing." Gil snuffed the candles and guided the woman up the stairs to their bed.

Late in the night, Ho woke with puny cries. Hanna tended him and brought him to the big bed to sleep between herself and Gil. She used the Beckett pitcher to feed him.

Gil was grateful that he would not be forced to tell the whereabouts of Henry's, prematurely. He had saved Elizabeth's story with his own for a better time.

"Gillie, can you turn your face the other way? I think Ho is frightened of your beard."

Gil covered his head with his pillow, too tired to retort.

"How does Beth do this, night after night?"

Gil emerged to see Hanna sitting against the headboard, holding the bundled child, weary enough to drop him.

"Shall I call for Priscilla?"

"Let her sleep, Gil. With all this company she'll be working tomorrow!"

Gil had regained the touch of his wife that night and would not show annoyance about Beckett's baby. He reached for his dressing gown.

"What are you doing?"

"We both tend toward overkindness. Leave young Beckett to me."

He carried the boy downstairs and found another night owl in the sitting room. "How do you put a kid to sleep, Doctor?"

"Don't ask me. I'm not much of a physician."

"Mac, people die. You never left Ann's side. Don't go like that on me. I need you."

The old man poured a cup of rum.

"I'll have one, too." Gil let the baby lie across his knees and drool onto the settee.

"It's no' for me, ye mad harper. It's for the bairn."

"Like father, like son."

"Tha's a two-edged jest, laddie. Israel ye know, he's gotten a great lot out o' travelin' with your wife. He's cum back with an idea. Dropped tha' preacher nonsense altogether. No, he wants to study doctorin'. I'm goin' ta teach him surgery. Meself. It seems foolish a boy with a Pa who's a doctor has gotta learn to cut people from a barber. An' haven't all of us doctors paid the barbers dear for their doubtful instruction. Israel can get his diploma anywhere he wants. But I teach him to cut this summer, before any butchers get a hold of 'im, don't ye know!"

"It is perfect. How did it happen?"

"Israel, you know," the father divulged with pride, "just can't stand t'see anyone sick."

"He's in the right business!" Gil laughed and the baby cried. "That remedy didn't do our Ho a bit of good."

"Mrs. Beckett died o' small pox. Israel's angry about that. The boy wants to wipe out the pox. Says there must be some way. He took care of this baby all the way, they say. Knew what to do, natural like."

"Born in him." Gil amplified the father's success. "Tell me, Mac, what do you think of 'Massa Ho'?"

"It's a good baby. Nice little baby. May not make it without a mother. What d'ye think of the father, this Michael Beckett, Gil?"

"I don't like him one damn bit." Gil's light lashes lowered over sleep-heavy eyes.

Dr. Mac pulled the sections of a silver flute from an inside pocket of his worn coat. "When all else fails, Gilbert, I take this an' sure as shootin' me audience goes fast asleep." The Scotsman began to play.

Gilbert Worth set the child on the couch, and ghost-like

in the unlit room, drew back the cover of his harp. The men made quiet music unaware that this midnight session was for each of them more than for the teething child.

In the morning, Gil begged the doctor to delay trying to get past Waban to see Elizabeth. "Help me make it easy on her. The child's had enough."

"An' more have I. Don't ply me with the English manner. She's me Bonnie. She's me patient. I'm her Scottish powaw, don't ye know? Tha's enough for the old Indian. I'm no' so clumsy as ye think. I'm takin' Israel and me friend Ho along. The kiddie needs woman's milk. Plenty of it there!" Mac winked.

Gil and Hanna had the house to themselves. He let her know about his week with Qunneke, and their settling of it as loved comrades.

"You know, dear, that is all I want with Michael. It is possible for me to have a friend who is not a woman. You do not seem to like that leaning in me as much as in yourself."

"It is not the leaning, but the particular friend I am cautious of. Perhaps tall, dark, handsome men who bathe in rye and sleep till midday make a threat to me."

"Silly old dear. Wakwa is taller, darker, and vastly more handsome than Michael."

"And Wakwa is Wakwa. I have no trouble over your deep affection and admiration for him."

"Gilbert, I cannot limit myself to friendship with the perfect. There are too few such people. I did not choose to care so much about Mr. Beckett. I have him well in hand. He is a product of the age, but growing, I think. He is in need of a firm base. He came half out of curiosity about you. I talked and talked of your virtues. . . ."

"Every last one?"

"I did not mention *that* specifically, but I am sure from my open devotion to you that he guessed. . . ."

They grew quiet as at the table the night before.

"Is this what you would be like without me?" Hanna looked sad.

"Dear wife, excuse my profligate humor."

"Not that. I mean the way you look. So strong, and rough, and. . . ." Hanna made wide gestures near her head.

"This?" Gil indicated his hair and beard. "Just a disguise. I'm off this very moment to get my wig out of the camphor box."

Shaved clean, Gilbert Worth was poring over the double farm accounts by noon, his natural hair trimmed, not covered but showing its gold, his costume exquisite summer wools in varying shades of blue.

Much at home, Beckett made his entrance without knocking. He went directly to the corner to pour himself a drink.

"Nothing like New England air to inspire an early, healthful breakfast," Gil muttered into the huddle around the account books on the writing table.

Hanna slapped Gil's hand.

"Don't mind our work, Mr. Beckett," Gil atoned to her, "make yourself comfortable, your son's been spirited off to my niece's people for an euphoric day of drinking . . . at the breast."

"Fine," Beckett said with the ennui which marked all his statements about his young son. "I will wait until you are through." Michael Beckett would not sit while Matthew sat.

"Don't do that, sir. You will be standing forever. The business of farming goes on eternally."

Beckett perused the books on the shelves in response.

Gil gave in and asked Matthew, with a lift of an eyebrow, to take the records back into the small office for completion later.

"Mr. Worth!" Matthew asked the master in and closed the door. When Gil reappeared, Beckett was already relaxing in a chair which faced away from the sunlight.

"You are the great democrat, sir," Michael criticized, genially.

"How is that?"

"Sitting with your nigger, answering beck and call. Very democratic."

"Polite, rather. Matthew is a freeman. He eats, sleeps, lives, and works where and how he chooses. He is not my property. Do not refer to him as such. I do believe he heard you."

"Your manumission is a dirty trick, Mr. Worth."

"Careful, Beckett." A tick showed in Gil's neck. "The man only wants me dig at you for information which may

189

lead him to a wife he loves and children he fathered some years ago. They are slaves and he is free."

"No nigger is ever free while there is one in slavery." Beckett delighted in his rhyme.

"The word 'nigger' is inequitable and therefore never spoken in this house. I am surprised at you, an attorney. . . ."

"Solicitor!"

". . . a Doctor of Law, using imprecise diction. Cut the word out of your vocabulary if you want your fee."

"Gilbert. Michael." Hanna looked up from her sewing frame.

"What do I say? Tell me! I am a novice in the colony. Freedman? African? Black bondsman? Indenturee?"

"His name is Matthew Freeman for your future reference. His position is called houseman. But he is so vital and integral to life here the title may soon change to something better fitting the services he rendered while I was away. In point of fact, he never was a slave. He was kidnapped, yes. And expatriated. But he never did a bit of work for us until he possessed his freedom papers and literacy."

"Illegal acts in the order you did them." Beckett shook his forefinger.

"Do not quote the letter of the law to Hanna and me! It has cost us a pretty penny to comply with the statute of this colony, written seventeen hundred aught three. What it has meant to us is a great out-of-pocket expense. All those words come together to mean that no slave may claim that he is free unless the said master assumes the complete and total burden of his sustenance forever, or two thirds of it plus gainful employment. My wife and I chalk up eight of these wretched people, snatched from gentlemen very much like yourself, and we totally supported them until such time as we could obtain them places and employ that met their wants. All done by the book, which to my mind was arranged so as to make it impractical and impossible to free a slave even should one want to do it! Very few with the will have the gold to pay for such a charity. The law perpetuates misery and gives no assist to the human beings it was written to protect!"

Beckett applauded. "Stand for governor! Learn when you discuss the law, sir, not to mix up human beings into it."

"Perhaps, Michael, if you had a piece of fish and an egg to start your day you would be less a pain in the ass to have around."

Beckett lifted an eyebrow in Hanna's direction.

"Dost mind my tongue, Goodwife Worth?"

"Both of you make charming conversationalists today."

Beckett laughed. "The cool head of the family." He sipped a second drink. "Have one, Gilbert. Gilbert is all right, isn't it? Nothing clears the mind like alcohol. Then you could follow your thought to its conclusion. The law you have spent your time and money bending is geared toward protection of property, before, during, and after freedom. As you say, it leaves much to be desired. The number of freed blacks in this country is too small to give them bargaining rights at any bar of justice. Free they have it worse than slaves, for they are a threat to everyone. Manumission is a sham."

"Stuff!"

"Listen to me! There is only one safe place for your Matthew. Right here in your nigger lovin' arms." Beckett assumed a drawl over his British English. "Where would he find work away from here with that independent eye of his? There is no way the nigger can free himself up to poke around the South looking up his relatives."

"He'd travel with his papers. No one could lay a hand on him."

"Papers!" Beckett shouted, then held his head against headache. "They'd be burned. He'd be hung. Just for living. His ambitions are dead as a skunk in a stew. Sign him up for the duration of his days. I'll do the contract this afternoon."

"Can it be that the world is better off in the hands of men who submit to its evils? Am I as naive as I seem? Or just a maniac who thinks he can move mountains? It is Merlin, Merlin, again and again."

"Here. Here." Michael poured him a shot of whiskey out of his own glass. "I have a foul tongue before two. I only tell you all this to move all your Bay Colony pretensions of integrity out of the way of the settlement of your brother-in-law's will. There has to be some fast stepping to clinch his land."

"You mean there is to be no justice there, either? Hasn't

anybody got rights to a thing on grounds of logic? Of simple dignity?"

"I'm not a wizard, but I have bent my mind around inheritance law from Georgia to Massachusetts. What a case! Can the biracial son of a common law plural marriage inherit the entailed estate of a natural-born American colonial, loyally subject to the king of England and the laws of Britain, who has named a woman as his heir. By God! We could set precedent!" Beckett picked Hanna's thread clippings from his meticulous, black mourning breeches. "Hanna, sorry, women do not make reliable heirs. Perhaps my hostess should not be bothered with legal trifles which may annoy?"

"Charles was my brother!" Hanna objected. "I have a right to know."

"Do you think, Mr. Worth?"

"Mrs. Worth thinks, Mr. Beckett."

"If you say. Before I speak, please both of you remember I did not write the laws which I research."

"And before you give us the benefit of your researches, I have a bit of unkindly news for both of you." Gil got up, reseated himself beside Hanna, put his arm through hers and held the hand against his breast. He made his way through the story of Panther Eye and his niece, thinking he had no right to delay anymore unburdening himself to his wife or his legal counsel.

Hanna retreated to the upstairs not to show them her grief. But Beckett relished the tale with another glass of whiskey, his delight in the case intensified.

"Your hands are tied, of course. Worth, poor fellow. You cannot sue for any kind of damages. The crime took place on Indian land, but how I would love to have had this copper missy out on extradition, up on the stand. Something smells about it. Why should the Indian chieftain kill one of his own over a simple assault of a white? He weighted Justice's old scale, but with what? The whole thing's more marvelous than any hypothetical case ever posed by an examiner. It may absorb my whole career."

"Beckett, you will have no career if you keep on absorbing liquor at your present rate. At first you made me angry. Now I pity you."

"I am deserving of pity. I live alone. I have that orphaned child to see through life. You do not know your good fortune to possess a wife like Hanna. I live in no Oriental harem as this native sachim you describe."

"Do you not, Beckett? How many are your slaves? I cannot imagine a man of your parts not taking out his frustrations on available material. Or doesn't it count when the object is black?" Gil struck hard in Beckett's weak moment.

The lawyer sat with legs crossed, giving his head gentle, drunken shakes.

"As you saw, Michael, my wife is no possession, but a free agent. Perhaps it is because she was born in Massachusetts. Do not wind yourself about her sympathies to seduce her. Can you see through your alcohol haze that sword above my mantel? I will use it to cut you fine for flannel hash if you debase her by touching her drunk. Do me the honor of sobering up and then just come out like a man and ask her straight to lie with you abed."

Gil called back as he left, "I'm sending Matthew for your coat. You will want to eat out of doors. You are sure to vomit."

The two men walked in the afternoon, southwest toward Dowland Farm. When he saw the house, straight and high, above the patchwork of freshly plowed acreage, Beckett exclaimed, "To have it in the family!"

"Yes. It is nice. Built in an age of innocence."

"Its value!"

"It is where my wife grew up."

"You wouldn't be willing to sell?"

"My wife, or my innocence?"

Beckett dropped the subject.

Inside, he was impressed again by the integral cleanness of the wooden structure. It seemed to Beckett that the place had lifted itself out of the surrounding forest as naturally as a spruce.

The lack of life drove them into the kitchen.

"It stays this way by magic?" Beckett asked.

"By the agency of a minor devil. She's out now, tending the bees, I suppose."

"Bees! Be serious." Michael Beckett began to snoop in the cupboards.

"Rigid Presbyterians, Beckett. Not a drop in the house." Then in an afterthought, "Make a good place to dry you out."

Beckett and Worth looked at one another in the same moment.

"I do not like to be forward . . . ," Michael hedged.

"Be my guest."

"Thank you then, I will. I will stay here. Out of your way to work. Dowland had an office?"

"Through there." Gil followed him, interested in the developing plan.

"I like this house. I'd love to have it. But if I can't get it for myself, I'll get it for you." Beckett moved with athlete's grace about Dowland's small, low-ceilinged study. "Did Dowland like horses?"

"My brother-in-law rode an ox."

"Great God!"

"Careful of your speech in here!" Gil snapped like a caretaker in a church.

"Quite right. It does reform one. Look here, Worth, Hanna brought me Dowland's very exquisite, operative will. If I am to do anything of value in Boston, I ought to know more. I need to go through his papers. I do have permission? There are cousins aplenty with their eyes on this, no doubt?"

"I can give you names in alphabetical list. I think I'd better tell you, among some of them there is a suit brewing against me for neglect they think I showed. I am an indirect heir. I was alone with Charles when he had his fall."

"Mort d'ancestor." Beckett dismissed this concern as elementary to overcome. "A property like this? Only a fool would let it get away."

"My niece may want to do just that."

"Yes." Beckett shook his head at the idea of Elizabeth. "You were right to wait to find the right lawyer. I'll need to talk to your niece, and this . . . this . . . sachim fellow." As he talked, Beckett walked about the room, appraising everything he saw for market value. He looked at the portraits on the window wall and knew the people who had made the house.

"I like you when you are working."

"I do not work." Beckett looked at Gil, askance. "I am a dilettante."

Gil left by way of the kitchen soon after. He pointed to the matron coming from the north meadow. "There she is. The formidable Mrs. Winke. Watch her like a hawk. She does not mind her business. What you need. She'll baby you to death."

Gil shut the door and passed the housekeeper on his way. "Winke! I have company for you. A Mr. Beckett here on legal business. Baby him to death."

_____ Chapter 29

THE SCOTSMAN got no further than Gil had in persuading Waban to let him see Elizabeth. He did prevail on Qunneke to take Ho to her breast. Stirling made himself useful, hoping that Wakwa would bring Elizabeth back while he lingered.

With Israel at his side, Dr. Mac reopened the ugly wound in a man's leg which had healed then festered in turn. He cleaned and cauterized the flesh and taught his son and this patient White Cat the art of winding a sanitary bandage.

He smoked with Waban. "Does your medicine feller, your taupowaw, have a son? Would his son sorta take over for the old man when he dies?"

"Mac, it is a thing for the spirit. Not only the will. The taupowaw is a seer. His sons, they hunt. He has a young nephew who shows talent for the plants—the way to talk beyond common talk. A thing of the soul it must be."

"Well, with us, it's some spirit and more will. Maybe your taupowaw wouldn't mind talkin' with Israel about plants an' such? I'm interested in anything that'll work. But I figure it is I got to teach the lad his surgery. What goes on inside. Not tha' I know much. I know what was taught to me an' maybe a little more."

"Mac, how will you teach Israel what is inside?"

"Well. . . ." The white doctor hesitated. "What we did at Edinburgh is . . . we used cadavers. Human bodies. Them who was poor, homeless, no one to bury 'em properly, don't ye know? Them bodies did more by lettin' us look inside 'em after they was dead than in all the time they was alive."

The two elderly men laughed together.

"You wouldn't have an animal about?" Mac's laugh trailed away. "An extra deer? A wolf? Fox? A dog? Anything? I could give ye somethin' toward it. I know ye need the beasts to eat."

"I can do better for you than a deer, Mac. I have for you a. . . ."

"A cadaver?"

"Cadaver. There is a corpse. A woman. A young woman."

"Not *the* one?" The physician's objectivity slid.

"What difference, white powwaw? I thought to give her to the buzzards. But what use is that? Neither can she have an honored grave. She is wrapped, with the red dust on her, ready. My son Nuppohwunau can show you where she is. You would do me a service taking her away. I thought to save her for Wakwa, but he does not return. What does he want to see her for? She is dead."

"Waban, it's two weeks gone now . . . two weeks an' four days!"

"She was more rotten when she was living than she is now. You will find her useful."

"All right, friend, Waban, we'll take the corpse off your hands, but. . . ." Now Mac drove his bargain. "I want to see me Bonnie, me Beth before the week is out. Call the lad an' her back. She's me girl. I want to see them eyes."

Panther Eye's moribund flesh became Israel Stirling's first classic study. Working in the cool of the glade where the corpse had been kept on a palette high in a tree, Dr. Mac uncovered sinew and tendon, cartilage and bone. Under surveillance of the taupowaw, Waban, and the ailing White Cat, he and Israel explored the inward organs, recording them with drawings, burning a part as it was used.

The heart was a loss. But Panther Eye relinquished a gift. The womb afforded red-headed Israel a precious look at the beginning stage of pregnancy.

Elated and exhausted, father and son returned to the Worths' on April thirteenth with the news that Wakwa and Elizabeth would soon be ordered home.

Waban lay sick for days in solitary realization that he had executed a grandson with the wayward woman.

"It's illegal." Michael Beckett settled himself on the settee while the others gathered around Panther Eye's scraped, scrubbed skull.

"Not to mention immoral," Gil put in from the corner where he worked at his harp.

"It's an amazin' symmetry." Mac praised Panther Eye's cranium.

Israel worked silently over it, measuring dimensions with his father's slender gold ruler.

"It is strange, one so physically perfect should be so twisted in her soul. What made her that way?" Hanna drew closer to Michael, and puffed at the wuttammagon, the little pipe that she had had from Wakwa.

"In Virginia, after dinner, men smoke at the table, and the ladies gossip over sugar cakes in the drawing room. What pleasant insanity in Massachusetts. Look at you all!"

"We are too busy, Beckett, to sit quietly on our aristocratic asses all night."

"Gil, if you don't stop. . . ."

"I can stand it, Hanna." Beckett turned his brown eyes on her. "If only you'll call someone to get me a drink."

"Could you get it, Michael? There's a dear. We do not bother Matthew, late, for little things."

Beckett took her remark for rudeness. "Matthew! Mister Freeman!"

The black man appeared, drying a tray. "Sir?" He questioned Gil, amazed at the voice.

Sweetly, Gil said to the guest, "Mr. Beckett, in Massachusetts we live quite plainly."

"Plainly, indeed!" Beckett put him off. "Yours is the only silver boot scraper I have ever seen in daily and general use."

"Well. Then try to fit in!" Gil plucked a long loose

string. "Matthew, mix our guest a flip. It's a man-sized drink, Michael, of rum and such. Sure to put you soon to sleep."

Hanna moved uncomfortably at the trend of the talk.

Beckett laughed behind his sleeve at the upheaval he was causing. "Rum, slaves, molasses. The eternal triangle of the Yankee."

"Michael Beckett, I have nothing to do with any commercial enterprise which would abet the ugly system to which you refer. I have carefully kept clear of the sea trade."

"Clean through and through." Beckett memorized the flip making, watching Matthew. "Worth, you wouldn't last a day in Jamaica."

"Shutoop, Beckett!" Mac struck the floor with his cane. "Never mind, I'll take her to my room."

Hanna swept over to the window and leaned against the little panes. She looked at the swelling silhouettes of the branches of the cherry tree and privately bemoaned the acrimony of the night.

"Does the bony lass bother ye, dearie? I'll take her out."

Hanna looked at the doctor, then toward the southwest and the home she had left to marry Gil.

Gil came behind her and rested his hands on her shoulders. She shrugged him off.

Matthew approached. "Mistress? They may bring the thing to my cabin if it would help."

"You wouldn't mind, Matthew? You are always kind."

"Horses!" Gil peered into the early night. "It'll be Massachuseuck telling us we may go in!"

Matthew went to the door with Gil right behind. Instead of messengers from the otan, four men from Wareham Harbor came, carting a long, wide crate.

"Nocturnal deliveries from merchant ships, Worth?" Beckett stepped near to see.

Gil knelt at the box, the Stirlings and Matthew working with him to pry it open. A letter appeared above profuse packing of straw.

Beckett saw over Gil's shoulders. "Marvelous engraving."

"A gift from Vaughan Thomas Kirke Ltd. Why?" Gil brought the large, folded sheet to Hanna.

"I hope it is not another gun."

Gil read to himself, then held the letter aloft and executed a quick little volta. He included the entire company in a letter from Locke. " 'You heard our bells, I surmise. . . .' Oh, Locke is dry. Great long peals went on for five minutes to warn us off and send us home. . . . 'They sent you home and tolled my diminution. Those were wedding bells. Mad Claude married me to the maid, Jeanette. Alleluia for the indefiniteness of the Old Style New Year. 1747–48 on the document put the fishers totally off and in the wrong. The case was dropped and Hal kicked by the town tribunal, inland and south to farm for potatoes. You can see why I will not be in Pemaquid for a long time. Married bliss does not suit me. This from Carolina at Kirke's suggestion, from his warehouse, a minor museum. I am here testing my well-mended leg at whatever parties are available to my like and at this time of year. Blessings on the Fox. Humbly, etc.' "

"Case? What case was this?" Beckett nosed for the letter. Straw flew. "A clavier!" Gil shouted. "Gilt!"

"Guilt by association, I'd say. Cozy with Kirke." Michael peered down.

"Say now, Gil, go easy. Don't break the box. Israel can keep the bones in it." Mac cautioned, "Lift, lift, watch out!"

"Ever get paid in claviers, Mac?"

Hanna watched Gil's abandon as he played it where it lay on the floor. She took his coat for him when he stripped it off, lost in the aptitudes of the keyboard.

"The very thing for composition. I have been struggling so!"

Hanna saw his well-made shoulders through the thin cloth of his shirt, moving in harmony with thoughts separate from her.

"What do you think of that, Hanna?" Gil took up his diary.

"I don't see how we can fit another thing in the room."

# Chapter 30

THE SCOTTISH DOCTOR had come and gone. Qunneke and Pequawus went east to bring Elizabeth and Wakwa home. But it was Wakwa and Qunneke who came into the spring otan, together. Elizabeth kept to the palisade days more. Then, without warning, she appeared in the freshly built town.

The first person she saw was White Cat. He was lying outside his mother's house in the sun. She hurried away from the spectacle of his leg, pared to the bone at the calf.

She paid her first respects to Waban's house. Her husband was sitting with his uncle. She stood easily, not deferentially, wrapped in a skirt and stockings of skin, and a wide chemise out of cloth the color of seaweed, wound about her hips with a belt of periwinkle. The falcon rode her shoulder. She removed the straw hat which put her eyes in shadow. Without hair, the grace of her neck and the face it balanced were ascetic sculpture.

Waban ran his thumb against her jaw. He looked into the eyes which had frightened him the night of their burning. Their containment of suffering lent them a mystery which she would never lose. She was sound, altogether improved, her loveliness exaggerated. The old headman conformed her fingers around his own so that they resembled the claw of a bird. "Manunnappu and Pequawus, they are attentive to their women. I will call for thine uncle, Kayaskwa. But let us keep you a few days to ourselves?"

The river streamed by, pink, below the rebuilt house of the younger sachim. Elizabeth found Qunneke seated outside her door, suckling a stranger baby.

"Who is this?"

"Ho."

"No. Who."

"No. Ho!" Qunneke happily took Elizabeth inside.

Clean, woven matting replaced fur for the floors. The mannotaúbana gave finish and color to the high walls. Baskets of dried fruits and herbs and drying feathers hung from the bent longpoles. The trunk of buckskin, storing the wooden bowls and carved wood spoons, stood open, ready to supply them for the supper simmering in the big copper kettle. Elizabeth stirred the stewing game and blueberries, slowly. Home was expressed in the roundness of the place.

She tethered the goat at a short walk from her own door. She watched her son and the white baby kneeling nose to nose, exploring each other's faces with dimpled hands.

"Two my wives!" Wakwa came in. He caught them to himself simultaneously. "Neese saunksquuaog nuttaiheog!"

Through their meal with their children and the motherless Beckett baby, their talk was what it might have been without the emergency they had withstood. Plans for the corn, predictions of the hunting bounty, discussion of the possibilities of the man root trade, were translated back and forth.

Elizabeth was determined to be of use. She arranged that Wakwa build her a wetu in Qunneke's field, big enough for herself and Sequan. It would make seclusion for the girl child's first lessons in reading, and every family had some person to scare the pests away from the corn. It was light work that Elizabeth was happy to do.

"A fit occupation for me. I looked in the glass today, and am the very picture of a scarecrow."

"You are so beautiful." Wakwa's hand strayed near to her flaccid breasts. He brought her to him and kissed the crown of her head. "Even bald, we three are the envy of every man and woman I know."

They laughed and smoked. Pequawus brought in a stand he had made for the bird and pounded the crossed poles into the dirt floor.

When the maids were gone and they were alone, Wakwa told his wives, "I think of leaving this position." Softly, he said, "I want to hunt my food, love my women, watch my children grow." He went even quieter and the wives waited while he took smoke. "Toward what do they grow? Reluctantly I accept power, and reluctantly let it go." After more time, he said, "You are tired, Elizabeth. Sleep now. Not so long ago you could hardly sit up at all. Do not overdo. I want you sparkling when Gilbert comes."

"I feel fine. Not at all tired."

Wakwa looked at her. "I will walk. I love spring best in the nights."

"May I come?" Elizabeth asked him.

Wakwa looked from wife to wife. "It is better I go alone."

The wives tried to combine their few commonly held words into a conversation. Qunneke began to unroll sleeping mats. Elizabeth looked for Wakwa from the door.

"Cowwetuck, Elizabeth." Qunneke held her fingers near her lips, then held them out, sending a kiss across the room.

"Good night!" Elizabeth responded in English as all her muscles shook. Information overcame her out of Qunneke's household courtesy. "Good night!"

She limped into her own room, bearing a new weight, found her mat and pillow in the dark, and lay flat. This was the night. No. It was one of other nights. "What a fool not to know!" Elizabeth thought of her staying with Pequawus on the eastern side, distracted by caring for herself, enthralled by important revelations, the sacred places, the grave of Nippisse. Qunneke and Wakwa had been home for days. Of course. They had been together. After four years. And now, tonight it was to happen again, a room away.

Wet from weakness, she stood and stumbled toward the passage to go reclaim her son. "Both boys should be with me." An anger held her upright. The curtain pushed against a clay pot. The pot rubbed another and made the only sound in the lodge.

Qunneke's voice came, surprised.

A man's voice soothed.

"He is back!" Elizabeth's voice caught inside herself. "Was he waiting without the door?" She stayed stranded, seeing through the loose weave of the rush wall. "I cannot get my baby!" Wakwa, came forward at the minute noise she made, a whir of wind confined, or the short song of the bow as it gave up its arrow. Elizabeth froze in fear of him. He disregarded the slight disturbance and spoke in whispers to Qunneke.

The curtain, opaque during the day, admitted points of firelight at night. Elizabeth saw more than shadows, yet not full flesh as the tall, straight man came behind Qunneke's naked form and let her breasts rest in his palms. Elizabeth tried to retreat, but the floor mats crackled like gravel. She heard her own name spoken. The man and woman looked her way, concerned about her. Elizabeth lent them peace of mind, stayed suspended, locked in the passage.

The pair was nearly indistinguishable in the way of the swans on the pond. Their color, their carriage were decreed by the same hand. In unconscious choreography, spines balanced their stance as they extended limbs or hands to one another in transmission of their spirits.

Qunneke leaned her shining, shorn hair against Wakwa's breast, amber in the firelight as her own. In gentle seizure, Wakwa bent forward from behind, caressing her exposed neck with his lips.

Elizabeth was rigid. They exhibited the special softness of their involvement.

Not hesitant, not hurried, Qunneke turned toward Wakwa's face and brought it down against her own, down to her breast, and down her body. His supportive muscles flexed, a foot moved back, his buttock caused a visible curve on the blank air as he bent.

Elizabeth saw abstractions of shape, crescents, active lines, fluid triangles where knees were raised by the arching of a foot reacting to small ecstasy.

But more, she saw the hand of Silent Fox cup Qunneke's round hip and loose itself in private hollows Elizabeth had somehow believed that only she herself possessed.

He pressed against lush shoulders to lie the woman down. Sound released from the English wife. No one heard.

Her eyes once blinded by sores recorded startling images from her cloister. Legs aligned and drew apart, then stilled, bulwarks for the fast-flying seed and their souls.

Elizabeth's imagination swung away. She saw White Cat's pitiable limb, the symbol of his hopelessness, as the human joining so close at hand attained to its perfection. Cries of happy confirmation covered her flight into her own room.

Blacking out the beauty of the act she had overseen, Elizabeth stared at stars through the skylight, sparing her spirit, planning for White Cat's survival. She designed him productivity, thinking of his strengths, his back and his arms, increasing in power from the use of his crutches. She settled him in the blacksmith's trade. In lonely satisfaction, she slept.

Elizabeth had appropriated every empty vessel within reach and hauled water and heated it by the time Wakwa called at her doorway. He bore a smile as radiant as his washed skin. Elizabeth turned her front away from him, disguising her confusion in the business of her bath.

Wakwa sat cross-legged, behind her. He expected that she would come to him.

"Sometime I would like to take a bath in a proper tub! Lead-lined and with sides high enough so that I could sit with water to my chin!"

"But you love the stream," he said.

"Damn the stream!"

"Elizabeth!"

"Where are your feelings?" She turned on him. "Shall I go down there with all those other women? A curio for them to study? The mother with no milk. The walking skeleton with a pate shining in places like a wigless old man. A little privacy is all I ask!"

"Shall I go out?"

"Do whatever suits you."

He watched her make a European toilette, her motions like a storm coming, ignoring the scrubbing clay to which she had willingly adapted. "I came here last night after my walk. To talk to you," he said.

She made bubbles of precious cakes of milled soap which had cost the price of many hunted skins.

"I found you asleep."

"I heard no one. I was not asleep." She stood in two separate pots, one next to the other, washed her body in two halves. "Ridiculous."

Wakwa watched muscles stretch in the back of her white thighs as she bent. Her slender arm, scrubbing, pointed his attention to dainty areas he had never had time to see in the usual course of their days. Her knee joint was fitted beautifully as a precision machine, drafted, it seemed to him, not of bone but of silver, like one of Gilbert's

204

English tongs. Her lax breasts fell away from her chest. He marveled at the ribs' delicate delineation of her girthless body. To him, she was white smoke, ephemeral, a spirit given humanity by weightless flesh. Her wrists, supporting cupping hands filled with spilling water, seemed too tiny to allow the lifting of the son she had borne him. He pined for her hair. But his interest was captured by the curling growth that was beginning to replace the luxuriant lengths.

Wakwa dipped his hand in the suds and ran it swiftly up her inner thighs, into the crevice that her buttocks made and on up her backbone.

She jumped away from him, falling, overturning the clay pots.

He went to help. She recoiled.

"Elizabeth!" He wrapped her close but she hunched, drew tightly in, exposed to his touch only parts that were bone hard.

She squirmed away, threw on a cotton sacque, and began to toss the remains of the used water outside the house. "I have had a brilliant idea. White Cat must not be let to waste away. Bad for his mind. Bad for his mother and the town. Don't forget he came to his condition because your father put him in your place at the bear hunt at our wedding feast. He made mistakes and got his legs nearly torn off. More than the wound the humiliation of it has half killed him. And he hates you for it." She moved around the room like light on water. "If Waban can tap my skill as a weaver to help the town, and use your speaking talent, why waste White Cat's enormous power which is stored in his arms? I have found a job for him. An indispensable occupation. What do we need more than anything to survive?"

"I do not know," Wakwa said out of familiar pain of rejection by one wife or the other.

"Think! We are dependent on guns more and more for our food and our trade. We have horses now, for travel and bearing. These luxuries are our new necessities. So, we need a smith! A resident blacksmith with arms like iron and a will to melt metal and form it into strength for the otan. We could stop depending on my uncle and rid ourselves of the curiosity of Sweetwood. We would not have to pay the prices they now ask of us for shoeing and sundry services. You have fields where metals rest underneath the ground. I saw iron powder cast over your dead. You make copper kettles and bracelets and bells. You kindly lead the English to these resources, but for their benefit. Use it for ours! Make White Cat into a smith."

"I came to you, last night, Elizabeth, and you lay so still. I thought you were asleep. Many times in the past day I thought you understood. Until last night when I bid thee to bed and you did not go. I could not say it just then." Wakwa recalled the tenderness of the night which might have passed them by in anguish. "I went to walk, I went to the river, I thought of your father. Of his need to know that you are cared for, kindly. I saw Awepu. He warned me to tell you what I thought you had seen for yourself. . . ."

"How lovely! I was the last and least to know."

"You did know, then?"

"Oh, I did." She crumbled near her mat.

"Then, if you knew . . . ?"

"I knew nothing. I saw."

"Saw?"

"Accident. I wanted Moses. Moses was my only thought."

"You were there?" Wakwa's voice was grieved for himself and for her. He remembered the sounds in the passage. He reached her and held the back of her neck with one hand and did not accept her revulsion toward him. He insisted that she let him close, and forced her head far enough back so that he could read her eyes.

She strained away, as if from dirty hands. "How could you do it?"

"She is my wife."

"Not that kind of wife."

"She was mine before I ever knew you. And before Qunneke there were others for short whiles. All of this you knew."

"That was then. How can you go from her in the night to me in the day? Touching me with the hand that touched Tame Deer? Is this cleanly? Is it . . . is it . . . ?"

"Is it what, Kayaskwa?" He held his face against her

206

bosom, moving her onto his lap, not letting her be alone with turmoil that involved them both.

"Love? Is it love?" She cried against him, not objecting to the petting he gave her head.

"Oh! It is love!"

"How can one man love two?"

"It has happened to me. I do."

"And how shall I love myself when you treat her the way that I saw?"

"Love yourself?"

"Are you surprised?"

"Do not stick at me with words." He held her tighter. "I wonder what there is not to love in you?"

"I wonder, too."

It was some time before the attempts she made became questions framed in words. The man drew speech out of her, leaving no part of her face untouched by his lips, as if taking nectar from a flower. For the first time since their scorching, he kissed her lowered lids.

She hid her eyes from him. "Do you compare?"

"What mean you?"

"It is another body. Lit by another mind. Am I not enough? Do I repulse you? When you come to me, are you only being kind?" The words wounded her throat as she formed them. "Her breasts are full, her skin is smooth and of your color, she is round where I am shrunk away." She permitted him to rock her. And again, they became still. "Having been inside her, are you the same man I have known? Is your body changed, somehow, in another forge? Does she . . . please thee more than I?" Scarcely audible she asked, "Am I ignorant of love as of all else? What did she do to cause such a look as when you came in to greet me today?" She turned her face from him, too proud to weep.

Wakwa watched the trouble boil from her.

"And does," the English wife whispered, "inside feel the same?" She turned over, lay face down across his knees, in her shame. "Are all women alike? Soft machines to bring forth your seed and then to sprout? How shall I live more ignorant of my secret faults than are you two?"

Unembarrassed, his smooth voice came. "Elizabeth, each one of you to me is like separate food. When I am with her, I see only her shape, I touch only her skin. I am told by her giving commands all that she thinks of me. No, I do not compare. Yea, there are differences between each person in the world. What comparison is there! You are two! Your perfection is your own."

Elizabeth groaned, disbelieving.

"Yea, you are both women with the same parts. But each same thing is also different. Do not think I use her loveliness and yours like a blind man in a brothel. All day I give to you and give to her, and only need to come sometimes closer to one, and then, sometimes, to the other. Do you not want me to have two such good friends?"

"It must be very sweet."

"Ah! It is."

Elizabeth relaxed and he let her go. She rose to soak up the bath water from the matting. "Why must this kind of friendship be reserved for men? Why two wives? Why not two husbands?"

"Elizabeth! That is not natural!"

"Ha!" The young wife caught her breath at this inequity. "Why? Do I love differently from you because I do not enter, but am entered?"

The man had to think long to respond. "It is because in our life, the way we eat is to have the man bring in the meat. The wife or wives take care the corn. One woman with two men could not raise enough grain for these husbands. And she could not eat enough meat to justify their catch. It would be like taking from other families. But when two women work the fields it adds, and blessings multiply."

"Blessings for the man."

"Yes."

"And children increase."

"Yes. That brings to mind, Elizabeth, when the woman with two husbands conceived, how would she know who was the father?"

"What difference if the husbands were friends?" Elizabeth pirouetted, billowing the wet rags on the air that she moved.

Wakwa was quiet, humbled by new thoughts.

"Was I cruel?" Elizabeth sat in front of him and briefly

stroked the back of his hand. It was as much as she could do.

"What is real is not cruel."

"You think I want another man? Wakwa! It is trouble to me, but I want only you. I wanted you to come to me last night. While she covered your back with her arms, I wanted you. Right then. If there were a way you could have both of us at the same time, I would want you." She ran her hands over the small scars on her scalp that she would always carry. "I have no pride when it comes to wanting you." She turned onto the center of the room, the white cotton sacque filled with yellow light. "What became of Qunneke's shyness? Why of a sudden is she warm as spring?"

"You might ask your uncle that for me when next you see him."

"My uncle?" Elizabeth examined pictures of Gilbert and Qunneke residing in her memory. She fell to kissing Wakwa's hands as they shared the mystery. She forgot her rending of the night before, and functioned in exotic regions Wakwa had broken open to her. The promise she had made him long ago to be the second wife of two had blossomed.

"I am shy. Yesterday I knew how to ask you. Now I am clumsy." She kissed his lips long. Fear kept the kiss closed.

"Dear little one. This is an unfamiliar thing to me, as well. It is the first day in my life of my having two wives." He chuckled a little. His fingers stroked each side of her face. "Another lesson. I cannot come. Not now."

She was wide-eyed.

"I have loved you once in many days, sometimes, and at others I have loved you many times in a day. But I cannot be ready to love at will. I am a man. Women are more lucky."

"It is a lesson for you, then! This arrangement is very poor. How shall we manage? I am reduced to begging and watching for you, and Tame Deer, too. It were better that she and I were men and you our wife. We could spell one another and you be adored at your caprice."

They were near her mat and he brought her down and fit her close to him and half covered her body with his legs about her. His shoulders sheltered her, above. "Please! All will flow when it is proper."

And, "Please! Please!" was her word to him. "I need you. Now." The pleading cut them each in the softest place, the part of a person that does not die, does not forget, and carries wounds, and spreads the wound. That place in her did not bleed; it welled with gall. She wept, and resented that he could see her weeping.

Their mutual grief subsided into rest. Under the warmth of him, her eyes closed. Her breathing slowed. After brief sleep she felt his wet lashes against her neck.

Wakwa's whisper begged, "Help me, please help me."

She turned around and saw his look, clouded as when she was his complete desire. She made a sound and turned away, too devastated to accept charity.

But he took her hand and held it against his penis and the weight of his leg kept her there. "Help me."

And Elizabeth began to ease him, gently, not to cause him pang, feeling the beauty of that part of him which had touched the innermost reach of the other wife so recently.

Long he bent over her. And, at last, let pour his seed, at home within her.

He backed away, breathless and exhausted, loose of limb, emptied of the stuff of his manhood, filled with humor. "I will not live the spring at this pace, but I will die in happiness." His hand came weakly to her shoulder where she sat, calmed and aglow. The hand slipped down.

Elizabeth walked out of the house for water with a swing in her movements. The acting out complete, the concept was not so hard to bear.

Wakwa woke to her washing him. "Elizabeth? How badly do you wish the lead-lined tub? The room with the curtains blowing in?"

"You do say silly things."

"I will be getting White Cat apprenticed to the Sweetwood smith. The plan is sound. More than your Christian heaven, it may be our salvation someday."

# Chapter 31

GILBERT WORTH rocked in the open air, on Sam Spinney's creation. His niece sat at his feet, her hand on his knee. They did not force speech but listened to the shouts of men working to push fresh long poles into the ground. The sachimmaacommock was torn in two. The space between the sleeping chambers was being filled by a round third room.

Worth smoothed the slender hand which rose and fell with his legs as he pushed to work the chair. The breeze from the sea stood his untied, uncovered hair high, and pushed Elizabeth's grass hat back from her face. He examined her through the lashes of his partly closed eyes. He found her to be beautiful, more hale than when he had left for Maine. According to Mac, her eyes were fine. Gil found them a tint darker toward true brown than he remembered.

With his eyes actually shut, he said, "My dear, what do you want with such a big house? Has it to do with Wakwa's being sachim?"

"The new house is only practicality, Uncle Gil." Elizabeth took one of his hands into her own.

"Seems very impractical. What an awfully big place to heat in the winter." Gil twisted around to see it.

The elliptical room which was Elizabeth's and the round one which was Qunneke's had been stripped of their bark skins. Their skeletons were being moved, now positioned as the legs of a *U*. A perfectly round room was being constructed to complete the handsome arc that would tie each wife's room together into one house. There was a yard for planting and playing between the east and west wings.

211

"The little, round room shall be where we eat," Elizabeth pointed out.

"When you are eating out of a pot, what do you need with a formal room for the purpose?"

"It will do us good!"

"I do not see it." His eyes clamped shut.

"I know." Elizabeth placed a kiss on the hand that she held. "Uncle Gil. . . ." Elizabeth's next words tumbled over her affection for him, and his affection for Tame Deer. "She is wife to him."

Gil's eyes blinked open. He waited for meaning to be fully delivered.

"Uncle Gil, dear, she lies with him. After so many years."

The runners of the chair sank somewhat into the meadow grass. Motion stopped. Gil looked through the face upturned to him. After a bit he saw Elizabeth again, and he said, "What happiness!" Then his arms extended down. "Oh, Beth!"

As he reached for her, she rose to him, and ended in his lap. They wrapped each other from dismay.

"She loves you, you know."

"I do." He swallowed. "I love her, too. We are a perfect match."

"Since you kept her, uncle, she has become the perfect match for me."

Their rocking resumed, too hard for comfort.

"True?" Gilbert's fingers undid the bow of her hat and it skidded away on a hot gust.

"Truly. Do you think me bad for loving him through it?"

Gil kissed the back of her graceful neck, as he had done when she was a young child. "I think you perfect."

"No!" She denied him this and straightened up, holding her legs out straight as a little girl's on a swing. "I am somewhat less stupid. Certainly feeling very kind. And more, I do not worry as I did."

"What worry?"

"Women's worries." She slid off his legs and away.

Both of them chased the hat, wobbling to a distance by its brim.

Gil reached it first, and retained it. "What worries are those?"

"Some are great and some are small."

"Will you tell me? I have a feeling that what a woman worries, worries a man, as well."

Elizabeth turned the hat around in his hands as she spoke, as if her life experience were pictured on a wheel. "The small—am I pretty, clean, interesting, special. Will he tire of me? Will I have time to comb my hair before he comes?"

They smiled. Gil handed her the hat. She tied it on.

"And the great?"

"Ah! There Tame Deer has helped me. Of what use am I? Do I act the worm, the slug, or the soaring bird? Will the love kill me or birth me? And this is mine—will I like myself when I come to die?"

"Fulfilling that last will make quite an uncommon etiquette. As you do everything with a flair," the uncle brightly readjusted the angle of her hat, "even Plant might approve of that." He stepped back for the effect.

"Approval I must learn to live without."

"That will make you lonely."

"I live perfectly well alone, you know."

"I know."

"But now there is Wakwa . . . you understand. . . ."

"Completely."

"And though it is very new . . . Tame Deer."

"Beth, how does that go?"

She answered as they began to walk to the unfinished house. "A jest extends further, a kiss spreads among three. I am confused in my numbers. I think of a couple as three. Of a wife as two. Of a husband as one. Seasons are four by three. My! Children! They are multiples of two by three, by three, by three. My own value is one third of three. An whole one. And should they be minus me, they will still be whole, the circle shrunk to two ones of two."

Laughing at these mathematics, Gill posed a riddle of his own. "Add this up. Elizabeth Dowland, Hanna Worth, Qunneke—Silent Fox, Gilbert Worth, and Michael B. Three women and three men round the fire for tea. How is it, one man will sit alone, that booby being me?"

_____ **Chapter 32**

BECKETT WATCHED ELIZABETH in the dusky light. "That one is dangerous." From his vantage point in Wakwa's partly finished house, he saw her in the field, bending, holding Wakwa's and Qunneke's shoulders. The evening breeze lifted her loose clothes like streamers. She kissed Wakwa's neck, and her hand rambled Qunneke's back. "Dangerous."

"Remarkable." Hanna defended her niece.

"You are remarkable, managing this madness." His arm stole around Worth's wife, across her front, pressing her bosom uninvited. "Hanna, marry me. I'll give you more children than you'll know what to do with."

"Michael, why do you bait me with maternity? I am already mothering each helpless thing that comes my way.

The arm dropped. "What do you want me to bait you with? Am I wrong to regard you as a lady?"

"Michael, you should not drink and talk." She took up one of his trembling hands, kindly.

His other arm immediately banded her hips and he pressed tightly against her from behind. "I know just what I'm saying. What are you saying? That I may have you in passing?" His tongue roamed about her ear.

"Go to the stream, Michael, and rinse your mouth. You will not impress Elizabeth if she detects the scent of gin about you."

Hanna bundled into Gil's blanket with him at the after-supper fire waiting for the solicitor to come. "Dear, Michael says that his research has put him onto something that should light up the New World."

"Pray share the good news with me."

"He didn't discuss it."

214

"Well, what was taking him all that long time?"

"He was asking me to marry him."

Gil and Hanna turned nose to nose.

"I was under the impression that you already exist in that state."

"But not with him."

"True. What was your reply."

"I told him, Gillie, to wash and be sober."

"Damn the sharper! Now I've got to kill him." Gil leaned close against her and said, pleasantly, "I vowed to him that I'd cut him a good one if he pursued his seducement of you drunk."

"Oh?" Hanna pushed her corner of the lap rug away. "Did you?" Her tone was acid washed. "Is there something catching in the air? Shall we start our own mènage à trois?"

They looked long at one another. Gil picked up the lax end of the blanket and offered it back into her grasp. "Only if you wish to."

Hanna linked her arm through his. "Gillie, I wish. . . ."

Beckett was standing over them. He slapped his tightly panted thigh for a gavel, and snapped, "If, Mistress Dowland, you had been born in Georgia, you would be sitting safely by the ancestral hearth doing your needlework tonight."

"Then I am much blessed!"

"Browneyes, first to business. And the business, the pressing legal issue is, WHO SHALL HAVE DOWLAND FARM. . . ."

"Mr. Beckett, I am all decided on that. I want it to go to. . . ."

"Seventeen hundred thirty-nine, a Georgia woman in your situation, that is to say, an eldest daughter, unmarried, possessed of no other land, and no brothers, of course, was allowed to succeed to full proprietorship of a piece of ground upon the death of the tenant."

"But I was born in Massachusetts."

"Yes, this whalebone corset of a colony where the laws of England are acknowledged. Hence your predicament. But the written law is not always put in performance here, or anywhere, my dear. And lucky for you. The law is become personalized, in out of the way places, due to exotic circumstances of life in them. I am counting on the common law to settle your father's farm on you in spite of a certain amount of untidiness in your private life. The doing of it will cause to be written at last a definite and very clear summation of what we practice. From such precedent is eventually born statute! Think of it! A victory for you means that the fairness of the Georgia common law will extend to the life of Massachusetts. Girls like you will not be put through the stultification of early marriage contracts with men like Hudson. They will be saved the effort of flight into the forest and an whole lot of pesty inconvenience." Beckett searched his pockets for a bottle of anything to drink. He came up with a perfume vial, unstoppered it and tried it.

"Sir? Why is it this new rule was never established before?"

"Because, Browneyes, the litigation I have in mind will become a life's work for the woman brave enough to undertake it."

"But I already have a life's work."

"So you think. Without a victory in the court, in writing, your life's work here, in Eden, will likely go up in smoke. The one depends on the other."

"Mr. Beckett, I failed to make my father understand me, though he loved me. How shall I succeed with harsher men than he?"

As if Elizabeth were the only person in the world, Michael Beckett came to her, folded his long legs underneath himself, and sat in front of her. "Now, Mistress, having seen the elegance of his will, it is my professional opinion that fail with him you did not."

"I thank you." Wakwa spoke up, and the solicitor looked surprised at sensitivity from such a source.

Beckett walked the outside of their circle whipping them all with legal jargon like an animal trainer among his beasts. "Charles Dowland has furnished us with an instrument, a grant in land of the highest order—a fee simple whose dignity is scratched with conditional clause, entailed out of sentiment, yes, but also utility, as his male issue failed and he was left *only* with a daughter."

Elizabeth made a slight cry.

Hanna said, "Michael will make it all right, Beth."

"That would be quite a feat, Aunt Hanna! There was

not a day in Sweetwood I did not spend contrite for my sex. I was fed my parents' disappointment with my mother's milk. I have even wished sometimes it were I died instead of Henry just to make things pleasanter for everyone about the land. I cannot abide that feeling anymore. I live here now. My decision about the Farm is . . ."

". . . to be carefully considered!" Beckett finished for her. "Young woman, I have mares ready to foal in Virginia. At great expense to your loving uncle I have trotted up here to inspire you to take this estate by the horns. Why should you not? You have taken your life by the tail and swing it over your head. Haw! While we talk of tails let me admire publicly the one on your father's will. He did more with the tail, the entail, that ornamentation which sets down a logical, orderly sequence of heirs, than many a sound attorney. Charles Dowland, studiously, imaginatively, used a five-hundred-year-old principle, De Donis Conditionalibus, upheld by Parliament, as the basis for his most particular entail. . . ."

"Mr. Beckett. . . ."

". . . As a perfect piece of silver is engraved with the initials of the owner without marring, Dowland has embellished the grant of his property in a purely legal fashion in such a way as to possess a daughter, you, of a vast estate, give her proprietorship in her life, and safely pass it on to the next responsible person. His will accomplishes this on paper. Half my work done for me. But it must be accomplished in fact. I am a student of the law, Mistress Elizabeth. I can guide you through the courts. We will set a precedent in American common law equal to or greater than the practice in Georgia. You have provided the country with a grander theme than paltry inheritance. Your choice of a mate could shake the whole colonial system. Quietly, without the firing of a shot, the ownership of America can be brought into question. Your marriage, and the issue of it, this Moses Bluehill, are an allegory so perfect with the struggle between the races, red and white, that a really clever judge ought to cite us for Feigned Issue. He might think you had concocted this whole affair just to try in court your inalienable right to ownership, whether you are a woman or your mate be an Indian."

217

Elizabeth shot to her feet and faced him over the fire. "It was by leaving the property that I assumed my rights!"

"What good are rights without legal sanction?"

"Sir, gaining this land will chain me, for rights have to do with persons first, and then the land will follow."

"That reasoning is not in the majority and therefore you will suffer for it!"

"Mr. Beckett, I would rather swing the tail of my life over my head than have the tail swing me!"

"Approach the bar! You talk like a lawyer even without your apprenticeship."

"I have had my apprenticeship, if you please, nineteen years of it. I do not study this case. I live it. I know what is right and wrong about it."

"I am at once confounded and fascinated by Massachusetts women. Though, alas, not charmed."

"Should you be? I am opposite to you for I feel the tying of a knot that I have taken great pains to loose. If inheriting land under the eye of a judge gives me freedom to choose a mate myself, a place to live, and habits of living, things that should be natural, then are you not saying that anyone's natural rights are rooted in owning property? Without a father like mine to grant me such a tract, I would have less dignity than any owl, or mouse."

"Or Fox."

"Then you understand. I am sorry that I shouted, Mr. Beckett."

"Well," Beckett stuck his arms back and took her in with a look, as if testing the bouquet of a rare wine, "I am not. We have cleared the air. And you have taught yourself that I am on your side. Believe me, Miss Dowland, you will be in a better position to expound your theories of rights and freedoms if you are visibly, and under protection of the law, vested of your land. Remember, the law learns slowly. Like the Church. And though you sound a Sophia, I look at you and I see a woman of passion. Guide your passions, Elizabeth, direct your just instincts, think of your son's future, and play along with me."

"I do not want to be balky. I only try to use my reason."

"Mistress Dowland, even here in the forest primeval, it is the eighteenth century. Reason is all. All our lives, though, are pregnant with opportunity, conceived by your courage. I beseech you to keep your wildfire alive." Beckett made her a courtly bow, but his eyes found Hanna's.

Elizabeth looked up at him. "Please, sir, go on. I will listen to the work of your winter."

"You give me Partible Consent. Appreciated. Here, young lady, pass this book around. Take care of it near the fire, it is nearly two hundred years old." Beckett presented her with a shaggy little volume. "It is the basis for the revolution I would have you cause. I am off to take a piss."

They all watched him straining to coordinate his liquor-loosened limbs to achieve the line to Wakwa's lodge.

The sachim put his hand on Gilbert's arm. "Is he going to pass water in my house?"

"Not at all, Wakwa, he's after a bottle. But I'd rather he took a leak on my rug than shit on my wife."

Not knowing for certainty which of the three wives present Worth meant, Wakwa turned his attention to the antique text.

"I say revolution, in the sense of turning, of exposing a new side of things to view." Beckett was back, bright and brittle. "Not a bloody revolution. Insurrections like that are theater pieces designed by Turks. Such revolting histrionics occur because the public remains chiefly ignorant of its powers under the laws of Nations. . . ."

Gil spoke up. "Michael, who keeps the public ignorant?"

Hanna claimed his hand. "Not now, Gilbert."

But Beckett answered Worth. "Whoever stands to make money by it, sir."

"Funny," Gil mused, "you stand to make money educating us."

"It is what I was retained by you to do."

"Funny."

"Why, funny? Are you calling me insincere, or a merchant?"

"I only marvel at profit-taking at both ends of the stick."

"May I finish my thought?" Beckett hissed at the fair-haired man. "May I have that book?" He took it out of Wakwa's hands.

"Be careful of it near the fire, Michaelbeckett. What I have read of your book makes much greater my respect for written down words."

"You read?"

"When I must."

"What an incredible order of things in this wood! He reads! What a delight! Circumstantial proof of the cogent philosophy of the wirter of this book, one Francisco de Vitoria, a Dominican priest. Yes, Gilbert, a Catholic, a Spaniard who was fortunate enough to spend much of his time, free and otherwise, in Paris. Thank your stars for him. He has prepared our brief for us. Here, still legible on the crumbling parchment, is a case mapped, crying loudly that the native peoples of the New World have first right to dominion over the land of said world. Vitoria was an original and liberal thinker in his own right, and God knows, liberal thought will not be amiss in settling the legitimacy of the principals who are claiming land out of the Dowland estate, but the Padre wisely leans on the shoulders of others, as well. Vitoria's supporting cast includes Biblical giants, as well as Augustine, Gratian, Aquinas, Bartolus, Wycliffe. Syllogism by syllogism, proof by proof, Vitoria established for the admiration of the students, scholars, princes of the sixteenth century, truths of dominion, discovery, ownership, and inheritance. He says, for instance, that if an individual can suffer wrong he obviously has rights over things; he says, wards *are* the owners of their property, he says that dominion is not, NOT— are you listening, Browneyes?—dominion is not dependent on natural OR human law, but on the ability to reason. In Vitoria's parlance, the possession of the image of God.

"But what is the use of explaining this to you all? I will teach it to some polly of a barrister. What you have to know is, that there is strong logical ground for you, Mistress Elizabeth, not to be disinherited either because you live with a nonbeliever of another race, or because you are a woman. The intellectuals are on our side. As for legal precedent, in the year sixteen hundred ninety-four, the English court sustained the principle that treaty agreements must not be crossed in order to change the customs and laws of correspondent nations. . . ."

"Oh, sir!"

Beckett began slowly for Elizabeth, again. "The customs and laws of nations who have signed a treaty are not to be changed, by the treaty, because each is still sovereign."

"Ah! Then Qunneke is safe. The court can do nothing bad to us because we are two women married to one man."

"Browneyes, you shall have to compromise there. Heaven knows you have compromised before."

"I have not!"

"Only yourself." Beckett quelled her disagreement. "I am trying to enlighten the whole of colonial law with this text! Polygamy will not represent an advancement in the mind of the man who is to judge your case. Tame Deer does not exist." Beckett blinked away the picture of Qunneke giving suck to his son.

"She does!"

"Who should know better than you!" the lawyer shot back brutally.

"Beckett!" Gil came between him and Elizabeth. "Go to have another drink. You are turning sour."

"My loyalties are with my client. Where, Gilbert, are yours?"

"You are both off the point," Elizabeth scolded. "I do not need my feelings coddled, only my reason aided. To my simple mind it seems that if I lie in the court, I will be lying when I am, again, back home. How shall I live?"

"Mistress Elizabeth, consider that Silent Fox might put aside his Indian woman."

"Never! Not because of me!"

"Your self-effacement could turn into self-fulfilling prophecy, so it does not impress me. Your defense must be the offense. Do not tie my hands with extraneous wives! You are the heiress, not she."

"Then what meaning Padre Vitoria and his talk of inborn dominion?" Elizabeth reacted. "Because my dominion is to be spelled out by written court papers, Qunneke loses hers? She becomes extraneous? That were a wrong to her and to me. And you said yourself that our wrongs establish that we have rights!"

Beckett raved, "Praise God, there are no women lawyers!"

"And should I follow you, Mr. Beckett, I am afraid that there never will be!" Elizabeth took Horace into her arms to raise a burp from him.

Beckett swallowed. "I think, Mistress Dowland, that we can work well together. I must only bear in mind your enthusiasm for your marital arrangement, and you must give some attention to what is the actual issue. The court will not rule directly for or against paganism, gentilism, or marrying and breeding across races. In Re Dowland Farm is the matter that is of the greatest concern to the court and to you. The matter is two thousand acres of prime land. All my fancy dancing on the toes of great thinkers and decisions of the past may serve only to keep your neck out of a noose. It may win you nothing but the right to live. But is it not worth a try to seek the highest justice? To frame our case to nudge direct approval of your principles, and allow for graceful acceptance of the indirect? I have already told your uncle that there is a risk in underfighting this case—the whole parcel of ground will revert to the Crown if there is neither an apparent heir nor a proven one. Tragedy. And God knows who will be your new neighbors after that, and all law shot to hell. Elizabeth Dowland, you must make an appearance before the court at Boston, prove your son's legitimacy, to have even the choice to give the farm away."

"What is the danger for her in this, Michaelbeckett?" Wakwa interposed. "Can you keep her safe though she is married into the Massachuseuck? Our treaty with the English is submission. What hope is there in the court if it shall consider her and us slaves? And what hope if they think us a nation of free men?"

"At last!" Beckett looked toward the darkening heavens. "A question containing legal substance! Fox, your son is your main hope."

"Wolf-of-the-mist He-hopes. . . ."

"Yes. Yes. But never forget that the treaty is a boon to you. True, you are subject to the authority of the Crown, but you are also entitled to its protection. You are under the wing of English law, stifling though it be. Nowhere does that treaty state that you Indians must be Christians. The treaty does not change your marital customs. Remember? 1694? Treaty agreements must not be crossed in order to change existing customs. . . ."

"But will English inspectors come on my grounds to see if we are a camp of warriors, not families who raise corn?"

"Fox, the court has no legal power not stated in that treaty."

"Will the court presume it?" Elizabeth joined the dialogue of the men.

"Young woman, you wander in a quagmire of suppositions. I deal in facts."

"Qunneke is a fact."

"Very well! If you MUST keep this other woman about you, do not let on to the authorities. I am not asking you to lie under oath. Only do not volunteer damaging information. If we cannot deny her, we will ignore her, overlook her. If anyone mentions this other wife outside the confines of this meadow, I am off the case. Float as you can."

Qunneke tied up her silk chemise, touched her husband's shoulder in a gesture of parting, and left the fire, Horace the motherless boy riding her hip. Elizabeth and Wakwa looked after her.

"Do not shilly-shally," Beckett persisted. "Who Shall Have Dowland Farm? Somebody will, you know, whatever road you choose to follow. Do not let it be some English cousin who never offered an arm to help your father's failing steps, some potbellied gentlefolk who will invade your clean house with their Chinese dogs and potted palm trees. That land belongs to those who have worked it."

"Then it belongs to Uncle Gil," Elizabeth said softly. "He has done double duty, farming his and Dowland lands for years."

"Yes. Yes. But that does not suit him. He wants it not for himself. Gilbert Worth's named heir is your son Moses."

"Then let that stand. What is all this for?"

"Browneyes, your father's will is this—if the issue of the male heir fails, and in this case your brother Henry was the male heir and is deceased and has no issue, the tenant in tail, that is you, a married you, could convey the land to a third person. The court may stickle about you there. Or, as in the condition your father lays on, if you should remain out of sight for two years, Gilbert Worth becomes the tenant in tail. That would be next January. Gilbert then could in law convey the Dowland estate to Moses Bluehill."

"Perfect."

"Sorry! Not quite. After the statute De Donis, which is

223

the basis of the will, the transferee, that is Moses, can acquire land only for your uncle's lifetime. I think this was done to protect you, my dear, if you wanted to throw your current adventure over and rejoin Sweetwood life. But it is no good to anyone. When it was written there was no grandchild. We fall back on an outright suit for the land or a conveyance. Wisely built in. I will never advise you to let Worth do the conveyance because though he looks now like he will live a thousand interminable years, the safer assumption is that his life will end in your son's prime. A bad time to have one's inheritance pulled out from under one."

Elizabeth held her head fevered by legalities and decision. "Then the statue, De . . . Donis is a burden to me."

"Not entirely, my dear. Alternatives sanctioned by individual cases in the courts for political reasons have the effect of completely docking the entail. That's where you need me."

"Now I don't understand, again!" Elizabeth groaned.

"These are abstruse niceties which you do not have to know. Know this. You have no choice but to go ahead and prove that Moses Bluehill is the fulfillment of the tail on your father's will. That is, that your red-skinned babe is the legitimate heir, male, of the body of Charles Dowland. Once proven, you could make the conveyance to Moses yourself, for after your death, or, if the judgment is for Moses Bluehill to inherit free and clear, the land could remain in trust of a capable executor until the boy is old enough to manage it himself. Your uncle could be executor, or if that is not convenient, or if, heaven help us, he should die, then someone else."

"Who, sir?"

"Oh . . . no need to go into that now . . . but oftentimes people select . . . their . . . lawyer."

Gilbert let out a long, admiring whistle. "Will you pour poison in my ear, Claudius?"

"Out of my way, Worth," Beckett snarled. "We are on the verge of a great moment." The solicitor crouched, close to kneeling in front of Elizabeth. "What's it to be, Mistress?"

Elizabeth looked Wakwa's way. It was painful for her to see the upright spirit in him which kept his body as erect as the guardian of a hallowed place. "I will not wound my husband."

Beckett hastily reassured, "That is what I am for. Roman law underlies the Magna Carta, doesn't it? With hardly a blink we will lead the judge back to the Roman Marriage Usus—common law marriage wherein even a woman was allowed the management of her property apart from anything to do with a male. I am a solicitor and I have confidence in the flexibility of the common law. Should not you?"

Tears began to show in Elizabeth's eyes.

"Here." The lawyer relaxed in front of her, sitting with his back to the flames. "It is not such great shakes. The way of it is, if *my* work is well done, is the case tried on a sunny day? Has the judge gas in his stomach? Is the plaintiff pretty? And you are, richly so." Michael bowed to Silent Fox for his leave.

Elizabeth turned to him, too. She had in her mind what Beckett said about politics and wills. She saw Wakwa's politics not bringing on special favors from the magistrate's court. Wakwa's march north could be seen as an infraction of the treaty on which Waban's name and Pequawus' were listed. "Mr. Beckett, all that you say makes very good sense, and I trust you completely. But you see, here in Massachusetts there is trouble brewing. The French and the English begin to fight in the forest over fur, when to my mind, if their wars were over fur they would fight upon the sea, and not destroy the homes of the animals and the fur itself. I think they want to take the land here, by force. Even Dowland Farm. You said yourself that Moses Bluehill being red and white was a perfect picture of the fight over this countryside. And that he was our hope. He is. But his father, Silent Fox, must keep the respect of all his neighbors, English and Indians and even French, so that when the fight dies down he can join with them in building a new kingdom, without a king. A new kind of governed place, a sachimauonk, as he would say. How will he do that if he makes a case now that being red he is the sole chief of this land? He will look a fool, or worse, he will become an hunted enemy in the place he dreams to preserve. I can only agree to do what will keep my son at peace with himself. My husband and I are different but we met in our child. Let him inherit. I offer myself to the court. I will go there and do what I must to prove that my father has a grandson, though they whip me for it. But I will have you do or say nothing to win Dowland Farm to myself. For I will not put my name above my father's door until the need for all the fancy stepping you describe is dispelled."

"By what?" Beckett's question was shaped by his lips more than pronounced.

"By . . . the outcome of the rest of my life."

The lawyer lowered his head and shut his eyes, foiled in his manifold design to win a name or a fortune in land to himself. The other people at the fire looked at Elizabeth in wonderment.

Elizabeth tried to comfort Beckett when he stood and backed away. "As I tried to say at the beginning, it was my leaving Dowland Farm to meet what lay beyond the established way that gave me new birth. Not grasping at English law, I, myself, set the precedent for an American."

The untwisting of the top of Beckett's flask was all that broke the melody of the fire's crackle and the tossing of the green, budding branches in the mild wind. He drank, then rattled at her without trace of emotion, "John Reade of this colony has done good work on joint deeds. It will help alienate this realty from you as soon as possible. You must each appear for separate examination and signing away to a third party after your son is judged legitimate heir. Special acknowledgment from you, the woman, is necessary that they will know you were not coerced into this conveyance. If you wouldn't mind giving me just a little help, see if the Indian can Anglicize himself for a day. Get him a proper suit and a pair of shoes. He will be referred to as Mr. S. Fox of Sweetwood, occupation, trapper. Appearances are all-important."

"Bizarre!" Gil breathed.

"There we are agreed, Worth." Beckett's handsome nose turned red. He kicked backwards at the spring dust before walking away, and said to Elizabeth, "It will be every bit as hard to bake half a cake as it would have been to bake a whole one." He pulled off his wig and threw his hairnet to the dirt. "Miss, *you* are a Turk!" He barged out of the circle toward the running stream. "Dammit!"

_____ **Chapter 33**

WAKWA LAY in the new room between the two women who were his wives. He could hardly see his hand in the dark. He turned to Elizabeth and touched her beauties as she slept. Against her skin, he saw himself clearly. "That is the secret of us!" He kissed the warmth hidden under curves of her female flesh. "You did well tonight," he spoke to her sleeping form, "wise woman and yet young!"

He lay back and lapsed into thoughts of Beckett's brief. English law did not seem to grow from the soft place of the belly, the home of honor, but was laid on the king's people like a lash, or a bridle, goads for horses in a race. Wakwa felt there must be a well of thought unplumbed by Michael, from where the English mind and soul received guidance for the management of life. It was the only way he could explain the English people whom he loved. As if the secret were within her, he gave in to the desire to waken Elizabeth. Her white body turned, and she nestled her haunch against his stomach, intent on sleep.

Wakwa moved the other way and listened to the breathing of Qunneke. He watched her breasts rise and fall. Her fingers curled on her abdomen, seeming to offer that part of herself she had denied him for so long. Qunneke's life, round and steady, gave shape to her flesh. Wakwa lay across her, lost into her hue. He tasted her firm contours with the flat of his tongue while she slept. His saliva ran soon, and he lay back between the women, a hand of each in each of his hands. Pleasant agony of desire came on him.

He marked the night as the first that they had slept, all together. The rebuilding of the house had put them all in one room, and him between them. He made noiseless

227

laughter at his blessing. Both sides of him were protected by the softness of women. They bordered him like wings, wings that would bear him through his future. Wakwa could no longer imagine living with only one wife. Poor side abandoned of a woman would be exposed, deprived, prey to aloneness. A woman on each side of him balanced him, made complete outlet for all his strengths. The harmony they struck within him rose out of him in a sweet sound. Humming from the idea of them, Wakwa touched Qunneke and Elizabeth simultaneously, while they slept. He would not tell them. He drew bravery through his fingers into his blood from double sensation. He looked forward without tremor to the coming summertime, and bouts with barristers, clerks, and judges.

Delight kissed the arches of his feet. Elizabeth once wanted him in conjunction with Qunneke. Now, Wakwa yearned after both women in the same second. Their dual presence lifted him to sitting, then to turning and leaning down to them with kisses. Elizabeth's hands came to the face which nuzzled the bottoms of her breasts; she blinked her eyes open and took the high-boned cheeks between her palms and drew Wakwa's mouth to hers. His outstretched arm was heavy on Qunneke's belly. Qunneke rolled away from it, and Wakwa's hand got closed between her thighs. He stopped her dreams with his touches of her there, and she drowsily folded herself along his back. Wakwa looked into her open eyes. She gave a languid smile. He drew away, fearing the weight on Elizabeth. Both women held to him as he rose up. Their arms dropped into embrace of one another with him gone, and they slid back into sleep. Wakwa would not divide them. Large from husbandly experience, he drank in the sight of them, drew on a blanket, and slipped into the cool of spring night.

He saw Beckett in silhouette, balancing on stones in the stream. He came upon Gilbert, a streak of white in his long nightshirt, lying flat, his back to the dirt, beating the air with nervous feet.

Gil's voice came at him like the dark. "Why are you, of all people, with double duty to perform, come here to the snake pit?"

"And why do you not lie with your Hanna?"

"Did."

"Good." Wakwa's chortle was covered by the tragic clatter of glass on rock, and the blubbering that rose from the throat of the sotted lawyer. He saw Beckett sit in the rivulet. "Michaelbeckett men trade dear, Nissese."

"Wussese knows." Gil rolled onto his side and propped his head upon his hand to see his nephew-by-marriage better. "She looks well. Elizabeth looks just fine. I had despaired. Thank you."

Wakwa's chin came up, defensively.

"June will be a time for joy," Gil reassured him.

"Gilbert, I am so happy tonight, I feel full enough for a life."

"Do not shortchange your fulfillment, my friend. Beckett might add to it."

"How can you trust him?"

"As I would trust a rat. He'll know how to gnaw the law and lead us right under the judge's chair through to where we want to go."

"To see your laws chewed away will bring us joy?"

"Bother the law! My mind is on music. There is more to this June than Beckett's legal puffery. June is an institution. I missed it last year, but I shall not, this. I am writing a piece. I told you that I would. I will present it to my dear amateurs in Boston, late in that lovely month. Each year these part-time musicians, male and female, farmer and physician, idler and craftsman, poets and I do not think any lawyers, gather and play themselves into a foam. I wish you could meet them. My friends." Gil sat up, his legs crossed at the ankles, his night rail stretching from knee to knee as tight as skin. "But why not! You and Beth will be in Boston just then! Oh, do come to the party!"

"Gilbert, no." Wakwa showed his face to the sky. "We will spoil your good time."

"You just have."

"Gilbert, you know we have a certain trouble. Not all whitemen are you, and not all Ninnuock are myself. I never want to see Elizabeth as I found her when I returned here from the Abnaki. You did not see. I saw. There is nothing I would not do, that she may avoid such hurt. No thing."

"Are you going to live under your Twisting River bridge like two trolls?"

"What are those?"

"Never mind. I am saying hiding away is not healthy."

"At whose house is this musical night to be?"

"No doubt, some merchant's place, or a tax collector's, they are the only ones can afford the big places on Beacon Hill. It has got to be big. And merchants have got to be good for something."

"I am a supplier, not a merchant, but I might be able to help you. I could get word to Crosswhite that you need his house. I have stayed there many times and tell you that it is very big."

"You see. You do not need introductions. You are already part of our party. Let me order you those shoes?"

Wakwa did not answer. He helped Gilbert up and stumbled through the dark with him to the water. He threw off his blanket to go fish out Beckett who was on his knees in the stream, progressing in a tight spiral, combing the sandy bottom with his hands to pull out the pieces of his broken bottle. "Not shoes," Wakwa finally said, "boots."

In the golden morning, Gilbert ate his samp and watched Doctor Stirling pick slivers of glass from Beckett's thin-skinned fingers. "Wakwa thanks you for trying to clean up their bathing place of glass."

A grunt met his politeness. Beckett would not open his mouth.

"Are you in pain?" Gil asked.

Beckett said between his teeth, "This Cape Cod air, the frigging peace of this encampment have got to be unhealthy for the mind."

"Open up, man. Do you think what goes into your mind gets there through your mouth?"

"Tell the Grand Sachim I kept house for him only 'cause I was drunk! And there's bad news for you as well. I'm giving up alcohol." Beckett winced at a nip from the old physician's tweezers.

"A mixed blessing for us both." Gil refused to back down from his handsomeness about Hanna's freedom of mind.

Under the sweetness of birds calling, and the running grasp of cloven feet in the forest, the Worths headed home.

Beckett packed up and left for Boston. He gave his son Horace to the mothering of a host of Indian women. He borrowed the Worth coach for his short journey and sent it back to them filled to the roof with Spanish sack.

_____ **Chapter 34**

IN MAY, while White Cat was hard at the hot fire of the smith, and Winke brought the profits from the first honey crop to Bottle's shop for Prue, Wakwa saw that there was no need to build the wetuomemese for Qunneke. His third child had been planted in her with the planting of the corn.

"I had so despaired of her!" Wakwa told his happy news to Elizabeth. Thoughtfully, he brought her the makings of a meal for her to cook. It was the delicate practice that had arisen, a signal to the wives of who lit his immediate longing. The wife with the duty of nourishing the family had her labor crowned by pleasure with the husband afterward. Closeness was kept for hours, sometimes for days, but all the while, the third member, whoever she was, was cherished. The wife alone was free from work, free to follow private pursuits, free to come and go. "Neesintuh! Lie thou with me, Elizabeth."

And she spent time with him, asking as she huddled in his arms in the small hours before light, "Let me be the one to tell Uncle Gil?"

Wakwa promised. But it did not happen that way. In the morning Wakwa and Awepu walked to Worth Farm to be measured for their Boston clothes. They found Gil in a strange mood, in the horse pasture, sitting a white fence.

"Awepu!" Gil yelled, "come see your foal!"

The Indian men sauntered over.

"Taste some." Gil plucked and passed around sprigs of flowering timothy. "Timothy is not native to America. Beckett thinks there is a fortune in baling it and selling it as hay." Gil bit the heads off the tips of the stalks that he held, and stripped them of lateral leaves with his teeth. "Others, as well as myself, hold this to be the best grazing around. May I?" Gil reached into the open basket Awepu carried slung over his shoulder. He took some of the wild raspberries meant for Hanna, strung them on the long, green grass, and held the succulent necklace to himself. It stained his clean, blue shirt. "I brought timothy in my pocket when I first sailed into this hemisphere. Seeds in my pocket." Gil sulked. A dimness like air before rain clung about his brows. His eyes were on his greenhouse. Then, he dangled the timothy high, along with its charms of purple fruit, and slowly engulfed the whole with his mouth. He chewed it to cud.

His visitors watched and did not move. When Gil finally made a sullen swallow, Wakwa touched Awepu's arm dispatching him to the house.

"It troubles me." Gil quit the fence.

"Timothy?"

"Seed. In general." Gil walked toward the greenhouse, his hands sunken deep in his pockets. "It is my determination to make an orchard under glass."

"Nissese, you have one," Wakwa said as they entered the humid growing place.

"I have nothing. An overgrown parsley frame." Gil jabbed a glass panel of the wall meanly with his elbow.

Wakwa hunched his shoulders waiting for the glazed structure to shatter above their heads.

"Do not worry, Wakwa. Old things are indestructible. It is the new which are fragile in the face of birth. No matter how splendid the germ of the idea."

They walked down dirt lanes between wooden boxes of seedlings. "I believe that there are untold benefits to the frequent eating of citrus fruits. I wish to create an environment where I can grow them here, without having to desert my home and fry my ass in Bermuda to do it, or to die of tropical cancer in Jamaica. I consult experts. Experts! What experts there are. I lay the idea of my horticultural womb before them and say, 'Work me out a machine, a device to heat my greenhouse,' and what do I get? Letters advising me to take a vacation at the south of France! I tell you, Wakwa, that there are no enquiring minds. Oh, mayhap I should go. Sit by the sea with my harp on my knee. But how can I? Christ! How the land chokes one. I do not blame Beth for sweeping it off herself. The effort to chain it to the proper master is making a slave of me!"

"Gilbert, is it Michaelbeckett? Is he what troubles you?"

"Hanna is a praiseworthy woman."

"I know. As is Qunneke."

Gil turned sharply to his confidant at that, but continued. "Michael tends to bleed all over beautiful women. Profusely. Try as she will, my wife cannot wash the stain of him off herself. She would have made a wonderful mother."

Wakwa opened his mouth to speak, but Gil cut him off. "I have deprived her that by marrying her. She never blames me. But the law punishes my sterility. That is the most grinding and public of embarrassments a man can ever suffer. My family in England have rendered service to the Crown from the Norman invasion, I have farmed this land all these years and paid every fucking farthing of my taxes, and yet they want more. Because I have no son the land-mongering king would just love to see this delicious and developed piece of ground revert. Revert! Think of that misnomer! It didn't belong to him in the first place. Michael was right about that. We should all have gone into the dock to prove that the royal sperm usurps. Englishwomen breed subjects to inherit stolen land, while I am told there is risk of reversion because I will it to a redman who has first rights to it, anyway! If Hanna would marry Beckett he could create on her a vast brotherhood of heirs in incontestable line. But again, that leaves me by the sea in southern France."

"Did you take Tame Deer in here?"

"What do you mean by that?" Gil's voice was severe.

"She asked me about sun on glass. Why it makes its own heat."

Miffed that anyone would invade his memory of March with Qunneke, Gil fluffed the leaves of his orange trees.

"I showed her these. My babies. Doomed to die. As is my name."

Pity overcame Wakwa's resolve to let Elizabeth tell her uncle about Qunneke. He set out carefully. "Gilbert, why say that you are sterile . . . ?"

"Because from the age of sixteen I have not got a woman with child that I have heard. And having money, I would have heard."

This was not the reply that Wakwa expected, and laughter cracked in him like breaking eggs. "Sixteen!"

Gil rubbed the beginnings of a grin from the corner of his mouth. "All right, fifteen. Well, a shade under fifteen."

Again, Wakwa stopped over the unexpected.

"There's little else to do in an English country house."

They feasted on this joke, and then took a long quiet look at one another.

Gil said, "I am getting old. I see how the elderly turn into crotchets. I have been one today. I do not ask that you understand my feelings. You have a daughter and a son, and if you didn't no one would put the squeeze on you for it. My empty balls have turned me into a pimp for the king."

Wakwa winced at this expression and brought one hand to the whiteman's face. "Do you remember Claude, and his talk of a Virgin who bore a son? A woman who was filled by a holy spirit, not by flesh?"

"That is a story."

"A pretty story." Wakwa added to its weight. "And who am I to say it is not true? I have seen a like one in my own wetu."

"What the hell . . . ?"

"The life of your spirit came into Qunneke when you had her with you. My power over her was nothing. Gilbert, Tame Deer has conceived! She goes no more to a woman's hut for her monthly sickness. Because of you, she is with child!"

Gil's surprise converted to white-lipped rage. "What the hell! What are you saying? I never . . . ," he corrected himself, remembering the closeness of her body, "I never touched her in that way!" Gil kicked water buckets out from under the flats and made a racket with them, abusing them with his work boots, forging through them to make a distance between himself and the husband of Qunneke.

Wakwa puzzled over his carefully chosen words, wondering how he had misused the other man's language in his quest to comfort him.

"Never touched her in such a way!"

"I know." Wakwa's voice was deadened by the porous earth.

"Oh! Fine! The description holds. I'm a pimp all right, but now, for you!"

Wakwa brought his fist down on the edge of a table of potting implements. Iron claws and spears of steel, and clay pieces jumped into the air.

Gil tore up tiny begonias from their shallow soil to the right and left of his path. Then he turned onto Wakwa's insulted silence. "Let me take that back. I am happy for you."

"And I for you, Gilbert Worth. You may never sire a son, but you have given rebirth to a woman. Whatever you say, her son is not mine, alone. He is, in the germ of the idea of him, yours."

They collected the foal from his pasture and, together, carried him into the kitchen to meet his master, fulfilling the promise Gil had made to Awepu, that he should have a colt by Grandee.

Wakwa said as they walked, "A round house is the warmest in winter, the coolest in summer. Good for your plants."

"A wetu of glass?"

"How to make it stand? Longpoles of wood will not suffice."

"Iron ribs!" Gil exclaimed.

"A center fire would dry out your trees." Wakwa abandoned the idea.

"Wait! I wonder. Hudson has all that copper he was to use for piping water out of Beth's bath chamber. According to the gossip, he has not used it all. If we could run hot water through a trough of copper, around the base of a glass dome, pump it, pour it, would it crack the glass in cold weather? How could we make such a trough?"

"Copper is my favorite metal. It heats quickly as a man,

LOIS SWANN

is malleable as a woman's body, and remains true to itself.
It does not rot away like iron. Copper is the color of Ninnuock."

"Wakwa! Let us ferret up old Israel. The kid is good
with his geometry. Dr. Mac can make the model of Israel's
design."

"But who to make longpoles out of iron?"

Both men turned to one another, White Cat, the appren-
tice, on their minds. "Hephaestus at the forge!" Gil
dubbed the Indian smith.

_____ Chapter 35

ANNANIAS HUDSON chose a table just out of the sun and
waited for his cider. He was at Bearing's Inn because his
house had a ghastly air, the furniture draped with sheets,
the cabinets and chests of drawers emptied of their contents and hanging open.

Every day, now, he came to the tavern at the Inn, early
afternoons, fretting until the postrider appeared and Bearing brought his mail to the table. Hudson was preparing
to leave Sweetwood lock, stock, and barrel. He was praying for word from some town, any town, that he had been
granted a ministry, a new congregation, a destination. He
would soon have to hire a coach to somewhere because
of his pact with Gilbert Worth. His neighbor to the north,
the gentleman, Mr. Worth, held a mighty stone over Hudson's head—the certain, provable knowledge of his dal-
liance with Prudence Hanson, and the bastard child soon
to result from it. But Annanias Hudson was not without
weapons. He held the keys to the smooth settlement of
Charles Dowland's will. He knew the name of the Indian
spokesman who had taken Beth to wife. A few well-placed

insinuations about that union could ignite racial riot in the out towns, and subvert the vast inheritance which had once been in Hudson's own grasp, except for Beth's last-minute capriciousness, and the clever-talking treachery of the heathen, Silent Fox.

Isaac Bearing's voice startled Hudson out of his meditations, and he answered the innkeeper with uncustomary candor. "I am very fit, Isaac. I will be sorry to go. Sell my furniture? Heaven, no! My writing table? Twenty-five dollars a leg, and a horse for it? Well . . . I don't know. All right, tell Goodwife Bearing I shall, at least, keep her offer in mind."

Hudson did not look at the post that Bearing left near his mug. The minister stared into the shaft of afternoon light, veiling other customers from his view. "Bay," he spoke bitterly within himself, "you are well-named for the buzzards who live in you. Sell my furniture . . . my writing table hold the guestbook here for an hundred dollars, indeed!" He shuffled the three letters, mixing them, paying no attention to their postmarks. "I wonder how good the horse is? Four legs that move for four that don't? Perhaps. But they shan't get my desk out of me. I will strap it to my waist and pull it to Ohio, first."

One of the letters had been hand delivered to the tavern. Annanias did not recognize the ornamental script. The sender's name was not above the sealing wax. "Local mail. Why was this not left at the meeting house?" Intrigued, he squared that envelope with the table's corner and examined the other two. Then Annanias began to sweat. One letter he held was postmarked "Boston," the other was foreign mail, three months overdue, out of London. Annanias sipped his cider. He put Prue's message exactly over the mysterious Sweetwood one, and broke the seal of the English letter.

. . . It is my sincere hope that my delay has not caused you hardship or waylaid other promising plans. The first ship out of port all but crumbled off the coast of Ireland. I am singularly blessed to be rescued and alive. In the one instance, I am shown how much He desires I fulfill my promise to come to Sweetwood, in the other, He detained me in England that I might linger at the bedside of my mother who lays adying. I ask your indulgence to let me stay until it best suits Providence to release me.

> Your humble and respectful,
> Mayhew Low

In a postscript, cautious in its cheer considering the body of the note, Low announced his marriage to his cousin, Dorothy, so attentive and loving to his failing mother.

Annanias glowered over his counterpart's success. "Calls her Dolly, I wouldn't doubt." Then a grin spread across his sober face. Mentally, he put price tags on each piece of his household stuff. "I consider it sold to the Lows. My marquetry table is saved from standing its life out in a public house." He was shot with a burst of energy and gained the courage to open the Hanson girl's letter, and hold the page to the slanting light with a steady hand.

Mr. Hudson,
Tell no one my predicament, but my money is running out. Can you ask Jack at Bottle's shop if Winke has been by with the profits from the spring honey?

I have passed through the black desert of sin and was paid by the tenth day of June with a changeling, conceived by my last summer's bewitchment. Satan stood outside my door during the birth of a boy.

I remain unforgiven and alone, when once I were *elect* as *anyone*.

> Deeply repentant, I am,
> Prudence

The Hanson girl struck just the right string in the disused instrument of the minister's heart. Before anything, Annanias Hudson believed in his vocation. From boyhood he had known that he was meant to shepherd, to preach, to elucidate Christian life for those lesser endowed with religious instinct. Even in his career's decline he was needed. A tortured soul cried to his ability to coax it back to safe pasture. Now, he saw himself, not dogging a paltry preacher's job, but retiring pleasantly to Philadelphia where people of breeding and import dwelled. He would write ennobling essays and publish in political circles, turning his back on the tirade of the pulpit to convert the larger audience. "I shall take my table with me! Dolly Low does not get it!"

Annanias was determined to tie all ends neatly before he left. He decided to go to Boston to rescue a soul. It did not even irk him too badly that he would have to ride to Worth Farm to ask leave to quit Sweetwood, temporarily, in accord with the strict bargain he had made with Worth the September before. It was not that he was curious to see the son of his seeding. Long ago he had elevated himself about guilt in its conception. But he was proud that the person he had been twelve long months before, had accomplished a thing that Gilbert Worth could not.

Giddy at this windfall post, he tore the fine vellum of the unmarked note. A gorgeous calligraphy which he discovered to be by Matthew Freeman, broached the topic of buying his extra copper from the bath chamber experiment. "Couldn't write it himself!" Annanias ground his teeth. "I must receive letters from slave-secretaries. What a blood! And why is it, today, I have what everyone wants?"

Within the hour, Annanias had dressed in new knee breeches, and got himself up finely with fresh bands. He combed his long, brown hair, and polished his shoe buckles. He passed by the unfinished dressing room, downstairs, on his way to the barn, and he stopped in to glance affectionately around at the incomplete dream. Annanias bent to pick up a hammer, never lifted from the floor where he had dropped it in his distress almost two years before. He was close to a rudely boarded wall. The flat head of an expensive iron nail slipped into the weave of his pants and damaged the fibers as crudely as a moth. Annanias did not breathe as he worked the fabric away from the rusted, ripping nail. He stood on his toes to ease the new breeches over the round head. He came away with a quiet curse. "It will mend. It will cover with the coat, but, by God, it is not fair!"

He rode up the hill into hellfire. Gaining the grassy high ground on his aged mare, leaving the flawless air and color of Cape Cod June suddenly for smoke and fire and demonic activity, brought him up short. Men, jacketless, some shirtless, scurried about heavy tasks in the north meadow of the town's northernmost farm. The carols of birds were replaced by the ringing of hammers on hot metal. Townsmen he knew who should have been home at tea, and redmen, more than he had ever seen in one spot, sweated over a pit of fire which looked like an impromptu forge. A great dome, ribbed and round as the thorax of an insect, rested on the landscape without visible means of standing.

Hudson scratched his sweating head under his hat and shouted at a worker, "Heh! You!"

The grimy, perspiring man turned fully around at the preacher's familiar bombast. It was Gilbert Worth. He wiped his mouth on the shoulder of his muslin work shirt. "Doctor Hudson, what are you doing on my land?"

"Mr. Worth! I did not know who it was, dressed in such clothes, without your summer straw."

"Then it were a lesson to address nobody as 'Heh, you'!"

"I thought we had called a truce on teaching one another etiquette."

Gilbert Worth would not reply. The minister dismounted.

"I repeat my question." Gil spoke now that they were at the same level.

Hudson peered over the master of the property toward the metallic dome. "Whatever that is, sir, it is too big to be kept secret, anyway."

"It is not intended to be a secret. Throngs of people will have passage here, to come admire it. You will be able to see it from your rooftop whenever you damned well please."

"Always your attitude. Your bitterness against me befuddles me. What have I ever done to you?"

"Annanias, I have got my end of an iron arch to hold up. What is your business here, other than curiosity?"

"I received this letter. You need to purchase my copper from me?"

"Oh, that! Of course." Worth was more pleasant. "Matthew is an efficient fellow. I only dictated that this morning."

Annanias's annoyance over short shrift from Worth was pushed out of the way by greater pain. Indians all over the field piqued him to wonder if one of them might be the man who had taken Beth from him. White Cat limped by with a bar of hot iron, which seared the smoky air as he passed.

"Hephaestus," Gil explained mischievously. "Greek name."

"I have my Greek well down, thank you," Hudson seethed. "I have seen Festus at the smith's, ever ready except when he's needed. I went there this afternoon on my way here, but of course, the shop was empty, the whole town being at your disposal."

"A late hour for a shoeing."

"I wanted an appointment for a shoeing."

"An appointment!"

"You are not the only one in Sweetwood worthy of courtesy. When I travel I need to know that my horse won't be kept penned up the day before. She's old, you know. I can't afford a young one."

Gil gave no sympathy. "When do you travel?"

Hudson jumped. "How did you know?"

"You just told me, Reverend Mr. Hudson."

Annanias's confusion worsened. "It is why I came up here. The other reason why I came up here. You see, I must meet a group of townsmen from Ohio who want me for minister of their town."

"Oh? Then this is goodbye?" Gil came forward, suddenly, with a ready handshake. "Well, luck to you!"

"It is nothing sure. It is a sensitive match, a man with his ministry. And a corporation with its minister. We are just to meet."

"Well, still, good luck!" Gil insisted on the shake. "What town?"

Annanias could not refuse this blush of warmth and blurted, "Chillicothe."

"Chill-i-coth-ee." Worth smiled impishly. "Indian name." Honestly inquiring he asked, "A trading town, isn't it?"

"It is more than that." Hudson's large head raised with pride over his fictional parish. "There are many people of merit there."

"Gentlefolk?"

"I presume, some. It is not Philadelphia."

Gil laughed at this gauge. "Good for you. Stick up for it. I should like to see these English trappers, and apothecaries, and smiths making a go out in that territory. Like Boston of a hundred twenty odd years ago."

Seeing how easily his lie was believed, Hudson soured. "You know I cannot sell you my copper for witchcraft. What holds that thing up? I see no pillars, no cross beams. We must have it understood—no Indian spells—before we settle on a price."

"Priest! Keep away from my physics and geometry with your supernatural moult. I want the copper, if you must know, to assist me in making a revolutionary system for heating the indoors of anything."

"What do you mean, 'revolutionary'?"

"Annanias, never fear. It is as old as Archimedes. If he could set the sails of enemy ships afire with sun and a directed lens, why cannot I start water into steam by the same method?"

The engineer in Annanias began to listen. "Still, why the copper?"

"You see, I am building a temperate greenhouse. We will fit it with invert lenses at intervals among the ordinary panes of glass. The lenses will capture the sun, cast its rays into troughs of copper run about the base of the building, and produce steaming heat enough to fill a jungle. Our idea is better than gold in a chest."

"What if the sun does not shine?"

"I will create an auxiliary heat source! I don't know! This is an experiment! We will work with it, figure out something . . . store the sun like jam in a jar, for God's sake!"

"An extravagant business."

"From which the thrifty will doubtless benefit. Refined, my invert lens heater may keep a man's bedroom warm, someday."

"I wish you every success, then, as I have nothing at all to heat mine, presently." Hudson put his shoe to his stirrup.

# Chapter 36

THE COBBLESTONE STREETS of the Boston docks were hot by noon. Toms in the alleys staked their territories, wrapped the base of the buildings with their urine, the odor diffuse in the evening fog. The sights of the harbor and its tides, visible from Prudence Hanson's tiny window, held no charm for her. The freshening wind would flap the shutter closed and she did not care. The miseries of past boarders scarred the yellowed paper on her walls. Alcohol, sweat, offal, and tears made a squalid pattern of their own. Yet, Prudence ignored the shortcomings of her hotel. There was no candle, but she had no reason to see in the dark. She kept to her straw bed, and passed the hours waiting the birth of her baby, decorating a clapboard house of her future, somewhere in Pennsylvania, its mistress, Mrs. Annanias Hudson.

While she invested her time in fable, Wuttah Mauo gambled to live. When he did not win at cards they ate and drank out of the reserve of Prue's money. He had no way of knowing that this strong currency was out of Annanias Hudson's savings.

After the gaming was done and the crowded tavern had quieted, Wuttah Mauo would linger below until dawn before joining his white mistress. Patty's Feather was his home, and Patty, his confidante.

He would tease and she would sweep, or when it was hot, sit with him and cool her bared bosom with ice from the bar.

"I have got a cousin with two wives."

"Like hell, you do."

243

"One Indian. Dark. Cold. Beautiful. The other English, white hot, rich, and beautiful."

"Yer full o' shit."

Weeping Heart pulled down on her loosened bodice and it tore.

"Fuck you! Yer just lucky it's on the seam. Last time somebody did that ta me, I had ta buy a whole new dress. That was an Indian, too. He paid me a solid gold piece."

"My cousin is the only Indian I know who carries gold around."

"It was that tall, han'some feller came to drag you home from here one winter day."

"That was my cousin."

"That was your cousin? Oh, say!"

"How did he get time to dirty his hands on you?"

"Must be an Indian thing, rippin' clothes. Sweet Jesus, it must cost him a pretty penny with that habit and havin' two wives!"

"Indian clothes don't rip so easy, Patty. That's why we make them out of skin."

"Oh," she said. "I always wondered about that."

"My cousin has two children. One a boy, who grows like a god. Goddamn him. This son is by his white woman, and the little yellow shit is going to get the place that should be had by a son of mine."

"Aw, what difference does it make! D'ya think these little yellow bastards is gonna rule the world? Ye want sleep. Go upstairs to that poor Prue. An' here take this up with you. It'll save me from seeing your face before noon, Willie." She brought him a bottle.

"My name isn't Willie."

Patty extracted the cork and poured two jiggers. "An' my name ain't Patty."

They lifted their glasses with happy snarls.

"This is my last drink," Wuttah Mauo said. "As soon as Prue drops my babe I am going to get married."

"Peculiar! Ye Indians make babies an' get married after? Ye mean if there's no baby ye don't get married?"

"Shut up!"

"Mean drunk! I was only askin' a question. If I was Prue I wouldn't hitch up to you."

"Stupid bitch!" Weeping Heart saw only Patty's sweating blue-veined breasts floating prominent pink nipples. "I've got me another woman. An Indian woman."

"Oh! Injuns do everything in twos?"

"She is beautiful."

"Here we go. An' what's to happen to Prue an' her half-breed kid? You two-face. Why don't ye do some honest work, buy an interest here with Pa, do the sweepin' up, take over the bar, run the craps, maybe?"

Wuttah Mauo's breath sprayed his derision. "Women's work!"

"Go ta bed, ye bastard!" Patty laughed, tucked herself up, and began to trudge the stairs.

Wuttah Mauo chased after her, grabbing the bottle on his way. "Patty, do me a favor?"

"Not tonight. I'm fagged out."

"Prue asks for milk, Patty. She says rum isn't going down."

"Stayin' down ye mean. You two better not be makin' a mess in there."

"Get us the milk, Patty?"

"Where in the hell am I gonna get milk? Ye think I got a cow out back like a country lass?"

Wuttah Mauo plunged his hand between her legs and kept it there while they mounted the narrow stairs. "You've cocks."

"What is the Indian woman's name?"

"Panther Eye."

"Jeezus! She'll fix ye! I'll leave the milk outside yer door, but ye jolly well better not let the cats get it."


One night, toward the middle of the month, Wuttah Mauo found Patty in the hall outside Prue's room. She rubbed her round, green eyes with the heels of hands. "Oh, Willie, I'm awfully sorry ta be no help, I ain't never born no kid before. I had ta cum out."

Howls of pain from behind Prue's door signaled the end of a pregnancy begun in selfishness and managed in ignorance.

Wuttah Mauo filled with a thousand regrets. "Is it dead?"

"Ain't born. Seems like it never will be."

Shuffling and curses from behind the door struck the waiting man and woman hard.

"It was not this way for my cousin's wife. They say not a sound or a sigh did she utter. She read a book whilst laboring. All was done with dignity. And she went alone. It cost my cousin not one cent."

"Well, this ain't your cousin's wife, it's Prue. She ain't readin' no book in there, she's dyin'. I gotta find somebody ta help. Do somethin'!" Patty ran down the hall.

Wuttah Mauo let himself into the place of confinement. It looked no different from any other night, except a whale oil lantern was lit and showed Prue lying on her side in the corner on the floor, for coolness. She hit her head against the wall to combat her inescapable agony.

"Out, out, you son of a bitch!"

Weeping Heart crouched over her, remembering the stories of Elizabeth. Awepu had it that she had entertained Wakwa, discussed their most loving moments. They had talked about a name for their child. Elizabeth Dowland had sent Wakwa away so that another woman could care for discomfort he suffered in his tooth. Wuttah Mauo saw the difference between Wakwa's second wife and this swollen pitiable woman, but could not tell why it was his part to end with someone like Prue. He found a clean cup and put it into Prue's hands. "I shall get you a pitcher of nice, clear water."

"Get out!" Her abuse continued after he had quietly closed the door. The metal cup clanged as it hit the panel.

He waited, alone, at a downstairs table. Patty passed him by with the wife of the owner of a nearby tavern. Not a sailor, or a woman, or a slumming student was left in the drinking room when Patty finally waved him up the stairs.

"There." She straightened the man's soiled shirt collar. "Now ye tell her what a good job she done. It ain't much of a kid, but it's there."

Wuttah Mauo whispered, "Is it a boy?"

"Boy? Boy. Oh, aye. A bitty boy. See ye downstairs fer a drink!" The innkeeper's daughter skittered away with a pail filled with the trappings of birth.

Prue's empty eyes seemed larger than the room. The Massachuseuck walked toward their centers.

"I hear I have got me a son!" He filled the silence with encouragement for her. "You are free. You have no more troubles. No pillory. No service. You may go anywhere you like. How soon may I take him?"

"Get me the sack from the hook," Prue said.

He brought her a store of precious writing materials. "You are a strange woman, Prudence Hanson. And always, you have bags filled with strange stuffs."

"You shouldn't pry into the belongings of others."

Wuttah Mauo looked at the baby. It was a series of lumps cradled in a packing crate. His head was large, over-sized at the crown, blue-veined and unevenly formed. His eyes did not turn toward the light. Small shoulders and hips trailed into tiny legs and feet. "He is pale as you," Wuttah Mauo forced himself to say. "He is pale as ice. Capat is the Narragansett name for ice. I shall call him Capat."

"We'll see about that." Prue turned from her side onto her shrunken belly.

Wuttah Mauo came quickly. "What would you like? To eat? To drink?"

Prue's head wobbled the negative on her crossed arms.

"You will get better," he comforted. "I will give you meat in the morning. Or fish." The woman unsettled him as much as her baby. "I will not bother you anymore. I will sit with Patty. If you need us, we are there."

Prue put her hand into the sack of paper and pens. Limp as leaves after rain, she stayed in that position, writing the letter to Annanias in her mind. "Pale as you" made a refrain which her imagination could not pass.

Wuttah Mauo uncurled some large notes from his purse, for Patty. "Here. Take it. For a new dress. It's old tenor. You'll have no trouble unloading it."

Patty toyed longingly with the paper money. "Ye don't have ta. Yer a good fella y'know? Panther Eye is gonna get lucky. Hey, drink yer drink."

Wuttah Mauo raised a hand. "I am through with drink."

"Tell ye what. I won't spend the cash till the kid pulls through. I never stole nothin' yet."

"It's yours! Use it. You did me good tonight."

"I hope so."

"Why say that?"

"Well, the kid ain't no prize. I ain't seen many his age

247

so maybe I'm wrong, but I wouldn't get me hopes up if 'twere mine."

"Hope. That is what my cousin named his son. Noh-annoosu. He-hopes. So seldom are my hopes up, I cannot let them down."

"I wish you'd forget your damned cousin, an' his damned baby."

"Noh-annoosu had hair when he was born. Much black hair."

"Bully for him."

"He cried."

"That ain't no blessing."

"Stupid woman! He cried like a grown man, a hungry man, never satisfied, even with two women to feed him."

"Sounds a spoiled brat ta me."

"When you are near my cousin's boy, his eyes watch you like an opponent in a game. This baby from this Prue lies like a fish, his eyes open and still."

"Did you see your cousin's babe the minute it was born?"

"Noh-annoosu had a skin with some little color in it. Even new, he looked like his father."

"Oh," Patty groaned, "now your kid's gotta look like ye, too! A minute ago you was happy enough it was a boy."

"Patty! I am an Indian!"

"I never would've guessed."

"Do you not understand? This boy has white hair instead of black. He has white skin instead of red."

"The kid is sick. How can ye tell what it looks like with its head all outa shape?"

"That head. . . ." Wuttah Mauo gagged. He drank his drink.

Patty poured him another. "What d'ye think this Panther Eye's gonna make of that there babe?"

"I don't know."

"I can't see the two o' you together." She meant Prue.

"Oh, Patty. We are like beans from the same stalk. I remember my times with her as the best season of my life."

"Jeezus, ye never know."

Wuttah Mauo remembered. "The first time with her . . . you call it February."

Patty looked at her friend openmouthed. "You got the same months as we got, where you're from?"

"A month for a moon. We have thirteen from winter to winter."

"Peculiar. We got twelve. Can you figure that an' Buzzards Bay only fifty miles south o' Boston?"

"I have never given it thought."

"Maybe you better."

"For what?"

"Nothin'."

"Nothing what?"

"Like ye say, I don't know shit about babies."

"Oo."

"But if there's one thing I can do it's add an' subtract. I add up Sid's take, did y'know?"

"So . . . ?" Wuttah Mauo clamped her wrist with his fingers.

"So, King Willie, ye bundle in February, ye ain't no way havin' no kid day ten o' June."

"Achh!" Weeping Heart was relieved. "I spoke of Panther Eye."

"You louse, an' with the farmer's daughter lying up there like that."

"The farmer's daughter I began with at Taquonk, Fall-of-the-leaf, late . . . October."

Patty checked time off against her small fingers. "It's close."

"Close?"

"Close enough. Christ, you got an extra moon, an' you expect a flesh an' blood woman ta be a clock. Ain't even no clock tells time right." She glanced at the one on her father's wall. "Course ye would have had ta get her pregnant, bam, the first minute!"

Weeping Heart began to move toward her, slowly, looming farther and farther over the table.

"Heigh, come on." The barmaid slapped his arm. "I know ye pretty well. Ye could o' done it!"

His hands began to ache, and he worked them hard, one against the other. "Count it again."

"I'm sorry! It's my fault for bringin' it up."

"It is not your fault!" He turned toward the stairs. "It is her fault!" The soles of his shoes pounded the names of the English months onto the steps as he mounted them. "November, December, January, February. . . ."

"Hold up there!" Patty raced after him. "So the kid came early. That ain't no crime! That must be why it's so little an' white!"

"It is white because it is the child of someone else! Get thee down!" He roared at her.

Sid's daughter cringed at the bottom step dreading the next moments of life.

Wuttah Mauo invaded Prue's foul room. The door slammed open and woke her. The exhausted woman saw knowledge in the face of the man who had been so easy to hoodwink.

"Coming to bed?" Prue issued the unthinkable invitation.

Weeping Heart stood over the tawdry crib of the baby. He waited for the pull of his vitals to the sad, pale form. It might have been a kitten spawned in an alley for the kind of sympathy it raised.

He came swift as he had been in his youth and pulled Prue from her untidy mattress to her knees. He struck her across her face, damaging his knuckles with the blows that punished the falseness she had perfected as other women perfected dreams. He used his arm like a pendulum, not missing her face at either end of his swing. He finally knew satisfaction in her flesh as he pummeled it, coaxing passion out of her with cruelty.

Prue accepted this defacement. It was true, no struggle was possible, the birth had been difficult, abnormal in tension and filth, leaving her organs sore and bleeding, her muscles torn from their unsupported effort. But, she actually submitted out of the dregs of her honesty, complying with his estimation of her, as other new mothers received reverence and love.

Wuttah Mauo dropped her down to regain his breath, and he hit her sensitized breasts with the flat of his hand as she struck the floor.

Prue floundered away on her back.

"Whose?" was all he said as he followed her on his knees.

Another woman might have wept, or from decency, lied. But, though it took time for her shocked brain to connect the question to an answer, Prue confessed out of pride, "This is Annanias Hudson's child."

Weeping Heart moved away from her, as if she were a

patch of ground he had just fouled with excrement. Dark paths that he had traveled in his life did not come close to the blackness of this irony. It was very bad to be the dupe of an English farm girl. His ancestors groaned in his ears. But worse, she had made him see himself as he was, an innocent. He had cultivated his toughness, had furrowed a division between himself and his tribe, to be harder, more wary, wiser than the English people, the hairy men from the east who had sailed their tall ships into the clean world of the Ninnuock.

It was now he felt kin to the damaged, helpless newborn, and he rid his purse of the remainder of Prue's money, threw Hudson's self-ransom into her lacerated face.

It was a terrible labor to drag himself from the hated room, because he was so drunk with defeat.

_____ **Chapter 37**

PRUDENCE AND THE NAMELESS BABY took shelter in a tumbledown shed on a shoulder of sand behind Patty's Feather. The wooden storehouse was pleasantly rotted by salt air, and smelled cleaner than the second-floor room. Ocean water made a little music for them on the beach.

"It's a changeling is what it is." Patty came every morning with a gruel for Prue. Both of them tried to fool the baby into sucking a teat of cloth soaked in milk. "The fairies left him for ye. Watch his ears. See if they don't start comin' into points at the top. It can happen."

"Do you think the fairies would take him back?"

Quite seriously, Patty said, "I'll bring ye some chicken blood this afternoon. We'll put it round the corners of the shack. If he really is yours, the fairies won't cross the blood marks, and they'll leave him alone." She stroked her plump, freckled cheek. "We really need someone knows how to do with iron. This kid'd be safe if we put some pieces of iron, still hot, near the door."

"You're making a spell. Who asked you to? Anyway, you could get hung for that."

"A bit o' magic ain't gonna harm the wee one. Ye're gonna kill him if ye don't feed him."

"Don't ask me why, but I tried."

Patty's eyes opened wide.

"Nothing came out." Prue was mystified. "I have all I can do to clean him, anyway."

"I can see that." Patty stood by the bed, hearing pain in the child's weak cry. Prue had devised a kind of litter, packing straw thinly covered with a layer of hemmed diaper cloths. There was no place to wash things so she disposed of the whole lining when it was badly soiled and made a new litter, again. "I think," Patty said, "his ears are a little pointed."

"Aren't any little people here, Patty, this is Massachusetts. Devils, maybe. Red ones. I have my money back. Do you think a wet nurse would come here? I can't move away until I get an answer to my letter."

Patty accepted a few of the Pennsylvania notes. "Willie gave it all back ta ye, huh? Not such a bad kind o' devil, I'd say. He been here?"

Prue backed into a corner, her hands at her spoiled, terrified face.

"Take it easy. I guess he's on a drunk. Too bad. He'd of given it up. I'll snoop around for a nurse."

Prue mended stockings in the sun. She wove saffron-colored thread through runs in silk, but her brain told her she was still working on Elizabeth Dowland's bridal sheets. "She's a crazy woman. It is a fact," Prue confided to a sea gull which was probing a clam shell for meat. "Beth Dowland lets her neighbors do the quilts, but she stays in the window seat with purest linen over her knee, working Annanias Hudson's bed curtains out of that, when fustian is good enough for every other bride."

The gull fluttered up an flew away. Prue shouted after it, "Disgusting! Wanton! Spending money on linen for such a thing when she hates him, anyway. Bitch! Sitting in the window seat working paschal lilies, with broad petals, mind you, bloomed out from strong leaves, and the stems growing straight up from the floor to the canopy." Prue muttered, "You can't stand it either, can you, bird, the tester was hung on three sides with valences 'broidered all over lily tendrils and buds, still tight, rambling 'round into words telling Annanias' favorite verses from the Bible! Madness! She's worked everything, the head cloth, the post curtains, the valences in white silk on white linen. It's snow on snow, light on light. You can't see a damned bit of all that work from far away, but come near. You can't take your eyes off it! Witch's work! So he'd look at her needlework and not touch her sainted body!"

Hudson's draped bed loomed on the purple sea, floating easily as a ship coming in to shore.

The white, Irish gelding, its mane blowing womanish in the ocean wind, marked the beach where King Willie baked in the sun. White Cat lifted Waban's first born off the shell-littered sand and threw him onto his shoulder. That was how the lame man appeared at the doorway to Patty's Feather. Iron thudded on wood as he came in. The Indian smith had fitted his crutch with a metal tip.

"Holy Jesus." Sid and his daughter watched.

For days, White Cat and Weeping Heart hunched over a dark side table. Festus spared his friend as little as he would an ingot. Panther Eye's death made meaty news.

"They made thin lines on her skull with a golden measure. I know because Gilbert Worth's black keeps it in his window. I do not know why but they have polished it to the shine of a painted pot. I lay you odds that the servant of Worth pisses in it instead of out his door in the middle of the night."

"Her bones? They have her bones?" Wuttah Mauo's voice was sucked deep by sorrow. "I shall go there for her bones. I will use her bones for clubs to kill them all. I shall beat Gilbert Worth to death with her bones."

Patty stayed close for the retelling to her in English. She hung onto Wuttah Mauo's forearm as he cried his pain. "Willie, you better worry about that country lass and that babe in the shed. It's dyin' fast enough. We got one body ta worry about as it is. What ye gonna do with more? Don't be behavin' stupid!"

"I shall run the bone of her thigh up their asses and turn it on a spit and roast them all and eat them!"

White Cat watched their shock. He had no plan. He had a need to feather his future. He did not see himself shoeing horses, forever. He had come to nudge to his favor whatever circumstances arose. But he dutifully manufactured the Celtic cross and placed it glowing at the shed.

"It seems to me, missy, that you had ought to of heard from this little feller's pa by now." The wet nurse talked as she fed, to pass the time. "No gettin' a letter is a bad sign. A nice girl like you deserves a second go 'round. This here's a big mistake."

Prue forced her eyes from the hut window to the baby. "It wants waiting. The letter will come."

"Do you want to marry this parson?"

"It is not up to me."

" 'Course it's up to you."

"I don't suppose you know much about ministers." Prue cut her.

"Listen, miss, I got a slant on them fellers enough to know ain't no minister can marry a woman with a round belly, or one that drops an infant far and secret-like, away from home."

Prue glared through her bruises.

"Now, miss, my heart's with you. You gotta believe that. This here's the parson's fault, to my way of seein'. Pickin' on a nice girl like you and preachin' in the church on Sunday. It's a regular crime."

"Leave off him!"

"Ah. Now we're gettin' somewhere. It's money outa my pocket, miss, it's food outa my own kid's mouth, but I'm not a selfish woman. This here ain't growin'. And ain't nothing wrong with my milk. Every kid I feed gets fat an' brassy."

"Do you want more money? Do you want to keep him at home with you to feed him more? I don't know anything about these things."

"I can see that. I can see. Now, listen, miss, I'm goin' ta treat you fair. Some other nurse'd say, 'Sure, pay me more to keep him home an' feed 'im.' But that would be like throwin' your money into an open grave. Get my meaning?"

"Is he going to die?"

"Look at his head! Look at the rest of his size! Has he ever tried to move? His little legs ain't uncurlin'. They's orange with the jaundice. This here's sick. He's comin' on ten days an' he ain't gainin'." Her crude face softened. "Money don't come easy. Hang on to yours. Look what I have to do for it. Money runs low, as money will do. I need a steady income, but I'm tellin' you, let nature take her course. There ain't no purpose force feedin' this here."

A thrill ran through Prue.

"You're a nice girl. Why should you spoil your life when you know your fella ain't goin' ta marry you with this here round your neck like a millstone. It's his office keepin' him away. He loved you once, didn't he? But there'll be no preachin' with this here."

"Annanias is not one to starve for love. No more than I."

"You're a practical girl. Good sense. So, if you could pass my name to some other lass, some friend who needs milk for her kid, I'd appreciate that. Even though this here don't make much of a reference."

"What are you saying? Won't you come anymore?"

"That's up to you, miss."

Prue pulled money indiscriminately from her apron pocket. She wrapped the woman's hand around the notes. Her eyes dwelled on the weak body of the boy. She saw Annanias's distraught face, as he might look, seeing this creature as his son. "Come as often as you think he is hungry."

"Very nice, miss. You'll always manage. You and I, we'll do our best for him."

The child's solace was his stupor. With a certain amount of grace he melted away as the governing factor in his mother's life.

On the twenty-first day of June, Prue's tiny son passed into death. She took the air on the rocks above the sea. Sunspots made her whole vision. She sat playing with bright light on the deserted spill of beach.

Patty was the only moving thing in the sunscape. "He's here! Your preacher's here!"

His black coat, full and fluttering, his walking stick,

straight and strict, defined Annanias as he picked a route toward Prue through the crust of salt and restaurant debris.

Prue knelt up, nearly invisible in the hay-colored sun. Hudson stopped in front of her. Patty and the two Indians descended from the tavern as the minister made reunion with his mistress.

He did not touch her, but his massive head pitched forward to examine her ruined face. The zephyr wind knotted his waving brown hair.

Suddenly, he straightened. The walking stick struck the hot sand. A barreling stride took him to the shack. Hudson kicked the iron cross and it rang a knell as it rolled like a jack down the rocks. He went in to the blinding dark where his baby lay. He made a stunned exit.

Prue tripped on her calico of yellow and green, trying to reach him. Patty and the Indian men hung in a half circle at the front of the storehouse.

Annanias Hudson fainted away in the sight of the four strange attendants.

_____ Chapter 38

GILBERT WORTH ricocheted around the anteroom of the courthouse.

Michael Beckett watched him with eyes calm as a cow's. "Hanna told me that harpers cherish long fingernails. I hope yours grow quickly, Worth. At the rate you are chewing you won't have one left to use at your music gala."

"Michael, I do not want them to hang." Gil slid his hands into his breeches pockets. "Elizabeth and Wakwa, that is."

"The judge's finances are in a very muddled state. We always have that road. Gilbert, be serene."

"It is important, Michael, that this case be won honestly."

"As you have allocated me no money to buy him, I have been forced to the expedient of plying the law."

"Forgive me, I was not implying. . . ."

"Certainly you were. It is the frustration of our friendship that you do not presume I would find buying a judge too boring to bother with."

"I have utter faith in your honesty and your skills, Michael. Yet, for God's sake, Silent Fox is not English!"

"You are beginning to have some command of the essence of this case." Beckett looked at the morning *Gazette.* Gilbert turned distraught, onto this casualness.

"Do not worry my dear third son-of-a . . . landed baron."

"Who told you that?"

"I just happened to come upon it whilst leafing through my pocket copy of the Domesday Book. Why won't you believe that I am thorough?"

"Beckett! This case must not turn on privilege and bluster. Do you not see how poor a man am I if I must court, and kiss, and eke indulgence, in a matter that should be one of simple civil rights and choices?"

"You want too much of me. I cannot reform and equalize the code of a people in motion for over seven hundred years."

"What of the precedent you were hot to set?"

"It is no longer worth my while."

"Drain me dry, Michael, but win this case."

"The matter is not one of fees. I am amply paid. The difficulty is this particular case in these particular courts. Your niece is a practical woman. I do not know one who is not. To sue for her rights under God, she sees as absurd. To sue for her rights under law and win, improbable. So we are suing for recognition of the obvious—that she is married after a style, and that she has borne a son out of herself, in the Dowland line. The basic step. And out of my hands now and in the lap of the court."

"I do so need a brandy. Michael, lend me your flask?"

"I can't. I don't keep a bottle about me. Like Ho, I imbibe milk. I do."

Gil was close to distraction. "I am a prisoner in this lifeless room."

"I am much at home, here," Beckett said. "It is done in quite good taste." He looked about them, admiring the pale yellow walls, the figured draperies, and the gold silk of the side chairs. He carried his blue velvet one near to the nervous landholder. "Take courage. Even if the Dowland place reverts, you will have yours through your life and can do an entail and hope it sticks in a storm. Fourteen hundred acres isn't thirty-four but it is a damned better chunk of ground than many a titled man possesses."

"I want to vomit."

"Would it encourage you to know that the beauty and the scandal of your American courts is that the judges are appointed personally by the Crown, and are not bred to the law? Do not know the least thing about it. They waddle through decisions as best they can on their dignity and the tenor of events which they find in the morning paper."

Gil untied his cravat.

"I have seen to it that the ass seated upon the bench today belongs to a man who has been known to bring casebooks with him on holiday. Mind, he is no lawyer, but he has a penchant for the classics, and no brothers who are in the Church. That is hard to find in a judge."

"That he likes Socrates?"

"That he is not connected with the clergy. In light of your niece, important. But Jeremy Duhmmer was connected with my father at Cambridge. Even better, he is slightly deaf."

"God, Michael!"

"Have you read the papers lately?"

"I have been working on the greenhouse to the exclusion of almost everything."

"Not of Hanna, I hope."

"I hope not."

"But assuredly not of your music."

"I manage to make the time."

"Well, that's your business. Mine has been to look up our dashing and talented Silent Fox. He is mentioned over a six-year period, by name, in no less than eighteen issues of news. While you have been luxuriating in the bucolic life I have been hard at work on some long articles which

I had published in the *Gazette* under a pseudonym. And I have paid Duhmmer's valet to push these articles under his nose with his morning sardines and coffee. Can you imagine sardines in the morning? Citing from printed reports of his fancy dealings with your Gov, I feel that I have established for the reading public and the judge, the economic advantages to them of the Fox's keeping the motley tribes of the area out of the fray with the French."

"Michael! What are you putting your hands into? Do not pin him down to a policy! Matters may change next year or the next. You could cost him his place, or his life."

"Or his wife. It will fall into place, Worth, believe me. The Harvard firebrand who is to be our barrister and argue the case has passed my most rigid test. He has the fine sense of when to break off political argument and commence to dance at a ball. Oh, it is all set to go off like a Chinese rocket. Getting a wife is much the more challenging pastime. Who is your tailor?"

People in the hall passed slowly by the open door of the room where Wakwa waited. He wore a nicely made linen shirt and a jacket and trousers of skin cut in the Indian style. His soft, low moccasins were black with periwinkle, it was so thickly sewn. Ropes of white wampum wrapped his fringeless clothes like honor braid. His obsidian knife, the sign of his occupation, glowed black at his hip. His black hair, pulled into a natural queue, gave every feature of his face to full sight.

"It is our time." Michael Beckett was there, admitting the others into the chamber where Wakwa stood. The solicitor was quick, low-voiced, smooth in his movements, a dance master before performance. "Why the bonnet?" His attention fell on Elizabeth.

"Her hair, Michael." Hanna tried to spare her.

Beckett said, "It is the perfect excuse for a wig. This is hardly the day to play the Quaker. She has problems enough."

"Should I go without?" Elizabeth lifted her lacy cap.

"Leave it!" Beckett shielded his eyes. "Only try to think as if you were wearing a wig." Under his breath, he said to Hannah, "I depended on you for that sort of thing."

Elizabeth and Wakwa met in the center of the polished floor.

Beckett placed the point of his mortarboard, carefully. "Our barrister is here!"

A young man, wigged and pulling on a black gown, nodded at them tensely, his blue brief bag sliding from between his knees to the floor.

Close to them, Michael chided Elizabeth and Wakwa. "For God's sake, do not touch each other."

"Michaelbeckett, are we not here to prove that we are married?"

"In Boston, Mr. Fox, it is an offense of statute to embrace one's mate in public."

"Ah! Is this why I so often see men in Boston embrace women not their wives?"

Beckett turned to Gil. "He has no respect for my work."

"You will gain respect for his. I so wish that the hearings were not private. I would like to watch how he takes the judge apart."

"Your friend, the sachim, is a cautious fellow," Michael complained, tripping and falling over Mosq in the upstairs corridor of his house.

"Was he unconvincing with Duhmmer today?" Gil was disbelieving.

"Very beguiling. I just don't see strewing my hallway with Indians to guard the guest rooms."

"Perhaps if the candles were lit, Michael. After all it is nearly dark."

"The maids here seem conservative of habit."

"Wakwa probably thinks you the cautious fellow. After all, you've split him off from his wife, and keep her here while he is alone, at Crosswhite's. He has concerns."

"I have concerns, myself. Problems which do not show readily, and therefore no one cares about them."

"I care. Certainly you must believe that Hanna does." Gilbert admired the staircase they had just climbed, which curved clear of the wall for two storys.

"I have Ho back. If the housekeeper will not light the lights how will she take care of him?"

"Why not bring some of your own people, more southern in their ways?"

"Slaves? You amaze me, Worth."

"Emancipate them. Then hire them on."

"Emancipation takes money. I'm short."

"This case should bring you others."

"I don't want to spend my life dickering over other people's fortunes. I'd better make one of my own. Remake the one I have spent on women and children."

"Something must have gone terribly wrong today."

"Right, rather. But I don't know how. Duhmmer got going with the sachim about what vermin foxes are, always stealing the choicest chickens from the barnyards."

"The fucker!"

"The sachim was impassive as that pillar. He simply said that if the farmers would leave the foxes their natural hunting grounds, that foxes would not have to eat tame birds. He noted that his wife, Elizabeth, had an Indian name, Herring Gull, because she was not tame but a free spirit. Whereupon Duhmmer asked why an Indian would keep a falcon in a cage. Their Moses made a great racket and the thing had been carried into chambers, hence the question."

"Wakwa's answer?"

"That as a hunter he moves about too much to keep a lap dog for a pet. Duhmmer seemed to like him better after that."

They looked into the unoccupied rooms to the left and right of the hall and saw north and south and east to the sea.

"It is no mystery then, how the case was helped."

"Ah, but it was Elizabeth who made an extraordinary little witness," Beckett said on their way back to the stairs.

Gil questioned, "How was Duhmmer's tone to her? As serious?"

"He is offering us that courtesy."

"He wasn't threatening to her?"

"He did ask her to tell how she lived."

"The premier question!"

"She said, 'Simply.' "

"Arch!"

"Astute. When he pressed her further about her house, she answered him, 'Your Worship, there is one room for cooking and eating, one room for me, and another that my husband uses at his pleasure.' I wanted to break open champagne!"

"But what about the marriage? There is neither a civil nor a church ceremony."

"Oh, he came at her with that like a javelin, which she turned aside with, 'Milord, I am not on trial for the type of ceremony, but for whether or not I conduct myself as a wife.' "

Gil edged close to the balustrade. "This sufficed?"

"It was perfect. All that lace about her head, the brown from those eyes stretching across the distance between them like a rug of velvet. . . ."

"He did not hold her incorrigible?" Gil leaned against the handrail of the stairs.

Beckett admitted, "He did say that were it forty years ago she would have been pressed to death for such a statement."

Gil gasped.

"Cool as julep, she came right back, saying that the Indian ceremony was all that was available to her for the Sweetwood minister would not perform the marriage, as he had long had an eye on her and the Dowland lands, and a civil ceremony required an oath of allegiance to the king, an oath which her husband's people had taken once, and would find it gravely insulting to have to renew."

Worth supported himself with both hands on the stair rail. "Was there no one to help her?"

"You don't break into testimony like that and disturb the progression of things. She was skillful as the devil."

"But every question a barb!"

"Yes. From behind a hay rick, dumb, damn Duhmmer out and asks if her running off unexpectedly to live with another race of people had not hastened her father's death."

"My God!" Worth slipped down a step.

" 'I object!' At last our Chancery junior jumps at a rare opportunity for speech. 'By inference, your Honor, you make the woman and a whole tribe accessories in a death, verified by two physicians as an accident.' "

"Thank heaven for him!"

" 'Have I done that?' Duhmmer piped up. 'Oh, dear! But I still want to know.' "

"You let her answer?"

"She answered, though my heart was in my mouth. She said, 'Yes.' "

Gil turned to cool his head on the thick marble railing. "I told you I was with Charles when he had the fall that killed him. It was my responsibility."

"She wasn't giving a coroner's report. She addressed the real substance of the question. Said she, 'Yea, milord, my leaving home brought my father to an early grave, because the laws he lived by made great obstacles to his passing on his land to a daughter, especially a daughter married as am I. And he tenderly loved that ground.' "

"Where was the barrister!" Gil demanded.

"There, but Duhmmer wouldn't stand an interruption. He begged to know if by this, Elizabeth was accusing him, Duhmmer, of killing Charles Dowland, because Duhmmer is the representative of English law in the colony."

Gil cast an arm across his heart.

" 'Yes,' she said, 'I believe that I am.' " Beckett undid Gil's stock and shirt front to relieve his labored breath. "Old Jeremy, honest Jeremy, doesn't flutter an eyelash but rejoins, 'Mistress Dowland, do you intend to sue the king about the matter?' "

"And she said?"

" 'This is my purpose in being in Boston!' "

Gil held onto one of Beckett's arms while the lawyer laughed in glory.

"Then Old Curlywig says, 'Mistress, are you attached to your old home as your father was?' "

"Every question a trap!"

"Yes, and I had the privilege of watching her step in and out of them like a Christ walking on water. 'Are you attached to your old home as your father was?' And she, 'As I am a Dowland, yea, milord. As I am a woman, nay, for the law alienated me from my home the moment I was born.' " Beckett moved Gil's hands off him to say with true reverence, "The decision. . . . Jeremy Lord Duhmmer said on the spot, 'We must uphold the law, because you are most definitely a woman.' " Beckett slapped Gil's back. "A victory in the common law! Duhmmer by this granted the land to the worthier title, that means a male one. Reversion is no longer a threat! The farm is at least in the immediate family. All we do now is prove that Moses is in direct line, and it is done! For this we trot out Doctor Stirling, and if we must, what's his name, the Indian who was inexplicably present at the birth."

"Awepu."

"Whoever. Duhmmer's due for his summer holiday. He won't malinger with his decision. We are days away from the final answer. Browneyes could have done it all without me."

Gil had regained his footing and his poise. "Michael, I think you have set precedent in spite of yourself."

"Better, I have joined the ranks of the Massachusetts liberals. I was saving this as a surprise for Hanna, but you look like you need cheering up. I no longer own slaves."

"A monumental step!" Gil's hands trembled in their warm shake.

"I have sold them off. Every last one!"

"Sold? They are slaves again?" Robbed of the sudden course of blood that had flowed fast at this news, Gil swooned back on the stairs.

"You'll go over! Damn you!" Beckett caught him away from the sheer drop, and pulled Gil along to his room. "How do you think I am surviving? The Virginia place is broken up, the horses come by boat. They are my means of living. They will be pastured at Rhode Island. They're to be improved by breeding on a little Narragansett pacer. Lift their legs higher on your stony high roads."

Gil shouted within his soul, "What on this earth could improve you!"

Awepu leaned around the door frame of the courtroom to look in. There was buzz and fuss at his elbow. Beckett's ear was being claimed by Mac and Wakwa at the same time. Awepu edged away from them all.

"Tha' judge threw me off the chair an' out! Ye saw it yourself. Dismissed everything I said as worthless, I felt a great fool and have done Bonnie disservice, sure!"

"It is unjust that Awepu be sent in there alone. My cousin is used to the woods, not places like this. And if his English fails him? If the judge tries to confound him? I must be there to explain to him, to interpret for him.

Surely, you can make request, Michaelbeckett, surely there is something you can do so I can help him speak!"

"I wish you could. I wish I could. I never thought Duhmmer would go this far. I never thought your cousin would be called. Who would have thought Jeremy would stickle over the testimony of a quite respectable, if Scottish, doctor. The old duffer picked right up on that tiny slip suggesting that Stirling was missing from Elizabeth's bedside at the crucial hour."

"What else could I say? I wasn't there for the actual birth. We rode like hell all day, and Gil both ways, from Sweetwood to Sandwich an' back, but I missed the birth by minutes. Wha' should I have done? Lied?"

Beckett was quiet a moment too long, then, "You did excellently well, Stirling. I want you to go back to the house now, and rest. You are nobody's fool. But you are overheated. You'd better save yourself. I may need you yet. For medical attention, myself. I am nearly an hysteric now that I see the whole of our endeavor rests like a crown of thorns on the head of this other fellow, what's his name —where is Awepu? Fox, the time to set the rules for the conduct of the hearing was before it began. My reasoning in agreeing to the regular rules was to avoid annoying the court. To slide in and out of there with the least hubble-bubble possible. Not making exceptions of ourselves. I see it as an oversight, now. I admit it. It is a flaw in my handling of this case. If things go haywire for us because I cast your cousin to the lions, I advise you to bring an action against me for negligence. That way, and with different counsel, you could get a rehearing. But I do not write the day off, yet. I'll be in there, and I'll see to it that the barrister never sits down."

Awepu stood in the quiet courtroom. He looked at the high ceiling. He found it good to have it far above like a clean white sky. Air and thoughts had room to play. The walls were paneled in cherrywood, and they gleamed like the rows of wooden seats ascending from the pit, where he stood, to the bottoms of the high windows. The windows were open, and wind and salt came in and mixed with the smells of wax and ink. The room was longer than it was wide, and it was quiet under the influence of blue paint.

Its heartbeat was the ticking of the tall clock. Its voice was the shuffling of parchment.

Duhmmer huffed in late, coughing and wiping his face of sweat with a big square of linen.

"Are you not well?" Awepu looked up at the judge on the bench.

Duhmmer looked down at him and rearranged his spectacles. The barrister shot over with apologies. Beckett turned aside where he was sitting halfway up the risers, crossed his legs, clutched his pen, and went as still as a painted image.

"Actually, I suspect myself of a stiff case of pleurisy, thank you for asking," the Bench decided to reply, "but nothing so bad that I cannot work. How are you?"

"My hands are cold. I am otherwise perfect."

Lord Duhmmer set his vast, curled wig. "Then, in that case, we will take you through the swearing in merely for formality."

"How do you know the daughter of Charles Dowland?" The questioning began.

Beckett's teeth locked onto one of his polished fingernails. He shouted in himself, "O! Do not say you met her while she was living in sin with your fellow heathen!"

Awepu waited before he spoke. "I know her as a good woman. An excellent wife. A loving daughter to my friend Charles Dowland."

Jeremy Lord Duhmmer coughed, and cleared his throat. "Though I was not after one, the character reference is appreciated. But understand. . . ."

"Awepu," the native man supplied.

"Understand, Awepu, for it to hold meaning, I would have to know you better than I do. Or get a character reference on you. Whether or not I want to know you better, and I think that I would, the situation right now is that we have only just met. Thus what you have said is rather light in weight."

"You had me swear on your black book to tell the truth, and now will not believe my words?"

The judge worked his handkerchief. "Awepu, many people swear to tell the truth, but what is truth to you may not be truth in someone else's eyes. The truth is a slippery thing."

"Father, if that is what you believe, I will not persuade you otherwise. But I believe that the truth does not slide and slip but is as easy to touch as a boulder in a man's path. But I am concerned that discoursing these things all day with me will make you overdo yourself, in your great headdress. You should get free of your robes and open your collar and have some hot tea. To make your day of work shorter I will tell you all I know about the son of Elizabeth Dowland, but only once, for saying it many times will not make it more true and will only delay you."

Duhmmer stared at the lean redman comfortable except for his braids which kept catching between his back and the back of his cushionless chair. The face was thin, easy to accept as the bark of a tree, not lucid, not dull, not exceptional in beauty, not insignificant in design. "Are you a man of medicine?"

"No, Father. The man you lately sent out of here in a fit, is. But if you asked him nicely, I assure you, he would attend you. I am the man among the Massachuseuck noted for good memory."

The judge sat back.

Beckett unwound, and sent a hasty note to his barrister by a clerk. It said—SIT DOWN!

Awepu spoke with each of his hands on each of his knees. "When I was a boy ten winters in age, I was told by my elders that the English king was to be thought the beginning and end of my food, my law, and my safety. For these things I was to call him father. This was the Submission of my Nation. Now, I can say, King George, I am not troubled by that. King George. I can say, my brother King George. That is fine with me. I see that in many ways he is a brother. And that was what before, he had always pretended to be. But what makes a man a father?

"A father hunts, gives attention to the corn, puts children into his wife. And when they come out of her fully formed, he cares for them, and mourns for them, and does not scar them in any way. And for this the children say, 'Father.' And more, 'Father, I love you.'

"I cannot say that of my brother King George. Quite honestly. But I called Charles Dowland, not father, but my father. You see, he spread his arms over his farm earth but left not one footmark on my forest ground. He kept his son who is dead with him in his mind, and set entirely free his daughter who is alive, so she might live with one of us, the man Silent Fox. And that man put in her a child.

"Now you know what is a father, and who is Moses Bluehill's father, and who is his grandfather. These hands," Awepu lifted them, put them into exhibit, "at harvest, last, received right from out the womb of Charles Dowland's daughter a man, the same little man you saw yesterday. These hands had him while he was yet tied to her at his belly, while he was wet and slippery to hold."

"So!" The English lord nailed Awepu with a pointed finger. "If that is the truth, the truth is as I defined it!"

And Awepu let Jeremy have his way. He sensed Moses' lineage would no longer be a stone around his mother's neck.

_____ Chapter 39

INFINITESIMAL CHARACTERS set in type in the *Gazette* were densely, darkly indistinguishable from one another as cobblestones of the street, to the casual observer. But opportunity seekers, followers of society gossip, and those who delighted in the general news, applied sharp eyes, extra light, and a magnifying lens to get their penny's worth out of the paper.

After his nights in the clean confines of a relative's Boston house, Annanias took in the morning news with his biscuits and jelly in the bald Eastern sunshine. On the twenty-sixth, just before his usual march through the filthy, narrow lanes of the wharf to Patty's Feather by noon, to work at bringing the soft light of repentance into Prue's gleaming eyes, Annanias caught an announcement run in lines of eye-breaking type. The musical fete, scheduled that night at the Beacon Hill mansion of Crosswhite, the merchant, took its annual place in the far right-hand column.

Hudson threw the paper down on the table at the tavern. Before King Willie or Festus could reopen the dreary subject of what to do with the corpse of his baby, Annanias clamored, "Worse things go on there during those cultivated Bacchanals than we could ever dream up!" Patty brought him a light so that he could check the guest list, again, for Gilbert Worth's name.

His angry page turning stopped at the report of the docket of the magistrate's court. He began to mutter, reading verbatim, " 'In Re Dowland Farm . . .' " The volume of his voice increased, sharing a psalm of misery with his companions, as he might to his Sunday congregation.

"Alienation Proceedings: In Re Dowland Farm: The local magistrate's court, today, upheld the conveyance of Dowland Farm in the region of Sippicon to the only surviving male heir of the body of Charles Dowland, late. The court placed Dowland's lands in trust with Gilbert Theodore Worth of that neighborhood by deed of conveyance executed this twenty-fifth day of June, seventeen hundred forty-eight, by E. Dowland, daughter of the deceased and by her husband, S. Fox, after private examination by Lord Jeremy Duhmmer."

Annanias put down the paper. He looked at the weary, creased face of Willie, the watchful young one of the smith. He saw the puffy, freckled, green-eyed barmaid, and he broke, and hid his face in one hand to cry. His lament over the report was more tearing to him and his observers than his sorrow over his dead son.

Prue rose from the table which she kept near the rear door, bidden to this distance because she made intolerable interruptions, singing at odd intervals, and sometimes vomiting her supper. She stood behind Annanias. "E. Dowland and her husband? Elizabeth Dowland and her husband? Beth and a husband?"

Hudson wheeled on her.

Prue looked into his water-colored eyes. "Little Henry died a long time ago. What male heir?"

The minister looked back to the tiny typeface, his vision stymied by his tears. Quite stately of carriage, Prudence Hanson departed the room to ponder these riddles on the beach.

Wuttah Mauo's hand covered the printed columns. "It is true. From what you read, I now have a very rich kinsman."

Hudson knocked the bronze hand off the paper. "Kin of yours, indeed!"

"Close kin, fat priest!"

"Liar!"

"The child of Elizabeth is more than the grandson of Charles Dowland! He is grandnephew to Waban! Smoke that!"

"That would be true if this Silent Fox has really sired her son. He is Waban's nephew. But who are you?"

"I am the son of Waban."

"You are a sachim's son?"

"Whose son are you?"

Hudson's head snapped back against the settle.

Weeping Heart punished him more. "Festus, here, guarded the grove where the saunks Elizabeth labored, and another man, another cousin, blood nephew of Pequawus, Awepu, the Indian who had his hand on the dying Dowland, held the grandson of the farmer, right as he came out of the womb."

Hudson squealed between his teeth as he tried to shut out such pictures. He slumped onto the table to ease his dragging heart.

"So now it does not look so good for you. We Indians stick close together. What belongs to one belongs to all. The big farm is in Massachuseuck hands, not yours, forever!"

Annanias breathed and sighed against his fist, pressed against his mouth. "They have left those rich and fecund acres to wolves and panthers?"

"He got it just right," Patty said.

"I will appeal in the name of the Colony! They have transferred English ground to another nation just like that? It will not stand an appeal!"

270

Weeping Heart hooted him down. "What appeal do you have? You fraud, you fornicator, you murderer!"

"You cannot talk to me like that!" Hudson stormed. He tried to get free of the table but he could not because the Indians were in front of him and his back was to the wall.

"I can too, because you need us to help you out of your troubles. You are a wanderer like Festus and me."

"That land, that house, a century of care and toil gone to beggars!"

Patty ran for whiskey to steady him.

He drank it, holding his Bible to his belly, leveling a curse on the ground that had been his passion for ten patient years.

"It will lie waste from age to age,
None will pass through it forever and ever.
But the jackdaw and the hedgehog will take posses-
    sion of it,
The owl and the raven will make their home in it.
"And the lord will stretch over it
The measuring-line of chaos and the plummet of
    desolation;
And satyrs will dwell there,
While her nobles will be no more.
Her name will be called 'no kingdom there,'
And all her princes will become nothing."

He toppled his glass and sprawled back, bleating out his air, from his slapping the face of the daemon that had lived inside him for so long.

Patty petted his shoulder. "Now, Reverend Preacher, ye shouldn't worry. She done all right. Willie's cousin is a prince. . . ."

"Miss Feather!"

"Oh, he's tall and straight, an' has a voice that reaches back to there in a woman. I seen him 'bout eighteen months ago, once, an' he's nothin' like these two horses' asses."

"Please!"

She mistook Hudson's delicate cringing. "I guess I've got a foul mouth?"

271

"He comes to this place?" Hudson blubbered.

An exotic cohesion bound the men in the instant of Hudson's careless question. From then, Wuttah Mauo kept up a steady stream of bilingual talk, so that White Cat could talk to the black-frocked man.

"He has been to this Inn before, to fetch out his cousin, this man you see before you. His figure is unforgettable. Now, how would you like to change the luck of this son-of-a-bitch, our fine sachim, Silent Fox? All we have to do is get him here, dump your rotten baby in his lap, and watch him try to get out of that."

Wuttah Mauo ordered, "Look at your paper. Is he at this music feast here in Boston?"

Hudson nearly tore it, finding his place. "They are all to be there, Gilbert Worth, Hanna, his wife, Beth . . . Beth and . . . imagine!"

"Then we lure him," White Cat said, "bait him with his cousin. We say that Willie is croaking and is calling for him."

"That will bring him?" Annanias asked.

Wuttah Mauo responded, "That will bring him. I know him. He is nursemaid to the People."

"And then?"

"Then, stupid priest, do not be waiting for him. We'll leave him the present of your dead babe, and after he touches that, he will never wash the stain of it off himself."

"I don't know about this. . . ."

"His ruin is your only chance to make your appeal, and get your woman back, and get her land." Wuttah Mauo looked proud of his scheme.

"What do you get out of this?"

"I get my father back. And I will fill that Fox's place."

Annanias began to neaten things up on the sticky table. "Very good. The outrage of it would hang the brute."

"An' you a preacher!" Patty slid off the settle away from him. "Mean. Mean and stupid you are. You'll not be believed. That baby don't look like no Indian. Never did."

Annanias looked squarely at her. "It's half rotten. Who's to tell what it was? And what does it matter as long as it's dead?"

"Mean. Rock mean. The lot o' ye. How dare ye mix up a man like that grand fella into a thing like this. Pack yer stuff an' get out. All o' ye. Drink somewheres else, an' take yer Bible with ye. Yer just jealous of 'is pecker." She raised a laugh and left them.

But White Cat snared her apron with the metal tip of his crutch and kept her there.

"Patty, do one more thing. Festus wants you to gather all the papers the priest has left. Every *Gazette* he has brought since his coming. There is one on the chair. Some are on the floor."

"Pick 'em up yourself. I ain't no housekeeper."

"Take the papers, Patty, wrap the kid in them. Well and thick."

"Aw Jeezus, you're cheap. I'll spare ye a blanket for a shroud. Just get the hell outa here! An' fast."

"Patty. Wrap up the baby and then get far from there yourself. I do not want you hurt. When my cousin comes the shed is to go on fire. Then no one can find whose baby it really was. Hudson doesn't want Prue to get flogged. She might squawk on all of us."

Patty tried to separate her petticoat from the crutch. "I just bought this, gimp. Let go! Don't dare set me dad's shed ablaze, his stock's in there. He'd kill me."

Annanias put in, "No one consulted me about cremation. I give no permission to burn the shed. Hephaestus, let go Miss Feather."

Patty tore the point of the crutch out of her dress and spat, "Yer full o' crap, minister, d'ye know? Gimme them newspapers. An' then get yer ass outa here. An' listen, love," she touched her lips to Hudson's quivering jowl, "my name ain't Feather."

Hudson bounced out under the niggardly light of the first quarter moon, on Weeping Heart's white gelding. Jobs had been neatly apportioned. Being English and presentable among the main of the population, he was to ride to Beacon Hill with the traitor's message for Wakwa, and from there, escape to home. Annanias knew all facets of fright as he began his errand. He feared for his health on this dank, night ride. He feared he would be stopped for questioning. He feared riding bareback, in his low shoes and good silver buckles, without time to fetch his boots at his aunt's.

He feared seeing Elizabeth in the midst of his felony against the man he had always wanted to undo. But he trembled worst at the thought that the plan would fail and that he would see Festus and Willie again.

Wuttah Mauo was to wait for Prue to come downstairs with her belongings packed. There was good hiding among friends in the forest of dilapidated inns sprawled on the wharf, where they could disappear like the rodents. He watched the front door for emergencies.

White Cat hobbled out back to see about the baby. Illumination was mostly the scant halo from the lantern that swung in his free hand. White Cat's crutch, the straight, peeled stick of hardwood with a natural fork at top for his arm, dug holes into the sloping sand as he searched for firm ground to carry his weight.

The lame man raised the lamp. Round as a bear, Patty came from the shed. White Cat did not like the way she walked. Her head was high and her back straight. She moved too quickly for safety in the near blackness. She did not pass up to her father's Inn, but chose a weedy way to the street, above. Her arms were crooked, bearing a bundle, a loathsome package.

White Cat called her. She screamed lightly but did not turn or stop. She went faster up the hill.

"Yo neepoush!" he screamed at her. White Cat began to cover ground.

Patty's stocky body was never stopping, and White Cat's was chained to the hill bottom by his lameness.

Instinctively, with a superior arm, he hurled his staff through the air. The long, lethal point stuck into Patty's back, dividing muscle and bone near the waist of her gown.

Patty flipped sideways into a bayberry stand. Her grizzly bundle struck the ground. She pulled herself free of the crutch, but instead of running, she angered, and stormed the man at the foot of the hill.

It was short work for the smith to wrest the flailing crutch out of her hands. He fell on her, pinned her underneath him, and jabbed her like a sturgeon until her life was gone.

_____ **Chapter 40**

"YOU HAD BETTER LISTEN to this, Sachim, if you are planning on studying law!" Beckett waved the penned decision as Wakwa swept past the drawing room.

"Be quick!" Gil warned. "You will miss the beginning of the music."

"Your clothes are laid out on the trunk!" Hanna sang from the bottom step.

With the judge's affirmation in writing, Wakwa had been admitted into Beckett's house. "Elizabeth!" His Indian politeness gave way. Wakwa opened her door before she had time to cross the room. His fingers aligned themselves with the fluted molding around the entryway, and he stayed there, awed. "Elizabeth."

Refined as a heron in the wilderness of rugs and curtains and gleaming furniture, she seemed as brave and as shy as when he had first seen her in his woods. She was alien in her own territory, but her beauty quelled any pity for that.

"Wondrous." Wakwa stepped a circle around the gown she had sewn. Dire Locke's sienna silk underscored her almost fully uncovered breasts, and rested tight as paint on her midriff. It trailed to the floor behind, in rich brown plumage, from high gathers at the small of her back. The fabric, showing copper where light welled in it, mirrored the varied colors of her hair, and its severe styling was unrelieved by any decoration. She was naked of jewelry too. But her coif gave a delicate completion to the study in form she had created out of herself. Rippling rows of tightly waved hair made the precise pattern of a shell from her forehead to the nape of her neck.

"How was this done?" One of his fingers touched a tiny curl.

"With a hot poker and rags." Her pain of remembrance of heat so close to her scalp left him embarrassed.

"You are the most beautiful now that I have ever seen you." He kissed her cheek, subtly powdered and rouged.

Elizabeth retreated to the window seat. "I want to go home."

"At this moment?" He began to remove his own clothes and prepare his wash basin.

"Let us put in an appearance, if we must, and then change our things and start back."

"In the night?" Wakwa played a shaving brush over his beardless face. He laughed.

"I miss Qunneke."

"I miss her too, Elizabeth. But we are here, now. Your uncle wants us with him. All he has fought for has come to be true. Tonight is like another birth for our son, and we will make merry, not have our bones shaken about in a coach, only to be turned aside at some public house. Enjoy your life." He lathered himself with English soap and troweled it smooth with his palm. "See?" He teased her, showing her his whitened arm.

She closed her eyes. "You are undressed before the window. Shan't I draw the drape?"

"There is nothing out there but water. The whales will not mind looking at me."

The wife took her own view of his body. She watched him wash, but saw him swimming in the river after pesuponk.

"Is there a special way to tie this string?" Wakwa puzzled over the fastening of the tightly tailored small clothes that served as underwear and lining for his knee breeches.

"A simple knot, I suppose," she said without care. "I have never dressed a man in actual clothes."

They locked glances. His nose wrinkled, and he began a grin. It stretched into a smile, and his tongue polished the fine edge of his teeth.

"It is not my idea that you do yourself up like a European doll Elizabeth retrenched. "Understand, I disapprove the whole thing."

Amused, he turned for other parts of his costume. "You

have made me a most excellent shirt, my wife." He admired the frail garment at the glass, happy with the effect of the embroidered eyelet which showed glimpses of his skin through the silk-bound holes. He drew on plum-colored hose. Then he fidgeted. "Oh. I have put on my breeches before the stockings. To get stockings bound up right one must have to put them on first. I do not see any garters. Hanna said everything was in this one place."

Elizabeth turned toward the evening sea.

"Look with me!" Wakwa moved the chest and checked behind. He hobbled through the dressing area holding both stockings up with one hand, searching for the elusive bands with the other. "My respect for the English grows by the day. It is a feat of intelligence just to put on their clothes in the right order."

"Dress is rather wisely called 'habit,' " Elizabeth said with her back to him.

"You will not help me, will you?" He folded his arms across his chest, and confronted her, his stockings riffling around his ankles.

"If these windows were not sealed solidly shut, I should throw these damned things out into the tide."

He opened her right hand and found the garters curling there. "What sucks the joy from your heart tonight, Elizabeth? Turn to me!"

She obeyed.

"Was it difficult to sign away your land today? Did it give you pain to write your name for such a thing?"

"I did it with a flourish."

"Then what is all this!" Wakwa took her wrist and pulled her to standing.

"I am not at home in this place."

"Nor am I."

"Then why do you pique me? I thought to find myself when I looked at you, tonight. I placed this night before me like the Grail."

"Do never look for you in me, my gull. You are full in yourself."

She recoiled, hating what he had said.

"Why do we pine after Qunneke?" He explained himself. "Because she is whole. We know even as she lives separately from us she is doing that well."

277

"You are more different from yourself with every silly piece of clothing you put on."

"How different?" His hands came to his hips.

"You were beautiful before the judge. You looked yourself. Natural. Now, I do not know you. I do not understand you."

He spun away from her. "You would disappoint me greatly, Elizabeth, if your knowledge of me rests only on what I wear upon my back."

"Then go naked to the fete. But do not play the Englishman on my account."

"It is not on your account. Nor mine. It is done on behalf of the People."

A chill passed through her.

"This going to law was not for you or me. It was for the People."

"Do you think of me as one of the People?"

He stopped, then said, "Because I am familiar with you, nux, yes, I do."

"I thank you for your favor."

"I pray yours."

Her strict stance softened.

Wakwa brought her against himself, carefully, mindful of her dress. "You live among my people, shall I not live among yours? Do not have shame over garters and small clothes, and coats and breeches. Could birds change their feathers, they would be safer at times." He kissed her neglected lips. "I have no need to beat upon my breast and say to your uncle's friends, 'See how I am an Indian!' It is important only that I act such. And if they are comfortable with me, they will come to know me, and so to trust. They will feel pleased with me, and with mine, and with themselves. We will be familiar. That word is like to family, sunnamatta? Is that not so?"

"Wakwa." Her penitent lips found his wrist. "I love you. You are better, more generous, and wiser than any man I shall ever know."

"My wife." His eyes began to gleam. "Those are good reasons for you to love me." And then his voice was raised, and thunder hit her. "But you do not love me because I wear the skin of a buck!"

"Mistress!" Priscilla said from behind the door.

Wakwa stripped off his hose and went to answer, himself.

Priscilla flushed and curtsied. "Master Worth is leaving, sir. He hopes that you can come soon after."

"Little maid, bring me a pitcher of fresh water, please. And linen cloths to dry. Stay by to recomb my wife's hair. Tell your master that I wish him to hold the music. I will be one hour late."

Priscilla hurried down the hall, forgetting manners.

"You are an overgrown boy." Elizabeth wrapped herself about Wakwa's arm.

"Matta. I am a man."

"That is what I mean."

He undressed her, hung each piece of her ensemble not to cause it any crease or damage. Her powdered skin glittered as she sat, bare, at the edge of the four-poster. Considerately, he drew the curtains, and joined her in the private rectangle.

"Will you not ever remove your new suit? It is my guess that most Englishmen do when they have a mind for love."

"I am not English!" His long body stretched above hers and with one hand he pulled open the buttoned closure of his pants.

Like novices, they found each other over the softness and slippage of the down. In the course of things, they became beholden to it.

He kissed her hello. "Now, are you home?"


Elizabeth and Wakwa crossed the crowded ballroom, splendent from candles, and marble, and jewels, and floating fabrics of sheer. Chitarrones and viols, flutes and harpischords tuning, outsang the announcement of their arrival.

But they were well observed. They used the forepillar of Gil's harp as their guidepost to his large party. It was slow passage through the thickets of rehearsing, drinking, conversing friends. "Stunning, scandalous, splendid," were whispers that streamered out on the serpentine path they chose. "Really!" "Do they think this is Jamaica?" "Charmers!"

Wakwa got picked off the route by Crosswhite acquaintances marveling to see him in genteel society. His reach for his wife came too late. She walked on into a clutch of hostesses.

"You have to be Gilbert's!"

"Your gown is French."

Elizabeth almost spoke.

"Is it smuggled?"

"How can you even think that? She's just back, can't you see by her hair?"

To defy Wakwa's choice of English dress, Elizabeth had tied a strand of purplish suckauhock around her forehead to hold a perky tuft of teal feathers Awepu had brought her from Maine. Her jest drew flattery.

"What an idea, the feathers! Imported from where?"

The words "they are American" nearly escaped her but Elizabeth threw that over. "From France," she said.

"We have been waiting to meet you."

"You are here through July, are you not?"

"I. . . ."

"We have heard you are an elegant needlewoman. Could you join us for a benefit?"

"For the poor."

"What could I do?"

"It's to be on Boston Common."

"A display of the best of every kind of needlework."

"Women of every class will mix there on the grass."

"Reserve a parasol for her," someone said, "she's so fair."

"Completed things will be displayed as women perform the skill involved. We'll have the usual fancy work, and spinsters, and weavers, but we need someone to show linen making."

"You do do linen?"

"I enjoy it."

"Heaven! It looks such tedium. Sign her on for linen."

Elizabeth glanced behind her. "I have lost my husband."

"Where were you finished?" They were after her schooling.

With a lilting laugh she philosophized. "I hope never to be finished!"

There was no response. She felt herself failing. Very quickly they began to leave her. "Is it like being married to a regular man, do you suppose?"

Elizabeth blushed to the limit of her curls.

"Sorry!" A stomach straining a previous summer's waistcoat blocked her way as Elizabeth started her search for Silent Fox.

"My fault, sir, I was looking afar instead of close by."

"Take care. I do the same and get myself the best trouble."

Elizabeth paid the man attention, now. She could not tell whether he was old and looked young, or the opposite. His hair was prematurely white and exquisitely curled, or he wore a very expensive wig. His nose was nice, short, his face was blocked square at the jaw and soft at the cheeks. He had eyes as blue as dye. The difference between him and the other portly men in the room was that his complexion was burnt raw by a stronger sun than the one that summered in Massachusetts.

"A typical Boston mob," he shouted down to her through a loud effluence from the brasses. "How did you wind up in it?"

Her reply could not be heard.

The young-old man filched two glasses of wine from a player looking for a safe place to stow them, and asked over the euphonic din, "Shall I guide us to the chairs?"

Gladly, Elizabeth followed him.

Away from the greatest outpouring of noise, he said in natural tones, "Thank you for talking to me without being introduced."

"I don't know any other way to behave. I was taught to reply when addressed."

The stranger mused, "I knew a girl like that, once. Nothing has ever been the same since."

"Because you married her."

"Because I did not."

Their laughter joined the rest.

"Why don't you sit and I can try to find your escort? He must be panic-stricken having lost you in this Orpheus' bazaar."

"Sir, my escort is not given to panic. We both came to see my uncle, but I know he is too busy to miss me."

"He must be awfully old."

They laughed again, and then they sat.

Investigation of one another's face kept them silent on

281

the prim chairs. Their testing silence, not their conversation, helped them to identify one another.

The man chanced, "Your uncle . . . could he be . . . ?"

"He is Gilbert Worth . . . Stephen?" Her hands rose on the tension of the air between them.

Stephen Poore stood clumsily in respect for the moment of their remeeting. And then he took the floating hands and touched them to his lips. "You always knew a fool! Beth."

Gilbert Worth wandered the ballroom with his score under his arm in search of a tenor. The amateurs were kind to each other. Practicing together for only a few days before their yearly concert, they let perfection of skill, and intent, outweigh accidents of execution. The performance was a good-natured game, release from isolation, the drear side of colonial life. At the last minute, musicians allowed themselves to be impressed into one another's service, risking nothing but a jolly time if they did not join the impromptu ensembles.

Gil's difficulty this year was that his composition was notated in an original way, using letter symbols instead of conventional notes. There was no key to speak of, and the combination of harp, violin, and trumpet required a human voice as the instrument for the obbligato part. He needed not only good will, but also a top musician.

"So! It is you."

"It always has been." Gil confronted the rudeness. "What the hell are you doing among the civilized, Stephen Poore the senior? I understood there was a run on Jamaican plantations and that you bought in. I have been picturing you beating drums in a field of sugar cane."

"You never change," the older Poore rejoined.

"Wrong. I change so fast you can't notice."

"If you want my violin you can't have it. I don't play her anymore."

"Lucky fiddle. I have a player, thank you. He goes on the flute just as well."

"Who is this?" Poore was vexed. "A lady, doubtless."

"A doctor. Stirling. From Gloucester and Sandwich."

"Reduced to barbers and Injuns?"

Gil waited. "Who let you in? You have quit the club."

"I am come to take back my wife. Our actual move is July first. Much to do. But Gwynn would not come away from Boston without attending this folly. I do suspect it is her way to sneak a talk with Hanna."

"I hope that they have more to say to one another than do we."

"You might thank me for Beckett."

"Thanks for Beckett. What I want to know is the nature of the deal between you two. You have bought his place. What is the rate of exchange? Black slavery?"

"I raise logwood! I sell ballast!"

"That is illegal, Poore. You know you are dodging the duty on black dye."

"It is you who dodges yours, my friend."

"What are you talking about?"

Poore grew smug. "Someday, you shall see. From the height of a gallows."

"Tatta. Injun for I do not know 'bout that. Stephen isn't here, is he? I need a voice. Countertenor'd do."

"What a face! If you must know, he is over there. I am encouraged to see him. That thing he is with is good to look at. Haven't seen him look at a woman since Cape Cod. The boy runs the risk of becoming a scholar. Wear glasses one day I shouldn't wonder."

"Horrible!" Gil twitted him and turned to find Stephen Poore, the son. "That thing he is with is my niece."

"Horrible!"

"You old fart!"

Poore sputtered, "Mixing decent people with a woman like that. Where is her savage? Chained in the cellar?"

"He is right there. Dark green. You do not rate an introduction."

"Tell the lad to bring his mother home. I won't breathe the same air."

"It has been five years for us, Beth. Twice in that time I missed my chance with you."

"Let it go, Steph."

"I did not deserve you."

"Steph, stop."

He went right on. "I am delighted to meet you, again. I have analyzed the business from one end of the Atlantic

283

to the other. I did not fight for you. I was too easily put off. That stinking marriage contract. And now, I must be glad, for I learn from your aunt that you married a man last autumn who makes you happy. Remembering yourself, I say he must be quite something."

"You will meet him. And you will meet my son."

"A son?"

"Last September, dear."

Stephen's lobster color blanched.

"And then, of course, there is Qunneke."

"That name, again?"

"Qunneke. Tame Deer. His other wife."

Stephen's mouth opened and closed. "At the same time?"

"And her daughter, Sequan . . . oh, Steph, I am sorry."

"Never be!" He stood and pulled her with him. "I am so glad you are not a Presbyterian anymore!"

They did not relinquish their embrace.

"Steph? Are you happy?"

"Happiness has never been one of my goals. Perhaps that is why I have never been at your side in time to catch you. But of late, there has come someone. . . ."

"You have met someone?"

"Shamelessly beautiful. . . ."

"Would I have known her? Will you marry?"

"Last to first, dear girl, no."

"Disapproval."

"Oh, yes."

"She's not an Indian, is she?" Elizabeth jibed.

Stephen looked from side to side. He began. He hesitated.

"It is only you are so dear to me, Stephen. Pay no attention to my nosiness."

He took her hands again. "Last year, Beth, in Virginia, two men were hung for such love."

Elizabeth comprehended.

"He is a great influence on my life. He always will be. He will lead the Paris Opera, someday. He is the son of a count and his concubine. He is visiting his parents in Jamaica, else I would never have promised father that I would go there to help arrange his papers in this move. You will meet him."

Elizabeth moistened her lips but found nothing to say.

"At least you do not pull your hands away."

"I am not letting you go again," she mothered him.

Stephen broke the clasp. "As soon as my mother is settled in the tropics, I go back to France with Alois, and there to stay."

Wakwa and Gil found them, then.

"Sachim," Stephen said, "I have loved your wife from childhood."

"I know who you are, Stephen Poore. I think that you must live with us."

"Wakwa, he is on his way to France. He is studying language. I have already asked him. He says that he cannot come."

"Stephen Poore, why study something that you know? Be with us and listen to the new. There is a place for you at the summer feast on the islands in the Bay."

"More immediately, Steph, are you up to this?" Gil stuck his score under Poore's nose.

"First my specs."

"Don't tell your father about those."

"I don't tell him anything since he's become a pirate. Is this notation Penllyn's?"

"Who is Penllyn?" Gil eyed his own work.

Stephen glanced from the music to the men.

"Take some time, Stephen." Wakwa was kind.

"Done."

# Chapter 41

CROSSWHITE'S HOUSE possessed a feature despised by the non-merchants who lived on the Hill. It was a glass-faced veranda, belted around the first floor of the tall brick structure. From there, its owner watched the maritime choreography of the harbor below. The continuous performance expanded his talent to predict the trends of the colonial marketplace. He trusted it as other men trusted their watches, and he prospered.

The "Crow's Nest," as Crosswhite called his observatory, was where his chronic guests found sun and fog. It was where Michael Beckett enjoyed seclusion the night of Gil's gala.

He swilled milk in a silver mug, with the pages of the court decision spread on his knees.

The Crow's Nest door opened. Wakwa walked quietly to the solicitor. "Michaelbeckett, I offer you my full heart, for your service to me."

Beckett did not rise or put out his hand. "I have made you a poor man."

"I say, my heart is full."

"Bring over my stick, will you?"

Alien feelings burst inside Wawka. Only equals did favors for one another. The scales between him and Beckett were always out of balance. "Mr. Crosswhite is wealthy. I have counted many of his servants where the people are at dancing. One of them will fetch for you." Wakwa crossed the narrow, painted floor to look at the stars.

"I beg your pardon, Great Chief."

Wakwa smiled at the glass. "I grant it you."

Beckett aligned the corners of the papers until they matched exactly. He set the pages carefully on the seat cushion of his couch and half stood, holding his temples tightly. Half upright, he shied toward the stick. When he had retrieved it, he sank onto the chair pillow, and the precisely arranged papers wafted to the floor.

Wakwa saw this exercise mirrored on the dark window-pane. Without turning around, he said, "For the first time since I have known you, Michaelbeckett, your clothes are not black."

Beckett untwisted the knob from the head of his cane. He put the stick to his eye, and looked down its hollow middle. Whiskey spilled onto his breeches. "Good enough!" He dripped some of the liquor into his cup of milk. Drinking the concoction, he sighed, "I have left off mourning. It is a year. Overmourning is lacking in taste."

"Have you chosen a new wife, then?"

Beckett considered an answer. "Would you spare me one?"

"Would you want her?"

"Why did you assume I meant the Indian one?"

"I did not." Wakwa faced him.

Beckett drowned his chagrin in a gulp of his drink. "You have the makings of a jurist." Without warning, he tossed the stick-bottle, upright to Wakwa. "Have a drink."

"Parity? I have no thirst." Wakwa gave it back to him.

"Thank you for bringing my stick." Beckett showed a dangerous smile. He bent and groped with imprecise fingers for the hand-drawn draft of the results of his work. "Not very fashionable. Not drinking. And you look quite the fashionable fellow tonight. But let me tell you, O great and mighty chief, the prevailing fashion in Britain is to have one wife."

"I am not British. I am not in Britain."

"As good as. If you would study the law, study the law in England. Forget Virginia, they'll hang you there though your son sits lord of the fucking manor tonight."

"I indulge your drunkenness. I have a cousin like you. He is ahead of you and no longer can kill pain with drink. It is all pain."

"Do tell."

"I am sorry for you. But to make you happy I agree with you. I cannot go to Virginia. I will not travel across the sea."

"You ought to think about it."

"Perhaps when Qunneke has her child."

"Her child? But I was told she didn't . . . why you old. . . ." Beckett shook Wakwa's wrist in prurient flattery. "Good boy! You really juggle two?" He stood abruptly to see him, eye to eye, but headache forced him to sitting. His mood reversed. "How dared you! You did not consult me!"

"About such a thing?"

"Consult me about everything! I thought I made it plain that that individual was out of the picture. With her pregnant . . . if it should come to light. . . ."

"It is no difference, lawyer. To the English, Qunneke is a she-wolf. And Elizabeth not much more than that though she is white."

"Nevertheless! You could have kept your cock to yourself, at least until the ink was dry on my conveyance!"

Wakwa forced his hands safely under his waistcoat. "Michaelbeckett," he trembled, "were you sober I would cause you to need that stick for something other than drinking."

"My dear Mr. Fox, gentleman Gilbert Worth will run me through if I do drink, and you will break me if I do not." Michael drank deeply of his toddy, then failed in trying to set the tankard on a nearby table. He settled for the expedient of harboring it between his thighs. "I have two punishments and I do not know my crime." He leaned his head back against the straw and summarily fell asleep. Wakwa picked up the court documents and folded them along the creases already existing. He slipped them into the pocket of Beckett's dove-colored coat. He opened a casement to let a clean salt wind freshen the atmosphere. He pondered the dimly glowing coastline and the dark sea beyond. His feelings toward Weeping Heart knew a softening. He involved himself in guessing which side street of the miniaturized city made the stopping place for his cousin's crippled dreams.

Awepu appeared at the door with Gil's Jaeger. "I told them I would find you here. Mosq, the Bear," Awepu said more softly, not to wake Beckett, "gave me this for you. I left him to watch the door."

Wakwa turned the small sheet of paper over in his hand.

"The gun is set for your part in the music. I knew if you began talking. . . ."

Wakwa read.

"Remember the hair trigger," Awepu instructed. "If the gun goes off too soon women will scream and faint, men will draw their pistols, and you and Gilbert will have started a war." Awepu laughed quietly as a cat. "Tell me, kinsman, what doth gunfire have to do with music?"

Wakwa looked from the message to his friend's face.

"Shall I stay with you so you do not miss your turn? I do not mind, though the prettiest English ladies have asked me to sit among them."

Wakwa tapped Beckett's face, needing to consult him, now. Beckett's mouth fell open and his breath drew more loudly. "Nux, Awepu, will you stay? You will do the part."

288

"What do I know about it? I have not once practiced music with Gilbert."

Wakwa led him along the porch to where bags of sand were lined against the outer wall. "You can see from here the spot where Gilbert will have his harp." Wakwa waved at Elizabeth's uncle, who was moving the instrument into place in the inner room. "His back will be to you, but he will raise a hand, thus, when you should shoot. There will be four firings in all. Two are close together and two are far apart."

"It is a thing for you to do." Awepu declined.

"After it is all over, wetomp, you can go back and sit with the lovely women. I need this favor from you for I must leave the house for a while, and it is only right. You are the best shot."

Awepu grumbled as he dried his hands on his shirt and eyed his massive targets. "Any boy could shoot, thus!"

Wakwa left, glad to keep Awepu, the father of four, safely at Crosswhite's while he answered the plea for help from Weeping Heart. The fewer on this dreary errand, the smoother, Wakwa felt. And if it were false, if the man only needed money, it were better not to spoil Gilbert's concert. Evading Mosq, Wakwa ducked into the concert room by another door and lost himself among women and men scurrying to their places with cellos and violins in hand. He clamped the shoulder of a man whose back was toward him. "Take care, Elizabeth, Stephen Poore!"

Slipping back through the rambling veranda, Wakwa went over the side into the soft dirt of the flower bed below.

Wakwa kept his saddle when he came to Patty's Feather. The message was still in his hand, the same hand that guided his rein. He avoided the uninviting doorway, and trotted to a side alley that curved about thirty feet above the beach. The horse dropped down the sandy bank, tearing bayberry bushes in his blind stride. Wakwa watched the lonely shore. The water rose silver to the sand, then receded to black under the setting moon. The horse reared and whinnied, and went out of control. Wakwa slipped off the stallion and let him run from his fright. He crouched on the rock-embedded sand trying to smell what the horse had smelled. The light wind hinted of fresh blood, and decay. Wakwa heard the quivering of Sucki's bells. He saw the black bulk of the shed. He carved the stuff to make a torch, but he was dressed in whiteman's clothes. No room for shells of punk in his pockets.

Wakwa stepped across the beach and rattled a shutter of the storehouse. It brought a scream like a girl's from inside. Wakwa jumped back, sweating. Then he approached the house, again.

He came to the front. High-pitched weeping met the dry sound of his steps in the sand. The sachim broke down the door. With his English boot he kicked apart the rotted wood roped shut from inside.

Wuttah Mauo came screaming out into the breezy summer night.

Wakwa pinned the stinking body of his cousin against the blowing sand.

From the reaches of his mind, Weeping Heart warned, "Musquantam Manit! Musquantam Manit! It grows large as God! Amaish! Go thou away!"

"You call me here to send me away! Drunken fool!" Wakwa held his cousin by the neck.

Weeping Heart sucked for air. "Get away from the shed! Get out of here! Get clear! I am sorry, sorry that I ever saw White Cat!"

"What does he have to do with you?"

"He has done too much!"

Wakwa pulled him up and dragged him to the little house. Weeping Heart struggled away as if from hell. He broke for the open beach while Wakwa looked inside.

Wakwa drew his knife and cautiously made his way from the door to the far end of the room. He found an oblong bundle roped to a keg of rum. He scored the paper and moved it away from the contents with his knife. Like garbage that townspeople wrapped to be carted away, the dead flesh of something was in it. Disgusted, Wakwa looked away, right into the round, green eyes of Patty. He remembered the barmaid from his other dreary errand to the Inn. He had pitied, then despised her. Now he knelt, desparate that she be alive. No heat or turgor met his clutching. The lantern light showed her clothes black and stiff. He saw the holes in her side and belly that had poured blood. Her eyes were frozen in the horror of her death. Wakwa closed them.

Wakwa went after Wuttah Mauo. The darting figure was splashing through the salty shallows toward a brace of rocks which protected the inlet from the open sea. Wakwa followed him, faster than he, the high bovine boots protecting him from barnacled stone, lending his agility power. He was first to the wild spot where Weeping Heart was fleeing.

Waban's son looked up the water-washed rocks into Wakwa's face. Wakwa caught him by his hair, and his head.

Over the rumble of the sea, he demanded, "Tell me!"

Sniveling, floating, treading water, the confession was made. Wuttah Mauo drifted away on the waves. Wakwa grappled through weeds and water as the tide tossed him back.

"If I find, Weeping Heart, that your open soul crawls with lies, I will hang you from a pole in the center of the camp, and face you toward your father's door, and rake you into ribbons with five knives for fingers, and use the strips of your hide for the fringe of my coat!"

Weeping Heart opened his mouth. Sea water swirled into it. Choking, he pointed like a watchman to the shore. Wakwa looked back. Fire outlined the dry roof of the shed.

Wakwa reached the sand and raced to salvage the bodies. Wuttah Mauo fought with him to leave them and run south down the beach, away. Burning shingles began to pitch down into the storehouse from the roof among combustible crates and kegs. Explosions began.

Wakwa hung back. "If the baby of Prudence Hanson is in there, where is Prudence Hanson?"

"There!" Wuttah Mauo looked helplessly at the inn.

Customers flooded down the hill, a motely brigade of firefighters, with buckets and spittoons and chamber pots.

Wakwa pulled his cousin behind the burning shack. He found two bottomless buckets in a refuse heap and ran among the crowd. They formed links in the chain passing water from the ocean to the fire. Befuddled Wuttah Mauo hindered the work.

"Who is that shipwreck!"

"Afraid of fire!" Wakwa yelled.

"Get him out of here! He's in the way!"

Wakwa guided Weeping Heart toward the path below the Inn. He bent for a brace of bells, the only sign of his horse.

Sid accosted them. "Willie, Willie, seen m' Patty? Been callin' her over an hour!"

An explosion sent dry boards flying, tearing into the screaming people, scattering flame.

"M' stock!" Sid held onto Wakwa's coat sleeves. "Gent!" he pleaded, "go for the firecart!"

Wakwa and Wuttah Mauo had reached the midpoint of the stone steps before the father's next scream. Wakwa looked behind. Sailors had brought out some of the cases. The innkeeper's daughter lay on one of them.

Wakwa moved. He played the helpful guest, shepherding his bedraggled cousin through the nearly deserted drinking room and up the stairs for Prue. He found her in a room at the hall's center, the one with the best view of the fire.

She moaned, "Let me stay to see the end?" as the two men took her from her vantage point.

A man remarkable for his height and elegance, his arms wound about a whore in green and yellow, faded into the general memory of Sid's fire. King Willie's familiar face was forgotten like the street posts as the back lanes filled with neighborhood people flocking toward the excitement.

The lavender lining of Gil's silver silk showed as he loosened the strings of his single-action harp.

"Don't his stockings set neatly?" a girl in the first row of the audience whispered to her mother.

Mrs. Sim returned, "Gilbert Worth is a marvel. You'd do well to settle for someone one tenth his like."

"Oh, mama, he is married then?"

"To that Watteau drape of pale blue with watercolor primroses. I have it from Gwynn Poore that she's worn it before . . . to an outdoor wedding!"

"Is he a miser with her?"

"What on earth . . . don't young girls know anything, anymore? There is a prince married to a Presbyterian."

Worth's strange piece began with a disclaimer from Doctor Stirling. "Doubt me if y'will, but I'm note perfect tonight. It's what's written is the trouble."

Following his lettered notation, his musicians gave aural shape to the American wilderness. Erratically pitched, designed according to no discernible scheme of related notes, the countertenor keened and the gun fired. The listeners were agitated to waking nightmare.

"Oh, he's a wit," men tittered. "Imagine such elegant humor living so brightly in Sweetwood."

Gil plucked quick breath out of the hearers, with his harp strings, taut now, sharing his New Year's Day with them, winding the coldness of the first passages with Qunneke's constancy of warmth.

"Naughty Gilbie!" Mrs. Sim clucked her tongue.

Gilbert kissed her hand at his rest.

The daughter breathed, "Maman!"

Women players surrounded him. "It was horrible!" The men asked, "Do you call it a string trio with voice, or a quarter of suffering cats?" But some, men and women, said, "Let us know theory."

Wakwa straddled the windowsill and maneuvered his long body back onto Crosswhite's porch.

Awepu reloaded the gun. "Wetomp, your boots are wet." He fired.

The shot woke Michael. "What do you say to some apricot ice?" He flexed his limbs and rose, tested himself in a walk to the window. "A good sign. A little nap and I am fit as fit."

Awepu left for the ladies.

"You smell of salt and horse and smoke, old fellow." Beckett breathed the air. "Where the hell have you been?"

"I was there." Wakwa leaned against the frame, pointing out a distant glow.

"There's nothing out there."

"There is a place at the wharf a cousin of mine knows."

"Why you old. . . ." Beckett hooked a hand familiarly over Wakwa's shoulder. "You are the sultan himself! I like you more and more. Took a little break away from this thrilling party to go down by ye olde wharf, eh? Anything good there? How long a ride is it? We could postpone the fruit ice. Take me."

"I much desired to do so. But you were drunk and asleep."

"Thanks for the thought. As sachims go, you would have made a good one."

"Sachimmauog."

"What's that?"

"More than one sachim are sachimmauog."

"As you wish. Anyway, you would have made a good one."

"I will make a good one, not would have."

"As you wish."

"It is not as I wish. It is as it is."

"You get pensive after a woman, eh? It suits you. Hell, if it helps you think, it's an all-around perfect experience."

"What helps you think, Michaelbeckett? Drink?"

"I get rather sharp."

"Then get you a drink and listen to me!"

After a hearing of the facts Beckett sat his chin in the palm of his hand. "How sly a fox are you? You have beaten the statutory law at its own game. But I do not see how anyone can beat out disgrace. You were seen by this Sid person with the accomplice of White Whatever. Doubtless the father's memory and affection will increase depending on the monetary loss he incurs. Of course, there is the stolen horse. A help to us. Let me work on that mess. My advice as your advocate is that you get the first ship to London and stay there. I am serious. Drop this sachim business. Disappear."

"Do you think I am a deer? That I should run at every sign of trouble? That advice is no help to me. What of the People?"

"You have done everything you can for them, Great Chief. I have in my pocket an iron-clad conveyance. They are protected from incursions as much as they ever can be. This is in the written record."

Wakwa strode away.

"I give you sound advice. Go to London. We'll fit you into the Department of Indian Affairs, the Board of Trade, some damn thing. You'll be useful, and married, married to a beautiful, if American, woman. Women. Take them both. You will be a dignitary and will get away with all sorts of extraordinary behavior."

"And the land?" Wakwa turned slowly on him.

"Oh, that. Hanna has the confidence of your folk. She

won't neglect her brother's farm. As a matter of fact, as long as we are all assembled, why don't I draw up a little thing about your having a second executor for Moses' estate. Avoid trouble in emergencies."

"You being the second executor?"

"I am the most obvious and best qualified person for that job."

"I see what has happened in Massachusetts, Michael-beckett. Holy men like Hudson no longer have their hooks in the land. It leaks like milk into the stomachs of the lawyers."

"Like milk with the kick of whiskey. You've come apace in a week. The land has got to go to somebody, and as much as I like the cloth Gilbert Worth is cut from, I must say that his semen runs thin as gin. He has no real claim."

"Do never injure Gilbert Worth. Every man of my tribe will swarm over you and your sons like bees."

"Fiddlesticks!" Beckett rose as the music stopped and the musicians surrounded Gil. "See how I am influenced by these highly cultured people?" Beckett dusted Wakwa's suit with his handkerchief and straightened his stock like a valet. "You have got a bow coming, Lord High Sachim. Stick by me. Together we will go receive the applause of two hundred highborn people who make your alibi." Beckett forced the Jaeger into Wakwa's hands. "Be sure to tell Gilbert, out there, what inventive flimflam that was he played."

"Everything is becoming lies."

"Lying is best done by honest men."

_____ **Chapter 42**

SONGS OF THE BEES lulled Massachusetts into satisfied contemplation of its own July. Afternoon fog chased itself through columns of sunlight, in the curls of land that fringed Buzzards Bay. Natural vineyards trellised the paths of the varied, sloping woodland. Wild grapes hung preternaturally from unrelated branches, vines of white or purple fruit winding maples, and birch, and elm. Sweet little pears, and a palette of apples from pink to bronze, soft to rock hard, all juicy, dizzied the picker with comfortable alternatives. Blueberries were ready. Roses were now fully opened, and their cousins, the raspberries, their clusters of red tears formed around their own ovaries, stained the skin of the gatherer who pulled them too slowly from their hulls. Wild cucumber brought green to the reflective waterways. Their fresh leaves stood straight out of the streams, showing off their ruby earrings to the fish that swam at their roots. And the bees supplied a canto of optimism to the warm world.

The bees had been introduced to the region by English farmers only a century before to pollinate the plantation. They had become more vociferous than the native birds or hard-shelled insects that had flown the Massachusetts forest since the origin of summer.

The honey makers knew a pleasant agitation. Like alchemists approaching the secret of rendering gold from dross, they buzzed about their work over the blossoms. They ate of their surplus supplies, packing their bodies with the elixir of May as a human would pack clothes for a journey. They ate honey. They declared out loud their abandonment of security, to chance their fate to unknown spaces, to transport their queen to an alien domain, to command the air, and sun, and flowers. To swarm.

Gil's face was upturned to the sun. He was transfigured by colored light. In the crystal palace for the plants, he was sealed from July's kind elements. He stood dead center in the Archimedian circle he had constructed by his force of will. "Icosadodecahedron." He hummed the structure's name to it.

Iron struts, precise of joint, made of hubs of many, many polygons. These polygons made the bones, the skeleton of the hemisphere. Great circular grids imitative of longpoles cut the convex solid into halves, and lesser iron grids added strength though they did not bisect the sphere. Geometry, faith in roundness, much sweat and smiling had created a net of iron that would counter exterior forces. Like women at knotting, Gil, Wakwa, and the Stirlings patterned their model with stable triangles, which poked into pentagons over the surface of the dome. It was a sturdy lacework fitted with glass.

But Worth had not wanted to fashion a void, a house without post or beam, a glass cage, all white glare and heat, to incubate his citrus trees. He chose to have the glass beveled at the edges, and when the sun's angle swung, the greenhouse was painted by light, shooting through thousands of prisms. This refinement of his extravagance tinctured him. Gil stood hatless in the house of growth, drenched in pure colors, caressed by shining shapes of sun rays, as a fish is touched by water gliding against it in a stream.

Poquahock and sukkissuog, the cherrystone clams and the longnecks, lined the beach in baskets waiting for the bake. While women and girls raked the seaweed off the tided sand and heaped it, slick, and salty, and green, to dry in the sun, men and boys practiced for the games with feathery light footballs they had made from deerhide and hair.

Wakwa walked the island with his wives. Stephen Poore came slowly behind, exercising his pencil across pages of a blank book. Sun heated the talc-fine sand, turned its beige to white, made it as painfully reflective as the vellum. Poore let his spectacles drop on their ribbon, and wiped away tears induced by light. He squinted to see. Qunneke toiled back over the sand to claim him from myopia. She brought him under ledges of gull-crowned rock to a shady, freshwater pool.

Wakwa and Elizabeth chose the western point of the humpbacked island, beyond the white drumlins that made its spine. Wakwa stretched out on the beach, stripped, willing to be burnt. Heat from beneath and above him began to penetrate his bones, which were cold from awful secrets. Elizabeth lay under his arm, shrouded in white gauze, protection from the beating sun, listening. Through the shouting of the herring gulls that circled above them, she heard the man start to sleep. And she was up. She built a lean-to of driftwood and tall, tough grass to protect her husband, her negligee hindering her, filling with wind, tattering as she worked. She buried his feet in the sand because the thatch roof did not extend over his whole length. Then she left him, before the sea mist could steam up the inlet and turn swimming into suicide.

She floated free. She was washed back onto the beach. She followed the rifting sea, again. She was caught in the stroke of a strong swimmer. Wakwa brought her to the foamy bed of sand that rimmed the rocks, and they began a strange delight. He had not shared his unspeakable troubles with her. The man and woman were clean of each other. Hollow as old wood, their bodies rang with exquisite, lonely tones as they drifted together by fortune of the sea. He came into her as worried with life as the water that rushed the beach. Like sand, she was momentarily quenched by his cares.

The tide receded, but they remained on the wet slip, stiff from sun and silver from salt.

# Chapter 43

"WHEN THE BEES ARE DAFT, like this, Mistress Prue, you can spoon 'em into a pail as easily as skimming butter off a chowder." Winke drilled Prudence Hanson in the method of collecting the honey. "You wear your . . . ?"

"Hat," Prue said by rote.

"Yes, and wet . . . ?"

"My hands."

"And . . . ?"

"And wash my feet before I stand in the house of the Lord."

"Dear, dear! Are you sure, Miss, that you can do this?"

"You did it."

Winke labored to keep back a retort. "Wet your hands, and immerse your arms in cold water."

"Up to here."

"Aye, to there. See you do, Mistress Prue, for though the bees seem calm, and clouds of them may settle on you like cherry blossom petals that blow in the spring, there's no need to risk a sting if you do not have to. And grab the wood bar firmly as you pull it from the basket so you can scrape off the wax works cleanly into the pails. Look here!" Winke held out a glass jar for Prue's inspection. "That's a chunk of comb sealed tight by the bees. If you mash the combs with the spoon the honey'll waste, for people will not buy honey with little bits o' wax sticking in it. And don't take all day with these buckets. Be back for more. I'm too busy to help you with this business. I've got the new minister, Low, and his bride due here, and I'm only one person. And if you malinger, Mistress, the mood at the hives might change if you think you can

rob them day after day and go scot-free." Winke looked
into the small-eyed face turned up to her. Prue's hair blew
across her forehead and strands caught in her lashes. Yet
she made no motion to rid her eyes of annoyance. "Are
you sure you can do this, Mistress Hanson? We could
wait and see if the bees'll fly away altogether as they
sometimes do. But that's no good, as I've seen they leave
some of their numbers behind, and tight and fresh, and
nasty are the young ones. Be off! I've work to do. Mistress
Low keeps a spaniel." Winke made a look of disgust. "I'm
going to put a basin of water and a clean cloth in a corner
of every room lest I run crazy from wiping up after
its. . . ."

"Cherry blossom petals that blow in the spring." Prue
wove away from the kitchen door, clacking out a tune with
the clusters of buckets that hung in her hands.

"Crazy." Winke looked after the shrunken figure of the
girl she had hoped to match with Annanias Hudson. "A
hat!" The widow pulled Gilbert Worth's French straw
from the kitchen hook where he had forgotten it at the
end of May. She caught up with the skipping young woman and tucked Prue's untended hair into the rounded
crown, and tied the black sash under her chin. "Use it,
Prudence!"

Since her return from Boston, Prue would wander the
neighborhood lanes and sometimes lose her way. Farmers'
wives, former friends, would lead her away from fascinated
study of calves sucking out milk from the full udders of
the cows, back to Nathan Hanson's door. But this day she
was successful in finding the sloping field where the bee
baskets were nestled. She put one bucket between each
two baskets and removed the hat to let the sun at her head.
She batted genial bees with her freed hands and swung
down the hill toward the dark, natural pool to wet her
arms. She passed Charles Dowland's smokehouse. It was
the most famous building of the famous farm, drawing
admirers, students of agriculture, from points as far away
as Virginia. Prue placed a hand on the rough wood of its
door and passed from the blinding brightness into the
dark, dry cool of perfect memory. The interior was hardly passable for the carcasses which hung down. Flitches
of bacon and sides of beef decorated hooks as thick as her

middle finger. The white fat and bones, and pristine floor, were sumptuous as they had been when she used to lie face up under the festoon of flesh. She did then. Put her back to the planks of pegged wood. But instead of smiles, a tear started in each one of her gray eyes. She recalled having seen a man's glowing face and not the drying meat as she used to look up. She ached, trying to remember why that man was not there anymore.

Prue toyed resentfully with the cold water of the spring-fed pool. The affrontery of this high-standing building presenting her with mysteries, plaguing her with puzzles she could not solve, brought on a tantrum. She refused to dip her warm arms in the frigid water just for the honey-taking. She folded her arms against her instead, showing her back to the silent house that was crammed with meat, and stamped her foot on the grass. The hot green blades hissed. Prue threw herself down on the slant and dug into the sod with a snaking tongue. She tunneled it into the soil, helped by her saliva until she gagged. Her tongue drew back and painted the roof of her mouth with the rich red loam as she swallowed. "Honey!" she cried.

Prue ran up, among the vacationing bees. Their insect song flared into the sun. Though she had never danced, Prue lifted her arms and let herself intend toward their delirious hum. She taught herself the rhythm of the swarm, letting her body move to the voices of bees on the verge of travel. She swayed in a reel among the baskets, partner to the ecstatic insects. Contingents of them floated about her shoulders like shadowy regalia, dipping, rising, swirling and swinging like a living mail, or epaulets establishing rank. If she stopped moving, they responded like drooping garb. Some of the insects alighted on her. Prue gurgled, tickled by their delicate touch. She cupped her hands, and clots of bees fell into the shallow spheres like soft fruit into a bowl. Prudence brought a palmful level with her eyes. For the first time she acquainted herself with the details of their form and color. An admirer of yellow, she was entranced by their buttery furze. She flung them to the broad azure, admiring the loyalty of the sisterhood which rose to follow the virgin bees she had scattered.

Sun laziness swept her. Prue Hanson sat and then lay on the Dowland turf, putting her awkwardly mended nose in line with the sun rays, as if sniffing out the secrets of light which had liberated the bees.

Bees came to roost on her. A peaceful throng blanketed her breast, rising and falling as she neared sleep. Prue turned onto her belly and some of the bees died beneath her. It caused no stir. Others swooped onto her back, obliging her need for a sun shield.

Prue craved rest. The bees craved company. A noisy clique of them walked the back of her hand in their loitering while the scouts found them a new and prosperous harbor. Prue flicked them away. The bees did not go. "Get!" She blew at them. They remained. Prue opened annoyed eyes to examine the insect knob. A large bee rested at its center. The exaggerated abdomen, the lavish yellow body, the dainty head presented no special threat or honor to the ignorant hand which was its stage. Prue did not recognize the marks of a queen. "Shoo!" The noble female chose to stay. "How's that, my pretty?" Prue took the languorous queen between her thumb and forefinger and squeezed the juice of life out of her.

Prue drew a first long breath in sleep, oblivious to her murder of all the future children of this migrant race. But some message passed from insect mind to insect mind. Ugly buzzing began over genocide. The cotillion converted into a horde. Stings that were to have remained disused on this unique day emerged poisoned. Bees already trapped in Prue's frightening net of yellow-brown hair dug them in. The terrible intelligence of the end of the tribe was received and then exuded from them. The doomed bees wreaked destruction.

Prue was driven screaming to her knees by a disgusting pressure from live matter. The burning thrust of the stings of many thousands of bees hit her like hail. Prue dragged some of them out of her flesh with stiff fingers, cursing at the feel of them. While she freed her face, her scalp was riddled for its blood; while she rolled to kill the bees lacerating her head, bands of them braceleted her arms and eked vengeance though it meant their deaths. Prue gave life up with them. At last she obeyed the fierce commands of nature whom she had offended all her life in great and petty ways. Prudence Hanson roasted in the sun all afternoon like beef, and swelled like leavened bread.

Matthew Freeman carted the Lows' trunks to Dowland House and went down the meadow at Winke's bidding to check on tardy Prue. Dolly's little spaniel tumbled over himself as he tried to match Matthew's long strides. Matthew saw only empty buckets neatly placed between the rows of baskets. But the dog smelled death and yapped all the way to the smokehouse where Prue had careened in her agony. Following, the houseman paused to pick Gil's handsome hat from among the fairy clocks. He grew solemn and his shoes began to stick against the black bodies of dead bees. He came to Prue's body and used the hat to cover her stung face which belonged now to the monsters.

"So close to the pond, she might have helped herself if she had only thought." Matthew tucked the trembling pet under his arm. He longed to confide the accident to his honored friend, the man who held his contract so gently. But Matthew took his own advice. Standing deep in dead bees, he thought. The freedman turned resolutely toward Winke and the Selectmen of the village, to protect Gilbert Worth from association with this malignant death.

"Whitened sepulcher," Gil whispered to Hanna about Hudson in their usually vacant pew. It was the second one, directly behind the foremost, the Dowland pew, which was paid generations into the future, and was occupied by the strong spirits of the Dowland dead.

Hanna leaned her shoulder into her husband's to silence him until the mourners could pass from the church to the graveyard.

Mayhew Low had withheld from beginning his ministry with a eulogy over a woman he did not know. He had not been in Sweetwood a day when she was found dead. He thought any words of his would be small comfort to the parents of Prudence Hanson and pressed on Annanias the most difficult duty of his long tenure. And Annanias could not refuse. He burned his light late at night, working on the ode, needing to win back his contract or to exit the town in glory. He spoke so well, eloquent in ethics and emotion, that the Elders were unable to remember why

303

all the expense and fuss of replacing him. They shook his hand as Prue's coffin was carried past their black stockings.

Gil's hand clenched and unclenched. Hanna took it and stroked it. When they had the church to themselves she confided, "Dolly Low has troubles with Winke, already. She has spent the last few days up in Mary's room sheltering from Winke's tidiness. And the dog cringes at her petticoat."

Gilbert laughed out loud.

"Dolly has an idea that Winke should go down to the manse as Winke is thick with Hudson and very grumpy with Mayhew."

"Dorothy Low will survive well in this atmosphere. That is a damned good idea. That way, when Hudson goes we'll be rid of Winke as well, and at no expense to me."

Hanna weighted the soundness of the plan. "Annanias' housekeeper kept dogs for him, great vicious ones. So she shouldn't mind little Poppy."

"Sweep one maid down the hill, and one maid up? Very neat. And I like Millie. She needs a rest from the Reverend Bombast. But I had a thought that we should send Winke to Maine in the dead of the next winter because Dire Locke is trying to rid himself of Jeanette-coquette."

"That is harsh, my love."

"Locke's discarding Jeanette?"

"Harsh on Thomas Kirke. I wouldn't wish Winke on anyone."

They slouched in the straight-backed wooden seat, happy sharing their naughtiness.

"I have a letter from Michael."

Gil cocked a blond brow. "Written proposal?"

"Dear, this was business."

"That is Michael's business."

"Gilbert!"

"Then why didn't he write a letter to me? I pay him."

"He knows you get preoccupied and needs some information right away."

"I have a secretary. He is so willing to push you into any role except that of mistress of my house."

"I will not argue it with you. And secretaries were the business of his letter. Neither Festus nor Weeping Heart can write. And poor Patty, according to her father, could do only numbers, though she read a little. His question is who wrote the note that brought Wakwa from Mr. Crosswhite's to Patty's Feather. And does Wakwa have the note to bring into evidence. Michael thinks the note was written by Annanias Hudson."

"Incredible."

"It is brilliant. Annanias was not in Sweetwood at that time."

"Bungler."

"Michael is not!"

"Well, why didn't he ask Wakwa for the note in June? I don't suppose the sachim keeps a file. It is most certainly lost now."

"He had not this idea then."

Gil turned to her and sadly shook his head. "Hanna, it is his job to have such ideas at the proper juncture. I cannot think of everything. Michael's victory in the conveyance shines convincingly now. But Wakwa is on the verge of making a clean breast of the tavern affair to the authorities so that he can sleep nights. Yet Michael says forbear. Tell you friend Michael Beckett he had better be right, for I see the strain of all these secrets telling on Wakwa and Elizabeth."

Hanna looked toward the altar, seeing more clearly the strain between herself and Gil. "Tell him yourself, dear. He is coming to us with Ho. The baby, poor lamb, was left alone, and dirty, and unfed for a whole day while Michael was out."

Gil was shocked into sympathy. "Why doesn't he fire the staff en masse?"

"Because, dear, they quit his service in a body and let this crime happen."

Worth's scandalized gasp disturbed the quiet air of the vacant church like stones that spread rings across water. "He ought to go to law."

"That would slow down our case. He says he hasn't the time. That is another good reason for our taking Ho."

The few, high windows showed the eastern sky paling at the southwest wind which warned of rain.

"What good will a few happy weeks do child Horace, Hanna?"

"Would you mind if it were for more than a few weeks?"

"Hanna?"

"You tolerate Moses in the house."

"Tolerate! I have bequeathed the place to him. I have canceled myself out for him. You might say that I worship the boy. . . . Hanna . . . we will raise Ho. Oh, my dear, foster him for long and you will never part with him. We will have adopted yet another orphan."

"Horace has a father, you forget."

"Not for a moment." Gil took her hand and they faced front, their gazes fastened on the panorama of the changing weather. "I think you had better consider if Ho's to have a mother."

"We were married in this church," she said, "and now we hardly come here. Gillie, are we sure that we are married if we do not believe what we used to when we took that vow?"

"You talk of form but the question is substance. I bed with a different woman every night, and always am vowing to cleave to her. I have had countless weddings to women who wear your body like bride-weed."

"How pretty!"

"Pretty, indeed." His lips entrapped hers.

She recovered from his kiss, haunted by the sexless sanctity of place. "What would you say to Madame Locke governessing Ho?"

"What an idea! Far surpassing Dolly's drab exchange." The building resounded with a single glad clap from Gil. Then his hands came to his face and he inclined forward, his knees down against the kneeling board. In delicate accents he proffered, "Take care for yourself. Michael is vulnerable just at this time, and Jeanette. . . ."

"Is dainty, dark, and deserted by Dire Locke?"

"Just so." Gil kept his suffering face covered from her view.

"Still, Jeanette will have the more difficult part for her employment."

"Ana, you are a very good woman."

The wife extended her arm and her hand soothed Gil's tense neck. "Being less generous than you, I do not feel good."

The townsmen passed by the great doors after watching Prue's coffin lowered into the burial place. They beheld the rarity of the Worths worshiping in public. "See their sorrow at such a thing happening on Brother Dowland's farm?" And the goodwives agreed among themselves. "Those two have had the hard lot, but I do not see that they should touch in the church."

Slivers of water broke out of the overcast. The caretaker came to lock the damp out. He fumbled at the doors, then cleared his throat, sensitive to directly disturbing prayer.

Gil was kneeling straight up, his face exposed to the rain light. "I prithee, my goddess, accompany me on a journey of the soul?"

"Where to journey?"

"To Nice, my Psyche, I am wanting one large-brimmed, blackbound, French straw hat."

"Sacrilege!" Hanna's breath inspired.

"Aye, it were that." The caretaker agreed to the only word of theirs that he heard, and he firmly closed the couple out.

_____ Chapter 44

ANNANIAS LOOKED DOWN into his front hall from the top of the staircase that led directly to his bedroom. "Those men are a sorry pair, Winke, certainly nothing to fear."

"Truly, Mr. Hudson," his new housekeeper declared, "this grows no better than working for the Worths. I'd never have let them in but one of them can't stand well, and the other said they are praying Indians. It's not my aim to interfere with your Church. Just know, I told them if they stole anything or broke anything with that crutch, I'd come after them myself with the broom."

Annanias hurried down. "William. Hephaestus." He

took a shoulder of each and propelled them into the privacy of his library.

"Fat priest," Wuttah Mauo greeted him.

"Not so fat!" Annanias sat at his writing table in front of a wall of books. "Sleeker these days than I have been for a while but surely not fat. We don't want to begin that way, do we? Now, my men, neither of you looks too well, nor too well-fed. I can give you a meal but do not ask for money for I am appreciably thinner in the purse than I am in my belly."

"Miserable holyman." Wuttah Mauo refused to sit though a chair was pointed out to him. "We are come to ask you for a higher thing than money. But we are Indian and know how to behave. Before we get, we give."

"I want nothing thank you. I returned the gelding to the smithy and am ever so obliged for the loan. You have done quite a bit for me, in your way. And I have kept my part with you. The receipt between us is paid. We are square."

"Shut up your mouth!" Weeping Heart jammed his hands into the loose pockets of his jacket.

White Cat shuffled past him and sat on the corner of Hudson's table. He shoved aside the array of quills and inks, sealing wax and paper.

"The legs won't stand it!" Annanias fussed.

White Cat sent a look his way and did not move off.

Wuttah Mauo primed his lips with his left hand. "What keep you to drink here?"

"In August, lemonade."

"What is that? Cheap stuff?"

"Not at all." Annanias scorned his addiction. "The chief ingredient is imported from Spain."

"Serve it up, then. Before I am through, you will want it, too."

Winke brought in a pitcher of the innocent drink. She stood with the tray, like a wooden thing, until White Cat vacated the table. She set the tray down, poured three glasses, offered one to Hudson, and left.

"Silent Fox is safe." Wuttah Mauo's face twisted up at the taste of the sweet stuff.

Hudson spat his on his black-coated front, caught between swallowing and speaking.

"He is a crafty beast. He has made friends out of a white forest of English people. Nothing touches him. Not your dead baby, not Patty. . . ."

"What would Patty have to do with . . . ?"

"Patty is dead."

"Great Lord." Hudson looked from one to the other of his visitors. His lower lip quivered out of control. "How was this?" His eyes followed Weeping Heart's glance to White Cat's crutch. "What stupid . . . !" Wrath clotted words.

"Not stupid." Wuttah Mauo took the crutch away from White Cat and swiveled the sharp, skinny stick between his palms. "The kid you made was in her arms to go to the constable. Festus saved your large wide ass."

Annanias's head bowed like a slave's at his continuing involvement.

"The fine people that my cousin knows, the gentlemen and ladies, the friends of Gilbert Worth, are footing the bill for new boards to rebuild the storehouse. And meanwhile, Sid is living off their money."

"Worth is silencing this?"

"Fat and stupid priest, his hands are clean of it! The story of the woman burned up in the storehouse was put all over your cursed newspapers. The rich ladies and gentlemen read of Sid's tragedy with tears in their eyes. And they took gold coins in their hands from out a huge pot of money made by their women who sewed their hearts out on Boston Common to pay Sid, the hosteler, for making his daughter a prostitute, and his storehouse a firetrap for bastard babes, and his Inn a shithole for Indians and English, together. If I had known that, I would have set fire to my father's house years ago, and put the story of it in the *Gazette*."

"How can such things happen!" Annanias raised his voice.

White Cat shook the Queen Anne table with both his hands gripping the edges.

"They happen," Wuttah Mauo shouted back, "because Silent Fox is protected. The fox wit sits always like a god."

"Protected by whom? By Gilbert Worth?"

"By Manit!" Wuttah Mauo screamed from Hudson's denseness. "Our great doer. A great spirit like your God.

For no bad thing will cross the path of this black fox who has married your woman."

"Do not say it!"

Wuttah Mauo began to turn the crutch tip against the rug like a carpenter driving a screw.

"Stop that! The rug you damage is not my property anymore. It is sold to Doctor and Mrs. Mayhew Low. Take care or you will answer for it before the circuit judge."

The elder son of Waban scoffed and threw the stick aside. "And what of damaging Silent Fox?"

Hudson worked his dislocated bands around to his coat front. "I am a Christian man. I am a preacher of the Light to the Elect of the Lord. I instill virtue into the souls in my care."

"Like Prudence Hanson. . . ."

"Keep off that!"

"And are you so good you will not put a stone in my cousin's path to stop him? What do you think, he is one of your Christians?"

"He is a thief!"

"Well, then, and what do the English do with thieves?"

Hudson calmed and cooled. "That depends on what they have stolen."

"He has taken your wife!"

Hudson shot out of his chair. "He has taken my land! My career! He has desecrated and scandalized a white woman and Christian, beside. How he was not hung on the spot by Lord Duhmmer, I will never know!"

Weeping Heart sagged and sat on the floor. "I need to drink."

"You disgust me."

"And not lemonade."

Something in the Indian's attitude, a private sorrowing, an actual pain, some disorder which gave his face a greenish pallor, made Annanias say, "For disinfectant I keep some gin about. Will that do?"

Weeping Heart waved a hand to make Hudson hurry.

Annanias went through his downstairs hall into the kitchen. Winke was already taking the bottle of gin from the shelf to have it ready for him. The minister and the matron stared at one another, appalled.

"What have you heard?"

"I am on your side, sir." The housekeeper took her chances.

"Winke, these are drunken men, nothing more. There is no truth to what they say. You will leave Sweetwood with me, shortly."

"When, sir?"

"Whenever you ride over and arrange two tickets on the Wareham coach to Philadelphia."

"I'll go now, sir."

"Do. Say anything to anyone and I will turn you over to the mercies of those two in the next room." He departed Winke with her mouth formed into a horrified *O*.

The gin steadied Wuttah Mauo like a translucent blood. Hudson buttoned up his coat, impatient to dismiss him.

"You have nothing to hit Silent Fox with, priest, unless I put a weapon in your hands. It is my gift to you, before I take anything. I give you better ammunition than powder and shot. Better than arrowheads carved by my own father. I am honoring you with the story of how Silent Fox spent his last winter. Keep pouring. Your gin is drinkable."

By the end of that glowering August afternoon, Annanias Hudson possessed the stuff of powerful allegation. Wakwa's first cousin delivered to the Sweetwood minister the names of all the men who had marched out of their villages and into French territory, and he made him write the name of each delegate down. In the political climate of Massachusetts, this information was thunder and lightning and flooding rain.

"Imbeciles," Annanias thought, "why do they explain all this to me? I simply have to drop this list of names in front of the magistrate." Aloud, he said, "Thank you, William, for your solicitousness. I am sure that I will find a way to bring these traitors to their duty under the Crown. The advantage of my office. . . ."

"My ass!" Wuttah Mauo capped the gin. "You can do nothing with these names without our plan, which we have not told you. Silent Fox has enough against you that you will go down with him, before him, and maybe without him, because there is no speaker like him, I do not care how many tongues you have in your head. And have you thought how to get the mistress of Silent Fox out? How will your stinking office do that, eh? My cousin is no vagrant in a ditch. He is more important than you. Do not think to snap your fat fingers and see the king's soldiers march into the summer camp and pick and choose who are your friends and who are not." Wuttah Mauo walked in front of the shelves and toppled the rows of books at his eye level. "It will take doing to make even the English cause a war over so good a friend of theirs as Wakwa Manunnappu."

"Who?"

"Do not mind. You could not say it anyway. Ask instead what is the price for this fortune of news I have placed in your lap."

"Well, state it, why don't you? If that is what is in the way of dispatching this robbing buck, Silent Fox."

With a little yell, Weeping Heart laid hold of him. "You cannot wait to fuck him! You great beast of a man. You English cattle bull of a fucking pigsuck of a man! How I wish I could feed Silent Fox to someone worthy of his sacrifice!" He gathered his spittle and hurled it from his tongue into Annanias's face.

Hudson surprised the Indian. He defended himself with efficient use of his elbows and his bulk. He toppled White Cat too, throwing Wuttah Mauo into him. Wiping his face with his handkerchief, Hudson accused, "I think that you want money. That you haven't any other plan than that. Well, I have no cash. I told you that when you got here. Let yourselves out the back door, now. I have correspondence to get to."

"He cannot wait," Weeping Heart mourned to his companion.

"Wait for what! Discussion of a plan is what we are about."

Agony of anger brought Weeping Heart's knee hard to Annanias's belly. The minister lay on his library floor gasping and thinking that their real plan was to murder him. Wuttah Mauo jumped astride Hudson's stomach. White Cat leaned his crutch between Hudson's shaking legs as high and hard as it could go without splitting his genitals open.

Weeping Heart pinned Hudson's wrists against the floor. "Fuck everyone, don't you. Everyone you get near. Everyone but smart Elizabeth. She ran far from you right into the arms of the great beating heart of my tribe. Because of you and this limp, fucking pecker of yours my own wife, my own life is destroyed!"

White Cat ground the crutch against Hudson's undefended parts and King Willie talked.

"You want to know what the price is for that, preacher? What is the price for tearing the heart out of everything you come near? You will carry us around in your pockets all your life. You will do nothing, you will not make a move without feeling us there, knowing we are there. And you will do this thing you want to do to Silent Fox the way that we say. There is no other way."

And Hudson's howl of grief filled hearing. Knuckle-bones, curled brown fingers, a long hard thumb invaded his mouth to stopper his calls of agony. A little liquid, the unlooked-for lemonade, gushed up from his stomach, and out from behind his teeth. He knew, remembered, struggled only for air. Thick as a steer in his thought, in his movement, he twisted away from the asphyxiating hand, and felt his knees against the cut wool of the rug. Even with White Cat still riding his legs, Annanias sucked and belched air in cattle's posture. Through the pain of refilling his lungs, he heard the dull scream of cloth ripping, and precious air palm his denuded buttocks. And the pitiful boots of the incensed Indians kicked the white skin of his posterior until it would bruise blue. Some knobbed, smooth-wrapped, unbending member pressed him, widened him, divided him, forced itself into the tight, exposed dark pit of him. The canal of his excrement became an obscene brain, hot with the fact of what was happening. The withdrawal of the fist gave him back to himself.

The two men who found they had attacked the kneeling Englishman in such a way squealed like revolted girls, and crawled as far from him as they could in the close, closed room. They tore their shirts off and wiped themselves, gagging at sight of the object of their lustless violence. They cried, inconsolable for their own imbruted state. Annanias wept with the voice of the unborn.

"In my condition, condition, condition . . . !"

Weeping Heart cried though he spoke. "Your condition

313

is that you are fucked, Annanias Holyman, we all are. Do you hear? Pull up your breeches! What are you? Are you proud not at all? Are you man not at all? What in hell are you?"

An answer was not expected. "I am a Christian preacher." Annanias struggled to his feet, streaming with sweat and tears, clasping at the waistband of his pants. "And a good one."

Wuttah Mauo trembled so that he had to lean on his crippled, filthy friend. "And that is why we have you in our hands. You will talk to the Namskeket, Half-Dog, the Nauset sachim. Explain to him the evil that Silent Fox is causing, selling out his tribe, with every breath, and every night he goes to bed. Half-Dog must be told that others besides him want Silent Fox to go. And Half-Dog will kill him."

"Thus, coldly?" Annanias limped to his chair, his jowls shaking.

"If an Indian does this thing, and he is in league with you and us, we will rule this region at his side when Silent Fox is stiff and dead, and his widow mourns in your arms." And Wuttah Mauo began to screech, his forearms covering his face. White Cat hobbled back to him with the gin, but the son of Waban kept on with the discordant cry of the owl and poured the clear spirits out, over his hair and his skin, anointing and bathing in the stinging alcohol, quivering at the vision of his father's bright, clear eyes, unblinking at misfortune. He washed in those liquefied eyes of memory, rubbing his skin with gin until his screaming stopped under the purge of that unencouraging stare.

Annanias was saying, " 'Hark! Someone is shouting in the desert, get the Lord's way ready! Make his paths straight. Every hollow must be filled up. And every mountain and hill leveled. What is crooked is to be made straight, and the rough roads are to be made smooth, and all mankind is to see how God can save!' "

"You tell Half-Dog that. Tell him that," Weeping Heart said. "He will do the right thing and you and us we will live in ease."

"Fool. Who is thinking of ease? If as you say the Fox is possessed, protected, I have got me a war with the Antichrist!"

When he had long been free of them, and Winke brought him his evening tea, Annanias put it to her. "Widow Winke, if a person were too ignorant to write, or let us say a farmer had some accident to his hands but could read, how could he correspond with a friend far away?"

"You are so delightful, Mr. Hudson. Always making me up puzzles." She tucked Hudson's napkin in for him, like a bib, and cut his meat, and jellied his muffins. "If it was me, sir, tell me if I have not solved it right, I would take the newssheet and some flour and water, and a manicuring shears and cut out the letters that I needed to make me my words, cut them out of the paper, and mix up a paste and fix the letters into what it was I wanted to say."

Annanias frowned.

"Have I missed it, sir?"

"Is the manicuring shears necessary?"

"Of course it's necessary. The print in the paper is small as a baby's tit."

"I do not have a manicuring shears."

Winke backed out of the room, wondering if her master were daft, since there was nothing whatever wrong with his hands. She thought more about this at ten that night when she watched him across the dark lawn, going gingerly with a torch, returning soaking wet, even his shoes, lavender blue to the tip of his nose. She was more comfortable that he slept on the settle downstairs.

# Chapter 45

GIFTED MEN, men who thought and spoke and dealt gracefully with people, were the ones the Ninnuock sought out for sachim. They lifted such men above them. They honored them not only for their elegance and eloquence, but also for their ability to follow the arts of woodland life. The things a sachim made with his hands identified the spirit of his reign. A paddle for a canoe created by such a man emerged as something more than functional. It was a unique beauty, carved, finished, and embellished in the manner of the sachim's soul. The People could touch and hold the true qualities of their steward.

When Wakwa had accomplished his primary chores, repairing rope and nets and arrows for the fall hunt, he resurrected his tools reserved for choice work. A curve of bone made his knife. He had a stone ax, and a polless iron trade ax. His awl was flint. His adze was a crescent of flint tied by hide to its handle. The objects he made out of wood took on a sheen from the caresses of stones and sand and oil. He was about making two gifts, one for each child, to celebrate the anniversaries of their births. He sat in the clearing in front of the big wooden hunting house, over the river, looking at a stump of birch wood, trying to devise the way to carve interlocking rings out of it for a toy for Moses. The partially carved paddle for Sequan lay on the dirt, beside him. It was nunnowa, September, and the present for his daughter should have been ready to give the spring before. It changed Wakwa's face to think that he had not had time to sit and simply carve for a long, long time. His sway over the People had been a mobile swung away from them. He had walked and talked to keep them abreast of the tide of things, but he had not sat. His was the lot of a sachim in wartime, to be watchful, light in his sleep, faster than his opponents.

Out of his assortment of tools, Wakwa picked up the one he loved best, his obsidian knife. As he began to peel the birch bark away from the wood, gunfire ripped the morning stillness. A ball from a smoothbore bit out some of the muscle of his forearm. Wakwa was slow to understand what the streaming red was, or why his arm smoked and sang as if someone had put it on fire. He was whipped onto his back and his head struck the packed earth. He rolled onto his stomach to watch the trees which ringed his sunny place, shouting, "Down! Down!" to Awepu who ran to him, cursing.

Then sun of the following day rose on Wakwa walking east. A fastidious guard of thirty went in front of him and flanked him, fanned among the trees. Awepu walked fluidly near Wakwa's poulticed arm, making his body the shield for it. "Wakwa, what do you say, was it a poacher?"

Wakwa kept his peace. They walked on, hundreds of steps, then Wakwa said, "Awepu, even if it were not, I have gained by a bullet, a fine moment to pay my respects to the new minister, this new man among us, this Mayhew Low."

They were going to Gilbert's house not only to pass on unsettling news. They wanted the old doctor to pretty up the bandage. Wakwa wanted his appearance at the door of Dowland House, where Low was being guested, to be even more imposing than if he had been whole.

Mac made much of the oak leaves plastered to Wakwa's wound with fine-grained clay that had dried in place. "Why, laddie, I bet that'll draw pretty well. But why not clean this up and give another remedy a try, too? Israel! Run! Go to my room for wood betony. Ye see, laddie, betony'll heal the cut veins and even sinew and suck 'er clean at the same time." The Scot worked over the arm at the kitchen table, and wound it with pristine muslin strips. But the sling suspended around Wakwa's neck across his deerskins was damask out of the dining room linens.

Hanna kept to the corner stool, her head leaning against her arm straight up against the wall. Gil paced like an affronted tiger.

Mac said softly to the Indian so the Worths would not hear, "Should it happen, again, old Fox, apply some pressure steady on, steady on, till ye stop spurtin'. I can tell by the way ye look, the way ye are, you've lost too much blood."

Wakwa let a respectful hand fall against the physician's neck, a comrade in the notion that damage to his flesh was likely to be repeated.

In the afternoon, Wakwa admired the late Charles Dowland's wing chair, the stone mantel, the furnishings, with a more aloof eye than he had at his first tender-hearted acquaintanceship with the place of Elizabeth's birth. There was so much permanence in these alien objects, though the faces that passed among them were strangers and new. And the objects served. Wakwa's body went cold.

But Low was so serious, so pale, so candid of feature and compact of stature, so white and gold and refined that the sachim was very tolerant of his jittery hospitality. Low called him "Governor," but kept him standing. When he saw open interchange with the Massachusetts man was easy, guided by elaborate courtesies, comfortable, he had Wakwa sit. Then Dorothy came in politely, bearing a headful of straw-colored curls, and shy smiles, and Low blandly forgot to introduce her. Dolly Low had the sense to offer the visitor tea.

Wakwa's voice warmed the farthest reaches of the room leaving Low spellbound. But on reflection, Low perceived that the disarming voice pronounced nothing that was not a direct, stringent demand. "So, Mayhew Low, the silence of the Ninnuock ends by my coming here. There are things to be corrected—black seeds your past minister planted in the minds of your village folk years ago, which must come to maturity and sprout poison fruit. There were false words about the way of our worship, about our feast at the-fall-of-the-leaf, about the Nickommosachimmiawene, the games and dances of the winter, and our summer prayer which we make out in the open under the trees. I invite you to all of these." Wakwa held his injured arm away from its sling for a moment, and then rested it.

Mayhew demurred at the invitation to strange rites. Dorothy insisted that he and she would be honored to go. And she was not shaken as her husband was when the spaniel fell to sleep across the soft moccasins of the dignitary from the wood.

"It is up to you only, Mayhew Low, to stop careless entry into our grounds, children playing hunter with their father's guns, poachers after our game, bounty hunters after our hair. All mischief makers must be kept off by you. The Selectmen of Sweetwood have a blind spot for these matters unless they have Englishmen policing our woods. That I will not allow. All our happiness is in your hands, Mayhew Low."

"Please, Sagamore," Dolly said as Wakwa rose to go, "remember me to your wife. I am a happy guest in the house where she was raised. There is not a space that is not beautified by her hand."

"Your thought of her will do my wife more good than any present I could bring her from the town."

Dolly looked up at his beardless face. She worked at a sentence of invitation to the true daughter of the house, but could not string a proper sentiment together for such a singular coming home.

Wakwa spoke first. "Littlewoman, if your dog should sire pups someday I should like to have one for my Elizabeth."

Dolly beamed.

He smiled. "And I shall give you a wolfling in its place."

This new ally of Silent Fox watched him down the lane with a palpitating heart.

When the farms were in the throes of harvest, Wakwa was shot again. He heard a resonant vibration, the melody most pertinent to the hunter, the singing of a bowstring as its arrow flew. He dropped the slipknot he was tying for a deer trap, and strained toward the sound of the unseen bow like a stag alert. The point and tearing flare of a flint arrowhead opened a course through his neck, pushing nerves aside on its escape, dissatisfied to implant anywhere but in his heart.

Wakwa fell with shock. He felt the wallop of the earth as he met it, and across the sightless light that flooded his brain, he heard feet pounding away. Then he gave up blood. His men were aghast at his plaint of terror and the rich red sloughing from his cored neck.

His guard, Mosq, had not been inattentive. He lived in a state of discreet, extenuated siege. He had heard the departure of the arrow from the alien bow too, and dived for the sachim, affecting the angle at which the arrow cut its hole.

Massachuseuck men descended on the spot. Awepu did not let them linger. He led a determined, silent mob out of the thicket, odd-looking in the emergency, like deer without fear.

Mosq's hands were wet, slippery purple as he fingered the arrow shaft, trying to break off the stone head and pull it out.

Wakwa held the arrow in for a painful plug. "Press, press, Mac said press!" He screamed because he could not hear himself make sound, but his scream was loud.

Mosq pushed against the arrow with both his palms, squeezing the severed veins together; his fingers wrapped the hideous holes front and back still filled by the arrow.

Men ran the deer path to Worth Farm, calling and hooting as they poured out of the woods and across the north meadow. The doctor was halfway to the barn for a horse by the time the young, frightened Indians gave him Wakwa's state. Mac yelled at them, "Blankets! Get a fire going! No movin' him!" The old Scot raced them the three unmarked miles down the sun-spattered trail.

Wakwa's eyes registered the image of Gil's cleanly shaved face close to his. He saw Israel Stirling kneeling at a little fire, warming water and poking at a block of salt. He felt Doctor Mac's hands, ministering from behind him, at his head. "This will not happen again!" Bound tighter than an Indian infant, he could not move his arms or his hands under the blanket. Instead, he took hold of the men with his English words and his oaths in his dialect.

Gil swore, too. "Damned right! You are going to hole up in my house until I get this son of a bitch."

Wakwa smiled. "Not you, Gilbert. This son of a bitch is an Indian."

"How are you so sure?" Worth bloodied his neckstock on the red-soaked banket, leaning close to hear the proof.

The physician quietly sawed away at the arrow shaft

with a carpenter's file to sever the flint head. Mac smoothed the raw, decapitated end with the fine-scaled steel, like a master silversmith. He blew away bits of wood dust and splinters that could catch inside the neck when he drew the arrow out.

Wakwa smiled at Gil through these aggravations of his wound, and tried to say an answer. A sad sound passed out.

Mac doused the headless arrow with whiskey, soaking the broken fibers of the wood to burn the filth out of them. He turned the bottle on the hole in Wakwa's neck and pulled hard and fast on the shaft, in the same instant.

For Wakwa only black was there. He lay in a nether state while Mac clamped a cloth-covered palm against the new flood of blood.

Gil made demands. "He must be gotten out of this target field! How do we do it?"

Mac said to Israel, "Sterno-cleido-mastoid," and to Gil, "Canno'."

"Cannot? What are you talking about? He's got to be moved out of here. He'll freeze or be shot again."

"Sterno-cleido-mastoid." Israel committed the name of the great neck muscle to memory, and took his father's place, taking a turn at holding back the massing blood with his hand.

The elder doctor sat back among the weeds, sighing in exhaustion and impatience. "Do you know how close that arrow came to his windpipe? He'll stay here until the bleedin' stops. Do ye want him paralyzed forever? He needs a dry wound and his strength back more than he needs a feather bed. Bonnie!" The Scot stood up and hurried his round body to meet the frantic wife. Waban and Pequawus gave up her sides as Mac took her. "Just the person I've been wantin' to see. I count on you to keep the big feller off his feet. Aw, now!" Doctor Mac brought her to his patient, in the bond of his arms.

It took fully thirty minutes of strong pressing, pulling back, testing, and pressing again, to reduce and quell the blood.

Wakwa heard their voices before he could raise his eyelids.

"There's goin' to be infection in a hole like that. Now,

you two, Israel, Bonnie, when I'm not about, ye keep a hot compress there and irrigate the wound like a ditch. It's a thing I'm tryin', salt water, warm, gently poured on the openin' to draw it. Sailors have known it for an age."

"How long?" Wakwa said.

The doctor whirled around and bent to him. "Hello. You're all cleaned up. A snip here, a scrape there. How long what?"

"To lie here."

Elizabeth came in front of the doctor to show Wakwa that she was there. He looked through her to the Scot. Mac held her, patting her hurt away, though she tried to escape.

"Two weeks on your back, laddie."

"Two days." The firm chin trembled. Wakwa closed his eyes for finality.

"Give it a dozen, why not?" Mac haggled.

"Seven only!" The tall, strong man was bled white, but he would not yield, or remember or groan.

Mac turned to the wife. "Don't expect him up and on his feet for three weeks. Fever'll drive him mad. If he doesn't swell too much, he'll talk and say the damnedest things. So pay him no mind. Tell me the instant that he canno' move his head." Like ants, men from the otan circled around to build a shelter over their leader. Elizabeth was left to strip bark off birches and fix it to the frame. Gil ached to help but did not offer after the warning from her eyes.

Waban and Pequawus left the scene of desecration. The old sachim searched his mind for who to blame, his brother-in-law went to reassure Qunneke. The pregnant first wife was kept well away from the wounding place. Days later Awepu returned empty-handed of the assassin.

Pooling of old blood turned Wakwa's shot flesh black. Grim and mysterious, the wound festered like thought did in the impatient, fevered brain of the man. The neck swelled obscenely. Over the week the trachea was pinched for room and got nudged out of alignment. The interference with his breathing held him paralyzed. Wakwa stared rigidly at the recollection of the assault.

Elizabeth clung to the work. She counted the times that

Wakwa had pulled her from the range of death and was given the strength to lift his body to help him to function cleanly or to organize the supplies sent from the otan, or to feed him, or to witness the grotesque shape of his neck and his suffering. She took the milk from Moses' goat to make a nourishing custard with wheat flour that could glide down Wakwa's tortured throat easily. His empty bowl was her source of joy. The day Israel replaced an old bandage with a fresh one, and showed her a stain of pale lymph and not blood, she laughed and sang.

As the morbid became outbalanced by health, Wakwa's sense sharpened. His suffering changed from the physical to a worming sorrow.

He came to himself, looking from tired eyes at an Englishwoman, a wife of his, he was quite sure, working over him, massaging his legs with oil to keep them supple and ready to run.

Elizabeth felt his hand come to rest on her hair. She looked up his body from under the waving mane neglected while she had cared for him. "O! Ohhh!" The intentional touch ended the doubt of her vigil. She elongated herself along his side and lay with him. She hid her face against his ribs, afraid to see in his eyes what he might have kenned from the climbs of disease.

"It is gone." Wakwa spoke in a weak-timbred voice.

"Aye, I can tell that it is." She looked at him and her worn face turned lovely with her smile.

Wakwa closed his eyes, unable to bear the light of her relief. She misunderstood him anyway. He shook his head from side to side on his blanket cushion.

"Freely, you move!"

He regarded her again, his glittering eyes fatherly in their indulgence. "It is gone. The blessing of Manit is gone. Musquantam Manit! What have I done that he be angry with me?"

Elizabeth wiped away the two thin lines of tears that overflowed his eyes. "Why do you say He is angry with you? If He is angry with anyone it is with the person who did this to you. . . ." Elizabeth passed over this in a hurry, sorry to touch on the burden her love for him had added to his life. "I am angry at the devil who hurt you for showing me you are mortal man. Mortal you are, but nonetheless, godly." She sat up sprightly as her young age and held his limp hand against her mouth. "Manittowomp!"

He took in a full breath at her act of faith, and air expanded his lungs as noisily as water filling dry ground. "How long? How long have I been dying?"

"You have been recovering, nine . . . no ten . . . no nine days. I am glad to be alone with you as you wake. There have been crowds of people here taking a hand in your cure. Uncle Gil has, at last, gone to sleep at home. Hanna they would not allow in, but you have been getting well from decoctions of her making. I have bathed you in yarrow for days. Soon I must bathe myself in anything!"

Wakwa passed a hand over his eyes to close out the picture of his helplessness that had been so well witnessed. "And my uncle? Waban? Hath he watched over me?"

"He has been here many, many times, very caring. . . ."

"No!"

"Wakwa, be happy. You are. coming well. Qunneke keeps Doctor Mac in our house. All are helping all, and that is as it should be."

"You do not see." Wakwa looked toward the sky but found only the dark dome of the hut. "A man did this to me. Did this thing to me. To me."

Elizabeth sat near Wakwa, clean, combing her wet, washed hair smelling of rosemary. She took her small glass from her lap and brought it to the man for him to see his own progress. She unveiled the closing wound and explained the stages of his healing. Wakwa saw exposed a raw, outstanding patch of himself, vulnerable, but clean and red. The new meat of him.

"Doctor Mac calls this that you see 'proud flesh.' "

"Proud." Wakwa turned it to the glass, examining the condition of his neck with short smiles, and a turning down of his mouth, and small bursts of vocal irony. "So, I am a brave man like other brave ones I have seen with battle scars. The battle is done, and yet I do not recognize the war." He appealed to her.

A numbness came into the thin bones of her hands. A pain began to climb her wrists and arms. She felt blame though he had dealt none. She retreated from him and breathed a long gasp out in the sun. The stupidity of conflict moved her to fury. "There is nothing," she declared into the crackling September breeze, "so wonderful as the curative power of the sun." And she tore at the walls and roof of the low hut, exposing Wakwa to rectangles of blue air and yellow light. She opened as much view of the sky as she could without risking him to a chill, and Wakwa seemed bettered by it.

The healing skin went yellow and green. Stirling and his son exulted. Buzzards caught wind of health and departed for the Bay.

On the thirteenth night, Wakwa pushed himself up. He brought his legs underneath him daintily as a maid. Then, favoring his sore left side, he squatted. He welcomed sweat.

"What are you doing?" Elizabeth stirred and found him out. "Lie down!"

He straightened his back and rose up like a growing thing, pushing on the muscles and tendons in his legs.

Elizabeth crawled over in the darkness, clasping him around his hips, her face against his thighs. He swayed but did not fall.

"One thing I am glad of." Wakwa felt her face turn up. "That this clumsy killer does not shoot below my waist." His hands capped her head and he lowered himself to her as at last she broke into tears. "Kayaskwa, tomorrow I go to pesuponk, and after that. . . ."

"For a swim, I suppose. Lie back. Don't you dare undo my work of two weeks."

"Do not undo that work yourself!" He scolded her in return, and reclined with aid. "It is much down." His good hand lightly felt the bandage. "Not too difficult to look at?"

She resettled him. "No, dearest, I see no swelling at all, though you may feel it. The skin is coming. But you must stay still or open up again."

He was peculiarly quiet.

Elizabeth left him for her own mat.

"Stay?"

"And if I move against you in my sleep? I will give you pain." The weak glow from their burnt-out fire showed his outline, his right arm slanted across his face hiding his distress. "Are you angry?" Her tears bloomed again.

"How I am angry!"

"But it makes no sense for me to tear you! If you are cold I can get you more blankets, but I was told not to keep a fire at night because of the sign of the smoke. There is only so much the guards can promise in the dark."

"Woman, I am not angered by you, it is, it is. . . ."

She came next to him, housed in her blanket like a snail. "It is what?"

"How a small thing like you has borne such heavy burdens these many days, I do not know." The arm of his wounded side came heavily onto her back. "Art very tired?"

"Would you like to eat? To drink?"

"Ah! Yes!" He turned his face away vehemently.

"Well then, I will get it you." She lay exhausted.

Wakwa longed for Qunneke then, stymied by this female. That she could not hear his meaning in his tone, which surrounded the inflexible words of her alien tongue, built into unreasoning annoyance. He covered his face with both hands, closing the Englishwoman out of his sight.

Elizabeth dragged herself from him and rifled through a basket of supplies. "From my aunt, some shortbread and a conserve out of white roses?"

"Put it away!" The loudness of his cry hurt him as it hurt her.

Stung, Elizabeth took comfort against a longpole. "Have you fever again? From the getting up?"

Assuming a face of quiet, a cry surfaced from inside the man, who mourned his untended need for quintessential care.

Elizabeth came back. She buried her face against his belly, ignorant of how to salvage him. She found herself pushed from his stomach to his groin. His phallus marked the side of her face with his message. "But how?" she whispered.

The limbs of the distraught man went slack.

Untaught, she received the surfeit of passion which he had just abandoned. Her mouth circled his phallus, the organ which had habitually reinstilled her life, and by the sweet pressure she gave him there, she escorted him past the bleakness of his isolation.

And he did not move at all.

She lost herself in acquaintance with the part which was the sum of him in his troubled state. She bent away, recovering her breath, not knowing that she was smiling, victorious, feeling personally responsible for the reprieve of summer. She brought her face to his face, her person lit and limpid, suspended over his darkness of expression.

His hand guided her to place her lips on his, and he brushed the interior of her mouth with his tongue and the words, "You can!"

Grasping that meaning was to sear herself. Such pleasure as she had known had failed with him. She began a second effort, knowing it would be tragic for the first. By force of bitter determination to please she summoned the pungent and potent semen, conjured it with the muscles of her mouth, and the viscous essence of the sick man surged and spilled, and she tasted the flux of his soul's debility, and swallowed it, and swallowed it for him, and gasped with him at the sudden making of space for true health to unwind.

It was a proper purge, and it equalized their partnership. She was raised up by his discipline, and he followed her by his mastering.

Wakwa stood outside the hut the next morning like an ancient man, sacked of strength, but settled of understanding.

# Chapter 46

THE LEAVES were off. October tore them from the branches, unfleshing the forest to its bones. The evening sky, October's eye, showed the month's delight over its repast. It glowed fuchsine, and russet, and aquamarine.

He had completed the harvest accounts for the two farms, and Gilbert Worth sat in Charles Dowland's study looking north, with little Henry's painting books on his knees. He compared the representation to the real. The scene beyond the narrow window was linear barrenness, but Henry's watercolor trees danced like straight-spined taupowaws clothed in blood-red sheaths.

"Yours was not a fledgling talent," Gil said to Dowland's dead son. "Old Henry, the man looking through your astounding work and out this window is not the same Uncle Gil whom you knew. . . . Massachusetts leaves her mark on the men who dare to engage her glance. By the looks of these papers, old chap, you did that every day. I begin to think this mighty virgin of a place buried you, under your lands of perfect title." Gil looked out into the blueing afternoon, and back to the book, out and back, and then he did not take his eyes away from the jumping, painted regiment of sanguine trees. They gesticulated with shocks of color where the ordinary eye recorded deep darkness. "So, dear boy, I perceive she did not kill you, she accepted you, gave you her hand in marriage, and you cleave unto your wife, the surrounding Mama Earth. You left us for her, and your sister left us for the Indians, but there is your legacy, these ruddy charts of this spellbinding wood. I am delighted to be English and yet able to read them. Wakwa and Awepu think I'm not up to it, to go hunting and get back in one piece. But the poetic eye, yours, nephew, has mapped my route." Gil put aside the books for his gun. "I'll go like an Englishman, with this map in mind, a-hunting my tea, assassin stew may it be." He slammed the kitchen door going out. "Like an Englishman, a red-coated fool riding to hounds. Better! I'll be the hound."

Gil raised his voice in a walking tune, and waded through dry leaves with the noise of ten, warning and frighting and drawing his prey.

Gil whistled a reel as he clashed with the trees and the lingering, decrepit leaves fingering his face. Loudly, then louder yet, his mood burst into words. " 'What shall we do with a drunken sailor? Put 'im in the longboat 'n let 'im lay there! Way ho and up she rises early in the morning. . . .' " Gil's song flowered into a bright inlay of tunes that told stories by melody alone. He sang la la's accompanied by the wind, rattling by above. His heart and lungs beat, blew like bellows, as he tramped without thought of safety. He was warm doing this foot patrol of his north-forested ground where the fauna shivered. He did not know any length to time, passing it with song. The light split in two, day turning away, night advancing. The sky went wan, still enabling Gil to see for a good fifty paces about him, but beyond that, avenues of sight closed off from him like clams.

Gil barged through the bewitching evening, excited to his heart that his American nephew, Henry, the child artist, had painted with such fluency, the fearsome view of the forest out his father's window, and that he had the luck to find those works. Henry's brush revealed the measure to which that north ground was wild space, unfarmed, unhunted, uninhabited, the dangerous zone between differing peoples. It was a tangle of ignorance, a trap, and avoided. Elizabeth had lost herself in there. Persistent, she had passed through to peace on the other side.

The lair echoed from Gil. " 'Take this for my farewell and latest adieu, sing willow willow willow, write this on my tomb, that in love I was true. O willow willow willow shall be my garland. . . .' "

The smell of smoke ended his lay. His fingers set the

trigger of his Jaeger, and he nosed the barrel through a hedge. Punk was smoldering out, and bits of roast flesh strewed it where they had been spat. A mat and a blanket were unrolled at the foot of a tree. The panting of men behind Gil brought him around.

He tripped the hair trigger of his German rifle. The air exploded into noise and glare. The stench of burnt powder, the scream of the missile, the separation of the features of a shot face from its skull took up the moments from Gil's shot to the reload.

Half-cock the firelock, handle the cartridge, prime and shut the pan, place the patched ball, draw the rammer, ram the cartridge down the gun's throat, return the rammer. Eight seconds. He shot, took no aim but toward a scurrying in the dusk. So, there were two. Gil should have been nailed to the ground by a bullet or a bayonet. But the testy smoothbore of his second opponent issued the fatal click, not igniting. The gunman fled a hand-to-hand encounter with a man who owned such a surefire piece as the Jaeger. And it was reloaded.

Luring Worth onto denser and darker ground became the strategy of the second stranger. The dry leaves announced the escaping man like clarions. Gil shot by ear, and stopped to reload. The stranger stopped, too. The comedy of the preparation of their arms, making the early night ring with speedily handled metal, aggravated their tempers and their hurry.

"Heh!" Gil's basso rose like a castrato's. He drew a shot from the other. Gil ducked and fired in the glow of the other musket. A man dressed in skins flared and faded, ahead. Gil missed aim and the running took up again. Chase was short. The course was too dark and the leaves were too loud. Gil battered himself in a fall and lost ground. The other man took a tree.

Gil was left guessing which one. "Goddam squirrel!" Loading and shooting, raiding his patchbox and loading again, Gil searched the area with the random hot reach of the bullets. He worked. The other man watched from high up. "Half-squirrel, half-ass!"

The irony of his attack was in using his precision weapon like a blunderbuss. The accurate fowler's piece would have allowed any marksman to snuff a candle at twenty paces.

Gil's adversary made no mistakes. He lay against the listing tree, still as a reptile in the black, one with the trunk, waiting out the storm of shot which he knew would eventually fail.

His tactic was not unsafe. But incautious Anglo-Saxon passion canceled out the cunning. The balanced, octagonal, seventy-five caliber barrel released its oversized, tightly fitting ball ferociously, at close range. Struck trees trembled from their bombardment. Smoke issued from the holes Gil gouged. The Indian hesitated between climbing higher or jumping down into the dark.

Gil loaded again, and then, fagged, caught his breath against a stout sycamore. A happy hissing brought him alert. Several leaves attached to a twig at his shoulder height had been sparked into flame by the flash of ignited powder from the gunlock. An idea caught fire, too. With bulldog belligerence Gil broke off the dry, burning branch, and flung it into the court of many familied trees. He set fire to his tattletale friends, the leaves. Their combustible thicknesses favored him with light. Gil brought the Jaeger to his shoulder in earnest.

Holding to life by his legs, the Indian tried a shot when his cover was gone. He damned the clever foreigner and his cannon, while he toiled over his own muzzle-heavy gun.

The Jaeger came into its own. Stiff trigger set, the nerve of the next touched, air parted with heat. Scream. Reload.

The wounded redman scrambled for any hold above the fattening fire. Gathering for a leap to solid ground, his back looked broad as the side of a barn over the bead sight of the Jaeger, now openly aimed from the tree's north side. Shot. The body tumbled down.

Sweating in the hot, orange thicket, Gil wrenched the corpse out of the flames and stared at the face. "Half-squirrel, Half-Dog!" He raised a yowl to the brightened heavens, then returned to the sachim's face, fascinated. Gil's exceptional physical poise charged by necessity began to fade, and he let the body sink down into the fire. The man had no ghost as he lay in the flickering light. But Gil's grew restless. This was only one of two dead bodies he had caused to be that night. It was the first time that he had ended human life.

He dragged himself to the site of the first killing. Worth fell to the ground when he discovered in the saffron glimmer that he had killed Jack, the cobbler. Two men dead and the job half done. There was someone in the ring who could write.

Gil lugged Jack's remains into the furnace of trees with the weary anguish of a hell-bound soul. Then he crawled with the dead men's weapons to the edge of the burning place to rest. He lay as if dead himself. He watched the sky, seeing stars through the denuded trees. He rolled over and brought his knees to his chest, yearning hopelessly for protection from the results of his vendetta.

The wood, burning pleasantly, like a censer, sent fragrance aloft. The dark wayside was soft and black as the lap of a priestly cassock. Gil thought of Thomas Kirke's room, of Claude de St. Aubin keeping watch of his sleep. Père Claude's bonus absolution cloaked Gil's head and shoulders, which were finally bowed. His slender companion, the Jaeger, lay next to him. Claude had censured this repository of grim power that had helped Gil to survive his deed, and to look ahead to a life lived under its weight.

Gil succeeded in a deep breath. His eyes smarted from smoke, not sorrow. A fit of perverse laughing grew as large in him as the cackle of the fire. Gil sat up in mirth. If there were devils in him, they frolicked then, not caring about damnation, but proud of their lawless, altruistic act. The words of a dirge flitted over his tongue, but Gilbert Worth refused to honor the assassins with song.

WORTH LET HIMSELF into Matthew's cabin without a knock. The houseman was sitting up, asleep against the rough wood of the back wall.

"Get a rake and a spade," Gil snapped him alert, "and we'll each need an ax. There's quite a fire on the other side of the hill. I did not know what else to do with these. Any ideas?" The trade guns made the thin mattress buckle as they were thrown down with force. "Clean his nibs, first. He's had a strenuous night." He stood the Jaeger against the work shelf.

Matthew gained his feet. "Fire? Sir! Shall I get the town?"

"Not unless you want me hanged."

Matthew's hand came across his chest and held his own shoulder. He studied his master. "The mistress is down with megrim. She won't retire, though, until you are found safe. I went after you at Dowland Farm, sir, but you were gone away. Mistress Worth felt it were the same as the night Mistress Beth ran away to the woods."

"Exactly right."

Matthew looked at his master's blackened skin, and smelled the smoke on him. He saw Gil's leather breeches mapped mahogany with dried blood. "Shall I go to the house for clothes for you, sir?"

"Please, would you?" Gil kept his eyes on the plank floor.

Matthew moved off. "If she calls me from the settee when I pass the door, what shall I say?"

Gilbert brought luminous green eyes to his servant's face. "To put an ice pack on."

Together with his houseman, Gil buried the charred bones of the two native men. He endured Hanna's small cry from the settee when he entered the sitting room without greeting her. He walked to the great south window and finally said, "There was a fire."

Her tremulous voice barely reached him. "What can I do to help you?"

"Pray . . . for rain."

The house hummed at a quieter pitch while Gil tried to swallow his secret. Ten nights later he still slept separately from Hanna. The wife would not pry, and Gil would not sully her with himself while he tasted the dregs of his own violence. Cooke's innocent gossip about the Indian cobbler not appearing in Bottle's shop, and the more serious whispers at the tavern, that the nearby Nausets were mourning their sachim for dead since he had not returned from a fall hunt, took neither the wife, nor the husband by surprise.

"Someone has to be responsible for our fire," Hanna said to Gil and Doctor Stirling the first November night. "Perhaps it were he."

"Astute guess." Gil's smile clashed with the look of the rest of his face. "In any case, the leaves were very dry. We are lucky that the blaze did not touch the house."

"Did it not?" She cut him.

"We're all stir-crazy, now, I'm convinced, with this rain keepin' us in." Doctor Mac suffered from the havoc Gil's melancholy caused their civilized routine, and he searched for a new topic. "Now that Madame Locke's arrived, I suppose Mr. Beckett'll be comin', eh?"

"I have written to him, Mac. I expect him any day." Hanna crossed looks with Gil. "*We* do."

"We *do?* Why don't I make it my opportunity to go into the otan with the things for Elizabeth's birthday. Michael may have Dowland House to himself for his reunion with his long lost son."

Hanna sank her needle into the stretched cloth in her sewing frame. "At expense to my heart I have let the poor little thing go to live at my brother's, a strange house for Ho, and a strange nurse. There is no need for you to see Michael if you do not want. But it is rude to go away just as he comes."

"I thought it would be seen as consideration." Gil looked straight at her. "Besides, my niece has her birthday each November first whether Beckett comes or not. I will be late as it is."

"We will be late. And she is *my* niece."

"Our niece!"

Stirling shouted, "Have you two thought about the advisability of takin' a boat out o' here before the ice sets? Your niece ain't providin' you with the sunshine ye both sorely need."

"Dear Mac," Hanna said, "it is light we need more than sun."

"Hark! A messenger comes. Bringing it, I suppose." Gil hopped out of his chair at the sound of a horse, and fogged the rain-spattered window with his breath.

"Maybe it is Michael!" Hanna clapped her hands, blushed, rose from her work, and paced between the window and the hall.

"I say it is the devil come to join this party," Mac grumbled into his glass of clary.

"Cooper." In unison, all three voiced their disappointment as the tither made his dismount and walked up the stone path to the house.

"Didn't even scrape his boots." Gil made a face and swung back into the wing chair.

"There might be something important, if he is in such a rush." Hanna sat on the settee.

"From Cooper? You make me laugh."

"That I make you do anything is a wonder."

"Children, children!" Mac made remonstrance.

Matthew opened the doors and announced Will Cooper. The petty official walked straight to Gil and delivered a large, sealed piece of parchment into his hands.

Gil turned the document over and over, then said, "This is addressed to the Selectmen of Sweetwood, Coop, why give it to me?"

The carefully suited man put his blunt fingers tip to tip, then let them slip nervously through one another down to his palms. "I do not recall, Mr. Worth, the Selectmen of Sweetwood ever having received any sealed letters from anywhere, let alone the court at Boston."

335

"But they have now." Gil wondered why Cooper insisted on a wig when he did not buy good ones.

"Mr. Worth, sir, it is a very few people in this village that reads the news out of the cities. Especially the Selectmen. Not to say anything against their honors, but they do not read. I think it is because they feel they are of moment and have no need to know of others that are."

"Cooper?"

"Meaning to say, sir, that being the tither, in effect the town's eye, I must read. It is a habit with me, now. My wife thinks a bad one. But it is my job. I am that happy to have seen the name of Dowland Farm in print last June. Sir."

"June?" Gil raised his chin.

Cooper looked about him, at Matthew and the doctor, and the mistress of the house.

"Be free." Gil shrugged off the tither's conspiratorial formality.

"I was that pleased to see the name of Mistress Beth listed as a married woman and a mother."

Gil's tongue ran the line of his bottom lip.

"Now, I have held that bit from the Selectmen, noticin' you never mention to the town about your niece."

"You are a most thoughtful man, Mr. Cooper."

"But I cannot hold the post."

"I do not ask you to. Take it to them. Do."

"I do not think that I should, sir, in the first place, and in the second, Isaac Bearing is most particular about how he keeps the mail. When I spied that come in, looking so important, I used whatever influence a man like me has, sir, to make him give that letter up to me. If I give it to the Selectmen now, sir, late, as it were, why there is no telling what would happen."

"Well, then Bearing can't be all that careful! Do you pilfer things that come in for me and send them off to the Selectmen, Coop?"

"Oh, no, sir. You know my job is to keep my eye on things pernicious to the public morality. I could never let them see the post that comes in for you."

Gil sublimated a smile. "You are an avid reader, Cooper."

"Well, sir, as I say, I must earn my salary, such as it is.

The way I see it is that letting this thing out to the Selectmen will cause more harm to the public morals than in keepin' it in between gentlemen."

"My God! What is in it? You know? Cooper! This whatever-it-is is sealed by the court!"

"Sealed and resealed, as it were, sir."

"Gil," Hanna suggested to the stunned man, "Michael is soon due. Why not save it for him to see? It is from the court."

Gil slit the wax with his harper's nail and trained his attention on the formal calligraphy. He opened his mouth to speak but he remained suspended, no sound issuing from him. Finally, he covered his gaping mouth with his hand and turned his face into the cleavage between the wing and the back of his chair.

The family surrounded him.

Cooper nodded, satisfied, and said, "Gentleman to gentleman, it is a rough winter ahead for me. I have two daughters going for marriage, a sick sow, and the Lord knows what. The town's a bit stingy with its allotment for me. Tell me, sir, at any time, what service I can be."

They did not see the tither leave. Gill released the mysteries of a sealed Information for their inspection, remaining limp against the high-backed chair.

"Oh, Bonnie!" Mac intoned when he had seen it. "The jig is up."

The court paper was a legal response to anonymous accusations concerning criminal acts alleged to Wakwa Manunnappu. It listed the Maine journey, the inter-tribal organization, and the actual contact with the Abnaki as proofs of treason. The names of co-conspirators, in alphabetical order, followed under the chief name, Silent Fox. Two names were conspicuous by their absence. Half-Dog, and Gilbert Worth.

Gil rose, blind to the others in the room. He proceeded toward the wide doors, elbowing the phantoms of new obstacles out of his way. "Who? Who?" He flailed the air with his arms as he went, striking and hurting himself on his harp, pulled out for playing. "Get rid of that!" he ordered nobody.

Hanna and the doctor caught up with him, amazed at

a rage in him great enough that he mistreat the instrument of his inner self.

Gil hunched in the hallway to summon control, and observed his own legs and feet as if they were attached to another man's body. Matthew stood in front of the master and his baize and hose and shoes entered Gil's circle of sight. "Matthew! Go onto the highroad and find Mr. Beckett. He is on his way here. If he has not yet left his house in Boston go all the way there and drag him back. Take Grandee. You'll meet Mr. Beckett halfway."

Tea was canceled in this crisis. With his wife and his friend using the dining table for support to help them sit and listen, Gil opened the story of the October woods. His confessions offered him no solace, and he looked at the objects in the windowless winter room knowing that if he had been wearing his sword he would have swept every piece of shelved porcelain and crystal to perdition with one pass of the blade. He ended his recitation, "There is only one farm out of these connected three which has not become a burial ground. The Hudson place."

The Scot, the sister of Charles Dowland, and the English landowner each looked at the round, silver bowl displayed at the table's center. "Annanias!" The trilled speech, the pure, plain American, and the comely clip of the British, each named the minister as the instigator of all their disaster.

Beckett was awaited like a Messiah.

He appeared almost too soon. Matthew, levelheaded in his service, slowed Grandee at the short lane to the Dowland place before speeding down the road through the village and beyond, and all night to Boston. There was rarely a day when Gil's houseman did not complete a precautionary circle around the old house, or knock for admittance to check on conditions. A black chaise at the front door rewarded his careful habits. He went to the kitchen entrance and heard from Millie that Michael Beckett had arrived in the early evening. Matthew took the four stairs out of the kitchen in one stretch, crossing a dining room, and looked in at the study.

The tall, fair-skinned, dark-haired lawyer was enthroned in Charles' chair, beaming, attempting to ingratiate himself with the Frenchwoman, Jeanette, Dire Locke's hastily wed wife.

"You look as if you need a tonic, Hanna." Michael kissed her lips on entering Worth's hall. "And winter has not begun!"

Gil let the light be low in the glittering sitting room, and alone with Beckett, tensely waited his verdict about the seriousness of the list of names.

Michael shook an expensively shod foot above the subtle figuring of the rug as he tested the meanings of the document within himself. Slight twitchings of the skin of his face recorded the darting of his thoughts toward the liquor chest.

"A shoddy thing," Beckett allowed.

"At the least." Gil drank of Beckett's attitudes.

"Lord Duhmmer sent this sketchy information to avoid assembling a grand jury to lay on a proper indictment. I venture to guess that he could not get enough members to prefer a charge against Silent Fox, and so, whipped off this handy paper to bring the sachim quickly to clearing or . . . to conviction. After all, Duhmmer's neck is in the noose if the accusations are proved true. He has not forgotten how it came to pass that the sachim's son is richer than he is."

"What are you going to do about it?" Words released from the vise of Gil's jaw.

"Put it in my pocket and go on up to bed."

"Help me, Michael. I am trying to be rational."

"I will help you. Be rational in the morning. I have done fifty miles in a rattling coach these past two days and a rotten hostel in between."

"Give the damned thing to me." Gil stood and put out his hand. "I took care of myself before you were my counsel. I will answer my own wants as usual."

Beckett held the stiff paper away. "Do not deceive yourself, good sir. Every time that you have the slightest need you ring either for Matthew Freeman or for me."

"Not quite. I do my own killing."

Michael Beckett uncrossed his legs and gave Gilbert Worth complete attention.

For the second time that night, Gil reviewed his lonely actions in the woods. He strode the darkened room and ended at the fireplace. "I let them burn despite Israel Stirling's insatiable desire to cut up and examine dead humans. Matthew and I turned their ashes under the earth the following dawn."

"The whole lot of you make my skin crawl."

"Michael, I did what I did to preserve life."

"Whose?" Beckett was impatient.

"Wakwa's, Elizabeth's, their babe's, the marriage, the tribe, for without an intelligent and recognized spokesman the Ninnuock are lost, worse, they will be dispersed, count for nothing more than the dry leaves which are rife for decay. Their like will never be seen on the earth again. A line of noble blood will be ended and they watch their race wither like a childless man."

The lawyer's long legs sprawled over the space between the settee and the wing chair, his left hand covered the lower part of his face, and his chestnut eyes marveled at the speaker.

"Michael, I do not require you to understand me. Only get Wakwa off. Sue for time, get the thing sunk, dazzle the judge. . . ."

"I am a solicitor, not a sorcerer."

"Pay his Lordship!"

"Your character is crumbling. Before you know, you will turn to alcohol."

"How can you be the way are, Beckett, and not be struck by lightning?"

"Well, you're the man to do it."

"Do not tempt me!" Gil lashed out at his unhelpfulness.

"You are in ruin, Worth, because you are quick to violence and yet do not want to pay the consequences for your acts."

"Have I whimpered over myself? Have I said one thing about protection for me?"

"O! I wish you had! That is the trouble. Do you never think to the second or third step? Do you have a care for your life or Hanna's?"

"We have had our life, and anyway, negate each other."

"That is the crux for you, isn't it? You cannot bear not being followed by a bunch of little Gilberts. But I tell you that the status quo, the reaching out for a little legitimate happiness, is as full of sacrifice and bravery as the hell you have created for yourself. You run about the woods breaking treaties, killing unruly Indians, endowing others, fostering the barbarization of English tradition and morals behind the veil of a gentleman farmer." Beckett raised the Information high over his head. "A revolution is here! And you are part of its muscle. Shed your disguise and remain in the wilderness, the savage you really are, and pull the thing together. Play bloody Robin Hood but do not continually ask me to make it all straight with the courts. Under current law it never will be. You want to wear two skins. My considered advice to you is that you choose one, creep into it, and behave according as it gives and shrinks."

"Do I understand? You think I should exercise my will outside the law? Not try to conform the law to what I think is just?"

"What you think is just? You are then a king?"

Gil came to sit in his wing chair. He pressed his fists between his knees and looked at an image of himself that he had never considered before. "How do I differ from one? Or how do you?"

"Are you bound by nothing? Zeus?"

"I am bound by . . . beauty . . . symmetry . . . light . . . love . . . right. And the rights to these."

Michael Beckett tucked the legal paper into his pocket and tiptoed to the door, not trespassing on Gil's insight with banalities of refutation. He gave a loud whisper before he exited. "Worth, you need a priest, not a lawyer."

"I have a good one. Père Claude by name. He is the Jesuit who saved the honor of Locke's parlormaid."

"Ah! I have met Jeanette."

"She seems sufficient unto the task?"

"At least the equal to it."

Gil retained a picture of the long shadow in the doorway for a good while after Beckett broke jauntily for the steps. He stripped off his coat and shirt, and worried the yellow silk of the settee he was using for a bed that night. "Poor, poor Hanna!"

And Beckett rehearsed possible defenses as he went up the short flight to his room. "Justifiable homicide. . . ." And against the Information and Hudson's probable part in it, "Hatred of a neighbor, In Emulationem Vicini. . . ."

Matthew met him at the landing. The houseman knew

his employer's need and he served Beckett as if honored by the task. He left him a bottle of fine spirits, pouring the first drink, and said after hanging Beckett's clothes and turning down the coverlet, "Anything that I can do for you, sir, at any time, do not hesitate. . . ."

"Hesitate I shall not."

_____ **Chapter 48**

PERHAPS because it was the time of her birth, Elizabeth found autumn to be more heady than soft, suggestive May. The falling of the leaves marked a yielding to an outside force. What fell would give rise to new life. Fall was to her an active, not an ending season. Its perfumes, dry and rarefied, exotic stuffs, acquired tastes, were prized by her every organ. The beautification in age of the leaves, the glide from glory to melding with the soil, was the direction she desired her life to take.

Elizabeth woke on her birthday to a dripping, fog-shrouded world. Light from the fire caught in her eye and she did not know the course of things outside. Wakwa smiled. Before she could speak he took taste of her mouth.

"I have not finished thee a gift. I offer thee the day." His lips followed the grace of her neck.

She touched the hollow of his with her tongue and then lay back examining the scar on him. The flexible neck skin had grown together into a flat, bronze seam as wide as her little finger and fully as long. He tossed his head to show off his soundness. He kissed her hair, relating the scars they both bore from violence. "You and I, keen kah neen."

One side of them was burning hot from nearness to the fire. The other was cooler. Wakwa nuzzled the breast that

342

was warm, then brought that heat to the other until it was more aglow than the side near the flames.

And Elizabeth gave herself up. She offered him space, a plain to till with affection. His tenderness knew no time. His fingers, his teeth, his tongue touched her center, the softness of her belly, her waist, her thighs, as if she were porous, and he were sinking hot stones in her to set her seething like a vessel of food, of clear water. And then he let that be and watched her while she pined and her full lips grew pink and pearly and they opened, and she gathered him against her with long white legs. He bent both away and to her, pulling back to put his mouth at her opening, the cloven heart of her. Then, without demand he drew on her, his mouth engaged in patient craft to create. As glass and music are found in blowing, he inspired at an empty place to fill it.

The gates of her went wide. She knew a startling pouring forth. A liquid essence, a secret honey, seeped from high. And the liquid ran, her liquid ran. It coursed the canal of her to meet the essence of him, the masculine brine that was building to release. His phallus sealed them.

They lay drugged with one another, letting morning pass into midday.

"Dearest," she said, "do I seem old now I am twenty?"

"You do!"

There was no greater compliment for Elizabeth.

They made no haste to wash or eat, but lounged on their separate couches of cushions, basking near the highest fire they had ever chanced in the sachimmaacommock.

Elizabeth ran her toes from Wakwa's knee down to the top of his foot. "It is quite late in the day."

He twined his ankle and lower leg through the angle formed by hers. "Kayaskwa, would you rush the day away?"

"It turns of itself. I smell the otan roasting meat. I have never known a birthday without my Uncle Gil. If he hasn't come by now, he mayn't at all." She drew her legs up against her front and hugged them, her forehead against one thigh.

Wakwa saw only waves of rich-toned hair, a bouquet above her knees. He pulled a tress to gain attention.

Elizabeth reclined again, and spread her legs toward

him. "You are well, Wakwa, what pours from you is better than nectar from fruit. It is . . . is . . . clean and silvery and a little wild, like wine."

Wakwa hid his pleasured smile against the arch of her foot. "Your uncle will come and bring a shower of presents for you."

One of her arms rested across her stomach. She said, "Suppose, dear Fox, that my calendar is wrong. Suppose a pin fell out of the embroidered number where I measure the days. I might have marked that day twice. My birthday might have been yesterday!"

"Would your uncle ever be two days late?"

"Unthinkable. I have perhaps marked ahead, put a pin through two numbers of a morning? That would mean my birthday is not yet. It is tomorrow."

"So you shall have two." Wakwa pulled her toward him by the ankle in his hand.

She laughed. "Might I? Then we will repeat this morning at next dawn?"

"Wamach! It is enough!" Wakwa toppled from his pillows onto the mats in mock exhaustion. "Are women never satisfied?" He groaned and sighed.

Elizabeth knelt near him, preserving his penis from the rush work, resting it in her hand. "It is the men who limit their imaginations as to the amount of satisfaction that can be had."

Wakwa opened one indignant eye.

Elizabeth kissed it closed, and pressed his back with lighthearted apologies from her lips. He grabbed with quickness and fit her next to him.

"If Gilbert does not come here first, let us gather up Qunneke and the children and go to see him."

"You and I? Go to his house?"

"To the very door."

"Today!"

"Not today. First we must ask Qunneke, then prepare a gift, then send a message ahead. We are many and must not take them by surprise. Rightfully, they would make us sleep out on the grass."

"I have waited over two years. I can wait for a few days more to see the changes they have wrought in the sitting room."

He turned and sat her on his stomach, and looked up cautiously, as if a tiny bird had alighted there. "If you could have anything, a thing, some thing, what would that be?" he quizzed.

The light of a wish encircled her face immediately, and Wakwa pushed himself up on his elbows to hear what he could buy her to bring her happiness. "I should like to have some silkworms!"

He remained carved in his pose even after she was up heating water for their bath.

_____ **Chapter 49**

"SUE THE BASTARD for libel. That is our first defense against what we have here. And what we have is a Criminal Information." Michael Beckett presided from the place of honor in Waban's house, the seat opposite the door.

The room was packed with men. And Waban had each of his sons within reach, and his brother-in-law, Pequawus, at his side, the side of his heart. Gil sulked against the entry, as far from the company as he could get. Awepu stood with him. Wakwa sat at their feet and trained his attention on the attorney.

"Where you have an Information, you have an informer. I would sue him today, but he has not the decency to sign who he is, so as yet we cannot take him to court. But we will ferret him out, won't we, men?" Beckett whitened the surrounding space with a quick smile.

Gilbert, in his buff breeches and kersey coat, hid behind his gun barrel as if it were a picket fence.

"Informers do not inform upon themselves, generally, and as I read this list there are some names conspicuously

345

absent. The sachim from Nauset, er, the sachim from Namskeket, you know who I mean. Half-Something, isn't it? And then there is missing the name of Gilbert Worth."

Worth crouched down.

"Gil, you haven't gone loony and pointed the finger at your bosom buddies, have you?"

Gil turned his fine-hewn face toward the silent crowd which looked back at him. He hated Beckett's game, but he played it.

"God! Look at that coat! Gentlemen, fellows who wear navy-colored cashmere on errands as hasty as this are not likely to need to sell their friends out for thirty pieces of silver, or for a song, or for anything. In fact good ole Gil is in the habit of giving things away—nieces, farm ground, movable property, even his shirt. Anything, in short, except his honor. We can count out Gilbert Worth."

Dense muttering told their complete assent.

"Still, I wonder why his name is not on this filthy paper. His name. Half-Dog's name. And Waban? What about your sons? I've looked again, and again. 'Silent Fox, Awepu, Bear, blah, blah, blah,' but Nuppohwunau and Weeping Heart are just not here."

Waban answered while his eyes traveled the faces of the sagamores and fighting men. "My sons did not make that walk."

"Oh, well! What a relief for you. No wasting fatherly anxieties on that score. They cannot possibly get into trouble. But you've got to have someone to sue in a libel, so all hands on deck and we'll find the wagging tongue, oh yes, we will. Why I say libel is this: The informer has named perfectly honorable people as fomenters of rebellion, and makers of traitorous alliances against the English Crown. . . ."

"False! False!" Gil stood and shouted.

Beckett blinked his black lashes at the interruption. "I had heard that the purpose of that chilly walk was to institute peace among all. That will be our countercharge. I will put you on the stand, Silent Fox, to witness to the real nature of the journey you led. You are the turner of phrases, the spokesman. If we prefer a charge of libel against the informer you would have to testify to the minute by minute history of that risky walk, and, of course, get Duhmmer to eat your story out of your hand like a deer at a salt lick. I like that . . . deer at a salt lick. I jot down a libel suit as a possibility." Beckett scratched away at his journal with a freshly dipped quill.

Beckett galloped on. "The second defense is an offense. And that is to dispute the treaty itself, as an oppressive instrument. It allows for no reasonable dissent when it says that right-minded adults may not meet to plan the redress of grievances without the suspicion of sedition. In other words, you are at the complete mercy of the English monarch if you may never make consolidated and reasonable complaints, or even changes in policies which no longer suit the times. With all due respect, Sachim, you have put your foot in it. According to the treaty, your inter-tribal conversations on political subjects, no matter how harmless, violate said treaty. Thereby, Sachim, by walking out of town you have forfeited the single condition laid upon the king by this instrument, which is that he protect the Indians of this area against unprovoked attacks. In other words, he can attack you himself, now, quite legally, and you are most likely a cooked goose the minute you make your body available to the court. This second defense presents some danger."

"I was a cooked goose, as you say, Michaelbeckett, from the moment of my birth," Wakwa said.

"All of us who are not kings, were." Michael looked at Gil.

"Just so," Wakwa continued to reason, "treaty or no. And as you may speak for me to a judge and not be hung for that which you say in my defense, so the spokesman for the Ninnuock should be free from tortures or wounds or punishments if he faces the court in behalf of his people. Why else do they bring meat to my door in fealty?"

"Well derived." Michael inclined his head in respect to Wakwa's attainment.

"Then," Wakwa announced, "I will trust my bones to Lord Duhmmer and answer this summons."

"Like hell you will!" Gilbert Worth made a stand in the doorway, his hands on his hips.

"Uncle?" Wakwa turned and looked back at his relation.

"Guarantees! You must have guarantees of your safety

if you are to walk outside your own jurisdiction. You have just been through holy hell with an arrow through your neck and are ready to throw yourself into the arms of some lout of a bailiff in the courthouse?"

"Gilbert, this is a business I cannot ignore."

"And I say the whole thing is nothing but a point of law. You are letting yourself get embroiled in a petty nuisance of a thing, just what your informer would have you do. He couldn't kill you, whoever he is, so he'll flush you out on a crooked account of private doings learned doubtless from some other Judas' tongue."

"That said," Beckett impelled Gil to sit by force of his frown, "we will write down answering the Information in person, as a possibility."

He inscribed his notebook in a graceful hand and then blew the ink dry and closed it, pointedly placing his pen in its box. "Number three." The solicitor's voice went solemn, and Wakwa leaned toward him, the fire toasting his face. "You may wish that I enter an Informatus Non Sum. Which is to say, I will go back to Boston without being apprised of your defense. The court will decree whatever punishment it sees fit, and administer it as it may. As your counsel I advise you, if you choose this alternative, that you not sit snug, here, waiting for reprisals. You may get off with a warning against seditious activities, or a crack over the knuckles. But if they want your handsome head on a platter, they'll have to go without if you are gone. Every last one of you. But I doubt it would come to that. Certainly, it is in Duhmmer's interest to bury this stinker of a criminal paper, because he was the one who let realty pass into the hands of your son. If he is seen by his colleagues to have abetted the fortunes of a traitor he would be drubbed out of his chair. Heaven, I am hungry!"

Michael Beckett was royally fed. A broth of varied kinds of fish, freshwater and salt, mixed with the breast meat of wild fowl filled the ample bowls of Waban's house. The corncakes were rendered into dainties, formed small and round, with berries thickening the batter, and baked and served hot in bubbling maple syrup.

"Tell you one thing," Beckett confided to Waban as they ate shoulder to shoulder, "I'd look out before I gave up daily lunches like these for any cause whatsoever."

Waban took a sweet and sticky cake between his fingers and let a knowing laugh roll up from his belly. He whirled the confection in its bath of sugary sap, and dandling it high, caught thick, dark drops on his tongue.

Across the big, round room Wakwa said, "Gilbert, you are not yourself. Find the stomach to eat. I need your strength behind me."

"It is always at your service."

Wakwa picked up Gil's neglected stew. "That is a thing for a nephew to say to an uncle. Eat."

To content the younger man, Gil forced down some bites of the meal, but he sickened. Taking up his Jaeger, he played with its inlaid design. He blew his breath on the fingerprints he made, then polished them away.

Wakwa sat with his shoulders low. "I wonder why it is that I eat, to fatten myself for the kill?"

"Don't worry about that."

"It is true, Gilbert, that woods are quiet, the children pick berries, the youths meet their young women there, the traps snare the deer. Yet, the killer is not caught. When leaves blossom in the spring, though, my wives will be made widows. So eat, and do not worry that I will make argument in the court to settle this trouble. I do not expect to live anyway."

"Taking your advice from Death, eh? A mistake. Really, you are quite safe. Let it all be. I know whereof I speak. Unless you have made more enemies than I know, you are safe for the rest of your days."

"How I wish I could be sure!"

"Listen to me. I know."

Wakwa shook his depression enough to study the whiteman who loved him. He was conscious of Gil's hands, toying with the gun, stroking it the way Sequan did the dolls she favored as constant companions. The green eyes held dense color as flourishing trees did, touched by sun and shadow. Nothing faint, unripe, uninitiated, or immature lived there. "Gilbert, you know things I do not. I would like to know what you know."

Gil raised a warning hand and said, "I know you are safe."

"How are you sure?"

"Because it has been seen to."

"Gilbert, by whom?"

"Why can't you take me at my word here, and let me eat before Beckett starts jabbering again?"

"How has it been seen to?"

Gilbert pulled the cold stew toward himself. Wakwa pulled it away.

"Definitely."

"He has been taken?"

"Done away with. Now, will that do?"

"When was this?" Wakwa groped for Worth's shoulders the way he reached for the truth.

"Weeks ago. Let it drop, will you?"

"So many days ago?" Wakwa looked over at his family and his friends like a cheated man. "Who else knows?"

"Only Beckett."

Wakwa looked from whiteman to whiteman. "Who here would tell Michaelbeckett without telling me first? Only you! Gilbert! What have you done?"

"For Jesus' sake! No! For yours! I shot them. All right?" Gil grabbed up the bowl and began to stuff his mouth, filling his reddened cheeks with food.

Awepu knelt down near the pair.

"You speak of yourself? You? With your hands? What are you talking about? You shot 'them'?" Wakwa kept prodding.

"There were two. Pop! Pop! No, only one was easy. It was the other took the time." Gil's chewing slowed with remembrance. "A little running, a little shooting, a little waiting, a little brains." Gold flecks began to leap in his eyes. "And the other son-of-a-bitch dropped, too." He was left with a lump in his mouth.

Wakwa's jaw went out of line from his astonishment.

Awepu whispered, "Who were they?"

"Oh." Gil shrugged and gathered the partially masticated food in his fingers and threw the flavorless mass into the bowl. "Jack, Jack the shoemaker, and your famous friend, Half-Dog. Nothing new."

Wakwa gathered himself, the balls of his feet and his fingertips touching the floor like a competitor about to spring. "You did it?"

"One might say I just followed a very good gun around."

Wakwa unflexed and stood and took a step backward. "For me you have become a murderer?"

Gil's lids went slowly shut. "You're welcome."

Wakwa was kneeling, kissing each one of Gil's shoulders and saying a word unfamiliar to the Englishman. He held a hand against Worth's fleshless cheek. "Two!" His lips pursed with pride. "Cowaunkamish, cowaunkamish, nissese. My service to thee, my uncle!"

"Ah, Wakwa, how I have feared to tell you! I thought to lose you if I let it out that I had killed men of your race. But goddamn! I am what you said, now. I've killed two fellows, sang-froid. I am no good, anymore, as a witness for your character, even if my name didn't make the mangy list. And how can you be a witness for mine? You have very little chance in the courts because I have this new thing to hide. I beg pardon for my offering. I have done a job of work is all, except we all must pay!"

Wakwa reeled away from him, found his father, and leaned on him in his upset.

Awepu escaped Waban's sachimmaacommock for the other one. Elizabeth ran to him and he held her tightly against him as a child of his own. He said in his calming voice, "I tell you to pull together warm things to wear and as many blankets as you can roll into one and yet carry them."

She cried out.

He stroked her cheek and a little behind her ears as he would any soft, small forest creature. "Put up some food, and be ready with Wolf-of-the-mist He-hopes. I do not know how decisions will go. If the English come they will take you with them and name you, everywhere, either a captive or a concubine. There is a field, a meadow with much rock hanging like caves, where you can pass tonight. And then tomorrow you will walk from there. . . ."

"Walk . . . walk from where?"

"From these caves. They are where the wuttahimneash grow, the strawberry hill. The women will be turning the dead plants under the soil. They will notice not that you are there, do you understand? Your dress may touch theirs as you pass by them, but they will not see you. You will

351

walk, taking my oldest son. I would send Tamoccon with you but he is too young and the council will be aware. You will find a place to winter, and my boy will find me and I will know of your place and keep you fed and warm until this passes. You must preserve yourself to Wakwa. This is the way."

"Awepu," something angry colored her voice, "why these guards around the house? I cannot go out or in to even fetch fresh water. Am I a prisoner? What have I done? All you will tell me is that there is a list of names and everyone on it is in danger of hanging, a thing I have worried about since Wakwa went away. Since before! I told him this would happen, I told him the night I conceived Moses, the very moment Wakwa conceived this monstrous plan. I did not write the paper! But if I do have a fault I should be going to the court at Boston to talk to Lord Duhmmer. He was very fair to us once before. Besides, I have told my husband, sworn to him that though I might be afraid I would never run away again. I ran once. Into these woods. And once, when I was afraid, I tried to find my way out. No more. I am frightened now, but I cannot, I will not go."

"Elizabeth Dowland, I do not know what you two have between you, but if you go you will remove a heavy weight from him. He will be able to think, a man unburdened. He can act any way he sees fit for the People, and mix you not at all in it. Like a cripple whose humps are removed from him he will walk straight to wherever he must go. You and he will come together, again."

Elizabeth turned away. "My father bore his burdens, his pain, his twisting, his lumps, yet kept the farm and our affection. Is Wakwa less loving, less wise than Papa?"

"As wise. As loving. Recall, my sister, your father did without you."

"This is different!" Elizabeth's voice pealed her anguish. "I am his wife. How can he be without me? I am the mother of his child. Will he send us both away? Who said these things? Who has thought such things? They do not know my husband or me very well."

"No one has said the least thing about you. That is what is heavy on my mind." Awepu let his hand rest on her breast for a moment and then slipped past her to go out. "Get thee ready. I will come if things turn for the worse."

Pequawus took Gilbert Worth's strong, slim hand into his and regarded it with a mixture of warmth and pain. He said, "Your family name, Worth, has meaning to me. Tell me why are you called Gilbert? That is your name special to you."

"Pequawus, I do not know if it means anything. My ear is used to it. I simply answer its sound like a dog."

"That astonishes me." Wakwa's father tilted his head. "The name has two parts," he pressed. "Gil meaning nothing?"

"I always supposed people say Gil because it is short."

They shared a look and a laugh.

Pequawus brought the captive hand to his chest. "That is not meaning enough. You gave yourself to the woods like any one of our stouthearted boys, and the woods has given you to us. You are ours . . . no matter how you have outcast yourself from your people and your law, by what you have done. You have a place here, always, with us. You are part of us."

The others in the room drew in around the pair, watching Waban's chief counsellor adopt the Englishman.

"From now, Gilbert Worth, you will be known as . . . He . . . He-who. . . ."

". . . Holds-the-stars-in-his-hand!" Wakwa supplanted.

"More than that!" Pequawus took exception. "From now, you are, He-who-holds-out-his-hand! Summagunum wunnutcheg!" The father of the sachim Gil had preserved bent to bless him with a kiss on each of his shoulders. And then he released him to the other men for them to honor him as a brother, born not of woman, but of men's blood.

Gil's marrow felt indestructible as diamond, and his heart pumped like a lonely man's who had found a woman.

When Wakwa took his turn, Gil caught him around the neck and held him down to whisper, "Is it all right?"

Wakwa looked his English uncle in the eye. "Were we Chippeway, it would be three days of ordeals before your new name could sit right upon you. Be grateful."

"Grateful I stand!" Gil searched Wakwa's smile.

Wakwa looked down and moved away.

As he performed the welcoming gesture, Waban's second son, Nuppohwunau, said, "I thought Pequawus would name you He-who-makes-music. Then you and I would be closer brothers, as I am He-who-hath-wings, for the way I lead the dancing."

Wuttah Mauo pushed him along. "I am your brother, do not forget." Then he placed his mouth at Gil's shoulder. "I spit in your face!"

Gil jerked himself out of Weeping Heart's reach. Harmonious chatter stopped. Gilbert and Weeping Heart stood at odds in the center of a sudden circle. Men sat to listen rather than standing to fight. Wakwa remained on his feet, behind Gil. Waban stood behind his son.

Wuttah Mauo cast a jaded eye around the serious company. "I spit in your face!" He sneered at them all.

Waban said in English so that the lawyer could understand, "Why do you not love the man who has saved Wakwa, our chief servant, kehche, one of our greatest men?"

"Father!"

"Why are you not happy that Wolf-of-the-mist He-hopes has his father restored to him in one piece?"

"Father! Do you not see since that half-breed was born the otan has bent to suckling him and nothing else?" Wuttah Mauo wiped his lips with the back of his hand. "This trouble we have over this paper today is because of the father. And the father's fall is because of the son. The court has a hatchet raised above all our heads because the brat has his name on a kingdom of ground that Englishmen would love to have themselves. Do not forget that! I am sick of succoring Wolf-of-the-mist He-hopes, and more I am sick of Silent Fox and his precious English uncle!"

Waban waited long to act for the first time in his life. The old joy in his firstborn child stirred. Weeping Heart was named for his mature vision of things, his sight of the sad, and Waban thought about what his elder son said. He watched the cousins take one another's measure as they used to before they vied in a game.

Wakwa moved to his own defense. "Weeping Heart, I

succor you! I have done all I can for you in your life. I have lifted you out of sickness and drunkenness, out of the arms of disgrace, and out of the arms of the constable himself! You envy me my son? Get one of your own! I cannot engender children for you, too!"

Waban's eyes went dead. Wuttah Mauo swerved, held his torso with his arms, keeping himself from tearing apart in his grief. But he rallied. "I have no interest in yellow children. To make them you need white women. I have had them in my time. They are nothing special."

At last, after a life pattern of patience, Wakwa lunged in temper. His reach and his weight leveled Wuttah Mauo. His knee pinned him to the floor. His left hand pulled the toplock of his hair, snapped his head back. His right hand tore his knife from his belt, and the cold hard blade slashed the skin above Wuttah Mauo's forehead. Wakwa ripped a second time along the scalp line, but Awepu's hands came under the cutting edge.

Men pulled at Wakwa's shoulders to get him away, but he held his cousin's hair tighter, and the skin of the scalp began to tear of itself.

Waban watched, not interfering, his eye hot with pride in Wakwa's swift response.

Blood rose in the trench cut across Awepu's fingers. Wuttah Mauo lay still, aghast at the run of blood which he took to be his own. Wakwa saw the line of running red and he dropped the knife to dam the wound of Awepu's wonderful hands.

Awepu pushed the knife back into Wakwa's grasp. "Only do not kill him yet," he entreated Wakwa.

"Nuppohwunau!" Weeping Heart called for his brother. The father ordered the younger son held away.

Awepu coached, "Ask him, Wakwa, now that you finally have him, how it comes to be that your stolen Sucki is back. Yes, Manunnappu, the horse has appeared, leaping the fence posts, black as the breath of fog. Ask him, did Sucki carry the Mattanit who has given our names to the judge. Ask him. . . ."

"Begging your pardon." Michael Beckett picked his way among the men. "I shall ask him. A confession made to me, however extracted, will be admissible in an English court." Beckett fussed with his wig and poised his quill.

He leaned his face close to the gore-stained one and inquired, "Do you feel alone?"

A shriek came from Weeping Heart.

"I do not mean do you feel alone here and now. I want to know, in general, in the main, with your cronies dropping like flies in the frost, do you feel lonely? Is that why you will not call Gilbert Worth your brother? Is he responsible, in part, for stranding you unto the island of yourself? The disaffected among the affectionate?"

Wuttah Mauo's eyes curved in their sockets to see the face of the lawyer.

"Put another way, Weeping Heart, I want numbers. How many are there left of the original conspiracy?"

Held down by the man he had failed to kill, Weeping Heart could not move or look anywhere. He closed his eyes and quaked.

"Now, you can't read, and I expect that you cannot write, but what kind of gambler cannot count? Eh? Shall I help you?"

"Manunnappu!" Weeping Heart wound his hands about Wakwa's wrist. "Help me!"

"I will fetch your head off in a trice if you do not make answer! I told you once, as I held you afloat, what I would do to you if you lied to me. . . ."

"I did not lie! I told what was true!"

Wakwa spat. "That is for your truth! Where were you when I took the People to the island in the summer? Telling the truth to men who can write and read?" Tears sprang and flew as he shook Waban's son, his hands around his throat, not minding that Wuttah Mauo's head struck the hard floor again, and again.

"Wakwa!" Awepu disengaged them.

Wakwa was collected into the ranks of his supporters, Weeping Heart was left to lie on the floor like a sack of rotten meal.

Beckett resumed with a clearing of his throat. "We were discussing numbers. And look, old man, if you are innocent of misdoing, I can help you. I come highly recommended. Why not talk to me? The circumstantial evidence is not pretty. Not so long ago, your brand-new frater, Gilbert Worth, was confronted on his grounds by two nasty fellows pointing guns. Alas, in self-defense, Worth blew their heads off. So far, I count two men dead. One of them, a nothing. A trigger squeezer. The other, a sachim, with the expertise to dominate this little band of Indians. But that possibility is as dead as Half-Dog, is it not? Are you thinking of being the sachim, here, instead of the card shark in residence?"

Wuttah Mauo uttered a cry and passed his hands over his red-washed eyes.

"Of your circle of acquaintances of the summer, very few are left. The girl you lived with, Prudence, died dotish with disappointment. Patty, the daughter of the innkeeper, is dead. Killed by White Cat because she was going to the authorities with your bastard baby. I am up to four."

"It was not my baby."

"Oh, come on." Beckett squeezed compromising information out of Waban's son, applying pressure in empty areas like a pastry chef forcing icing out of a bag. "What sort of fellow lives eight months with a wench who's all puffed up if he is not anxious for the puff? Tell me that?"

Men held Wuttah Mauo so tightly that he could only tear the air with his teeth. "She lied! She told me it was mine! But no more it was! I should have killed her instead of trying to get Manunnappu!"

Beckett winced at the sloppiness of Weeping Heart's divulgation. "Now we have that, may I say, if you had killed Miss Hanson you would have saved a lot of busy people an appreciable amount of trouble and expense. But that does not seem part of your life design."

Wuttah Mauo eluded the restraining hands and crawled to Beckett's feet, the skin of his scalp streaming and askew, his arms clinging like weeds to Beckett's fine, straight calves. Michael tried to step out of this embrace.

"You who can just live! What do you know of why I needed to stay with her, tearing myself away from a woman of beauty whom my father slew with a knife? What do you know?"

Waban pushed his derelict son away from the solicitor with a soft-shod foot. It was the moment for approaching his lost boy. Waban knew. But Prudence Hanson had made a double fool out of him, a sachim for thirty autumns. And

Waban clung to his office, and his primacy. He looked his dearest son in the eye. "Well did I name thee, Weeping Heart, for that is your future. Weep over this, that you wasted so many seasons savoring the thought of a mixed-blood son to contest Moses Bluehill. Mauo! Mauo! Cry that you left in the woman you debauched here, at home, a son, a baby son, a full-blooded Massachuseuck, kin of Silent Fox, not unnaturally of a line to hold sway, here, by the river. You stupid! You killed Panther Eye the day you left her for the holyman's whore. You killed her by leaving her to her devices, and I saw their marks on Our-Elizabeth, an whole and splendid woman!" Somehow affection crept into the father's curse. "If I did not know otherwise, I would blame your creation on another man. I own you, though, as you did not own your own blood. And you make me sick that you are my son."

Wuttah Mauo took his father around his waist, clinging and groveling at his condemnation. "Is it fair? Is it fair?"

"Fair! I should kill you with my own hand, son or no, for what you have done. What you have tried to do. You treat the People with as little reverence as any woman whose clothes you have stripped off. You hate Gilbert who has held back your crimes with his two hands so that better men than you might live and prosper. I praise Gilbert Worth over you! Like Moses in the whitemen's holy book, he has held back the ocean of horrors you have dreamt up for all of us. Now, he is my son and will sleep where you are no longer welcome! There is no home for you among Ninnuock, anywhere, forever. You have not regard for yourself. How are you of any value to anyone else?"

"Is it fair? Is it fair? Think on my sorrow! My woman! My son! And now, no father! Pushed out by farmers, and farmers' daughters. Is it fair?" Weeping Heart dottered to Wakwa's side. "Can you see how I have suffered? Is it right that my father has always loved you more than he loved me?"

Wakwa held his cousin steady, astounded by revelation of Panther Eye's secret, and by how much regret could drain from a man.

Waban committed himself further, not chancing doubts in the mind of the council about the honesty of his rule,

358

or more questions from Michael Beckett. "Stand you up. Stand straight!" The old man searched his longpoles, looking for his favorite club, the one it had been his pleasure to use to finish off the mad bear who had eaten his sister's face.

Pequawus begged Waban to forbear.

"It was your son mine has tried to kill! What is the matter with you, Pequawus?"

Wakwa backed away, as Waban approached Weeping Heart from behind. But Beckett stayed, pressing the sorrowing man for the final detail. "Did you talk to Annanias Hudson at any time? Did you talk to Annanias Hudson? Did you give him names, places, times, anything he might have used in a letter to Lorn Duhmmer? It will help you if you tell me! It will help us if we know!"

"Michael Beckett!" Waban's arms were raised.

Wuttah Mauo looked behind. He knew his father's face. It told him why the heavy club was threatening his head. In an act of love to his father, Weeping Heart stood firm, revealing nothing, giving no proof that could strengthen the case against Annanias Hudson, because he could see it was not to Waban's advantage. Safety for the People was in simplifying, in cutting cords that chafed.

The whole of his responsibilities gave his shoulders power as Waban brought the club solidly down on Weeping Heart's skull. He looked at the body of his son.

Nuppohwunau made his light way through the company to listen for life at his brother's heart. "It beats!"

Waban emitted pride. "He has his strengths. Let him wake where life will be the worst for him. He does not have the brains to make trouble anymore." Waban did not glance Weeping Heart's way as he was carried from the room.

Wakwa said into the hush, "At any time, Waban, I am ready to give over the small powers that I have, out of service to you. They press against me, having as I do a wife who is white."

Waban crossed to him and rubbed Wakwa's neck at the place of the long scar. "I know, nephew, I know."

Wakwa went home, alone. "Weeping Heart is gone," was all he would say to his wives about the grueling day. He was bathed by them, and fed, and he kept their society, saying nothing, laboring over the canoe paddle which he was lavishing with relief-work.

"A grand jury could be forming at this moment, and you take the morning shaving!" Gil berated Beckett.

"The appearance of control may mean control. We must look fresh, or that crafty old chieftain will pounce on us and serve us round for lunch."

"What nonsense! You saw what he did to his son yesterday, out of deference to me."

"Out of deference to somebody."

"He knows the bad apples from the good. Second thoughts, Michael, you'd better shave."

"I don't know how to manage these things. Come and heat water for the soap."

"Don't be prissy. What's to manage? Here, make a little fire, heat up some stones, hang the damned birchwood kettle over the stand. Oh. Water."

"Yes, the water." Becket relieved himself of headache, clamping forefinger and thumb at the bridge of his nose.

"They've always supplied me amply. Pretty young things carrying it in and in."

"Perhaps the stream ran dry, blood brother. Or they have run out of pretty girls. Don't bother to look out the door. Only guards."

"They won't carry."

"Bad hospitality. Worth, I'd wager Silent Fox is under siege as well."

"Then, of course, we'll have to shave."

"Alack, the water."

"The water."

Beckett wheedled when Worth would not budge. "If you'd brought Matthew, he could go fetch. . . ."

"If I'd brought Matthew he could shave us with a dry razor without the least discomfort."

"I wouldn't offer that black bastard my throat at any time."

"With reason. I would slit it myself if I did not need you, as I seem to do, regularly."

"And all the time. You ought to be locked up, you know."

"You need me, too, Michael, and I do not speak about

money. What a drab life would be yours, but for me."

"Debatable. Nevertheless, I'll give this case my all, but I am not about to fit my neck to a noose for any poet."

"Obliged for the compliment."

"Not meant as one."

Gil wound his cloak around his naked form. "Anything you wants besides water, Massa?"

"It would be dandy if you could bring me White Cat on a silver platter."

"Do you want me to try? I will. I'm only standing around."

"Don't trouble yourself, Gilbert, the idea is that White Cat be brought here alive."

They risked killing themselves working their razors without mirrors. Neither offered to shave the other.

"For what it is worth, Michael, to you, and to all of you," Gil volunteered when the principals greeted one another around Waban's morning fire, "I am willing to open up the whole ugly business between me and Hudson. If Annanias did this thing, wrote to Duhmmer, he has broken our agreement. A gentlemen's agreement. I could damage him. I would even if it landed me in a jail. Better me than Wakwa. I could start on Hudson anywhere, illicit liaisons, the mess in Boston, his hounding Charles to death because of Beth. . . ."

"I am not willing to let you testify to anything, Gilbert Worth." Beckett would have stamped his foot had he not been sitting Indian fashion. "And, Hudson has kept his gentlemen's agreement with you. Your name is not listed with the others."

"Exactly! I was there! I walked that course proudly with thirty-eight other men who are listed. There are plenty of witnesses up the coast. Ask the shire-reeve of Pemaquid if he remembers me. It will be clear to Duhmmer that Hudson left me off the Information to protect his own ass."

"Why don't I borrow some rope from one of these hunters and hang you myself, this morning, along with a deal of unnecessary paperwork. And Hanna, too! Save her the grief of watching you ruin yourself and her."

"Hanna I will hide, release her from her bond to me if that would make her secure, but I will not let that great walking carcass of a preacher trample on Wakwa's name and get away."

"Gilbert, will you impoverish the woman you love, lose through forfeiture the lands you paid dear to save, reopen graves that you dug, bring infamy on every Indian you would honor, all to tell the world that a fat and failing priest deflowered an overripe virgin in his barn?"

"Michael, are you saying it is impossible? Can I be of no help?"

Beckett altered his hard tone. "I am saying, sir, that you have done what you could. It is my business to keep you alive so that you may exercise your highly civilized political theories at a more propitious date." The lawyer readied his writing materials, setting himself to explain another route of defense. But he interrupted himself to say, "Why would the sheriff of Pemaquid remember you, Gilbert?"

"It is no matter."

"I'd like to decide that."

"It really is not all that I made it out to be. I brought in a few furs, was looking for someone, asked for a brandy, the barkeeper was uncordial. Nothing else."

"Gilbert, I am not the judge. I am your advocate. Why would they remember you in Pemaquid?"

Worth removed from the group. He occupied the doorway again, and related the tavern brawl.

Beckett took notes. "Cut him with your sword? Not seriously, of course."

"I nipped his hand."

"Not off," Beckett quipped.

"Not quite."

"Your diary would make a Turk blanch! How can I prepare a brief if your bloody . . . zeal . . . foils every defense we have?"

"Oh, what is the difference about Fisher Deil? What would you have done to a surly bastard stealing your property, probably to shoot you?"

"I do not put myself in such situations. Drab though I be."

"That can't be helped. Anyway, Dire Locke settled it out of court with a blood-wite."

"Oh, fine! Amercements paid by third parties! You have hung me. How can I act for you?"

"Listen to me, Beckett." Gil possessed the place where he stood like a man of larger bulk. "In this wilderness there is no iron control, there are no masters, no slaves, no gods, no kings! We are, each of us on our own, which is why Wakwa made that journey in the first place. There is your defense! If you are going to shed the dust of other places from your shoes and live on the mainland of America and practice law, you had better accept little accidents along the lonesome ways with a more masculine grace."

"There is bile enough in that last remark to make a duel," Beckett said smoothly, then winked to cover wickedness. "I may not have as fancy a gun as you do to settle quarrels of manhood, but I am not without ammunition."

A change was effected in Gil out of his horror at having his rallying speech turned against his vitals, open insult against his childlessness, in the sight and hearing of other men. Withstanding the troubled gaze of the Massachuseuck, his primal senses, at last, looked up. They led him beyond frustration, beyond chagrin. Gil laid his desire to produce offspring to rest, along with the pleasures of vehemence, like clothes out of style. His emotions cut loose of Beckett. Quietly, he returned, "I will trust, sir, that you will use those vital balls against the enemies of Silent Fox," and assumed a place among the others.

Less irritably, Beckett reasoned, "I suppose that I could bypass your dispute with the fisher as an example of the feuding Silent Fox attempts to quell."

"Do better," Wakwa spoke up. "Tell Sir Jeremy because of it Gilbert was saved by Dire Locke, who then came into the woods for our discussion, and ended having leased an island from those French Indians for Vaughan Thomas Kirke to build ships on."

Beckett was overcome. "That is a marvel! Do you know what you have done? You have begun commercial cooperation between political enemies. Certainly the profitable exchange of goods is the basis of lasting peace. Do you know?"

"I know," Wakwa twinkled back. "Do you know that is how the Iroquois have kept their treaty with the English kings for one hundred twenty years? Michaelbeckett, as well, I have made arrangement to harvest ginseng root for Locke."

"Another very advantageous arrangement for everybody. What do you say? Shall we meet this head on? Drop the libel? Go in with a plea of innocent?"

"Will there be searches? Seizures? Will they arrest my women? I will not injure those two."

"Sachim, what you and Gilbert want guaranteed, it seems to me, is that you have the right to act outside the norm, to be different, to think independently of the mass, and go unscathed. At present, no safeguard for dissent is written into the law. But in each territory under the thumb of one judge or another, cases are heard on their special merit and decisions are handed down . . . so common custom forms. So, if I broach it to Judge Duhmmer that he really ought not to raise his eyebrows at an Indian sachim who is not Christian, is married to two women, and walks on water over the fault in unenforceable treaties. Duhmmer might assent, guest you in his house, give you the key to the city. But only if the common custom in your neighborhood can be shown to tolerate freethinking. Short of statutory law, there is common law. Outside of that you are an outlaw. Solicitors have obligation to turn to someone familiar with common legal practice in his clients' region. I ask for the Sweetwood tither, Mr. Cooper."

They took him away from a hot meal, a game of beans-in-a-bowl, and the society of soft-eyed girls who had sung and danced for him, making their music with their bodies covered by copper bells.

"How are you, Cooper?" Gil encouraged him when he appeared in the torrid room full of troubled men.

"Bat-blind. The town's eye can be blind. I were never here. This is an experience not given to the likes o' me."

"Gather your faculties, Will."

"Here is the man who prevented justice miscarrying herself," Beckett introduced him. "Will Cooper brought the Information directly to me because he bears you all a friendship."

"Begging your pardon, governor, I bear a friendship for Gilbert Worth."

"Same thing." Beckett saved his face.

Less a liability for his influence in Sweetwood, Gil remarked, "Will, you are a good egg. Friendship or no I want you to answer Mr. Beckett with complete honesty. It will go the worse for me if you do not."

Beckett began, "Mr. Cooper, has there ever been a court action in this region concerning a marriage of mixed blood?"

"Oh, aye. I tell you how I know. . . ."

"Favor us by staying to the point?"

"Sure, gov. About ten years ago it were. Thirty-eight. Over to White Island Pond at Agawame."

"Yes?" Beckett leaned forward eagerly.

"I answered the question, sir."

"You did, indeed. Try another? What happened to that husband and wife?"

"Now, sir, it weren't a marriage. The woman, she was English and married to someone else, a farmer by name of, I don't suppose it matters, well, her husband, he was a hard worker but drank on the sly. Now that matters, 'cause it's forbidden by law. A little cider was all they was supposed to take. But no one made mention of his infraction nor his resultin' bad temper. Well, sir, up from the woods the buck come, regular . . . the feller, the Indian feller, he come regular ever' ten days or so. They was real attached, I mean like regular folks who. . . ." Cooper made meshing gestures with his fingers.

"One might assume that, Coop." Kindly, Gil said, "What happened to them?"

"Well, sir, Mr. Worth, I tell you when it came out, the husband, he put the matter directly to the Selectmen, he did. And they put the lady in the stocks, as directly. Now you may not think this is to the point, but what they did was to turn the stocks toward the place where the man used to come out of the woods. And then, you see, she'd get ten stripes. Ever' day for a month. A stripe for each day she'd a-been hankerin' after the buck. The feller."

"And the fellow?" Beckett drew Cooper out because Gil could not speak.

"The Indian? Banished. The deal was if the Selectmen promised to keep their hands off him, the tribe, whichever, was to see that the buck was never to be, or to be seen in his region again."

Worth did not like the story a bit. "I've lived here since twenty-seven, I've never heard of any such thing!"

"Why, Mr. Worth, that was what I tried to tell you first. Only reason I know of it is because they called me over there to bury the lady."

"She died of the lash!"

"Some say. But she lingered over a year. 'Twas no infection sent her to her Maker. I dressed the body. 'Twas scarred but healed. That lady died of a broken heart."

"The facts are all we ask, Cooper," Beckett cut him off. He said to the rest of the men, "It does not pertain. In our instance there is a recognized union, in the Massachuseuck form, I grant you, but recognized, nonetheless. Duhmmer himself let it stand for purposes of the land conveyance. Our complication is too many marriages. What of that, Cooper? What instance have you of Massachusetts women who are untraditional? Not members of the Church. Let us say, a woman who brings no harm to anyone, yet who lives unawed by civil statutes?"

Cooper considered. "I could give you men." He laughed. "I give you Gilbert Worth." No one responded to his humor. "It is hard to find a woman in these times is willing to do without a full belly and a full trunk o' clothes, for the darin' to be different."

"When, Cooper, was that ever easy?" Beckett made a joke of his own.

"In the sixties and seventies before the Great War with Philip! Aye, there were women, dozens I could name, hundreds I cannot. I'll give you Mary Fisher. There's Ann Austin. Had their books taken the minute they landed in Boston. No, before they docked. And then they was examined, I won't say how, by the Elect of that place to see if they was witches. Why, ye see, they was locked up, and one by one the officials, they came and each man. . . ."

"Cooper, it is not necessary!" Gil shut him up.

"Gilbert! We are there!" Beckett hushed him. "Mr. Cooper, what was their offense? What law had they transgressed?"

"Why, sir, none. They was just different. Those two did not fit in the mold, as it were, sir, if y' see."

"Quite." It was Beckett.

"I see." Gil whispered.

Wakwa watched Waban.

Cooper worked to regain attention. "I give you Alice Ambrose. . . ."

"Do we need more, Michael?" Gil asked.

Beckett raised a hand for general quiet. "Tither, be brief."

"Alice Ambrose sentenced to be flogged for preachin' the inner light, sixteen hundred sixty-two."

"Wait one moment." Michael referred to some notes. "I have here there was general toleration for all Protestant sects by then. On the books."

"Alice Ambrose sentenced to floggin' for preachin' the inner light, walkin' to Dover and preachin' Quakerism, sixteen hundred sixty-two, in the winter."

"King Charles expressly said that all Protestant sects would be permitted to preach and take on members. . . ." Beckett fought for his point.

"In all sects save Quakerism. Y' see, sir, he reconsidered there. Vagabond Act went back on the books as pertained to Quakers."

"Charles II intervened, personally?"

"A liberal soul, he was. Said y' couldn't hang one."

"Well, thank you, Cooper. That is fine. We appreciate your substantial help." Beckett dismissed him.

"Alice Ambrose sentenced to floggin' in the winter for preachin' Quakerism, sixteen hundred sixty-two, by the Reverend John Rayner."

"What difference, Will?" Gilbert Worth shook his head until his gold hair rippled.

"Have y' never seen a person flogged in cold? Alice Ambrose was tied to a cart on a December day, stripped to the waist, though the snow was comin' down. Alice Ambrose was made to walk all the way to Dover behind that cart, flogged from town to town, ten stripes at each town she would pass along the way. There is eight towns on that road. That is eighty stripes in the cold."

"We thank you," Beckett said. "We have the gist. Good afternoon. You will be escorted back to Sweetwood, immediately. We have kept you long from your duties."

"Alice Ambrose was whipped in December cold by a rope as big around as a man's little finger. Not counting knots. It was so cold that no sooner than the whip was laid on, the opened flesh froze, then," Cooper clapped his hands, "the next one. There's no tellin' the pain."

"Goddamn you, Cooper." Gil clenched his fists.

"Alice Ambrose went all the way to Salisbury at the tail of that cart, walkin' through the snow, her bare feet froze, her body all blue and blood, a pulp."

"God!" Gil covered his face.

"Cooper, this is old news. Give us something from this century or get out!" Beckett's hands were black, his cuffs dripped the ink that spilled.

"But the people of Salisbury, and here is what I'm gettin' to. . . ."

"Please!" Beckett pleaded.

". . . The people of Salisbury had what it took to cut ghastly Alice from off that cart and they set her free whether or no she were a Quaker."

"Praise be for that!" Gil looked up at the curved roof.

"That is important!" Beckett wrote, "PEOPLE OF SALISBURY BREAK THE MOLD!"

"No matter that in the night," Cooper took up the slack, "that other constables come and found poor Alice at prayer and they took her out, dragged her with arms tied, face down across the snow, over stumps and fallen trees and dead wood near a mile. She were stuck in a house there, and the next mornin' which was very cold, the same two constables pushed Alice into the frozen salty harbor, and her with them fresh gashes from the rope, and made her swim for her life next to the canoe they paddled."

"They killed her after all?" Beckett's professional detachment gave ground.

"Well, sir, a storm came up and the constables had to get out of that canoe or drown so they took Alice Ambrose back to the house with her clothes all wet and built her no fire and when it was dark midnight in the woods, turned her out with her clothes frozen stiff upon her, . . ."

Beckett lost his breakfast. Awepu boldly broke from the group and left Waban's house for Wakwa's.

Pequawus said to the disturbed sagamores, "If we would, we could trade stories with the tither. We all know that in the Great War, a woman, a pretty woman, a white captive, was cooked alive and eaten for her skin. Let us not be frightened. There are men, red and white, who make nightmare out of gentle lives."

"Brother-in-law," Waban took exception, "in a war between nations many atrocities can happen. What worries your son is that Elizabeth's people make war upon themselves."

Awepu and Meadow-in-the-Night, carrying their youngest child, found Elizabeth huddled against the far south wall in the dark, Moses asleep in her lap. She was painfully idle as a person bereaved.

"Now, Elizabeth. You must remove. Do not ask me why this mountain giving way under your husband is falling on you. I hear it rumbling. Come away. My wife will stay in your house to fool the guards. You wear her cloak about you, and her blanket across your shoulders and around your babe, thus. I will shelter you with my arm. The guards will think you are my wife, and Moses my child. And you will pass to safety. I will keep you like a precious thing, and when all is smooth I will return you to Wakwa, wherever he may be."

Elizabeth looked at her friends with eyes aglitter from slight fever. "I have a complaint for the women's council. I have done nothing wrong. Yet, I am kept caged by my husband as if I were a vicious thing."

"Elizabeth, let it go. The guard is but a warning to Waban. Wakwa has put those men about you like stakes about a town. Waban has disowned one son and I would not expect him to stop at cuttings bonds where no blood binds. There is no answer to Wakwa's trouble. The troubles only can be chopped off him like vines that strangle the green tree."

"I am a trouble? How do I trouble him?"

"They rake over his heart with talons of iron. They furrow his insides with grim fangs. They seed him with horrors. I tell you, Wakwa will never scar you with his hand. Let me take you away. I will save you for him like a choice nutmeat. You will come together in happier times, for with tears in his eyes, Waban, the sachim, his uncle, is moving toward you with his ax ready."

"Oh, am I a sweet, then, for tasting on sunshiny days? Awepu, I am a woman grown. I see trouble in the life of every grown person I know. Why shall I be preserved from my part in Wakwa's life?"

"It is enough he loves you as he does. Do not ask him to kill you."

They fell together, and Awepu's wife took Moses and began to bundle him for a night walk.

"What do they say is my part in this? What crime have I done that Wakwa will not speak to me? Why cannot I see Waban or Uncle Gil?"

"Elizabeth, soon they will come for you. Come away."

"They said that they would come? I can answer for myself?" She took no hope from Awepu's face. "How do you know they will come?"

Awepu brought her to the courtyard made by the house. He wrapped Elizabeth in his arms in the dank night. Where they stood there was no human sound. But wolves passed along rumors of frost, emptying prophetic cries out of their bellies. The pines sieved the warning of cold times to come, and let it sing up against the black sky after the wolf voices echoed away.

"They will come," Awepu assured.

Elizabeth leaned against him, not wanting to stand on her own. "Sure as our breath, I feel it, too."

"I must take you at your word. After this I cannot help. This council will not end until all is decided. No loose string will be left untied. Tell me now. Will you save yourself?"

"Awepu, had I thought of saving myself I should never have left my father. And I never would have known a friend such as you."

They stayed bound by irony. When their arms untwined, it was Elizabeth who helped the grieving man to go inside to reclaim his wife and baby, to bring them home.

# Chapter 50

WAKWA DID NOT LISTEN to Michael Beckett anymore. The fire burned high, feeding on his trouble. The second day licked at the third, flamed into it, consumed it, became it. Haggard, Beckett negotiated solutions, forgetting sleep. Wakwa faced the reason for his dilemma.

It stood in front of him. It was a beautiful thing. It had a changing shape like a light, far away. It stayed bright no matter who or what touched it. All else was shadow when Wakwa acknowledged this peculiar flame. It was never snuffed even in a tight place. It illuminated one vision—a sight of certain love, a will. It lived without him. He did not know life without it.

"Non Sum. How about it as best under the circumstances? Make no plea, Fox. Disappear for a while and I put Duhmmer through his paces."

"Then I am no sachim, for evermore. Who will serve?"

"I am afraid you are up a tree like Half-Dog." Beckett searched for some device. "If you are going to give yourself to Duhmmer and take on the burdens of your office, you must let a wife slide. Nicely. But let her go. I need some range."

Gil snarled, "Damn your eyes, Beckett. How dare you confront him with such a choice!"

"The choice is not his," Waban said. "He will give up the one who would come to the most harm."

"I will give up nothing!" Wakwa fought to control the moment. He saw them escape, he and Elizabeth and the children, all together. South they could not go. East across the sea was certain death now, for the lot of them. West would bring them into the Mohawk region. Elizabeth, by

371

treaty, was their enemy, forbidden access to those lands. He saw the hand of the Six Nations turn her white face up to horrors and himself suing for the rest of their lives at the Onondaga fire. North was the only way, into the cold with Qunneke big with his child. Claude would give them sanctuary if they could reach him. If the French found them first they would shoot him but, far worse, make his wives parlormaids in Montreal and teach his children tasks of the stable and the scullery.

"He will give up nothing," Waban agreed. "One wife will be taken from him."

"You will take a wife from me?" Wakwa was on his feet.

Waban puffed his pipe. "No, nephew. She will be claimed by her own."

"When finally she is complete, and mine? Lose Qunneke?"

"What kind of fox bites onto a bit of tasty flesh, and pulls at it to take it to his den when the morsel is attached to the leg of a man? A whiteman. Elizabeth is a limb from a different tree caught in our branches. Will you break her off to keep her in your arms? She will be deadwood. You will divorce her while she is yet full of life."

"Elizabeth!"

"You would be sachim, yet would not waste her. Being the one you must do the other. So divorce her. For I will not let you away from your duty. I did not beat my son over the head so as to lose you, too."

"What is going on here?" Gil took in first one sachim and then the other.

"Old man, Waban, here is the answer. You will take my wives and the People for the winter remove, but you will take them far, high into the White Mountains where no whitemen go. I am the spokesman. I will go to Boston and speak. Lord Duhmmer will not touch me. I have too many friends."

"Will they hang with you?"

"I will not hang."

"You have not, in Gilbert's word, a guarantee."

"I will act as I please! You made me what I am. I am sachim."

"I am the old one."

Wakwa was confounded.

Gilbert Worth was not. "You are also the sachim who promised me on the day I told you that my land and Charles Dowland's lands were yours, that my niece would walk always in the sun, protected by Kautantowwit. Well, I've kept my bargain. You've got the ground signed and sealed. Now you want to spit her up. Well, swallow hard, Waban. Because she doesn't go down easily, anywhere, now."

"As to the land, Gilbert Worth, you have never done us any favor. You are a good man. You have done what is right. And we will do right by Elizabeth."

"By giving her the shove when the going gets rough? That kind of protection is just not good enough! Let me hear one of you praise the sanctity of the spoken word, now! Give me an old-fashioned, hard as rock, Saxon marriage contract any day!"

Beckett motioned Gil down. "That is what Hudson had." The lawyer turned to the ageing head of the tribe. "Friend Waban, I was moving your nephew to drop the first wife. After all, Elizabeth Dowland bore him his son. That must count for something. It is not to your financial advantage to turn them out."

"Them? I did not say, Michael, that I would let her take Wolf-of-the-mist He-hopes with her. Whereas her skin will blend with other white ones, his will not. If I am to care for her shall I let her child be stoned in the streets? We will raise him. He has a second mother. He will be a great man. He shall have been loved."

Beckett put his notebook into the breast pocket of his coat. He was the first to see that from that moment the council would be a staged affair. It was a matter of balancing tragedies.

Wakwa saw Elizabeth brought to the entry. The life in her eyes set his special light to flickering over the fire. He began to believe that knife of brightness was in her view, as well. It was the superior life that kept her supple, shining, manittoo. He and she could walk separately for a thousand years, yet be unparted. And they were joined though they had never met.

"Awepu." He explored a different way. "If I ask it, will you borrow Gilbert's gun? Would you keep it near you until I can take Elizabeth to sleep with me one night under the stars, before it becomes too cold? Could you watch for day? And before she woke, could you . . . shoot first her . . . then me? I trust her to you. You would do it so she would never flutter an eye."

Awepu's mouth seemed to swell as the juices in him waned. "If you ask it, if you wish it, I can do it. You are the one I hold above me."

Neither man could see the other behind tears that would not drop.

"That may be." Waban's close voice surprised them. "But shoot the nephew I have groomed for my post, Awepu, and I will shoot your whole family. All their eyes will flutter."

Wakwa swayed and pressed his weight against Awepu.

"At least a little, let him be a man!" Awepu cried out darkly to Waban.

"I force him to be one."

Elizabeth's voice invaded the silence of the hot room. "What have they done to you!" She forged a crooked way to Wakwa and he caught her against the thud in his chest.

"Wakwa!" Waban scolded and a din erupted. Men grouped into factions. Beckett pounded points home to Waban, fist to palm.

Despondence turned Gilbert Worth toward the semi-dark tunnel of the hall.

"Can't we table this? Vacate your grounds. Let me go to the court and file a countersuit. That will give us the power to investigate and come up with the informer. I tell you, if this is a simple case of spite, Fox won't have to say a thing about where he spent last winter!" The whites of Beckett's eyes broke into red threads of blood.

"No! We will be turned over like a turtle to the sun!"

"You have to take some risk!"

"Michael, I take risk when the risk will bring benefit. What benefit is there for Wakwa in this union? Torment only has been his headdress since he has had her! The union itself is a risk which I took for him. Its benefits fall short of ones that yet await him in his life! And you see, Englishman, they will never be separate though they never touch again." Waban gestured toward the whispering pair.

Michael Beckett turned on his heel and absented himself

from the rest of the proceeding. The camp was still, a living thing listening. Only the quash of the stones against mortars crushing the corn told its pulse. Beckett followed that rhythm to its source and sat at the periphery of the group of women barning the last of the corn, and drank his flask until his shaking stopped and the sweat dried above his upper lip.

"You are so beautiful." Wakwa could hold back no tenderness as he touched her.

"Let us go to the court, together. We have done that before."

"You are so strong!" Wakwa lifted her, face to face with him.

This height, his admiration, gave her hope.

"Tell her, Wakwa!" Waban insisted.

"Let her go away." Pequawus continued to try. "I shall live with her and keep her. Do not tear them apart! I know what life is, lived longing for love cut while green."

"Pequawus, I would remove her from the clutches of the bear before he strikes. The difference between you and me is that I act to prevent the wound, and you live to wipe it."

Pequawus was stricken by this hardness.

"You will do better to hold your son in your arms after this, rather than his white woman. Else he will fail and forfeit the place you never could have." Waban elbowed his way to Wakwa and Elizabeth. "I am sending for your wedding reeds to get through with this breaking off!"

Wakwa let Elizabeth slip down. "That is not up to you! That is my decision. Kitchize! Old man! How long have you to hold sway?"

"Until I see you able to do so. Qunneke!" Waban fretted after her.

"Hold me." Elizabeth took Wakwa's naked, sweating sides.

The groups of men watched her, in quiet.

"Hold me!"

Wakwa remained loosely attached, his arms circling her back.

"Hold me!" Elizabeth wrapped herself round his slippery torso.

Wakwa took her shoulders and bent down and drank

from her mouth. "Long ago I nursed you from a wounded thing, so you could fly. And now you must."

Waban tussled with Qunneke for the reeds. "My sister! My sister! Weetahtu!" She lost them to him when pain struck her great belly.

Wakwa held Elizabeth's face so that she could look at no one but him. "It is my will that I do not drag you in the dirt I will walk through for the Ninnuock. Let us cheat them who will extract payment from you because you have received love from me. We will keep that which we have had at its high peak. Here is where you always are." He crushed her to himself, and said, "Unscathed! So, my promise to your father!"

Waban wrapped Wakwa's fingers around a painted reed. He conformed Elizabeth's hand around hers. She let it fall. He picked it up and held it in her hand with both of his.

"My wife! Nehyewgh!" Wakwa's reed remained intact.

Waban pronounced, "Nequt oukauau. He has one wife."

"Wenygh. You are woman." Wakwa's subtle change of consonant came with the snap of the dry reed in his hand.

Elizabeth screamed at him, "I do not let you go! You are the knife in me. Do not draw it away!" The heart of her slender stalk of marsh grass crushed under her desperate hold of his sides.

Waban ordered Awepu, "Take her away from him!"

Wakwa's lips touched the crown of Elizabeth's head. "You may!" he said to Awepu.

Gilbert and Qunneke stood like one being, their hips, and shoulders, and heads touching as they witnessed. Wakwa's arms were held aloft over Elizabeth's clinging.

"Hold me!"

"Divide them!" Waban shouted in fury.

Awepu lifted Elizabeth, pulling her away by her breast and hips, stretching her out like a line of willow. She fought his muscle, digging her fingers into the skin of Wakwa's rib cage. Four faint, red tracks appeared. She was adrift of him.

Pequawus went after her. Young, strapping men caught him away. Elizabeth saw him, and beyond him to Wakwa, bowing to the elder sachim, kissing his shoulders in ritual obeisance, saying cowaunkamish, "My service to thee!"

A squad of men bundled the uncle and niece together

onto the back of the bay. Grandee whirled and dragged men with him as they tied Worth and Elizabeth to one another, in the saddle. Beckett drooped from his horse, green as a seasick man.

"My child!" The knell of English fell on the little houses like shade.

They were led across the bridge without him and up into the trees.

Wakwa ran into his house and faced Qunneke's eyes. The taupowaw put a dusty, wrinkled hand on each of Wakwa's torn sides. "She is untouchable. You will nevermore mention the name of Elizabeth to those who look up to you. When the blood dries, deepen the cuts with your knife. Never let these heal until the flesh refuses to forget its harrowing." The wise sayer pressed a skin bag into Wakwa's hand. "Here is your balm. Use it."

Wakwa and Qunneke stood in the center of the barren room. He saw nothing in her face but himself. "Burn it! Burn everything," he screamed. He tore down the entry mat and then bolted away, never stopping at the precipice. He threw himself down into the turmoil of black water.

Torchlit by Mosq, Wakwa grappled his way across, and up and into the hunting house. His dripping knife redrew deeper the marks Elizabeth had made on him. He staggered out into the utter dark, calling, not his butchery, but the agony of a full self never to be tapped.

These sounds crept over the skins of the passing horses and their riders.

Elizabeth strained against the ropes to listen. Closed against her, in the coil, Gil comforted, "A frightened animal is all, dear." He kissed her where he could reach her.

She wept, and the uncle did not try to stop her, thinking tears were good for her just then.

# Chapter 51

DOCTOR MAC resolutely overpowered Elizabeth, dosed her with opium, believing in his soul that violent passion matured into acute illness. He linked arms with Hanna in the sitting room, where Gil lay.

"He looks like a dead man." She watched her husband, stretched out on the settee in his boots.

"Some part in him is bound to die after the likes o' this, but knowin' Gil, somethin' else more wonderful will regrow. He needs ye, now." Stirling went to rest.

Matthew hovered between floors, keeping watch above and below.

Hanna turned from the couch to the corner where Michael Beckett had strewn himself. Notebook in hand, he drunkenly tried to compose a brief from the written tatters of Elizabeth's short marriage. His black hose were ripped. Hanna covered an open spot with her hand, feeling the white skin and soft black hair of his leg for the first time.

"You think me despicable." Michael worked his tongue and teeth around the word which seemed to have grown longer since he had last used it.

Hanna did not offer to help him. She did not suggest a chair. He was comfortable on the floor. She went for a bottle and a glass. "On the contrary, Michael, I am an admirer of excess." She returned and helped him sip. "It betokens something that is worth doing."

"Aren't you fine!" Beckett leaned his sweaty head against the wall of books behind him.

"I know that I am sad. I do not seem capable of excess, myself."

Beckett threw an arm over her near shoulder. "Com'ere."

He curled up in sudden pain, not finishing his phrase. In short vocal pushes of his larynx he told her, "See what it gets you? See the stomach it gets you? See what it got your niece?"

"We do not know what it has gotten her. The years will tell. But it got her something."

Michael eased back against the angle of the shelves. Perspiration sluiced from his pores and he covered his eyes. "I did try. Tell me, tell me you believe I did try." He did not give her a chance. "But, the savage will out." Michael caught Hanna's brown hair with fingers that could not quite hold. "I am coming back when you have more time for me. I'll dance for Duhmmer for a while, then I'll take you back to Boston, for Ho cries hard for his 'Ani.'"

Hanna slipped her fingers between the touching of their lips. Blood rose in Beckett's cheeks.

He belched. "Your husband said in front of fifty men he'd divorce you jus' to kick Hudson's ass. 'Release her from her bond to me,' how he put it. Fact. In the note-book."

Hanna hobbled away to a cabinet to get a rug for him. Beckett assured her as she tucked the thick spun wool about him, "I am not despicable!"

Noon of the second day, Gil entered his front hall softly, mired from riding. His face was bleached of color. He heard Hanna's skirts, not her greeting, and he croaked wearily, "They are gone. There is not a person or a thing there. You look over the river onto virgin territory. All that is left is the smell of char."

"Gillie? I want to awake. This is real?"

"It is passed." Worth's eyes went red at their rims. "Beth and I are like boats bailed. Safe enough, but empty." He put his hands over his face. "I'll be demned, but you know, Hanna? I am glad to have her home." Then he gave way to his grief.

His male sobbing brought Elizabeth to the landing. In shadow, above them, she bore no expression. Her borrowed dressing gown engulfed her figure. "What is the matter?"

Hanna looked up. "Your uncle has been gone overnight, darling, looking for . . . your family."

"He did not find them," she said, sourly.

"Oh, Beth." Gil came to the bottom step, shaken to have to say, "They are not anywhere to be found."

"They are out in the swamps. Freezing. Out of fear. Fear of me. You rode right by them." Elizabeth made a light laugh.

Gil looked to Hanna at this exquisite rudeness.

Hanna kissed his cheek, and said near to his ear, "It is the drug."

Beth's hearing was acute. "I did not take it today."

"Then do," Hanna said.

Gil climbed halfway to Elizabeth, but stopped his progress when she drew back from him. "Dearest girl, I searched all the routes I searched for you, long ago, and more. They are not in the swamps. We must imagine that the old ones, the babes and the mothers soon to be confined, are not freezing but managing well, on their way to winter quarters. Your baby is not with you, but we must assure ourselves that he is being tenderly cared for. A little food, a little sleep, and I will look again."

Elizabeth eyed a small bundle tucked against Gil's breast.

"This!" he said, recalling it. "In the center of the open space, bare ground where once your house stood, I found a jar. This was in it. Here, it must be yours."

Elizabeth shied when he baited her down toward him with the sack. Then she ran the few steps and snatched it and sat on the stair. She hunched lovingly over the soft deerskin, ashamed that they should see her eager. She undid the string and stretched the bag wide. "It is a little root, is all." Her hand searched the bag in her great disappointment. "What am I going to do with a little root? A root!" She let it fall, and the man-shaped thing bounced down to Gil. Elizabeth buried her head under her arms and gasped back sorrow. She looked up at her aunt and uncle, recognizing them. "Excuse me!" Rising before she knew she had, she ran, gained her room, and released the sounds of a hellion.

Gil started after her.

Hanna held him back. "Mac is there. He will attend it. Soon she will be asleep. Could you possibly rest?" Walking a step lower than he, Hanna propped him up the remaining way to their bed. She undressed him, tended him as if he were a soldier. She lit a candle though it was bright day. "Just for a moment to bring on the bayberry." The wife smiled for his labors in behalf of her brother's daughter. She bent to blow out the flame.

Gid did not permit it.

Hanna found herself lying with him, exposed to the smooth linen of the bedclothes, and her husband's soreness of heart.

Gil did not let her go lightly. Through the short, eastern afternoon, he sighed out his troubles, and as they struck her he petted her, and his anguish flowed into her, and ebbed. As day dimmed, outside, Gil raised up to snuff the candlelight, not caring to let its smallness assume the place of the sun. The man root lay at the base of the stand, surrounded by fragrant smoke. He brought Garent-Oquen into bed with himself and his wife.

"Tame Deer left us wild Seng. There is some message here." Gil turned the valuable plant over in his hands.

"Gillie, plant it."

The husband looked at his wife. "Plant it. In the greenhouse. Of course! Pot it. Make it grow. Keep it alive. Cultivate it. And in four years. . . ." Gil stopped speaking and held onto Hanna with a force applied by the whole length of his frame. "Hanna, I want Qunneke here to harvest it!"

# Chapter 52

ELIZABETH ATE apart from the family, walked close to the walls, performed tasks of the house that could be done near the chill north windows, the ones that looked to the tree line.

She was tender over Wakwa's lack of faith in the potency of their union. It was how she explained the slackness, his letting go. In hiding her from trouble, he mangled her days with his own hands. A pod of bitterness burst inside her and left an acrid taste on her tongue. What right had he to decide which kind of pain to spare her or which kind she must endure? She knew pain was in everything, excepting in star points of ecstasy, exquisitely in what was held close. That sharp edge woman held against her soul calling it love. Groundstone of life. And its grace was only at the edge of risk. She left her golden needles with their silver eyes at rest in their case, and did wild things in thought to force the man to take her back into his life.

The great glass dome seduced her from the kitchen, one afternoon, to see its strangeness. From faraway it was a belly, a breast. Elizabeth was drawn to its roundness as an infant is drawn to the nipple for milk.

She lay her body against the firm glass skin and saw someone inside. She found the segment that opened and went in. Liquid dripping, rippling gently as the coffee falling in the innards of the Worths' Italian pot, scents like spring from plants wrapped like the dead, and unseasonable warmth teased her neglected flesh.

She saw her uncle bent over a frame. "He may come, don't you think? You do think as I, that he will come for me?"

Bound in her dismay, Gil did not greet her. "He will love you always. That is why I cannot imagine his ever crossing the barrier he has erected between you."

Elizabeth turned away and walked out into haze light. Her uncle seemed old with his succinct, correct view. She was seeded with it now, herself, and felt the tumor grow at a monstrous rate.

Gil closed the greenhouse and walked at her side, pulling off his coat, placing it on her. "You shouldn't come out without a wrap, you know, when the day is gray. There would be shadows if there were sun."

Elizabeth punished him with poetry he had taught her in delightful days.

> "Hark you shadows that in darkness dwell,
> Learn to contemn light,
> Happy, happy they that in hell
> Feel not the world's despite."

"We have lost her," Gil said when Hanna joined him after helping Elizabeth into bed. "Had this house been built with an attic she would be roosting there, quite mad. I fear she will do damage to herself. Keep sharp things out of her reach. Take her needle brooch away. She longs for hell. She does not know, even yet, we are all born into it."

"She broods, Gilbert, she is a mother. She does not know where her baby is. Her fortitude is inhuman."

"Think of his. Having to be the one to inflict lifelong torment on the person he loves past anything. How sublime in cruelty that all their great striving is crossed off by a stroke of Hudson's pen."

"That was never proven. Michael did not have the chance. Oh, how I would like to have been there when all the great men's minds broke off this most becoming match."

Gil pinched a string of his harp between two fingers and ran them up and down, tight on the wire-bound gut. An abusive vibration shot up their spines.

Hanna held her temples against the return of debilitating headache. "Apologize!"

"I will be doing that, I suppose, for the rest of my life." Gil stamped away from the instrument and sat so hard next to her that the settee nearly fell backward. "It was he, Hanna, whether or no Beckett ever proves it."

"Gil, she wants to pray."

"What does that mean?"

"To pray. She is desperate."

"Can you see her in the church? I say, let us charge admission. It will be like a fair. They'll come from Plymouthtown to gape. We shall abandon the spring crop and cruise the Mediterranean on the proceeds of our sideshow."

"Matthew counted twenty carts on our road in the past two days come to catch a glimpse of her. Sweetwood knows that she is back," Hanna said.

"How?"

"Shan't we indulge her?"

"With pap now she's through with opium?" Gil scoffed.

"She does not want to go to service. She wishes the minister up here."

"I'll send a note to Low in the morning."

"Gil. She wants Annanias."

Worth stood away from his wife.

"It is untoward," Hanna admitted, "yet, it is those two who began all this history. If she talks to him, if she can stomach to talk to him, something might be said, disclosed, that would be helpful. . . ."

"To Michael."

"To the case."

"That great gutted beast in my house?"

"It is ours! And the less it is a home, the less either of us owns it."

"You are acquiring the legal mind. But no matter, you are not kept by me. Ask the hangman up to tea!" Gil's doggerel brought him into the hall for his fur-lined cloak. He twirled the circle-cut garment from his shoulders with a dandy's flourish. "I am gone for a day. Collecting tunes from simpler folk who live about the Bay." Less caustic then, "Please have him gone before I come home tomorrow night. And if he must sit, do put him on the yellow settee." He turned his back to exit. "I will be interested to see this thing solved under the sole management of women."

# Chapter 53

"YOU ARE HERE," Annanias said in the sitting room in Gilbert Worth's house.

"I know your voice," Elizabeth said to him.

It was the first time that Annanias Hudson and Elizabeth Dowland had ever been alone with one another. The house Hudson had publicly denounced for its splendor had been darkened for his visit. Drapery muffled light and sound. The faint gleam of solid objects was the result of their quality, not any reflection. The wing chair was turned toward a cold hearth. Annanias saw the chair only, in profile. Gradually came the impression of the edge of a gray petticoat and a slender leather boot. He accepted what was granted.

Tiny blood vessels burst under Hudson's skin. He groped for the courage to ask why the sudden summons. But Elizabeth spoke to him again, and like a boy, his past was swept from his memory, and he smelled the smell of roses.

"You should sit." Elizabeth watched him covertly, one eye looking past the right wing of the chair. She saw his cane.

He sucked his breath as she leaned beyond the blind of the chair to look at him fully. He fell onto the settee, then stood immediately, abashed and attentive.

"Sit," she said.

Hudson did, and put the cane across his knees. She disappeared behind her shield, but the minister clung to his new apprehension of the woman who was his idol. The modeling of her face was the same as it was before she had run from marriage with him. The fine shaping of feature was untouched by the cruelty of circumstance Annanias invented in his phantasma of native life. But her cheeks were lovelier for their loss of girlish roundness. Her eyes seemed to have grown and darkened. The long amber silk of her hair was transformed into short, free waves like the feathering on a setter. Annanias smiled. "Presbyterians would never think of bright yellow for chair silk." He tried to correct the clumsiness of his compliment. "It is the rare color that would show through this gloom."

Elizabeth leaned across the arm of her chair as a woman leans out a window to see into the street. Two years told a grim tale on Annanias's face. Its moon blandness had puffed under his opal eyes. The eyes themselves and his mouth had thinned into slits like tears in weak cloth. His middle was taut with the substance of his pantry, but his bones sagged. His curling hair had lost youthful oils and flew dryly, a whitened brown. His cleric's black was brushed, passably, a new practice. She looked with dread for his silver shoe buckles, and found them decorating his black vamps as they always had.

"So, you are here," he said.

"You sound the same."

Annanias was dry in the mouth from curiosity over why she had sent for him. "Do you visit this house often?"

"Never in all these years. I have dwelt close by, yet very far."

"A matter of some considerable inconvenience for so many who knew you."

"Berate me?"

"How shall I berate another man's wife and not a Christian, at that?"

"I am a divorced woman."

Annanias gripped his walking stick. He put it aside. Gratification put another blush on his skin. This change was to his credit. "The inevitable end to the ill-begun."

"Nothing ill. Nothing ended," she contended, quietly. "Annanias."

"Beth, do you wish to pray?"

"I pray all the time, thank you. Do you wish to pray?"

"There was a note from your aunt. . . ."

"We will get there, dear."

"You say that!" Annanias's chin touched as far down as his bands.

"Art offended?" Concerned, she put herself in view again. "I meant nothing by it."

He swallowed a cry. "Beth Dowland, you have not changed."

"Should I?"

"I do not understand you!"

"Then you have not changed, either."

"Changed enough to know not to suffer women's abuse. Over two years I have suffered things, and seen and done things that would give even you great pause . . . perhaps you know . . . ?"

"I know nothing." She brought him up short. "And more, I do not want to know. I did not ask you here, Annanias, to vie with you. Even I."

"Why did you ask me here?" His bluntness with her thrilled him.

"Another thing I do not know."

"You are incorrigible!"

"I am willing to admit that. But myself is not my concern."

"In the twelve years that I have known you, Beth, I never could decipher what your concern was."

"The despond that you signed with my father. That is my single concern."

"The despond? The marriage contract?"

"What is its state?"

"State?" He was hurt and bewildered.

"Have you got it?"

"You want it?"

"Does it exist?"

Annanias looked at his shoes. "Your father had me over to the house one night to tear it up and burn it."

"Unfortunate."

"You have the most amazing gift for summary." He gazed strangely at the fragile woman.

"It does not matter. A new one must be drawn."

"Are you mad?" He came to her chair. The buttons of his breeches were at her eye level as she sat.

She looked away and his hand came near her full, free hair. Then it dipped and chose one of hers from her lap. Small inspirations of her breath at the touch of his soft, wet palm gave him mistaken incentive. He put the hand to his lips and smiled broadly when he was done kissing it.

Wakwa's white, even teeth ghosted her.

"It were a dangerous thing for you to toy with a man's feelings after what you have done."

"Then we will be married." A chill climbed her spine, then took her whole body.

Hudson let her go. "The room is dark. You have an ague. You should take a cold bath. If I were home, I would get you some yarrow and milk and put a plaster of it on your wrists."

"That is very nice of you, Annanias."

"Always 'you.' Never the tender 'thee.' "

"Thee."

"Eh?" He flinched at her sharpness.

"Thee." This time the word was soft.

"I cannot fathom you."

"Thee!" She bellowed at him. "I have said it three times. Do you wait for the cock to crow?"

Mean as a Hereford bull, Annanias looked at her and said, "Who put you up to this?"

"Say nothing more. I will retract. I am destitute. Deliberately dispossessed of land. Perforce freed from servitude to any person. My only possession is a private burden of which I will dispose, very soon." She let Annanias replace her hand between his two trembling ones. "Having nothing, I can afford to squander. I am a vagabond."

"You are a gentlewoman born. And always will be."

"Misfortune, sir."

"I liked it better when you said 'thee'!" He knelt and put his heavy head on her knees.

A certain sympathy for his deserted state let her be gentle. "Is that your answer?"

He left a kiss in her lap.

"Please!"

Hudson lumbered away, wiping his perspiring face with his sleeve. "I forget myself. But to think, after such a period of time! You see how a man's pride is whittled with waiting."

She saw the woods. "A woman's, as well."

He took her words as a compliment to himself. "It is settled then."

"There are conditions."

"Of course." He hastened her along.

"There is to be no question of ground. The land is eliminated as a consideration between us."

"This is an affair of the heart, my Beth."

She remembered hers. "O, indeed!" She repeated the points she had devised. "I must have free passage in and out the house. I will not be asked whence and wherefore."

"Quite right. You have always been independent."

"The last. . . ."

"Quickly!"

"Annanias, I have come recently from a most gentle existence. Thoughtfulness and care are expressed from man to woman in some regions as could not be believed in any other place."

"Do not tell me." He would not listen.

"I will have complete say as to when to bed with you. I am used to no other way."

Had she risen and beaten him with his own stick he could not have known more pain. He saw the breastless child, the ten-year-old his eyes had caressed. She was unblemished, transparent, in equilibrium as exquisite as a work in glass. He had spent his prime doting on dreams of her. Every lonely night of every lonely month for ten hard years he had placed her mentally in the chair opposite him at tea. He had furnished the manse with her in mind, doing without editions of books he would like to have had, materials for experiments he designed during solitary nights. The nights. Picturing her there, talking to her, taking her memory into bed with him. Dreaming, waking from his one dream into the knowledge that she was not there and was glad not to be. The rolling Massachusetts ground he owned was a Sodom of creation in the spring, even the dogs romping in full view, yet Annanias had held fast to his legitimate prize, did not court another woman, did not consider any other marriage. Prudence Hanson was the blur on his soul's record for which he did not take blame. She was the trial sent him to purify him, and he had surpassed it. His reward was now, and he gulped it even though its edges were sharp.

Annanias had no strength to refuse Elizabeth's proposal.

He said with his eyes closed, afraid to pay her while looking at her face, "Thy father's despond offered thee as a virgin. Your consorting with the heathen, the savage, a specimen of American life profane in every lineament, I excuse as a trial sent to both of us to supersede." Then he watched her. "Had it been a goat, a pig, a wild wolf, or a very fox, it were all the same. Your spirit is a perfect flower no matter the degradation of any other part. I consent to the decrees of your spirit, which is what I will wed. Say you, when."

"Pray first that I may be forgiven." Elizabeth did not say for what.

_____ Chapter 54

"I APOLOGIZE."

"O, sit down, Gil." Hanna discounted his attempt at grace.

"I never thought to offer anyone I loved such offense."

She extended her hand to him through a steel sunset light.

He shared her couch with a grand sigh. "You are the Baths of Caracalla, a mineral spring, the river never turned off course. You are like your brother. A constant. I love Charles and I love you, and need you both." He kissed her bosom and let his face slip down against her trim stomach.

Hanna carded his gold hair which was hot in the white sun. "I know this separation from Wakwa means more to you than that he is divorced from Beth."

His arm slid around her waist.

"I know that this division goes hard, for you love him better than a brother. And you miss Qunneke." She stroked him strongly as his other arm came around her knees. "It is a divorcement for you, too. Elizabeth is of my family. I take responsibility for what she does and will do to you."

"Hudson showed his face here?" Gil nestled further into her belly and knew his answer when Hanna's hands held him there.

"She is a desperate person. You and I and Wakwa do not deign to tell her Hudson's crimes, but she suspects our secretiveness. She is after the mystery that broke the back of the beast that has borne her through paradise."

"Waban forbade us to say. Shall I break my word? Will that help?"

"Now is too late. The Ninnuock are dispersed and Wakwa has a new dedication."

Gil sucked air, not to weep.

"Now, now, as you are divided from Silent Fox for what you did to save him, Elizabeth divides herself from you. I know how she loves you despite what is coming. She says that before new moon she will marry Mr. Hudson."

Gil drove his head against the giving softness of Hanna's abdomen, pushing hard, as if he would wend his way through her body into another kind of world. She let him cause her extreme pain.

"She thinks by this means to call Wakwa back to her."

Gil sprang away from his wife and stood in his illuminous window, saying, "Massachusetts can be very cold even with the goddamn sun shining like that. I know this place is your home, your soil, but won't you come away with me for a time to someplace warm? Italy? Greece? We'll rent a place all marble and at sunset instead of hay and shit and balsam and frost, we'll smell ripening peaches in the atrium. And we will eat of them without care as we used to do."

Hanna stayed quiet until the dream he had conjured slipped weightlessly away.

Gil sought the fireplace warmth. "Writing down tunes over other farmers' fences has been restful. I think I know now why the musicos in Boston have been sluggish with their praise of my first piece. It was a matter of. . . ."

"The matter is, do let the marriage be here, in this house, in this room?"

"Ah!" Gil cried out, held his forehead, pranced to the

doors and threw them wide. "Come in, Mr. Gooseguts, soil the place at your pleasure, my niece is on a silver tray, room center, apple in mouth. Cram on my heart for your dessert!" Gil banged the double doors closed, causing paint to chip. He leaned his head against the place where they met. "I sought to learn and I have been taught in the past thirty hours that melody is the thing. The most important thing. No matter a key, or a scale of notes, the truth is, it is melody that brings meaning to man. And if the melodies will not come from inside me, I will seek them out from other men."

"I feel that way, too, asking help is most important. I thought of bringing Michael in to secretly draw the contract and perform the civil rite, but I will not burden him with a task so loathsome to yourself. Mayhew Low can do the Presbyterian ceremony in the manse. That way, without a civil service, the match can be annulled at a later date. I won't bother explaining to Elizabeth."

"You will let her do this?" Gil was past believing her.

"No guests. We can be the only ones in attendance."

"Neither I nor you will go near them."

"Gil, she needs our support."

"She hath not mine, in this instance."

"You sound like her father."

"Hanna Dowland Worth, for all intents and purposes, I am."

Hanna thought, "Without me, I wonder what else might be," but she let opportunity for argument pass. "I wish that one of us could be there," she said. "At least, we could send them down a supper. She is dowerless! A pheasant's breast. Some relishes."

"Stop! I cannot prevent you from attending this sham, but you will not expend the least penny of my resources in behalf of Hudson's blasphemy."

"See how you favor her!"

"Now, you are sounding like her mother."

"How clear it is what happened between Mary and my brother."

"What would you have me do? Work up a little charivari? Compose a wedding march for pot and pan and kettle top and spoon and serenade this incongruity? I wouldn't give them a nod. If you want to shoot a wild pheasant with a gun that is your own, and pluck it, and stuff it yourself, and roast it in a stove of your making or your purchase, you are perfectly free to do so. No servant I employ or implement I own will be wasted on such mockery."

"I only thought to discuss it with you."

Immediately gentled, Gil took the brass latch of the door in his hand. "I suppose I ought to go up and talk to her."

"You are a dear, but it will have to be later. Beth is at the printer waiting for the banns wet off the press, and then to post them at her haunts in the woods."

# Chapter 55

SALT MIST hid the vales. The soil was like pudding from rotting leaves and rain. Mud at the bottom of the rocky slope where the Massachuseuck kept the bodies of their dead held the perfect cast of a foot. Beside it, the clay was punctured as a belly is with a navel. Wakwa's long, powerful limbs stayed folded like an insect's, his hairless face did not flinch, and the tea clearness of his dark eyes did not cloud as he looked at the sign of White Cat. Then, he and Mosq went after him.

Drizzle fine as baby's hair effaced any other marks. But the fright of hawks high up the burial hill and the descent of smoke under the suffocating sky led them like senses.

They spiraled the cliffs and found nothing. Then Wakwa got a notion. "We go to my mother's grave."

"But Wakwa, those lastmost places are small. White Cat is a tall man. And, he is something of a brother to you, he was your father's ward."

Wakwa waited a night and a morning in the rain outside his mother's resting place. He kept his hands warm and his knife handle dry without the privilege of fire. Blood deepened the color of his smooth skin as the rock seal of Nippisse's tomb rolled toward him. Fingers of smoke grasped the lip of the cave entry. Like an animal rewarded by nature for patient stalking, Wakwa burst toward his prey with a yell. He crossed the rocky rampart and was through the opening.

White Cat was settling down to his meat near Nippisse's wrapped bones, her perfume, and her purple shells. The baby carrier which weighed her eternity blocked the cooking fire from draught.

White Cat's knife held raw meat over the small flame. His dilated eyes blinked. Wakwa kicked the steel out of the vise of White Cat's hand. He opened White Cat's throat with obsidian. Struggling with the cripple's heavy, living weight, Wakwa dragged him out through the hole in the rock hill and threw him bodily down and down into the running river.

Wakwa and his man cleaned out and reordered the desecrated grave. They sealed tight the opening into what Wakwa came to feel was his faceless mother's womb.

Smoke from the farm fires caught the silver of the last quarter of the moon. Rectangles of parchment tacked to the trunks of the trees attracted Wakwa's hand. He ripped one from its place. Wakwa kept this paper under his skin shirt through excited hours of his watch over Gilbert's house, until dim dawn. His breakfast was the reading of it. The black words of Elizabeth's misalliance quivered in him, spun him on the clammy red soil like a fish hooked.

# _____ Chapter 56

ELIZABETH CHOSE RUE for her wedding flower, and dressed in the plain dove gown she had sewn over years, for this occasion. The marten fur lining of her cloak with its depths of brown softened the sorrow in her face. The fields that were pearled with gray every day in the low temperatures taught her what was real and what was desire. Winter would come as surely as the harbinger mist had shouldered out the sun. Cold would descend on the farmland, and snow would spread white for miles, unrelieved by the patterns of passing carts, or horses, or persons. Privation stood very close to rich memories of other seasons. But there would be no whinny from Sucki, no call from the man on his back, no reach of arms down, or pull upward, no fitting body against body. The warmth by which she survived would not return in spring as with the countryside. More useless than frozen ground, she dressed in richly simple, dense, dark clothes that would help drag her underwater when she went to drown. She had set this fate for herself, but went to give at least vows to Annanias.

Her aunt was waiting in the hall. "I have Matthew out keeping the road clear if by any chance. . . ." Hanna turned the hood up over Elizabeth's loose hair.

"Thank you for that, Aunt!" Elizabeth loved Hanna freely then, like a friend. "Knights and their great deeds are things of story. We live in a practical time."

They kissed through their terrible disappointment.

"May I say goodbye to Uncle Gil?"

"Oh, my dear, he left last night. There is a gathering in Rhode Island at an inn. Gentlemen go there, and yeomen, to share some music. Not a party, but serious talk and exchange. Perhaps a little singing and playing. Your uncle needs that. He said that so civil a gathering must not be disregarded as it was the only sign of hope he saw in the country. I am sorry."

"He did leave a message for me?"

"He thought of it, Beth, but there is none. The ink froze in the jar yesterday and he took it as a sign that he should not write anything and left right after."

Elizabeth walked the cart road alone, composed as a criminal. The black headstone of the Dowlands in the churchyard revealed the diary of her father's life—Charles Dowland, Christian, Elder, farmer, husband, father, just and kind. "Tell me, Papa, why do I feel like myself when I stand near your grave?"

Priscilla's sweet, frightened face appeared at Elizabeth's knock. Marley had been sent in to serve Elizabeth, and Winke required by Hanna to go. "Mayhap, mistress, he will come at the reading of the vows!"

Low was unhappy to see Elizabeth Dowland alone. "And no one here to give the bride away?"

"That seems to be the habit of my weddings, Mr. Low."

Annanias caused the stairs to creak as he came down, slowly, after a lengthy toilette. Elizabeth forgave his lateness and smiled at him. Today he was the bride. Annanias took her hand and the pair stood in the parlor. Mayhew opened his own Bible when Hudson refused to bring his into the ceremony. Dorothy observed the sacrament. Vows were read and repeated, and Annanias, overwhelmed by this change in his life, turned his wife's face to his.

"I am sorry, Annanias," were her words to him.

He mistook her and shed a kiss on her mouth.

The house's sheer curtains diffused the day's gray, turning the room bright. Elizabeth did not fall when his lips touched hers. The loving expression was from a man honest in his love. Her disgust was not in him but in herself.

There was no festivity. Just cider, hot and spiced, was passed around. Elizabeth entertained new knowledge with its fragrance. The charity her father had spoken of as the highest requirement of any married union was an actual, living thing. She saw how other women could marry lesser men than Silent Fox and live in love. Elizabeth respected the longevity of Hudson's devotion. She was like that herself. She cast a glance at the happy husband. The Lows were thanked and paid, and ushered out.

"Mrs. Hudson, it is not the Worths' luxurious board, but our wedding lunch is lobster. You know the fable about the foods of love?"

"I thought to rest. I am not hungry."

Hudson's pale eyes took on a glow.

Elizabeth went toward the dining room. "We will eat what we can."

Neither could or would talk about their pasts, and the future was too far away to touch. Their pewter forks clattered through their silences like wagons on an empty road.

"I usually read at this time of the day," Annanias tried.

"I walk alone."

"So soon alone after this occasion?"

Elizabeth checked the light from the window. "I'll go. I take long walks."

"Must you?" he pouted. "Today?" He toyed with the cake on his plate.

"I will walk out." Elizabeth was gentle.

His head turned quickly up to her.

"I could sit awhile in the house if you would like to have me here. But I do not want it to be too cold before I go."

"I could walk with you!"

"I go alone."

"Of course. We have agreed. Do as you like."

Elizabeth saw his side of it. "I hope it is all right."

He looked at her in such a way that she pushed out her chair and rose away from him.

"You have never seen the effect of the purple glass in the window that I had put in for you on the northwest steps. It glows most wonderfully when there is sunlight. But this stuff won't burn off down here till tomorrow. Fog's longest in the lowland. I am sorry about it."

"Annanias, you must not be. I shall close my eyes as I go up the steps. I will not look at the window without you."

His head tipped to the side as he considered the charm of her statement.

Only certain rooms in the manse had been hurriedly unveiled from camphor and muslin for the hasty wedding. Empty cabinets, barren shelves, vacant chests made pockets of echoes in the rooms. Barrels of Hudson's packed belongings had been secreted in the downstairs bath chamber, and that plumbing rigged. But the floor above the rugless stairs was a vault. The weather had left the wainscot damp under its varnish. The smell of talc exuded from plaster surfaces. The grates in the bedrooms, long unlit, ticked with the drops of rain that slid down the chimney.

Elizabeth saw the door to Annanias's room opened, the bed hung with the white curtains she had made herself. She avoided that place though it was southerly and firelit. She chose the northwest room that looked out over the Sweetwood road and up toward her father's farm. Like a mouse, brown and gray, she slid a rush-seated chair under the eaves, and wrapped in the quilt from the bed, watched village life from the window. The sound of horses brought her to her feet. But only village people had come, church members curious about her, as eager to set eyes on her as to give congratulations to Hudson. Elizabeth saw him from above, striding out with his hand ready for shaking. She thought how strange it was that Annanias did not ask his visitors in, and stranger still that this cold etiquette was not seen as rudeness. The part through his long brown waves reminded her of which world she was in and she saw the minister behaving well, in his way, like a new father, keeping the nursery hushed so that the baby upstairs would not cause tumult. He waved his neighbors off, promising something in words Elizabeth could not hear, and then, with his arms bent and his shoulders hunched, he made for the protection of his house to mend the continuity of his reading.

A rapping at her door startled Elizabeth. She made a shrill noise as she gave up the bliss of sleep for the blindness that comes on waking in the dark in strange surroundings.

"I did not mean to startle you!" It was Annanias. He lifted the latch but found the bolt in place.

"I am fine." Elizabeth filled with regret for what she might have missed outside the window during her nap. Hope made her say as she stumbled through darkness to the bed with the coverlet, "Is there something wrong?" She was poised to hear that the parlor was crowded with Massachuseuck men.

"Nothing wrong that won't be righted. The day has slipped away." He was peeved. "You haven't got any fire and have hardly eaten a thing. Come, please, to the library. There are hot milk and biscuits for you there."

"How kind." Elizabeth thawed her fingers with her breath.

"It was Marley's idea. Don't let it get cold. What could you be doing in there? You haven't got a light."

Elizabeth did not move at all until he relented, and retreated back down the stairs. She opened his library door alone, soon after.

Annanias was at his writing table, his Bible before him. "Do I come too soon? You are still working, Annanias?"

"Mrs. Hudson, feel free to come in."

"Thank you. I had never seen this room. It is very nice. And warm." Elizabeth stepped a few steps inside the door, not far enough to reach the rug, or a chair, or the pretty tray.

"I am sorry about your fireplace, but you were locked in. How could I set you up with wood? You must be freezing. Have your supper, Beth."

"You are worried. That is sweet."

"You are reputed to be so."

Elizabeth hung her head. "I try to be, but results show some lack there."

The Presbyterian priest shuffled pages. "I imagine that you have suffered much. I have thought about it this long day. You have been very self-contained and dignified about whatever it is that your trials have been. I admire that."

"Annanias Hudson . . . thank you. When you want, you talk exceeding well."

He looked away from her flattery. "No one ever said things the way they are said here, though. The very printer's ink is unction to me. Ah! My!

When I remember the tears you have shed,
I long night and day to see you again, and
    have the perfect happiness of being reminded
    of your genuine faith. . . .

He paused, and watched her the rest of the way.

> . . . for the Spirit of God has given us a
> spirit not of timidity
> but of power, love and self-discipline. . . .

Beth, that is you."

"There is breadth in your ability, Annanias. I am sure that is what Papa saw in you." She colored. "Above all men I have known, you are the most loyal to your love." Her face changed, and she covered half of it with one hand, seeing him through free, hot tears.

His peek at her passions embarrassed him, and he looked to the book. "This is not the result I hoped to produce."

"St. Paul always does that to me."

"Try again. Which Epistle, Beth?"

"Philippians. No! First to Timothy."

"Second letter to him, it was."

"No matter, dear, it gave me comfort. I give you short shrift."

"We are about correcting that."

"Leave it go, Annanias." Her eyes went moist again.

"Now, come on, Beth. Eat your stuff. This were only hunger pangs."

"There is no time to eat. I should have gone long before tea. It is a long way where I am going and I do not know how I shall find it."

"You are going to walk out now, in the dark?"

"I said that I would."

"You have kept the whole day away from me. Now you are restless."

"I am at perfect peace, Annanias."

"Can you guess why I am not?"

"You ought to be." Elizabeth quivered and took a backward step. "We are not children. We have an understanding."

"I have understanding. You are the child who will have to acquire it. Believe me, I have danced like St. Vitus on a very string for you for ten long years. Twelve, now! I am nearing forty! Some men my age have children ready for marriage. If you are going to walk anywhere, walk up the front steps to the chamber where the large bed is hung with drapery of your making. Be ready for me, for when I am done my prayers, I intend to finish today's work, today."

Elizabeth clutched the door frame for support. "Why do you dispute your promise! I cannot respond to you as you wish me to do. More, I could never after a speech like that! I wish that I had a line from Scripture to comfort you. But you would not hear it for you are made to preach."

Annanias's big face went plum color and he ripped the lace-edged bands from his neck and tossed his Bible on the table hard enough to close it.

Gilbert Worth's words of years before sounded to Elizabeth and softened her: Doesn't mean Hudson wouldn't like to throw his bands out the window. "Annanias," she cockered him, "can you trust me that I know how you are feeling? Only recently I have been turned away. I have told you that my life before this was gentle. It was! True, I have lost that, but, when two lives are so tightly and exquisitely bound to one another as were mine and my husband's, there is no right, or reason . . . or way that it be trespassed."

"For a woman lately dwelling in the smoke hole of a bloody savage, you are passing delicate about the forms of love."

Elizabeth was thunderstruck by his extension of his bigotry to her. She was fused to place.

Hudson chewed his cheek. "I realize that I do not have a swarfish skin to give me beauty or a wicked black eye to lend me style. But, I am a man!" Annanias began to attack the buttons of his waistcoat. "Don't look round for Marley. She and Sam Spinney are by the hearth in the kitchen, most likely hard at what we should be doing. The surprised eye! My wife, my mistress, my Beth, I know a great deal more about the process than you give me credit for doing." The wide-built man got around his table, pulling his shirt out of his breeches. His throbbing belly showed.

She ran from the evidence of her abuse of him. She flung the front door wide and it marked the wall it hit. She passed out of the house and crossed the halo of light on the lawn into the dark, toward the cart road which bisected Hudson's land, leading to Worth Farm and the woods.

The slanted field hit her in the face, rising up at her out of the dark. She ran again.

Hurrying after, carrying his stick, moving too fast to use it, Hudson chose a route at random. Pneumonia-weakened lungs made him wheeze.

Elizabeth looked behind her into black blankness at the noises, shocked to hear that she was not running alone. "Wakwa!" She screamed his name in anger, struggling to untangle herself from dried pumpkin vines that looped her ankles.

Hearing how close she was, Annanias threw his stick away. His short-fingered hands were on her back, at her waist, in her hair.

Elizabeth left him with a fistful of the waving stuff. Her tearing away left her reeling. She foundered.

Hudson hurled himself at her, bringing her down under his rolling weight. "Oh, Beth! Oh, Beth! 'Tis kindly meant." He made excuse, closing her throat in the crook of his left arm. His right hand worked to tear away the thin cotton of her drawers.

She remained face down, struggling against his arm which stupidly cut off her wind. His fingers broke the seam and made stabbing exploration of delicate membrane.

The blackness of the night broke up into tails of eerie light over the hill. Elizabeth saw the fog burnt as fire would have eaten gossamer stuffs she sewed.

"Wake up, get up! Get higher!" Hudson moved his arm to aid himself, and he plunged into her frighted, dry flesh, bestride and behind. And she breathed. He used her hair like a rein, stretching her throat to its length, then letting it shrink, catching her chin against the crusty ground.

She knew him through the gouging he administered. The slender chamber into her was rifled by him, deeply as a gun barrel. She was gored by hard horn, invaded high enough that blood was drawn. Both shrieked with the gush of red that met her subjugation.

Hudson's grandiose relief left him unaware that Elizabeth pulled herself out from under him by force of her forearms against the dirt. He discovered her hips between his hands. Perverse adoration of what he had tortured made him follow along, behind her, as she crawled away, loosing him from her opening like a bung from a bottle. He walked upright, a master with his bitch, now and then reminding himself of the completeness of his achievement, bathing his fingers in what spilled from between the spheres of her buttocks.

"There's my dear." He passed his hands down her front as she tried to stand and failed. "Go home. I will meet you there, as soon as I locate my stick."

Elizabeth had to move downward, it was so dark. She went down, not able to make the hill to her uncle's house for help. She went down, rolling and slithering toward the manse like an aquatic creature.

Annanias kept one hand inside his breeches, caressing the viscous honey, his penis thudding softly against his fingers as he walked. He lauded its toughness, a worthy implement for a landowner's use, a precision earth-boring auger. Its stemming reached over a dozen years of denial and conquered the distance to a spirit that had stood him off all his life. Now Elizabeth was his private field like the one he trod in his search for the great adornment of his loveless past—the walking stick. Annanias kicked his shoes against the dirt like a bull on a spring day. He wondered that warm dust did not spray up.

Convenient illumination suddenly made his stick plain. Annanias stooped for it and looked around for the source of light in the same labored movement. Rags of mist were scorched out of existence by a hand-held torch nearing him. Country blackness allowed his eyes nothing but the flaring gold, a slow comet, flowing unnaturally near the ground. And then, sinews of a darker wrist and arm than his clarified out of the night, and a face, long and smooth, carved into terrible beauty by pain.

Sounds outside the Dowland house woke Dorothy Low's spaniel. It ran yapping to the kitchen door, and Dolly went after her pet to quiet him, looking anxiously at the closed door to Dowland's study where Mayhew worked on a sermon. The spaniel raced for the forest sound when she opened for him. Dolly looked after him to the grove of pines. She had heard the stories about Dowland's dining with Indians there, about the slaughter of his ox in those green trees. She saw them weirdly lit now, and the barking stopped. She followed her dog, and found him there, licking Wakwa's feet.

Dorothy bowed her ringleted head on her way home. She made a major decision in her marriage. The information she had given the fugitive in the glade was not for Mayhew's sake, but she would keep him clear of having given it. It was better that way for Low's career.

"Dolly, what was all that riot about?" He looked out of the study when she came up the kitchen steps.

"I think it time we moved down to the manse, dear. Poppy is hearing ghosts here on the hill."

Torn like a leaf by the news that the banns were real, when he had hoped they were some official's cheap lure to force him out of hiding before his statement to the court was properly prepared, Wakwa moved across the shrouded fields toward Hudson's house. He and the light. Each step came hard, confounded by fog and his vast frustration. Steadily he climbed the hill. His name, wailed bitterly, passed him with the nasty damp. He thought of it as the ghost of his marriage wailing to him, its heart split by his own knife. From high above, he saw the flat walls of white clapboard glowing from fires and candles and lamps, inside, and a slender small thing, a woman, creeping toward the door. Gull's cries from her, her horror at his having set her free, deafened him. He could tell how fully she was debased and he turned his sorrow against himself by not going to her, lifting her, taking her, making her a safe nest. Such marks of his care were past, by his own will. Instead, Wakwa went toward the portly man strutting nearby.

Wakwa seized the walking stick before Annanias could. "Askug! You snake!"

Annanias looked up to the angular face of an Indian man. His bowel rumbled but he found the grit to say, "Trespasser! Get off my ground."

"You trespass on mine!" Wakwa touched Annanias Hudson, wrapping his massy head with his arm, bringing their faces close. Then he pushed Hudson against the earth. "Elizabeth Dowland is this!"

Hudson wormed himself away. "Oh, I see. You think I've got to put up with more of you drunken animals, now

I am married to Dowland's girl. He may have abided you people, but I do not. I'll whip the last of you out of the town."

"Use your tongue more wisely, preacher! Say any one thing that can save you."

"Who do you think you are to use the English language as a rule for you to save me, you heathen." Hudson was up, straightening his dishevelment, brushing himself off. "Drunken savage. Wizard! Devil! Antichrist! That is all I have to say to you. Get off!" Annanias boldly turned and started down his hill.

"Ahhh!" Wakwa bared his teeth from misery. He caught Hudson by the scruff and slapped him hard across his ear. "Hear me, I will be between your woman and you from now until the time that the sun shall die. Yet, salvage yourself. Give me the reason that I should not kill you."

"If you so much as mention Mrs. Hudson again, I will have you policed. By your own. Ah! You think a minister of God has no friends outside his church? I know a man twice your strength, a smith by trade, Hephaestus the name. I know a lout of your color, one Willie, a sachim's son. I know a chief. A right-minded one. The Nauset sachim happens to be a personal friend with whom I have had some rather successful business dealings, so do not bully me. I will snap my fingers and they will go after you with your soft voice and your pretty manner. Worse devils than you have sat in my parlor."

"Walk over to the tree." Wakwa's voice broke over the continuance of his duty. From Hudson's mouth had come the full proof of the conspiracy. Dependence on English law was a fool's tie to honor, to justice. From Beckett's helplessness he could tell. "Walk!" he ordered.

Annanias began to shake so that he could not move without help. He refused Wakwa's touch and was handed his cane. There was no point, Annanias saw, in trying to defend himself just yet. The Indian was too large, too strong and quick to bring on anything but a bludgeoning.

"Go to sit under the tree!"

"You realize that I only humor your drunken game."

Wakwa tripped Hudson's feet out from under him at the crab apple and tied his hands to the trunk, high over his head.

"Foolish little boy's games." Annanias sweated then shivered in the chill. "You bucks have to realize you all can't get your hands on her just because she suffered one of you, once upon a time."

Wakwa bound Hudson's feet at the ankles and tied the end of that rope to a neighboring tree.

"Who are you to do this to me?"

"I? I am he whom you have injured most. You have seen me every day in the red earth of your meadow and have not recognized me."

"Eh? What does that mean? Damnable Indians never speak out plainly. I say who are you?"

"English call me Silent Fox. Die like your dog."

"Dearest God!" Annanias looked at his soft middle, exposed and ripe for the ripping, and he screamed.

Wakwa forced his hand into Hudson's open mouth, not to strangle the man for air as he had done to his hound to keep him from Elizabeth, but to sever the tongue, the instrument that had brought down his pure hopes with misinformation. The knife of volcanic glass cut it like dinner meat.

Gagging on his own, profuse blood. Annanias watched the careful work of the native man by torchlight. The black blade opened Annanias's clothes from his throat to his groin. Blood and inarticulate cries choking him, Annanias endured the redman's hand probing his white belly. He saw his she-dog, dead in the woods the morning he had searched with Gilbert Worth and Matthew for Beth. The red cavity from where Princess's gut had been lifted yawned before him.

Wakwa felt above the navel for the hardness of the day's food and he made a small incision, just big enough for two fingers, side by side. He fit two of his in and took hold of the intestine with them. He hooked the firm, full gut, nudging a loop of it outside Annanias's body. He began to pull on it, hand over hand like a sailor, disemboweling Hudson inch by inch.

Annanias witnessed his mutilation without amazement. In the cool night, the sleek gut grew into a steaming pile on his legs. It lengthened like a serpent vacating the pit of himself. A terrible tongueless howl lent eloquence to Hudson's parting spirt.

Wakwa sliced the connection from the stomach and gathered the hot, heinous bundle, winding the coils like a hunter bringing home his rope. He knelt close to the speechless, gutless man. "You ask who I am. In my language which you never learned, and alas, will never, I am Wakwa Manunnappu, the-black-fox-who-waits."

Annanias looked at him with full recognition. Fright stopped his heart.

_____ **Chapter 57**

UNSEEN SUN burned the mist from the valley bottom. The vapor lifted away from the frost. Grandee bounded out of this eerie silver toward Worth Farm, scenting out his home and his comforts. Gil did not stop as he passed Annanias's corpse. The empty belly, sagging, was red and dully gleaming as a hollowed ruby. It was not a repulsive image to Worth. What roused him out of delectations of finding Hudson obscenely murdered was the rime which etched the gory cavities of mouth and belly. The frozen dew glittering in the heightening light was real.

"Whoa!" Gil commanded the bay as the animal, too, became conscious of death. Horse and man fought and spun, Gil needing to ride back, the horse needing to escape. Gil loosed his boots from his stirrups and helped Grandee to throw him, pushed himself, and slid free, hitting the brackish grass like a load of bricks. He stood at the center of Hudson's dead stare.

The body was like that of any well-butchered bull, if Gil avoided the eyes. This domesticated animal dressed in human clothing, his ankles aligned closely as a prudish woman's, had his forelimbs extending skyward, not hung to the ground. Had the body not had three dimensions, Gil could have mistaken it for a caricature in a misanthrope's notebook.

His eyes followed the passage of the ropes around wrists and ankles, tied the knots again, visually. He knew the knot. He knew the rope. His niece had wound thousands of yards like it at her lodge. He sank onto his heels, thinking that he should untie the ropes and guard them from identification. But he saw Annanias's black shoes, frozen to garnet with blood. The buckles were missing.

Gil's strained face smiled. "What an attention to detail." He took the clotted shoes and worked them away from the stone feet, huffing with effort. "Common theft the motive. Some people will do anything for a pair of silver buckles! Foxy work."

Gil walked briskly down toward the manse, his heart beating fine, his body stimulated by hope. He had sensed that Wakwa hovered. He knew it now, for fact. "Where are you, O Reverend Annanias's Tongue? Boiled and reboiled, sliced thinly for a rich meal? Go ahead, Wakwa. Do it. Eat his words." The other side of things turned Gil properly sober when Sam Spinney, gray as gray, passed him in the dead minister's cart, heading toward the corpse with a tarpaulin.

"They know at the house, Sam?"

"Yea, sir."

"How long?"

"Only just. It's only Priscilla and me on the whole place, sir. Irishers gone for the winter. Told Mistress Beth . . . Mistress Hudson. . . ."

"Mistress Beth."

". . . And brought her there in the cart. She's in a rough way. . . ."

"I'd imagine so."

"She does not walk."

"What?"

"I cannot tell but that she was attacked, too, sir, by the look of her face."

"What went on here? What went on?" Gil dropped his idea that Hudson had been paid by Wakwa. "What were you doing when hell broke loose!"

Spinny went sullen. "I slept in the barn, sir, I worked late on some panels the Reverend ordered for the unfinished bath place. Pris was peelin' apples for this mornin's sauce in the kitchen about dark. We were each doin' that we are paid to do. I hope . . . I hope, sir, I shan't lose your investment in my furniture makin' venture because the hand of God has struck this place."

Gil studied the square, shiny-skinned, young face. He decided there was wisdom in the Charter with the Crown which gave the vote only to landholders. Sam's uniquely selfish viewpoint left the aristocrat aghast. "Continue about your business, Spinney, lest the hand of God strike you."

Mayhew Low opened Hudson's door. "Terrible, the hand of God, Mr. Worth."

Gil said dryly, "When that theory wears thin, Mayhew, see you tell the town the cause was robbery. Money becoming the God of the country as it is." Gil deposited the buckleless shoes on the woven rug near the door where Winke insisted all muddy footwear stay.

Dorothy Low left the side of the chair where Elizabeth huddled. Priscilla drew her soft wool shawl back from Elizabeth's injured face and whispered, "Your uncle is here."

Gil went down on one knee to see her. "What has happened?"

"I bathed her, sir, as soon as she came in. I put her in the lead tub as it was ready, Mr. Hudson having rushed Sam so about it."

"But her face, her hands . . . how did this happen?"

"Mr. Hudson went out the house with her though I made the bed ready."

Gil turned his face up to the little maid, engaged to wed the carpenter.

"I know how she was hurt, sir, as I was the one who bathed her. And she does have pain. It took both Sam and me to fetch her out of the tub."

"Poor Pris, any more such observings and you will never want to be a bride. Did no one call my wife for help? The doctor and his son are there."

"My mistress said to call no one. And sir, I did not." She curtsied and left them alone.

Gil put his cheek to Elizabeth's hair. She was bent down into her own lap. "You were right, dear," he said, "he did come."

"O uncle!" Elizabeth slid from the cushion, lowering herself to put her face against the tops of his boots. Gil tried to lift her but she mourned, "I made it so that he can never come again!"

Down with her on the floor, Gil corrected, "He will always keep his part with you and be where you need him. But I know he trusts, and I do too, that you will be strong after this and not force him to you. It will take your lifetimes, but you will meet again."

Gil brought her to her feet and held her against him as she whimpered. He thanked the God he often derided that the woman mishandled let him near.

"Annanias took all I had left. All I had."

"I know!"

Gilbert and Mayhew took time in the study. Dolly held Elizabeth's hand, profoundly silent. She kept her word to the man she had seen in Dowland's trees the night before. It was not fear for herself but fear she would undo some good that forced Dolly to let the memory of the meeting fade her like food.

"Yours is a difficult work in which you will do well. Better than I would have." Elizabeth's voice surprised with its calm.

"No. I admire you. Your . . . ," Dolly faltered over Wakwa's name, ". . . home shows what you are. I am honored to meet you. I shall be sorry to leave your house for this."

"Dolly, there are pleasures here. I would show you to them, but . . . ," Elizabeth looked away, degraded by the source of her pain, ". . . the sun has come. Look up the stairwell. The colored window will be lit. I have not seen it but I think it will be nice."

While Dolly was away, Gil came out of the library with Hudson's Bible. "Mayhew says that you should have it."

Elizabeth watched the black book in her lap as if it were some incendiary thing. "What shall I do with that?"

"Read it. You were always fond of Isaiah."

Dumbly, Elizabeth opened the weighty volume by the ribbon marker that lay at the heart of her favorite verses of prophecy. She bent to see the vellum better. She examined the quaint type as if she were reading an orthography unknown to her. She felt the fine parchment with her forefinger. And then she turned page after page of woeful prediction in an excited heat. Forgetting her face, she looked at her uncle. "It is all cut up! It cannot be read. There is not a passage whole."

"Except at the Day of Vengeance." Gil set his hand over the verse. With cantor's depth he said from memory,

> For the Lord has a day of vengeance,
> A year of requital for the feud against
> Zion; . . . Edom will lie waste from age to age,
> None will pass through it forever and ever.
> But the jackdaw and the hedgehog will take possession
>     of it,
> The owl and the raven will make their home in it;
> And the Lord will stretch over it the
> Measuring line of chaos and the plummet of
>     desolation; and satyrs will dwell there,
> While her nobles will be no more.
> Her name will be called "No Kingdom There,"
> And all her princes will become nothing.

That is how his thoughts ran. Take heart, the beast is dead. I believe this is how Annanias sent a letter to the court. Cutting and pasting each separate letter of each separate word of his message, he delivered Wakwa up. Unlike Judas his prize was much more valuable than money. His prize was you."

Elizabeth pushed the book into Worth's hands and rose out of her chair. Without support from him or any of the others she limped toward the door. Hudson's walking cane poked out of a china urn and she took it, using it to aid her ginger steps down the path and up the meadow.

"People are gathering at the site. Do not let them see you. Wait for Matthew, he is coming with the coach. Be glad! You have saved the name of Silent Fox. Beckett will have this within two days to present to the court. Unless Hudson had died this proof never would have been found."

Elizabeth raised a shoulder against the caress of the man. "Do not touch me! Can you not read the sacred book? Because of these feuds it is I am laid waste and am possessed by jackdaws. It is I who am no kingdom any-

411

more. I am a lonely haunt, a shell. I shouldn't wonder if vultures do not already swim in my womb."

Stirling said, "Bonnie's comin' with me to Sandwich. I'm no' so old that I should go dottering down to my people in Pennsylvania to die. I've got a little farm with an ocean view and I'm bringin' Bonnie back there. And no interference from you two. Israel's learned enough about broken bones and powder burns and open wounds. I'm gonna show the boy how t'heal a mind. An' you, Gil, an' you, Hanna, get some peace. Sleep late in the mornin'. Don't answer your mail. Stay in bed. Eat. Mend your nest. This wee bird, me Bonnie Beth, will need one when she's well." The old Scot put his plum hand over his red face.

Hanna sugared his cup. "I hate to say it, Mac, but you are right. Beth should go away. Right now the town seems satisfied that Annanias's death is a sign from God of something. But should they turn against Beth . . . what do you think, Gil?"

"I think I would like to taste that dessert! Bring on the cakes, Cooke!"

"I would like to, sir, but how shall I?"

Worth crossed the sitting room to her to help. "Mrs. Cooke, you should say if the tray is too heavy. We would have helped you." Gil relieved her of it and his arm levitated at its lightness.

"Twice now, sir, something has happened. Two nights in a row I have baked with ginger and set the cakes outside to cool for the icing's sake. You see, I always give Matthew extra of what we have in the house, for him to have late at night at the cabin."

"So, Matthew went overboard and took the lot." Gil twinkled. "I'd be the last to blame him for wanting your ginger cake at midnight."

Cooke curtsied. "But master, he never got it. The first night when he went out for his portion, the tray was bare."

Gil guffawed. "We are descended from high treason to the pilfering of goodies. Write Mr. Beckett, Hanna! Roust out Cooper! Shouldn't wonder if the tither stole the cakes himself for his consideration."

"I did not know the cakes got stolen until the next morning, and that was time Mistress Beth was leaving for the manse and you were not here to tell. . . ."

"Cooke," Gil reassured her, "a lucky raccoon has had a windfall. Do not worry."

"I do, sir. It were not a raccoon. I know that now, sir. I wish it were a raccoon." The housekeeper lifted the hood from the cake server. "Tonight's cake is gone too, missing from outside the kitchen door here at the house."

Gil looked onto the crumbs and sugar remaining on the plate that he held. At center was a silver buckle, one of the pair Annanias Hudson had proudly worn through his adult life. Gil picked it up and gave the dish away. His fingers touched each rosette and rambling relief of the baroque and heavy thing. "Wakwa is hungry. He has been here. He subsists on stealing cake. And has paid for it with this."

"Gillie." Hanna smoothed his hair. "It is another sign. What can be done about it?"

Gil went to the settee to check Elizabeth's sleep. He put the buckle in his pocket. "There is no question. This precious thing must be matched with its mate."

"It is much to be regretted that a careless habit of thought takes it for granted that a good Indian word of one locality is a good Indian word of another, and that names may be transferred from North to South or from South to North at the free will of an innkeeper or of a poet. Such transfers of words, which in the beginning amount almost to falsehood, cause more confusion and more as time goes by."

—Edward Everett Hale, 1901
from the Introduction to *Natick Dictionary*

# Glossary

ALL NATIVE AMERICAN WORDS used in this book are of Algonquian stock, represented mainly in the Narragansett dialect. All spellings are taken from *A Key into the Languages of America*, by Roger Williams, 1643, and *Natick Dictionary*, by James Hammond Trumbull, 1903, using English orthography, approximating actual Indian pronunciation. The asterisks mark proto-Algonquian words found in *Contributions to Anthropology, Linguistics I*, National Museum of Canada, Bulletin 214, Series No. 78, Ottawa, 1967.

*Abnaki.* A nation or tribe native to Maine
*Agiocochook.* The White Mountains of New Hampshire
*Ahquontâmah.* Forgive thou me
*amaïsh.* Depart, go away
*appu.* He is, continues to be, lives in a state implying rest; he abides

*askùg.* A snake
*awêpu.* A calm

*capát.* Ice
*cheepe.* A specter; something separated from life; preternatural
*cowaúnkamish.* My service to thee
*cowwêtuck.* Let us sleep

*garent-oquen.* Signature plant, ginseng; "man's thighs and legs separated"

*kah.* And
*Kautántowwìt.* The great southwest god
*\*kayaskwa.* The herring gull
*keèn kah neen.* You and I
*ke ná eh.* Thou seest me
*kihtuckquáw.* A virgin marriageable
*kíkkita.* Hearken thou to me
*kitchize.* A man exceeding in age

*mamunappeht.* Spider
*manit.* He who exceeds the normal; God
*manittóo.* Apprehension of excellency in any being; it is a god
*manittowomp.* Godly man
*mannotaúbana.* Embroidered hangings
*manunnappu.* He has himself, is in possession, remains quiet, sits patiently
*Massachusêuck.* A small nation or tribe of Massachusetts
*Massasoit.* Seventeenth-century sáchim of the Wampanoag Nation
*matta.* No, not
*mattannit.* Bad spirit; devil
*máttapsh.* Sit thou down
*meninnunk.* Woman's milk
*Metacom.* Second son of Massasoit; King Philip
*miâwene.* A court, a meeting
*Micúkaskeete-Nokannáwi.* Meadow-in-the-Night
*mishe-miawene.* A great assembly, a grand council
*mockussinchass.* Shoes
*mosq.* The bear

416

*Muckquashím-ouwán Noh-annóosu.* Wolf-of-the-mist He-
   hopes
*musquantam manit.* God is angry

*Narragansett.* A nation or tribe native to Rhode Island
*nasàump.* Pottage of meal, made soft, thinned with water
*Nauset.* A nation or tribe native to Cape Cod
*neèse sauncksquûaog nuttaiheog.* Two mistresses mine
*neesintuh.* Let us lie together
*nehyewgh.* My wife
*nen not appu.* I am home!
*nequt óukauau.* He has one wife
*nétop.* My friend
*Niantic.* A nation native to Rhode Island
*nickómmo.* A solemn feast
*Ninnuock.* The People; the natives of America
*Nipmuk.* A nation native to central Massachusetts
*nippisse.* Little water, a pond or pool
*nissese.* My uncle
*nòsh.* My father
*nunnaum.* I see
*núnnowa.* Harvest time
*nuppohwunau.* He who hath wings
*nux.* Yea; yes

*otàn.* A town

*paewe.* Little
*Passamoquoddy.* A nation native to Maine
*pauquanamíinea.* Open me the door
*pemmican.* Cakes of a paste of meat, rendered fat, and
   berries
*Penobscot.* A nation native to Maine
*Pennacook.* A nation native to New Hampshire
*péquawus.* A gray fox
*pésuponk.* A sweat hut
*pígsuck.* Swine
*Pocumtuc.* A nation native to western Massachusetts
*poquâhock.* Round or cherrystone clams
*powwáw.* A priest, a wise speaker

*qunnèke.* A doe.

*sáchim.* "He prevails, has mastery"; one who governs
*sachimáŭonk.* A governed place
*sachimmaacómmock.* Large house of a headman
*sachimmaŭog.* Leaders, governors
*sachimmiawene.* Assembly of headmen
*saunks.* "She prevails, has the mastery"; mistress, wife of the sáchim
*sauncksquŭaog.* Wives of headmen, headman
*Scatacooks.* A nation native to the Eastern woodlands
*séquan.* The spring
*squàws-powaw.* A woman wise sayer
*súcki.* Black, dark colored, purple
*suckaúhock.* Black shell money
*sŭkkissŭog.* Longneck clams
*summágunum wunnutcheg.* He holds out his hand
*sunnamatta.* Is it not?

*tamóccon.* A flood
*taquònk.* Fall of leaf, autumn
*tattâ.* "Of doubting"; I know not
*taúpowaw.* A wise speaker
*toh kutapin.* Where art thou?
*touohkomuk.* Forest; wilderness

*waban.* The wind
*\*wakwa.* Fox
*wamach.* Let it suffice
*wame.* All, wholly
*Wampanoag.* A nation native to Massachusetts, east of Narragansett Bay
*wampum.* White shell money
*weatchimin.* Corn in the field
*weechauau.* He went with him (her)
*weetahtu.* A sister, half-sister, one of the same household, family
*wehpittittuk.* Let us eat together
*wenỹgh.* Woman
*wetomp.* Dear friend
*wetompauog.* Dear friends
*wetu.* A round house
*wetuomémese.* A little house for women
*woi.* Oh that it were

*wompan-anit.*   God of daylight
*wosketupam.*   The surface of the sea
*wússese.*   An uncle
*wuskannem.*   Semen
*wuttàh mâuo.*   His heart weeps
*wuttámmagon.*   Pipe

*yò néepoush.*   Stay here

"A rich, stirring novel of the westward
thrust of America, and of a dynamic woman
who went West to tame the wilderness within her."
*The Literary Guild*

# PASTORA

## JOANNA BARNES

The passions of two generations, and the rich,
colorful history of 19th-century California, are
woven into this 768-page epic of adventure and
romance! It follows one strong and courageous
woman through tragedy and triumph, public scandal
and private struggle, as she strives to seize a golden
destiny for herself and those she loves!

"Blockbuster historical romance!"
*Los Angeles Times*

"Readers who like romantic sagas with historical
backgrounds will enjoy this."
*Library Journal*

**AVON Paperback**          56184   •   **$3.50**

Available wherever paperbacks are sold, or directly from the
publisher. Include 50¢ per copy for postage and handling: allow
6-8 weeks for delivery. Avon Books, Mail Order Dept., 224 West
57th St., N.Y., N.Y. 10019.

Pastora 12-81

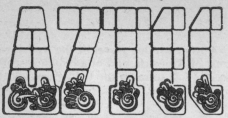